VOICE OF THE TIGER

MARKHAM TURNER

VOICE OF THE TIGER

To Carol,
boleh jad kamu nyawa
ada bahagia

[signature]

HAZARD PRESS
publishers

*This is a work of fiction. Every effort has been made to make it true to
the localities and situations of the period but, other than historical figures,
all characters are imaginary. Any resemblance to actual people living
or dead is coincidental and unintentional.*

Published by Hazard Press Limited
P.O. Box 2151, Christchurch, New Zealand
Email info@hazard.co.nz
www.hazardpress.co.nz

ISBN 978-1-877393-39-6

Printed in New Zealand

For Louise, my wife, in appreciation of her love, encouragement and help. Also for the thousands of young soldiers from Britain, Australia and New Zealand who served in Malaya. Especially those who, like Vince, as the song says, '…found love by the heartful in a far-off eastern land'.

acknowledgements

I would like to acknowledge the patient professionalism shown by Hazard Press in guiding me along the steep learning curve of publishing my first book.

Special thanks are due to Fiona Gartland who, as production manager, exercised commendable patience and restraint in dealing with an elderly, peripatetic and neophyte novelist. Thanks are also due to her team of editors and proofreaders. They managed to trim away much of the dross and present me with a text and a cover of which I can feel proud.

I should also express my appreciation to Stephen Stratford of Write Right. He took my original manuscript, ungainly and overweight as it was, and demonstrated how to strip away unnecessary fat, reassemble it, and turn it into a leaner, more publishable novel.

Thanks guys.

Markham Turner

introduction

Set in Malaya during the early years of self-government, this story clings as closely as possible to the reality of the times. As Malaya transformed into 'Malaysia', it underwent enormous changes to become a modern, thriving, industrialised nation. An economic force to be reckoned with, it is now a regional power with armed forces that contribute to UN peacekeeping around the globe.

Modern highways, towering city buildings and enormous hydro-electric dams have created incredible visual changes, as has the swing from rubber production to producing palm oil. Lake Chenderoh, which features in this book, is now Tasik Cenderuh and closed by a dam to river traffic. Taiping has become a bustling university city; pressures of prosperity have stolen some of the lustre from people's smiles and the BMH Cameron Highlands is once more a school.

The Malayan Emergency began on 16 June 1948 and concluded twelve years later, on 31 July 1960. Because the Malayan economy, still struggling to recover from the effects of the Second World War, required that it be so, it was called an Emergency rather than a war. Insurance companies would provide indemnity for property damaged or destroyed during civil unrest – but not during wartime.

This benign deception extended to all military activity being under the direct authority of the civil jurisdiction. When the High Commissioner Sir Henry Gurney was assassinated in 1951, a soldier, General Sir Gerald Templer, was appointed to replace him the following year. Awarded wide political and military powers to lead the country to independence and to bring the Emergency to an end, he had the confidence of the armed forces. When, after a very successful tenure, he departed in 1954 he left a country largely united against the insurgents and headed towards full political independence.

With delegated power and the experience to use it, he forcefully pressed the policies of both his predecessor and those of (Lt General) Sir Harold Briggs, his Head of Operations, who also acted in a civil capacity. He recognised the importance of winning the support of the Orang Asli, the indigenous people, in the jungle war and developed policies to enlist their aid, while denying their assistance to the rebels. At his departure, the end of communist rebellion, although still distant, was at last within sight.

At the time in which this book is set, there were an estimated forty-five to fifty thousand aboriginal (Orang Asli) people living throughout the Malay Peninsula. This number was spread across some twenty individual groups divided by ethnicity and/or language, but only three of these are mentioned in this story: Negrito, Senoi and Temiar.

It would perhaps be more correct to call the people I call Senoi, Semai, as both Temiar and Senoi are of the same stock and known collectively as Semai. The distinction I have made, despite its inaccuracy, is that which was made by the Security Forces of the time.

The Negrito people are from an entirely different race with quite different physical characteristics and culture. In the early 1960s it was still normal for the Temiar-Senoi (Semai) to live in longhouses and practise 'slash and burn' agriculture. At the same time small family groups of Negritos lived a completely nomadic life of hunting and gathering, essentially a people of the jungle.

Many Orang Asli have now adopted the Muslim religion, but they were by tradition animists. This means that their spiritual life revolved around the notion that a spirit, either benign or malicious in nature, might inhabit any environmental feature – a stream, a rock, a tree – or an animal.

An integral part of their culture is a belief in the power of dreams and the halak, or shaman, who orders their spiritual life is a very important person. Halaks also advise on dreams, which are of great importance in the social and spiritual lives of the Senoi. Nocturnal memories are discussed at regular morning gatherings and these dream conferences help to create the enduring bonds that keep a saka, an extended family, united.

The halak, as he develops his power and influence, needs a gunig. This is a spirit, similar to the familiars of medieval witches in the western world, which acts as an adviser and guide. The gunig of choice is feline, and in the jungle it is a giant cat: the tiger. Gunigs may however be anything possessed of a co-operative spirit, even another human. From his gunig, the halak may learn a special dance and song. This will be performed to facilitate entrance into a trance state during which the spirit of the gunig possesses the halak and provides advice on any subject that affects the welfare of his people.

On ritual occasions, the halaks typically dance themselves into a catatonic state. During their trance they are believed to be under the control of their gunig. Their movements are slow and jerky as they move amongst their adherents, giving advice, suggesting subjects for dreams that might help their saka, and interpreting past dream experiences.

Such experiences are considered to be of great importance. Senoi believe that jungle spirits may be either mischievous or helpful. If a spirit is encountered in a dream it should be challenged, for if it is hostile it may steal the dreamer's soul. If on the other hand it is benign it may lead him to knowledge that could improve the lot of his saka and his own wellbeing.

Children discover resilience and courage through participation in these morning sessions. They learn that if they find themselves sinking in water during a dream, then they should become spirit fish and explore the depths. If falling in a dream, they must soar as birds to conquer the currents of the air. If a dream involves forbidden behaviour, the dreamer should not blame himself. Erotic dreams involving close relatives, or dreams of violence – particularly against a family member – indicate the work of an evil spirit that has assumed the identity of a real person in order to steal the dreamer's soul. Such demons can be confronted without guilt at breaking the incest taboo or using violence.

During the morning group discussion of dreams, their contents and meanings are carefully analysed and questioned. Antisocial behaviour, within the context of the dream, is severely criticised, but the dreamer is reassured that he is not at fault. The criticism is directed at the evil spirits responsible. Thus these morning conferences help to eliminate subconscious antisocial drives without inflicting feelings of guilt, while also enhancing group bonding.

Prior to the invasion of the valleys of the Orang Asli by the communist insurgents and the security forces, crime was virtually unknown. In his book

Noone of the Ulu, Dennis Holman attributes this to child-rearing practices. In the 1930s, Pat Noone, a young British anthropologist, became the first person to make an in-depth study of the indigenous people of the Malay Peninsula. In 1939 he was appointed as the first Protector of Aborigines in the State of Perak. Noone gave credit for the remarkably high standard of social behaviour of the Temiar to their social cohesion. The group is all-important. The most horrific punishment that could be meted out to a Temiar is expulsion from the group. This is rare and usually results in the exile's suicide.

Temiar children are as aggressive, selfish, self-centred and demanding as any others, but adults typically treat such behaviours with good-humoured tolerance. However, if as children mature they persist in such behaviour, they continue to be treated as children. If they continue to be greedy and selfish into adulthood, they are considered to be insane.

Sexual behaviour is not repressed beyond the usual taboos against incest and some experimentation among young people is considered natural. While people behave with normal modesty while attending to bodily functions, bathing or making love, there is not a lot of drama if they are accidentally observed. The limited privacy inherent in longhouse life, inevitably means that children see adults engaged in sex and imitate them. Sex acts are not copied furtively, and adults treat such imitation tolerantly for what it is: children at play.

Once a partner is chosen, however, the couple are considered to be married and in a lasting relationship. Even then though, provision is made for human frailty. If a couple are parted for more than a few days it is considered acceptable for either to seek solace with a relative of their spouse until they are reunited. For either to display jealousy as a result is thought to be bad form.

glossary

ana laki laki	son (Malay)
bhaju khabaya	sarong and blouse, worn with shoulder sash, or sleeveless jacket (Malay)
bapu	father (Malay)
basha	building constructed solely from jungle resources (Malay)
boohai	remote area (NZ slang)
cheong sam	elegant, tight-fitting Chinese dress with slit side
Chin Peng	Secretary General, Malayan Communist Party
CTs	communist terrorists, sometimes referred to as 'bandits'
gunig	spirit familiar of a halak (Semai)
gunong	limestone feature remaining after erosion of surrounding terrain (Malay)
halak	spiritual leader, shaman (Semai)
hongi	touching of noses (sharing of the breath of life) in greeting (Maori)

JGs	jungle green uniform
kuala	confluence of rivers (Malay)
ladang	jungle area cleared for cultivation (Malay)
makan	food (Malay)
NAAFI	Navy, Army and Air Force Institute
pano hut	small building used by halak for solitary trance sessions (Semai)
peh	younger brother (Malay)
perempuan	woman (Malay)
puan	contraction of the above
ruwai	group spirit (Semai)
saka	tribal land (Semai)
sankal	female ogre, guardian of the underworld (Semai mythology)
sam fu	Chinese trousers and tunic
selemat pagi	good morning
selemat siang	good day
semangat	spirit (Semai)
SLR	self-loading rifle
sonkok	Malay man's hat – similar to Egyptian fez, but oval
sungei	river (Malay)
tai hoa	'wait, friend' (Maori)
tepeh	older brother (Semai)
terima kaseh	thank you (Malay)
tidak	negative (Malay)
tuan	a title of respect (Malay)
ular sedok	king cobra (Malay)

chapter one

'Wait on, you jokers!' Short Storey's anxious whisper from the back of the file was punctuated by a metallic click-clack.

'Storey!' Brian Jones hissed softly. 'That rifle better be on safety.'

'But – but Sarge, I – I – something's moving beside the trail, behind those bushes. I reckon it's a tiger – I can smell the bugger!'

'Shut up, Short.' Joe sounded resigned. Short was in his section and he was used to the man's odd ways. 'Come up here, and if you don't belt up I'll tie you to a tree for bait. I've got uses for a tiger skin rug.'

Jimmy Te Pania's lecherous snigger suggested he had some too.

The Penghulu, the headman, of a Senoi community close to where they had camped, had invited them to a ceremonial dance, or jin-jan, to celebrate the return of the new moon. Lieutenant Tom Andrews, the platoon commander, had given permission. 'Just remember,' he had said, 'the reports of terrorists around here. Even though we've seen no sign, keep your weapons handy. If the girls have nice tits, look but don't touch. Don't laugh at butterflies, piss on the roof, or marry anybody.'

A young intelligence officer, during an orientation briefing, had exhorted them against such behaviours. He had not explained the first two. Longhouses were built on stilts with roofs usually twelve feet off the ground. But butterflies?

And cigarettes offered to single women would supposedly indicate a romantic interest. Jimmy and Short both carried extra cigarettes with that in mind.

They halted not far from the longhouse and waited, barely touched by the firelight that flickered through the walls. Vince Tanner's head throbbed as he squinted at the structure in the uncertain light. It was about thirty yards long and twelve wide. The roof was steeply pitched, with wide eaves to keep out the monsoon rains.

They were from five platoon, Bravo Company, of the New Zealand Regiment. Together with Australian and British units, they made up the British Commonwealth Brigade, assisting the recently independent Federation of Malaya to bring the twelve-year communist insurgency to an end. During the final days of a patrol they had been diverted to the upper reaches of the Sungei Temor to investigate reported sightings of terrorists. They had found no sign of them, nor had they expected to. It was 1961. The Malaya Emergency was officially over and most surviving guerrillas had sought sanctuary in Thailand. Those bandits still south of the border maintained a low profile; the purpose of patrols such as this was to harass them and prevent them from re-establishing their jungle bases.

Vince wiped the sweat from his face. All day he had felt ill. During the descent from the central ranges he had kept stumbling and knocking into trees. Maybe, he thought, I should have just crawled into my hammock? Too bloody late now – wish this bloody headache would go away. When Barry said we'd been invited to a jin-jan, I should have said I felt too crook. It should be interesting though – as long as I don't pass out.

He turned to his mate with a croaking whisper. 'Hey, Barry...'

Vince's voice died away as a figure appeared to wave them forward. A man of middle years, sinewy build and not much more than five feet tall stood at the entrance. His features were unclear in the gloom, but he wore an appearance of confidence and authority that defied the grubby loincloth, which with a leafy headdress was his only clothing. He descended to meet them, stepping on the notched log that was a primitive, but tiger-proof, stairway.

He was Busu Ap, the penghulu, or headman, of this ladang and others in the valley. Joe Savage, who'd led the earlier patrol of the camp perimeter, introduced the small party. With much grinning and nodding of heads, they handed over the gifts they each carried. Candy bars from ration packs, a tin of cigarettes, packets of fishhooks, an army-issue clasp knife. All were accepted politely but inside, in the better light of the long house, it was clear that the knife and hooks were the most highly prized.

The communal area seemed to be crammed with bodies, including the members of an orchestra. A group of young women and girls crouched near the wall, clutching varying lengths of bamboo with one end of each length having been cut off at a joint. In pre-determined sequence, each player dropped her bamboo vertically onto a hardwood log to produce strangely compelling music not unlike the sound of a glockenspiel.

Nearby, two young men stood against the wall blowing into nose flutes. Their melody slipped between the bamboo beat and wove a blanket of sound, eerie and seductive, that drew their listeners to emulate its undulating rhythm.

The young women wore posies of flowers and leaves in their hair. Some had necklaces of coloured beads, woven grasses or other trinkets hanging from their ears, and multiple silver bracelets. The men wore headdresses plaited from green leaves; all were bare to the waist, the men in simple loincloths and skirts of palm fronds. The women had patterned sarongs tucked into woven cords strung around their waists. Each attractive face stared blank-eyed into the shadows. Vince peered through the smoke. Jeeze, he thought, they look as though their souls are away dancing to their own music, somewhere in the shadows...

The room ran the full width of the longhouse and was about eight yards deep. Another floor was raised some eighteen inches and appeared to lead to family alcoves, semi-partitioned for privacy. Each had a small cooking hearth of river stones before it. The floor was a framework of logs supporting saplings laid crosswise and covered with split-bamboo panels. The same framework supported walls clad to head height with split-bamboo panels in chequered patterns. A steep gabled roof framed with bamboo crowned the building with a thatch of attap palm. Lashed together with fibrous vines, the resilient structure lurched and swayed with the movements of the dancers.

In front of the orchestra a long, low fire provided uncertain light: it was not needed for warmth. Guttering flames reflected on the sweating bodies of the musicians and four dancers who swayed and stamped on a small clear area nearby. The performers seemed oblivious as they stepped out their movements, yet their obedience to the insistent beat remained in complete harmony. With steps as carefully choreographed as those of ballet dancers, they traced a predetermined path across the uneven floor.

Vince peered through the shifting shadows, the smoke from the fire and half-cured hill tobacco, watched the dancers and listened to the strange, haunting music as though in a dream. It was so alien, yet strangely familiar. He experienced a sensation of déjà vu, a feeling of having returned to a half-remembered place he had left a long time ago.

He sat on a rough bench of saplings, between an old man and a young nursing mother. His comrades dispersed amongst the thirty or so of their hosts to watch the dancers. Vince exchanged smiles and muttered comments with his neighbours. Uncomfortably aware of the mother's milk-filled but comely breasts so close, he patted the baby and let it grip his finger. The old man tried to tell him something, but he felt nauseous and light-headed again and the rough tobacco the old man smoked did not help. It was like sitting next to a burning compost heap. The odours of sweat, smoke and tobacco felt thick enough to shovel and he was grateful for a breeze that carried some of the fug through the gaps in the walls.

Reality drifted away. Part of his mind urged him to rise and dance to the insistent beat. Another saner part suggested he lie down and sleep. His eyelids closed. The building swayed and with the beat of the music insistent in his ears, he dozed – only to wake marinated in sweat, head aching, eyes burning, his throat dry and raw.

The music had stopped and all eyes focused upon where the oldest of the dancers convulsed upon the floor. This was a halak: a spiritual leader who had led his acolytes in the rhythmic dance and into a trance state. Dazed and at last convinced that he was seriously ill, Vince fought to recover his wits. He burned with fever, his eyes smarted and, worst of all, it seemed to him that he was staring down from among the rafters at the activity below.

There was his own body – slumped between the old man and the young mother. There were his mates scattered amongst the tribespeople, and there the halak lay twitching on the bamboo floor. The man's convulsions diminished and he uttered throaty, snarling, coughing sounds like a tiger. His eyes opened. As he climbed slowly to his feet his companions stepped back, watching him carefully. The shaman gazed unhurriedly around. He made eye contact with his audience and began to utter a high-pitched, incomprehensible chant. With unnaturally slow movements, he reached into a woven bag at his waist with his left hand and withdrew a green leafy whisk. With his other hand he took out a handful of seeds.

With careful steps the halak moved to face the bulk of his audience. His body tensed and with a shrill shout he threw the beans from his half-open hand into the crowd. There was a deep hush as, with arm extended, he gradually spread his fingers. Four seeds remained. A collective gathering of breath and a chatter of approval said it was a favourable omen.

Confused by his dream-like state and the events unfolding below, Vince watched the halak cross the floor. Over some people, he waved his whisk; onto others he blew through hands that formed a tube while addressing them all in that same strange voice.

Intrigued, Vince saw the halak approach his own body, still slouched upon the bench. The shaman gazed intently into the inert face, looked upward into the rafters, passed his hand over the body and gestured for Vince to descend. He felt himself falling into eyes like pools of orange fire, sensing that he was being told things he could not understand.

chapter two

A voice called urgently from far away. 'Can you hear me?'

'Wake up! Doctor, I'm not getting life signs!'

Yet another voice asked, 'What's wrong? Why are you doing this?'

Vince was troubled. He was in the longhouse; the halak was speaking, almost singing instructions on how to approach a gunig – a familiar – while fully into a state of trance. These other voices disturbed and distracted him. He tried to sink deeper into the trance but now something pushed violently and rhythmically against his chest. Irritated, he opened his eyes.

Startlingly, he was in a hospital bed surrounded by white gowns and nurses' uniforms. His chest was sore; a man in a white gown was pressing it vigorously with both hands. Another gripped Vince's chin with one hand while the other pressed on his forehead. His lips were only inches away from Vince's own. They were beginning CPR, while several nurses stood by ready to assist.

Vince jerked his head away. 'Not you', he croaked. 'Her.' He indicated with his eyes a nurse on the other side of the bed. The doctors straightened with astonished grins.

'Well,' said the chest-pounder dryly. 'This'll be one for the medical journals. If patients won't return to consciousness when required, get Willie here to threaten to kiss them.'

Vince soon realised that he was in the Taiping BMH; he had been here before with malaria.

This time, he was prescribed bed rest for two weeks. He slept most of the first week – and thought. He remembered the longhouse and the halak's eyes. There were also flashbacks: unclear memories of being half-carried from the longhouse to the camp and then from there to a landing zone. An injured Senoi soldier, a member of the Senoi Praak, an armed unit of Senoi soldiers set up by the security forces to counter another recruited by the rebels, also waited for the chopper. He recalled being helped aboard along with the Senoi, being unloaded and the Senoi being castigated for spitting betel juice on to the floor of the aircraft.

When he awoke, he lay there in his bed and tried to understand what the halak had told him. In his dreams, he danced to a bamboo beat and talked with the shaman, conversations that, though intelligible and lucid in his dreams, had now become incomprehensible fragments.

Vince had no recollection of eating, defecating or washing for the last several days, and he was embarrassed to realise that he must have been fed, put on bedpans and given bed baths by nurses. As soon as he was able, he would quietly shuffle down the ward to the toilets and showers during the night shift.

One morning, he was too late. The Australian ward sister came on duty, saw his empty bed and stormed into his shower stall. 'Come out of there, you silly bastard. You know you're on bloody bed rest!' The remainder of the ward was entertained to see her dump Vince naked and dripping onto the bed and dry him vigorously.

Struggling to preserve a shred of dignity, he murmured soulfully, 'Oh, Sister! Please say you'll still love me in the morning.'

'Watch it soldier,' she warned grimly, 'or I'll have your balls for yo-yos, and there'll never be a better opportunity than now.'

A puzzled Gurkha patient asked, 'Why is Memsahib being wet and wrestling with the sick Kiwi?'

The senior medical officers told Vince that he was recovering from scrub typhus, a disease caused by a tiny mite. 'It enters the body through the smallest of wounds and lay its eggs,' he explained to the junior medical officers during ward rounds. 'The fever is the effect of antibodies produced by the body in response to the hatching eggs.' As though producing a rabbit from his hat, he would deftly flick aside the sheet and declaim the ulcer on Vince's right shin to be 'a classical mite invasion site'.

After two weeks of bed rest Vince was relieved to be permitted to get up and wander around the hospital grounds. To have the freedom of the latrines and the showers was bliss.

Strange dreams, centred on the evening in the longhouse, still haunted his sleep but the fever and headaches went. As his strength returned, he felt better every day and the shuffle, when he first got out of bed, became a normal walk. By the end of the second week he felt fit, and he was happy to be loaded with others onto a bus to be sent for a week of recuperation in the Cameron Highlands.

Vince sat alone on the bus. He did not feel like chatting. As the countryside passed by he reflected on the changes since they had arrived in Malaya. 'Black roads', where vehicles must travel in convoy and under military escort had gone. School buses no longer needed an armed guard and the vegetation, cleared back from the roads to avoid providing shelter for ambushes, was growing back with tropical speed.

They passed Kuala Kangsar, the home of the Sultan of Perak, wove their way through flocks of cyclists, some carrying all manner of cargo, and between the rows of Chinese shop-houses that formed intermittent townships on the tin-rich plains around Ipoh. At last the bus turned east. It ground its tortuous way up an alarmingly narrow road to lead them past tea and coffee plantations, alongside terraced gardens of temperate climate produce, and finally reached its destination.

chapter three

BMH Cameron Highlands was a converted school, perched on a slope overlooking the township and a nine-hole golf course. In early afternoon, the bus parked at the rear and they clambered out to stretch and stare curiously around. The remaining day was taken up by lunch, followed by roll call and assignment of beds and lockers in the three wards available. Kit issue and orientation took up the remainder of the afternoon. The blankets and pullovers, both rarely seen at lower altitudes, intrigued them.

A nursing sister, crisply uniformed and bearing the two stripes of a lieutenant on her epaulettes, provided the orientation. She introduced herself as Sister Mathews and was clear, concise, informative – and very attractive. Vince noticed slender ankles, shapely calves in their white nylon stockings and found himself distracted by the way in which the otherwise severe uniform tightened over her breasts when she moved her arms.

He admired her hair – light brown with undertones of gleaming red. Would it look blonder when brushed out of its rather severe chignon? He was startled to hear his name.

'You – Corporal.' She glanced at her clipboard, 'Corporal Tanner, do you have any questions? Do you know the time for lights out? When is reveille?

What is the dress for convalescents who visit the town in the afternoon and when may they do so?'

Despite her severe tone, he could see an amused glint in her eyes. A whisper came from behind him. 'Ten, six, pyjamas and dressing gown, one to five.' She waved him back into his seat and he cleared his throat.

'Yes ma'am.' He echoed the information he had just received.

'Well, thank you Corporal.' She smiled with exaggerated sweetness. 'You have been most attentive, and thanks to your friend behind you for his contribution also.' She looked around briskly. 'Are there any questions?'

Normally shy with women, Vince found he wanted this one's attention. 'Uh, yes ma'am,' he coughed and cleared his throat. 'Sorry, I, er – we, wondered if there were any recreation facilities available between dinner and lights out.'

She regarded him thoughtfully. 'I don't know what sort of recreation you have in mind, Corporal, but by the cafeteria where you ate lunch there are two dartboards and several card tables. Darts, playing cards and chess sets are on racks nearby.' She hesitated, glanced around the room and added. 'There are usually off-duty nursing staff around after dinner if you want any help.' She smiled again. 'I shall be out there tonight if anyone wants to challenge me at canasta. I must warn you, however – I think that I'm rather good at it.'

Vince watched her dreamily. Her dark brown eyes contained orange flecks and he thought for an instant of the longhouse and the eyes of the halak, boring through a smoky haze and into his mind. He threw off the thought and studied her lips. Sweetly curved and pinkly luscious, especially when not drawn into the uncompromising line they had been in earlier. Her make-up was sparing. Not, he thought judiciously, that she needs much.

Diverted by a slight tic, a vein in her throat, he noticed a line of pink scar tissue below her right jawline, bordered by pale suture marks. Unobtrusive but visible, it caused Vince to speculate with unaccustomed concern: how'd she get that? Dreamily, he wondered at her age – somewhere between twenty-five and thirty?

Chairs were being put away and the briefing was over. A tap on his shoulder turned him towards Bryson, one of the Aussies he had met at the Planters' and Miners' Club in Ipoh some months before. Bryson had been the helpful whisperer. He was beaming. 'How ya going sport?' He pumped Vince's hand vigorously. 'Haven't seen ya since Ipoh. What a night, eh? Those old jokers had some pretty interesting stories eh? Too much booze and no sheilas, but.'

Vince did not know Bryson well, but liked him a lot. From Brisbane, he was large, ginger, freckled, enthusiastic and at times overwhelming; any room he was in seemed crowded.

After some mutual reminiscence, Vince moved to leave. 'See you later, mate. I better sort out my gear.'

Bryson looked earnest, took him by the arm and steered him towards the door. 'I reckon I got you out of the poo just now. You was dreaming 'stead of listening. What's the deal with the nurse sheila, eh?' He had a whisper that made public address systems redundant.

To Vince's horror, Sister Mathews turned and quizzically raised her eyebrows. Blushing, he seized Bryson by the elbow and hustled him into the cafeteria. 'For Christ's sake keep your voice down,' he whispered.

Bryson nodded his satisfaction. 'I thought so. You've got the hots for her, you randy bugger! For the last half hour you've been looking as though you was going to jump on her and commit an unpardonable act right in front of the troops.' He looked serious. 'Don't forget, sport, she's an officer. If they catch you poking one of their own, they'll have your balls gift-wrapped and sent home on a different plane.' He grinned again, kindly. 'Cheer up, soldier, I think you've fallen in lust – and we all know the cure for that, eh?' He winked, punched Vince lightly in the ribs and walked off, calling slyly over his shoulder. 'See you at canasta – lover.'

Dinner was like mess-call in camp. Patients queued, plates in hand, to be served by mess-helpers. The food was good and instead of on benches, they sat at tables set for four. Vince's meal companions were two Kiwis, whom he knew slightly, and a Brit. Kevin had arrived in Singapore as reinforcement for a REME – Royal Electrical and Mechanical Engineers – unit and was promptly knocked over by a taxi. As he exclaimed with righteous sorrow, '…and I never got me end in or even got to Bugis Street before I was clobbered!'

After dinner some patients moved to the side of the room to play darts or cards, read, or just to sit and talk. Vince realised with disgust that the hollow feeling in his gut indicated he was anxious to see Sister Mathews. He thought of going outside for a smoke, reading a book or drinking the bottle of Anchor beer that had been issued that afternoon. Instead his legs displayed a worrying independence and carried him falteringly, but remorselessly, to the table where the sister was about to sit.

'Good evening, Sister,' he quavered. 'Do you feel up to teaching me how to play canasta!'

'Good evening, Corporal,' she replied sweetly. 'I'd be happy to, but won't you need your friend to prompt you?'

Unable to simultaneously force a smile and grind his teeth, Vince mumbled, 'I'm just a simple Kiwi, Sister, but I'll try to manage on my own.'

Others drifted over. Soon they had four, only one of whom apart from the lieutenant had played before. They drew for partners, the novices to be paired with the more experienced. Rangi, a rifleman from D Company, was Vince's partner while Ernie, a young national serviceman from Leeds, was paired with the lieutenant. Sister Mathews sat on Vince's right, with Rangi sitting opposite him and Ernie on his left.

As they played, Vince became increasingly aware of her closeness. He sensed the heat of her body against his cheek. Her sweet musky woman scent made his heart race distractingly. Sometimes when she moved her sleeve would brush his bare arm and deliciously disturbing tingles ran up his spine as the short hairs on the back of his neck bristled with pleasure. He tried to concentrate on the game and not appear to be too inept a pupil, but despaired that he would again make a fool of himself.

Occasionally he imagined a warm pressure against his right knee, yet when he sought to return it there was nothing there. Once, when she dropped a card, she put a hand on Vince's knee for balance as she retrieved it. Although the hand was quickly withdrawn with a murmured 'sorry', he tingled with delight.

With mingled relief and disappointment Vince realised that the game had come to an end. He and Rangi had lost, but not by too great a margin, and they both swelled with pride when the sister complimented them on their play. Vince glanced at his watch when the cards and the chairs were back in place: there were still forty minutes left before lights out.

While he fumbled for a way to retain Sister Mathews's attention, she turned from Ernie to Vince with a sunny smile. 'Let's go outside for a cigarette. I'd love to hear about New Zealand.' They went out to the concrete steps as Vince fought to control his right arm. Like his legs earlier, it had developed a will of its own and wanted to slip around her waist. They sat on the steps in the cool evening air and chatted idly. He lit cigarettes for each of them and for the next twenty minutes, they subtly probed each other for background information, exploring each other's views of the world, likes, dislikes and other trivialities.

She drew pensively on her cigarette. 'You know, I've wondered about emigrating to New Zealand. Is it difficult to find nursing positions there?'

'Gosh no – with your qualifications I'd bet you'd have no trouble at all. You'd want to go to Auckland though.' He rushed on. 'It's a sub-tropical climate.

Although it can get a bit rainy, the summers are beaut.'

She looked up with a quizzical smile. 'Beaut?'

He grinned sheepishly. 'Yeah, we're like the Aussies, our slang's a bit different. Means "good"; short for beautiful, I guess.'

She smiled encouragingly. 'Well, what do you do in this "beaut" summer weather?'

He laughed. 'There you are, Sister, you're practically a Kiwi already. You'd love the beaches, but the best in the world is Onetangi.' He described gathering tua tua, fishing for snapper and camping on his family's section on Waiheke Island.

'An island?' The idea intrigued her and he enthused over the islands of the Hauraki Gulf.

'Are there any snakes?' He shook his head and shuddered. 'No snakes, but you've got to watch out for wetas.' He grimaced.

She looked alarmed. 'Wetas! What are they?'

'Oh,' he shrugged. 'Just large insects that look like unusually ugly lobsters. Occasionally a dog will go missing, but it's a long time since a child got carried off. I…'

Her face wrinkled in horror. 'What! Insects that…' Her voice trailed away. 'Corporal, I think you're pulling my leg. That's not fair.' They exchanged grins.

Their backgrounds were disparate, but they had discovered feelings and thoughts that were surprisingly similar. A primitive part of their brains might have understood that they had launched on a mating ritual as ancient and stylised as that of courting albatrosses.

When they stubbed out their cigarettes in the ashtray Vince had fetched and prepared to go inside, she said with careful casualness. 'I've a day off tomorrow. I could show you around the town if you like. Perhaps we could have a game of golf?'

Vince nodded coolly and fought an urge to break into a dance of triumph. 'That'd be great, Sister. Until tomorrow then – goodnight.' He paused shyly. 'I've really enjoyed talking to you.'

When he stood aside to allow her to precede him up the steps she hesitated and turned her head quickly, 'I've enjoyed it too – very much – in spite of your teasing. Wetas – ugh!' Another pause. 'Let's meet at the bottom of the steps out front at 1400 hours tomorrow? Goodnight.' She moved up the steps and disappeared through the door.

Vince's euphoria disappeared when he saw his bed. The ward was small, containing twelve beds, with a door at the far end leading to the ablutions. His bed was immediately to the left of the door as he entered, the two beds opposite being vacant. His displeasure was caused by the bits and pieces of gear that were scattered across his. Comics, a sock, the mate of which lay on the floor, a toilet bag and other odds and ends lay amongst the debris.

He glanced about; everyone else was either already in bed, or about to be. Some men he knew slightly, others he had barely met while they settled into their new environment. They seemed pretty good guys – with one notable exception.

Stan Danty was an uncouth lout. He was pimply, slovenly and despite the climate, pallid. His skin, like his coarse black hair, looked greasy and unwashed. A man who would without hesitation belch, fart and pick his nose in public. He was close to six feet tall, and his mother, in a good mood, might have described him as 'plump'.

Everyone was watching. What should he do? With a deep breath, Vince said as evenly as he could, 'Danty, please get your gear off my bed.'

Danty looked up indolently from his comic. 'For fook's sake man, if they're in yer fookin way, just put em on me locker.'

Controlling himself with an effort, Vince spoke quietly. 'Have your junk off my bed before I get back.' He carried his toilet bag into the ablutions, wondering how a day could go so wrong so quickly. Teeth cleaned and face washed, he was back in the ward within four minutes.

Nothing had changed. Ignoring the air of expectancy, Danty lay back and gazed at his comic. Without comment, Vince put his toilet bag in the nightstand and glanced at his watch. Seven minutes to lights out. He turned back his bedcovers and, with a quick flick, sent all the mess onto the floor.

Danty sat up, outraged. 'You fookin Kiwi prick! Wot the fook do you think yer doing with me gear? Yer joost a jumped up fookin' lance-jack, don't you come throwing your weight around with me.' He leered. 'Joost because yer tryin' to slip it to that nurse tart, yer think yer better than us.' He grinned nastily. 'Don't worry, we'll all have our turn with her. Everyone knows she roots like a rattlesnake. Now you pick up my kit!'

Slowly Vince walked around to where most of the gear lay scattered. Danty, with a smirk of smug satisfaction, lay back on his pillow. As a very junior NCO, Vince was quite proud of his command voice. For a man of moderate stature, he felt that he could produce sufficient decibels to get all the attention he needed.

In his hospital pyjamas he stood at attention between the beds and took a deep breath. 'Atten'shun! Get-your-arse-off-that-bed-Private-Danty-and-get your-heels-together! NOW! I may be "*joost a fookin' lance-jack*," but I'm ready, willing and able to put you on a charge! At-the-double now! MOVE!'

Shocked and bewildered, Danty found himself impelled into a position approximating attention. Vince, however, knew better than to accept that as sufficient. 'Stand straight, man. Pull-yourself-together-get-to-attention!' he bellowed. 'You're only a make-believe soldier, but try to look like a real one!'

Regaining some composure, Danty straightened his spine marginally and sneered. 'Wot yer think yer can charge me with then?'

Lowering his voice, Vince stepped up close and spoke with all the menace he could summon. 'In the last few minutes you have: defamed an officer whilst under her authority, behaved in a manner to the prejudice of good order and military discipline, trashed a hospital ward and defied an NCO. Worst of all you have severely pissed me off! What else do you want?' He locked eyes with Danty and only permitted himself a luxurious blink when Danty finally looked away.

'You've got two choices. Apologise to me now and to Lieutenant Mathews tomorrow in my presence, or I'll designate an escort to march your arse down the street to the provost marshall's office – I'll think up more charges along the way.' Vince glanced around the ward, delighted to see eight enthusiastic hands waving in the air.

Danty measured the strength of feeling against him and, choking on the words and probably unwilling to resume an acquaintanceship with the provost marshall's department, mumbled a reluctant 'sorry'.

'I can't hear you, Danty! Want to try again?'

Wearily, but a little louder now, 'I'm very sorry, Corporal.'

As Vince was about to dismiss him, the night sister bustled into the room, looking around sternly. 'What's going on? You're disturbing the whole hospital and it's time for lights out.'

'Sorry, Sister,' said Vince humbly. 'Private Danty was anxious to improve his military manners. I was trying to help him. Sorry about the noise.' Mollified, she wished them goodnight. As the light flicked off, Vince was intrigued to intercept a wink between the sister and Angelo in his bed on the opposite side of the ward. He tried to compose himself for sleep, but it was difficult to settle. He was upset by his confrontation with Danty. The offensive remarks about Sister Mathews were more disturbing than Vince cared to admit.

His stance, although largely bluff, seemed to have worked. What else could

I have done? he asked himself. If I'd backed down, I'd get no respect from anybody and the fat bugger's got the weight and reach to beat the shit out of me. I bet he'd fight dirty too.

Vince sighed. I did the right thing, he thought, and he wished he had persevered with learning judo.

With some mates, he had joined a judo club when they'd first arrived in Taiping, without realising how regular absences on operations would inhibit their progress. Consequently, when they did attend the classes, they were so far behind that much of their time was spent merely practising 'break-falls'. Sometimes an astonishingly adept adolescent deigned to face them on the mat and proceed to throw them all around the gym. Tired of being demonstration missiles, most had returned to brothels and bars for recreation.

It was doubtful that he could have made the charges stick, or even certain that he could exert authority over a soldier of another nation, even if they *were* part of the same Brigade. His main concern was that the others would think that he, a mere lance-jack, had overstepped the mark and gone mad with the power.

Vince pushed Danty from his mind to turn his thoughts to Sister Mathews. He was amazed, even frightened, at how much pleasure he gained from thinking about her. Suddenly he was terrified. Bloody hell, he thought. I can't be falling in love!

He knew that he handled rejection badly. When a relationship ended, if it were his own doing, he would feel sad. But if a girl dumped him, he might be devastated for months. It was a sickness that he traced back to childhood. When his parents' marriage broke up, his mother had departed the family home leaving only a note of regret and farewell. For a ten-year-old boy it was not enough and the sense of rejection ate at his soul.

In the morning Vince ignored malevolent sidelong glances from Danty, but there were no comments about the previous night's upheaval until Danty had hurried through perfunctory ablutions and scuttled off to the cafeteria. Once he'd gone, Angelo joined the others in slapping Vince on the shoulder with mumbles of, 'good on yer mate' and other approving noises.

A Brit, whom Vince had noticed on the bus with two stripes on his sleeve, shook his hand. 'Sorry, I didn't jump in meself, but you sorted the bastard any road.' He laughed. 'Yer had us all jumpin lad. I had me feet on the floor a'fore I knew what I was doin. Any road, if tha' has more trouble wit' the 'erk, I'll back yer all the way.' He paused. 'I'll take 'im over any time yer like, but yer sortin 'im out right well.'

Bryson followed him from the cafeteria after breakfast. Angelo had mentioned what had happened and he was after the full story. It was not something Vince wanted to pursue, and at last Bryson gave up to go and prepare for ward rounds. He said as he left, 'That Danty's a real prick, don't trust the bugger an inch. Why don't I arrange a little accident? He's the sort of bloke who's likely to fall down the stairs.' Vince declined with thanks. 'Think about it, sport,' Bryson advised. 'It could keep the bastard out of our hair all week.'

Ward rounds passed without incident. The ward sister wheeled a cart stacked with medical charts and accompanied the MO conducting the rounds. When the procession stopped at the foot of their beds, patients came to attention until the MO murmured 'at ease'. Charts were glanced at, patients examined and asked a few questions. The Sister made notes and the circus moved on. It was a tedious business that continued for half an hour.

With ward rounds over, the patients were encouraged to play badminton or netball behind the hospital or just watch from the sidelines. Vince joined the badminton players. He hoped it would take his mind off the confrontation with Danty, which he knew was far from over.

Nervous about his afternoon rendezvous with Sister Mathews, he worried that he might develop a hopeless infatuation. Hopeless, first because she was an officer, which made her off-limits to a very junior NCO. And, second, because he had no reason to believe that beyond some curiosity about New Zealand, she had the least interest in him. Third, he was uncomfortably conscious of the difference in their backgrounds. And fourth – he sighed deeply – it'd just make life too bloody complicated.

While he waited to shower before lunch Vince chatted with Jeff Jarvis, the Brit corporal who had spoken to him that morning. Danty had been absent during ward rounds and Jay-Jay, as he was known, reported. 'The sneaky sod's bin shif'ed to ano'her ward. Told Sister he had awful pains in the gut and doctor told 'er to admit 'im to an investigation room. Good riddance', he sniffed. 'Tha's a nasty 'un an' we're be'er off without 'im.'

Vince wholeheartedly agreed. He regarded the bed next to his own – neat, tidy, sans Danty – and hoped fervently that it would remain so.

After lunch Vince fidgeted. It was a good meal by army standards, but his stomach churned uncomfortably. At 1345 hours he searched for reason and opportunity to cancel the appointment. At 1355 hours he was at the bottom of the steps in pyjamas and dressing gown, self-conscious and afraid she would not arrive. By 1357 hours he could not keep still. He walked around the corner and came back as she descended the last few steps.

He gazed and gulped. Commonsense doubts evaporated like morning dew. She was gorgeous! Out of uniform, the transformation was remarkable. A beige cotton skirt reached to just below her knees, the short-sleeved blouse of ivory silk, soft collar half turned up to cover her throat, and beige rimmed sunglasses made her look like a film star out for a casual afternoon stroll.

The severe chignon was replaced by wavy brown hair, the ends, blonded slightly by the sun, bouncing lightly against her shoulders and afternoon sun struck golden highlights from her hair. Her legs were bare and her small delicate feet were clad in light sandals.

'Sister!' He gaped at her. 'You look truly lovely. Did you step off the set of some glamorous movie? I'm' – he looked down at his dressing gown, pyjamas and issue leather sandals – 'a stand-in for *Lost Weekend*.'

She gurgled with soft, pleased laughter. 'Why, thank you, Corporal. You say you're from New Zealand, but that sounds like blarney to me! Now, it's a lovely afternoon and we're away from the hospital. Please call me Audrey and I shall call you Vince. Okay?'

They strolled down the main street with Audrey acting as tour guide. She pointed out the stall where 'they make the best nasi-goring in Malaya', her favourite vendor of Chinese noodles and glazed duck, and the shop where the knowledgeable could eat 'the greatest tandoori chicken and dhal outside India'. 'And there,' she pointed to the other side of the road. 'There's the vegetable market. Early in the day you can buy almost any tropical or sub-tropical fruit that's in season.'

'Do they sell durian?' Vince asked innocently.

'No,' she shot him a suspicious look. 'It's too early in the season. Nasty smelly stuff anyway.'

The durian season had begun about a month after the battalion arrived. The green fruit as large as a watermelon was forbidden in camp, and hotel signs prohibited it on their premises, for when the hard spiky skin is punctured a terrible stench evocative of open drains almost stuns the senses. Because of its local reputation as an aphrodisiac, everyone had to try it. The Malays were said to have a proverb: 'When the durian comes down, the sarongs go up.' Short Storey, the platoon clown, described it best when he exclaimed in disgust, 'Jeez, it's like eating fruit salad in a shithouse!' Bobby Kendrick claimed to have eaten one that kept him and the entire staff of a knocking shop occupied all weekend.

Vince was happy to stroll beside Audrey and enjoy her cheerful chatter.

He had grown accustomed to the theatre of Malay street life and he never tired of it. He enjoyed the spicy smells from the food stalls, the scent of joss sticks wafting from open doorways, the mixture of races and the colourful variety of their dress.

Plump, dignified Malays in sonkoks were followed at several paces by a wife or two and scampers of bright-eyed children. Vince and Audrey acknowledged 'selamats' from others and continued on through the throng. Graceful Malay ladies in traditional baju kabaya of fine fabric slid sinuously past, in contrast to their peasant cousins in similar but less elegant garments.

Today Vince continued to be amazed at the colour and variety of the crowd. There were Malay men and women in Western dress, and Chinese or Indian vendors passed by delivering meals in banana-leaf packages. The Chinese women were dressed sometimes in formal and attractive cheong sam, form fitting and split to the thigh, or beautifully brocaded silk sam fu, but more often in the utilitarian cotton 'pyjama suits' of Chinese workers. Indian ladies drifted by like colourful butterflies, sweeping the ground with their bright saris. Turbaned Sikhs with authoritative beards and Hindus in white dhotis and shirts added to the mix.

Audrey nudged him and nodded towards the other side of the street where a small procession of Aborigines trudged towards them. Unused to paved surfaces, uncomfortable between buildings under the curious gaze of strangers, they kept away from the crowded footpath.

At their head was an elderly man with a walking staff in his left hand and a whisk of twigs and dried grass in his right. Like the other men, he wore a loincloth from the top of which protruded a dangerous-looking parang. A sarong was rolled and tied across his body. Despite his age and apparent frailty, he had the air of dignity and authority of a penghulu, or a halak.

Behind him were five others: a sturdy middle-aged man in a torn khaki shirt, two women and two handsome youths, one of whom carried a blowpipe over his shoulder and the other a hunting spear. One of the women looked old and tired. Worn from child bearing and the pressure of years, her sarong was raised over pendulous breasts that hung to her waist.

The other, perhaps her daughter, was young and nubile. Probably no more than sixteen years of age, she carried herself like royalty. Brown rippling hair hung below her shoulders. Coppery, Mediterranean-like features, together with a sarong rolled down to her waist to reveal pert young breasts, formed a picture that Vince found totally charming.

An elbow in the ribs diverted his attention. 'Isn't she lovely?' Audrey smiled.

'Just don't get too carried away! I think I know that group. I recognise the man in the shirt, and the old lady too. I think they belong to a ladang in the Berincang valley, about eighteen miles north of here in Kelantan.

'Nursing and medical staff at the hospital are divided into teams,' she explained. 'We have a rota and when choppers are available and there's a landing pad near population centres, the teams try to hold clinics a few times a year. My team is scheduled to go up that way on Thursday – if the chopper we were promised is in service.'

As she spoke the group of Temiar drew level with them. The man in the shirt glanced at Audrey and grinned in recognition. He spoke over his shoulder and the women smiled shyly and waved. Audrey beamed appreciatively. 'That's nice, I'm not always sure if I'm getting through to them, but I believe they understand more than they let on. At least this shows that they do recognise us. Oh…' She faltered for a second. 'If we turn right here it will take us towards the golf course.'

Vince nodded. 'Yeah, I reckon most of them understand more than they let on. I was with a patrol looking for a landing-zone the SAS set up a couple of years ago,' he said. 'It was marked on our map, but we couldn't find it. We were just about to give up when we ran into a couple of Senoi guys crossing a stream. They seemed friendly, but not too bright, and they were carrying hunting spears. Their hair was too frizzy to be Temiar and they both had skin infections over most of their bodies. They'd rubbed mud onto their sores and didn't look very pretty. We took up the usual positions for halts on the trail. The medic got his kit out to treat their rashes and Neil, our patrol leader, tried to question them.

'Neil got his thoughts together, faced them and waved towards the sky, speaking slowly. "Many moons ago whirly-birds come here." He swung his hands around and pointed at the ground, "From the sky. Where they land?"

'The guys leaned on their spears and looked blank. They looked from one another to the Corporal. Neil whirled his arms and made motor noises until he was hoarse. At last the eyes of the scruffiest one lit up. He looked at his mate doubtfully: "Helicopter?"'

Audrey laughed. 'Yes, that's exactly the sort of thing I mean.' She touched Vince's arm. 'Look,' she said, 'there's Mr Wu. Mr Wu is a good friend and also my landlord. I must ask him if he has been able to repair the door lock for me.' Impulsively, she pulled on Vince's arm. 'Come and meet him. He's a lovely man. You'll like him.'

Vince followed her gaze. Mr Wu was a short, slightly rotund Chinese man of middle years. He had a round cheerful face and dark eyes that flickered with intelligence. He greeted Audrey with an enthusiastic delight that Vince thought must discredit forever the trite phrase, 'inscrutable Oriental'. Clad in blue overalls liberally spattered with paint, Mr Wu was busily scraping at the flaking surfaces around the front window of a small shop. Vince assumed him to be the owner and peered inside. Seen from the sunlit street the interior was dark, but a number of objects were displayed around the room. He sniffed at the scent of joss sticks that drifted from the open doorway. Suddenly, he realised that Audrey was speaking to him.

'Vince, I'd like you to meet Mr Wu,' she said, rather formally he thought. 'Mr Wu is my very good friend, and a wonderful landlord.' She laughed. 'He's just fixed my door lock so I had better praise him up. Mr Wu, this is a new friend of mine, Vince Tanner. Vince is with the New Zealand Battalion and is recovering from one of the nasty tropical ailments we get here. We are just getting to know one another and I think we are becoming good friends.' Vince was charmed by the flush, which spread up her neck as she spoke, and his heart leapt at the hint of a developing attraction.

They shook hands. Vince murmured the usual pleasantries.

'Velly please to meet you, Hon'ble Sir. It make my day; delightful to gaze upon your esteem' countenance,' lisped a beaming Mr Wu. 'Some time you mus' honour my humble premises with your esteem' person.' He added a little bow for good measure.

Vince gathered his wits and replied with equal solemnity, 'Kapai, e hoa. She'll be sweet eh? Too right, flaming oath, you beaut,' and returned the bow. Mr Wu's eyes grew round as his mouth fell open.

A chortle of mirth erupted from Audrey, in which Mr Wu ruefully joined. 'That was wonderful, Vince,' she spluttered. 'Mr Wu, you have been asking for that for a very long time!'

'You may be right,' confessed the grinning Chinaman. He winked at Vince. 'I like your young man, Audrey, don't let him get away. In future I shall be careful to avoid putting on my act for Kiwis.' All of this, Vince noticed, was spoken in faultless English, with a very slight accent he could not identify. Mr Wu wished them both a pleasant afternoon and returned to his work as Vince and Audrey resumed their walk.

As she led the still bewildered Vince away, Audrey giggled and whispered, 'I should have warned you. He loves to speak to new acquaintances as though he's escaped from an old Charlie Chan film. You were a picture when he went into his little act. Did you see his face when you set him up so beautifully?

'Mr Wu's family,' Audrey continued, 'were among the many Chinese who settled in Vietnam centuries ago. His family seems to have been pretty well off, but he got caught up in the anti-colonial war against the French. After Dien Bien Phu he found communist rule in the north no better than that of the French and left. Disillusioned and looking for a new start, he obtained residency in Malaya as a businessman.

'Apparently, his anti-colonial feelings don't extend to the British,' Audrey chattered on. 'After the last war he obtained a degree in business management or something, from the LSE. His dislike of the French is still profound. He won't even speak the language that was his own second tongue. Because he's of Chinese descent and Special Branch found out that he'd fought with the communists against the French, they're suspicious of him. Anyway, what was that nonsense you said to him?'

'Aw, just "friend" in Maori and a jumble of Aussie and Kiwi slang.' They waved at a group from the hospital, including Bryson and Angelo. Vince noted that these two were making up a threesome with the dark-haired sister with whom Angelo had exchanged winks the previous night.

Vince was content to stroll around the nicely laid-out nine-hole course with Audrey, but was pleased when she flushed in the way that had charmed him earlier and said casually, 'Whew, it's hot and I didn't bring a hat. Let's wander back. I'll check my new lock and we can sit in the shade with cool drinks while you tell me all about your wicked past.'

He grinned. 'Cool drinks in the shade sound great! If we're going to talk about a wicked past though, it'll have to be yours. I don't have one. I was perfect as a child and it continued into adulthood. See, totally boring.'

Audrey gazed majestically down her nose. 'Reticence and evasion will not be tolerated!' she warned with a mock scowl. 'Ve haff vays of making you talk.'

Vince brightened immediately. 'You cannot force me to talk against my will,' he declared. 'Only kisses and prolonged bodily contact can break my silence.' He flung himself to his pyjama'd knees and cried piteously, 'You couldn't be so cruel to an innocent youth.'

Red-faced, Audrey looked around wildly. People on a nearby green watched in open fascination. 'Get up, you silly bugger,' she hissed, whirled and stalked away.

Alarmed that she seemed upset, Vince scrambled to his feet and hurried after her. When he drew close her head was down and she seemed to be sobbing. 'Good one,' he muttered miserably. 'I've stuffed up again.' When he drew level to apologise, he realised that she was sobbing with laughter, real tears running down her face. He was relieved. 'Really Sister, language! You've been talking to too many Australians.'

She stopped, shook her head in frustration, and wiped her eyes with a handkerchief. 'Oh! Oh, you're incorrigible. You deserve a beating.'

'Mmmm, that could be fun. But could I have that cold drink first?'

They strolled towards the main street while Audrey explained why she rented her 'retreat', as she called it. 'I'm not really anti-social, but I like to have a little privacy sometimes. The other girls are all nice enough and our quarters are all right, but sometimes I like to read and listen to music. Whenever I settle down with a book, or to listen to a record, someone wants to chat, borrow nail polish, lipstick, or talk about her love life. Now I have the best of both worlds; whenever I don't feel like company I just come here and relax. D'you think that's unreasonable?'

'Absolutely not,' Vince declared stoutly, 'I really hate it in the barracks when I'm reading and someone wants to borrow my lipstick or nail polish or even – would you believe it? – my mascara!'

'Just vait until I get you inside, you vill pay for this foolish levity!'

Across the road from Mr Wu's shop, they stopped beside a wooden door that opened directly from the street. Audrey slipped a shiny new key into the lock and opened it. 'Now get inside,' she ordered ferociously, 'and prepare for your punishment!' Inside, he looked around as she closed the door. She gave his shoulder a gentle squeeze. 'Welcome! Please make yourself at home while I get the drinks.'

He took stock of his surroundings. It was a pleasant room, rectangular, airy and quite large. A kitchenette, with a tiny sink-bench, fridge, stove and a small wooden table and chairs, was partly concealed by an ornately carved Kashmiri screen. The wall on his right was taken up by two sets of triple glass doors. Before disappearing behind the screen to get the drinks, Audrey drew back colourful batik drapes to reveal a small garden beyond.

A large rattan settee with a coffee table beside it faced the glassed doors. It matched the two chairs against the opposite wall; their comfortable-looking loose cushions were covered with the same fabric as the drapes. That door in the opposite wall, he thought, must be a bathroom.

A bookcase supported an electric record player and a pile of records. Several shelves of assorted Balinese woodcarvings and a set of ivory globes stood on a carved stand of the same material. Walls and ceiling were painted in shades of ivory. The floor, of some beige material, was broken by a large woven brown and orange mat, and line drawings, in gold on black paper, of Thai dancers in traditional poses decorated the walls.

Audrey returned and handed Vince a glass beaded with moisture. He accepted it with thanks and took a sip. 'Ahhh', he sighed contentedly. 'Mango and orange, delicious!'

Her eyes sparkling, Audrey gestured towards the settee. 'Sit,' she commanded. 'Wicked past: confession to begin – now! Questions may be asked for clarification as required.' She turned towards him with raised eyebrows. 'Yes?'

Vince took a deep swallow, placed his glass on the coffee table and leaned back smugly. 'Sorry, nothing to confess except a life of purity and good works. I could make it more interesting with the right incentive. Remember? Kisses and prolonged bodily contact.' To his delighted surprise, Audrey turned to put her hand on his shoulder and leaned forward to kiss him lightly on the cheek. Oh God, he breathed. Even her sweat smells heavenly.

She pulled away with a serious stare and whispered. 'All right, are you certain that's what you want?'

His throat went dry. 'Yes,' he croaked, 'oh yes!'

'Okay!' She jumped to her feet and headed towards the door.

Confused, he sat upright. 'W-what's the matter, where are you going?'

Audrey paused. 'To fetch Ishmael of course.'

Thoroughly bewildered, he clutched his head and fought a rising irritation. 'Who in heaven's name's Ishmael?'

'Oh, he's a Malay boy who rents a room over Mr Wu's shop. He too, wears lipstick and mascara. I'm sure he would be happy to provide all the kisses and prolonged bodily contact you want while I go shopping.' She burst into laughter and ran for the bathroom.

Vince caught her before she reached the door and they collapsed giggling onto the settee. At last they fell silent and looked at one another. She lay across his lap as he leaned back on the settee. 'How did you get to be such a tease?'

'Easy,' she grinned, 'I've been learning from an expert.' She reached up, put her arms around Vince's neck and drew his head down until their lips met in a long, sweet kiss.

After a time she wriggled away. When he protested, she said she had to blow her nose and wipe her eyes. She returned with a box of tissues, handed it to Vince and together they repaired the damage caused by their laughter. For the rest of the afternoon, while the ceiling fan made faint thunking sounds, they snuggled together and exchanged reminiscences of past lives. After a time, Audrey stirred and looked at him. 'I'll bet that your mother wasn't too pleased if you teased your brothers and sisters as you do me.'

He glanced away, towards the bookcase. 'Mum left home when I was a kid, taking my little sister with her. I've another sister, Bernice. She's a teacher in Whangarei.'

Audrey placed her hand on his arm. 'I'm sorry, I didn't mean to pry.' She was silent for a moment. 'Life's not always easy, is it?'

'Yeah.' Vince nodded at the bookcase. 'Omar Khayyam, good stuff – and Kipling too!'

She looked surprised. 'Do you read poetry?'

He shrugged. 'Some, only the bits I like. Most of Kipling and Omar too.' He put his head back and looked at the ceiling. '"Awake! for Morning in the Bowl of Night has flung the Stone that puts the Stars to flight: And –"'

Audrey cut in quickly. '"And Lo! The Hunter of the East has caught the Sultan's –"'

'"–Turret in a Noose of Light."' They finished together and exchanged grins.

'Okay,' he said, feeling himself blush. 'Here's one about you.'

She straightened. 'Me?'

'Yeah,' he gulped, wishing that he had kept his mouth shut. 'Uh…Keats… I…I think. 'Um… "She walks in beauty, like the night of cloudless skies and sunny climes…" ugh,' he stumbled, 'that's probably not quite right…'

Audrey's face was pink and her eyes glistened. 'Not quite, you got "climes" and "skies" back to front – and it's Byron, but it's lovely and you're making me cry.' She dabbed her eyes with a tissue. 'Well I suppose that we'd better be getting back…'

'I guess so,' he mumbled.

In each other's company, they had found an unexpected freedom that neither wanted to end. At the door Audrey paused shyly. 'If I can swap duties I could be free again tomorrow afternoon. I'd love to spend more time talking to you – that is, if you have nothing else you'd rather do.' Pleased by Vince's obvious delight, she handed him a key. 'Let yourself in and make yourself at home. I'd like to think of you being here. If I can't get away stay as long as you like, but please leave me a note so I'll know you've been.'

They held each other silently for a few minutes before walking back to the hospital side by side.

At dinner Vince was too distracted to hear when spoken to. His table companions eventually gave up and talked around him. He completed his meal without knowing what he had eaten and went outside to smoke. Where he and Audrey had sat the previous evening, he sat and wondered at how quickly life can change.

Bryson came and sat down beside him as he began his second cigarette. He lit one of his own and swore Vince to secrecy. Angelo and Sonya, the dark-haired sister, were actually married. Bryson had introduced Angelo as a cousin of Luigi, who Vince remembered from the Planters' and Miners' Club.

They had broken the news to Bryson on the golf course that afternoon. It seemed they were old friends from schooldays. When Sonya, a career army nurse, was posted to Malaya, Angelo had hastened to enlist in the next Battalion being formed for service there. Thus, in Bryson's words, 'leaving all the sheilas in Melbourne with their knickers in a twist.' A couple of months earlier they had found a Filipino priest in Singapore who was willing to marry them in secret.

'Saw you and Sister down on the links this arvo, sport,' he remarked casually. 'You was kneelin' on the grass. The others reckoned you was proposing, but I told them you wasn't that sort of bloke. I said you was putting a Maori blessing on the place.' He looked doubtful. 'I'm not really sure they believed me, but... what *was* you doin', sport?'

'Well, uh, we – that is... I was just showing the sister how I played Al Jolson in a school concert.' He spread his arms. 'You know...Mammee, how I...'

Bryson backed away, holding up his hands. 'Yeah, yeah sport, okay. See you later.' Vince felt guilty. He longed to share his feelings with someone, but was too confused to speak them out loud – and Bryson was a great guy, but garrulous. He rose, sighed deeply, stubbed out his cigarette and went inside to bed.

Sleep was elusive. He thought about Audrey and burned with honest lust. He also ached with a great tenderness for her. He thought of her sweetness: her candid gaze, compassion, companionship, her humour, and was soothed. He remembered how she had set him up that afternoon. His chuckle provoked mutters from the darkness. He imagined her soft lips, the swell of her breasts, her sweet womanly odour and the way her hips undulated when she walked. An agitated groan provoked more muttering.

At last he fell deeply asleep, only to wake again in a sweat of horror. In his dream he had been sprawled with Audrey on her settee. Surrounded by discarded garments, they had made joyous love until she threw back her head and opened her lips in a moan of pleasure. Suddenly her fragrance was overwhelmed by a feral reek of tiger, her eyes had burned like embers and a throaty roar had erupted from her open mouth.

He sat bolt upright as a voice hissed, 'For God's sake shut up – lie on your back.'

Deprived of dreams of passion, but released from shock, Vince composed himself again for sleep. He shuddered as he drifted off. Holy hell! How would that guy Freud interpret a dream like *that*?

His waking emotions were balanced between ecstasy and stark terror. Every instinct drove him to make the first part of his dream come true, but a niggling doubt persisted: listen to that tiger – back off. In any event, he spent the entire morning fidgeting anxiously, waiting for the moment when he might see Audrey again.

All through breakfast and ward rounds he suffered, then through a game of badminton that left his partner exasperated. Somehow he got through lunch. At 1400, he shot down the stairs and into the street. Strolling yesterday with Audrey, absorbed in its ambience, he had enjoyed the walk. So much had changed. Now he strode urgently, heedless of how incongruous a figure he looked as he strode along, sandals slapping, dressing gown flapping around his legs. At Audrey's door he impatiently knocked twice.

There was no answer. His heart sank as he slipped the key she had given him into the lock and entered, waving back to Mr Wu in his shop doorway. The drapes were closed and he stood for a few minutes in the shadows. He felt like an intruder, disappointed that Audrey was not there but enjoying the lingering presence of her scent.

He turned on the ceiling fan and examined the ornaments. Beside the record player on the bookshelf, a Malay kris attracted him. A beautifully-made weapon with a hilt of lustrous ebony inlaid with silver, the sinuous curves of its blade were etched with delicate designs of crescents and stars that made it a work of art as much as an instrument of death.

He set the kris aside and examined the stack of records, delighted anew at the similarity of Audrey's tastes to his own. He put a disk of Ella Fitzgerald singing a selection of Cole Porter songs on the turntable and lay back on the settee to enjoy her rich, sultry tones. As Ella assured him: 'Though it was great fun, it was just one of those things', a key turned in the lock and Audrey stepped into the room.

She stood by the closed door. When he rose and crossed to her, they stood awkwardly, unsure and unspeaking. Not touching – just staring at each other. She had on a pale green, knee-length cotton dress with white buttons down the front. He reached to take her hands. 'Audrey,' he whispered with awed sincerity, 'I didn't think it possible, but you're even more lovely than you were yesterday.'

'And you, Vince, are still full of it,' she added with a tight smile. 'The blarney, I mean.'

The smile, such as it was, faded quickly and trembled. 'I am so pleased you came. I've been thinking about yesterday and wanting to see you. Then I started to worry that you'd changed your mind and wouldn't be here. Damn it! When I reached the door and heard the music, I knew you were here – but suddenly I was too nervous to come inside.' She sagged. 'I might still be out there if Mr Wu hadn't been giving me funny looks. I must have caught some virus; I'm not usually this stupid.'

Vince wondered if he too was ill. My mind's gone numb, he realised. How'd her head get tucked under my chin, and why am I giddy?

In order to think, he needed to stop the flow of her words and he bent to kiss her firmly. It did not work very well. When he opened his eyes again they were sprawled together on the settee.

For a time they lay close, held hands and stared wordlessly out the window. Then she turned to look solemnly into his eyes. 'I'm sorry I'm so silly. Maybe I really *have* caught a bug.'

'Yeah, maybe we both have. Perhaps we could be quarantined together?' He paused awkwardly. 'Look, I'm not very good at this, but there's something I should tell you.'

'Vince Tanner!' She dropped his hand. 'Are you going to tell me that you're married, or… or', her voice quavered, 'just having a fling?' She looked miserable. 'When I was outside the door and heard that song you were playing I felt sick. You were trying to give me a message, weren't you?'

He reached for her hand, but she jerked away and stood to remove the record still revolving mutely on the turntable. He waited for her to return but she remained staring, head down, at the record sleeve. He rose to stand behind her and place his hands on her shoulders. She did not pull away but beneath his fingers her flesh was tense and ungiving.

'Audrey,' he whispered. 'I've never had a wife, there's no message. I just like Ella – as you seem to. What I was trying to say is that I can't stop thinking about you. Ever since you spoke to us on Sunday and you were so stern with me.' He smiled weakly. 'Maybe I'm a masochist! I don't know what I'm eating, when people talk to me I don't know what they're saying. I only seem to be happy when I'm with you.' His voice rose. 'Bloody hell! You're the loveliest, sweetest, most beautiful woman I've ever known and you're driving me crazy!

I dream about you day and night. How the hell could you think that *any* man could be crazy enough not to want to be with you?'

He lowered his voice. 'Sorry, I've made a fool of myself again. I'd better go. Sorry about the speech too.' Audrey faced him and grabbed him by both arms.

'Oh please don't go. I started all this with my silly insecurity. Those few hours yesterday were more fun than I've had for years. I – I hope I haven't spoilt that! You haven't made a fool of yourself. I...'

She caught her breath and smiled wanly. 'Did you put some awful Maori spell on me to make me your slave, or slip a magic potion into my fruit juice yesterday? Anyway, I'm getting used to feeling like this – I might even get to like it.' She led him back to the settee, drew him down beside her and regarded him appraisingly. She spoke slowly, almost to herself. 'I've only known you for a couple of days, you're only moderately good looking and sometimes you're a real smart-arse. The army forbids us to fraternise; we only have a few more days to get to know each other before you'll go back to your unit. I dream about you too and I can't even contemplate not seeing you again. I *must* be crazy. Oh Vince, I want you to make love to me. Please!'

What did she say? His ears heard her words, but his brain could not process them. Blood rushed from his head for urgent service elsewhere as their meaning sank in. His fingers fumbled nervously with the buttons of her dress as they kissed. With her guidance they gained confidence until the dress fell from her shoulders. Now more dexterous, they unhooked her brassiere. She threw it aside as he buried his face in her soft, sweet globes. Rapturous, he inhaled the fragrance of her skin. The rigidity of her nipples fascinated him and he caressed them with tongue and fingers until, with a tormented groan, she drew his hand down her body. He exulted when she lifted her hips to aid the removal of her panties.

They lay length-wise on the settee naked, but for the underpants caught awkwardly around his knees. He kicked them away to nestle between her thighs and she guided him eagerly. A few wild thrusts and their bodies united in rhythmic harmony as though they had made love together for years. Too soon he shuddered as he approached orgasm and attempted to withdraw, but her arms around his neck and legs firmly locked around his waist forbade any retraction. Grateful, he thrilled, and thrilled again as their bodies shook together.

Glowing in the aftermath of love, they shared the touch of their bodies. For a long time they remained as they were with the ceiling fan swishing idly above them. Sometimes they would kiss whatever part of each other was immediately accessible, while the draft from the fan caressed the dampness from their bodies. Face cushioned in Audrey's breasts, he listened contentedly to the steady beat of her heart.

When she rose to go to the bathroom, he released her reluctantly. Disdaining any awkward scrabble for clothes, she walked with natural grace to the door, reminding him of the young Senoi girl they had seen the day before. She reappeared looking like a young girl in her white towelling bathrobe and, considering their recent activities, absurdly sweet and chaste. He had recovered his dressing gown and as they passed in the doorway they shared a smile and a loving kiss.

When he returned, Audrey was in the kitchenette. Biscuits were on a plate; cups, saucers and a freshly brewed pot of tea were on the table. 'I hope tea is all right. Would you rather have coffee? I have coffee for breakfast but I like tea during the day.'

'That's wonderful, me too. D'you think we were twins, separated at birth?'

'Don't even think it,' she said forcefully, 'then we couldn't…well,' she reddened. 'I don't want us ever to have to stop making love together.'

She hurried on. 'Now sit down and drink your tea before it gets cold… darling.' She used the endearment hesitantly, experimentally and with a pleased smile. Vince too rejoiced in domestic intimacy and returned the fondness. They sat close and spoke the language of lovers, with touches and whispers.

They drank their now tepid tea. Vince, suddenly ravenous, devoured most of the biscuits. Returning to the previous day's conversation, they explored the hidden world of each other's past. Vince told of his childhood: his siblings; being brought up by his father; summer holidays spent camping by the beach; traditional English Christmas dinners cooked in camp-ovens among the heaped embers of an open fire beneath a hot southern sun; and of the beautiful islands of the Hauraki Gulf.

Audrey recalled the villa in Wimbledon where she grew up, her favourite teachers at primary school, the grammar school she had attended. Her sister Gwen, two years younger, who, if she could get away with it, borrowed clothes, cosmetics and boyfriends. Their post-war holidays, school trips to France and Holland and her schoolgirl horror at the sight of men urinating in the canals of Amsterdam.

Her family, it seemed, was affectionate but not overly close. Her mother was still a keen club tennis player and devoted much of her time to fundraising for various charities. Her father was 'in the city' – a partner in the firm of stockbrokers for whom he had worked since the end of the war.

At Audrey's insistence, Vince revealed his few serious love affairs. He answered her questions reluctantly, but as honestly as he could. Pleased that she did not question his sexual behaviour since arriving in Malaya, he did not press her when she appeared unforthcoming about periods in her own life.

She spoke openly about schoolgirl crushes and about young men she met while doing her nursing training at a hospital in Great Ormond Street. Her training completed, she had worked as a registered nurse at Brompton Road Hospital. Vince knew that as the lovely young woman she was, she would have explored relationships with men to whom she was attracted. Unable to suppress his jealousy, he wanted no details of such affairs.

Later, accepted into the Royal Nursing Corps and her training completed, she was posted to a BMH in Cyprus. At this point Vince became conscious of reticence and evasion. Apparently unwilling to discuss it, her voice fell to a dull monotone. 'Soon after taking up my posting I met a cavalry lieutenant.' She shut her eyes and bit her lip. 'I thought he was wonderful and we became as they say, "interested in one another".' She stared at the table and continued in the same monotone. 'It was a whirlwind romance and we became engaged that same month.' She gave a shudder, grimaced and hesitated for a moment. 'Only weeks later I became ill and was evacuated home. I was in bad shape and admitted to an army medical facility for treatment. It was a long time before I was declared fit enough to return to duty. After recuperation, they offered me a medical discharge or another posting. I chose to be posted here, and here I've been for nearly two years.' No further mention of the lieutenant – or the engagement.

As she spoke, Vince became worried. Suddenly unwilling to confide in him, her whole demeanour had changed. Gone were her warmth and sparkle. She sat hunched and stared at the table as she spoke. It was as though a bright, sunny day alive with birdsong had become a sombre world of muted shadows. Afraid, he ached to help her. But he knew no words of comfort for a sorrow he did not understand, and sensed that anything he asked might disturb her further.

She interpreted Vince's expression, forced a smile and reached for his hand. 'I'm sorry, sweetheart. Please be patient with me. There's a lot I'll have to tell you and it's not easy. I'm scared that you won't understand and I might lose you. At least I'm sure that you're honest and won't just sneak away.' She paused. 'Please… can I write down everything you need to know so I don't have to see your face while I tell you? You can ask any questions you like after you know the sort of person you've hooked up with. If you don't want me then, please tell me so to my face and I'll understand.'

Mystified and disturbed, Vince felt relieved not to be fobbed off with an incomplete story and that Audrey seemed willing to invest emotional pain in maintaining their relationship. The worm chewing at his bowels reduced the intensity of its attack.

Unable to endure the sight of a solitary tear that had escaped her left eye, he stood, held her tight and bent to kiss the top of her head. For a few minutes she kept her face pressed against his body, then stood with a nervous smile. 'Let's talk of nicer things. I forgot to tell you earlier – well, ask you rather – will you come on a picnic with me tomorrow?' Before he could speak, she rushed on. 'Sonya says that no one will notice if you aren't there after ward-rounds. Mr Wu will lend us his car and I'll make a lovely lunch.'

Pleased by the invitation and Audrey's obvious delight in her planning, Vince hugged her. 'Sweetheart, what a wonderful idea! I don't really care – but where to?'

'There's a place not too far up into the hills. Its not much of a road, but it'll only take about half an hour to get there and it's a lovely spot; I'm sure you'll like it.' She hurried on. 'One of the girls took us up there weeks ago. There's a waterfall with a big pool and it's a lovely place for a picnic.' They fell to making plans. Audrey had negotiated another day off, would arrange lunch and all would be ready when he arrived after ward rounds.

With an abrupt gesture she picked up her watch and glanced at it. 'Oh, just look at the time! We have to get you back to the hospital. Who's first for a shower?' With only token reluctance she was persuaded by the entirely spurious claim that showering together would save time.

After a little initial shyness they undressed together and were soon soaping each other happily in the warm water. Unable to restrain himself any longer, Vince wrapped her lovely, slippery body in his arms and kissed her greedily. She returned his kisses with equal fervour then slipped from his grasp to stand back and view him with a proprietorial gleam in her eye.

'Well,' she whispered, 'Vince Tanner, just look at you! I can't send you out on the street like that – Ishmael would whisk you away in a minute – come along.' With his nearest extremity in one hand and a bath towel in the other, she led him, not entirely unwilling, into the other room.

She tossed the towel over the settee and pushed him gently backwards onto it and, as sinuously as a snake, slid wet and glistening on top of him.

Lovingly, she kissed his mouth, raised herself on to her knees and then lowered her body until he was securely within her. Strands of wet hair swayed across her shoulders as, with a gentle smile and closed eyes, she rocked forward and back until he could hold back no longer.

Their bodies dried and began to chill in the draft from the fan. Audrey slid from him. 'Come on, sweetheart,' she murmured, 'I hate to move, but if we don't get you back soon we might put tomorrow at risk.' Firmly resisting further blandishments, she pushed him back into the bathroom to complete his shower alone.

Vince emerged with the rumples in his dressing gown smoothed out as well as he could, but still looking somewhat unkempt. Audrey had recovered her bathrobe and was trying to smooth creases from her cotton dress.

'It's no use,' she giggled. 'I'll have to sponge it down and iron it. If we walk back separately people won't guess how we spent our afternoon. I need to tidy up here anyway. Now, please go before I jump on you again.' She kissed him without allowing their bodies to touch and eased him towards the door with a whispered. 'Tomorrow after ward rounds, my darling – I love you.'

He wanted another kiss, but instead he whispered, 'I love you too, sweetheart,' and headed towards the hospital. He trod the now familiar route oblivious to his surroundings. Curious looks from passers by, prompted by his rumpled appearance and contented smile, went unnoticed.

Minutes late for dinner, he tried to appear nonchalant as he took his seat at the table. With some reserve because of his earlier obtuseness, he was included in the conversation. He learned more about their day than he wanted to know, and that he – and by extension Audrey – had become a subject of speculation.

Resolved to be more discreet, he took his beer ration and went outside for a smoke. Thinking about the last few days, he was awed by how his life had altered. He had fallen in love with a beautiful and passionate young woman who – incredibly – seemed to reciprocate his feelings. Her perturbing reticence about her earlier years had largely been addressed by her offer to put that which worried him on paper, for him to read. At the back of his mind, however, there remained a nagging fear of the unknown. And like anyone with an inaccessible itch, he tried to scratch the source of discomfort.

Had her fiancé in Cyprus made her pregnant and deserted her? His blood raged! Perhaps she'd had a baby – or an abortion? He ached at the thought of her undergoing either ordeal alone. The thoughts upset him with outrage on her behalf. It was beyond belief that Audrey, his Audrey, could be guilty of anything more than the minor sins to which all of humanity is heir.

The nagging worries persisted until after lights out, but he managed to set them aside and fell asleep wrapped in the warmth of reciprocated love. He dreamed of leisurely lovemaking, of Audrey's sweetness. To have discovered her was the unexpected realisation of a neglected fantasy. In the morning he woke happy, confident and secure in the belief that while there were difficulties ahead, Audrey and he together would endure and prosper.

chapter four

Wednesday morning passed in a glowing cloud of semi-euphoria. Even the dragging boredom of ward rounds could not dent his benevolence. When they were completed, he slipped inconspicuously out the door and down the street. Outside the flatette a fairly new green Austin Cambridge sedan, presumably Mr Wu's, stood at the curb. Audrey opened the door in response to his knock and looked so delectable in issue jgs – jungle-green trousers and shirt – that he felt momentarily dazed. Oh my God! he thought – she's lovely!

'G'day soldier,' he nodded. 'Is the lady of the house in?'

'Flamin' oath mate.' She attempted a low register. 'I'll get her for you.' She turned away and immediately turned back. 'Taa raah!' she clowned, and flung her arms wide. 'My new boyfriend said you were here.' Laughing, she threw her arms around him and kissed him thoroughly. They separated at the applause from the other side of the street. Mr Wu and a young Malay, presumably the androgynous Ishmael, stood grinning outside the shop.

'Get inside, you masher.' She dragged him through the doorway. 'There goes whatever was left of my reputation!'

She handed him a pile of issue jgs, with instructions to change in the bathroom. The clothing fitted tolerably well, even the issue basketball boots.

He did not ask who they belonged to; he might not want to know.

He was changed in time to help to load the last few items into the car. There seemed a lot for a picnic, including two 38 packs, full of folded ground sheets and, Vince noted with interest, a few towels. Mr Wu and Ishmael waved them on their way, having clearly found the whole performance vastly entertaining.

Audrey knew the road, and was an able driver. Vince was happy to sit beside her and gaze out the window. There was little other traffic: a group of Senoi, some cyclists and pedestrians with produce for the market. Only two other cars passed them on the narrow, winding, unsealed road.

The day was clear, sunny and already quite hot, but the heat haze obscured views of the distant valleys. Except when another vehicle approached in a billow of dust, they kept the windows open for the resulting breeze. Past the tiny village of Berincang the road became steeper and the surface deteriorated still further. Soon Audrey dropped into low gear and swung the car onto a barely discernible track that branched off to the left.

Their new path, cut into the steep hillside, was barely wide enough to accommodate the car. Vince tried not to think about meeting another vehicle. They moved at a moderate pace down a precipitous incline where vegetation brushed both sides of the car. The fall to their left was steep and he took comfort from the thought that if they slipped off the track the car just might lodge against a tree trunk before it fell too far.

From the corner of his eye he watched Audrey. Her sangfroid amazed him. She seemed quite relaxed, but for a small frown of concentration. About half a mile from the road the track ended as they bumped into a clear flat area the size of a football field. She drove to the far side of the clearing and parked in the shade of a large tree.

'Is it safe to open my eyes yet?' he quavered in mock terror, then lowered his hands to grin with great sincerity. 'Let me kiss the best driver I've ever ridden with. Did you learn to drive in the Tank Corps?'

With a laugh she leaned over and kissed his cheek. 'We learned to drive ambulances – we're better than the Tank Corps. Now out you get. I'll give you the guided tour.'

They climbed from the car and stretched their legs in the long grass. 'Come on,' she said. 'We'll unload the car later.'

She led the way through the trees towards sounds of falling water. A faint path led them to another much smaller clearing. From far above water poured from a sheer rock face to splash off the uneven stone, creating clouds of spray before falling into a large pool.

Sunlight wove rainbows through a cloud of mist. Vince stared. Above the pool myriad brightly-hued butterflies created another rainbow of gauzy wings. Bright sunlight sparkled on droplets of spray that hung from rocks and greenery, and the pebbles in the clear water shone.

Vince turned to Audrey and shook his head. 'All right, I give up. Where've you hidden the fairies? Bambi must be somewhere. I want to see him too.'

Audrey smiled with pleasure. 'That's exactly how I felt when I first saw this place, and there were no butterflies then. But it was soon after the last rains and although the falls were more spectacular the whole area was soaked with spray. It's much nicer now.'

They touched shoulders, enjoying each other's company and the perfection of the scene. When in unspoken agreement they moved back towards the car, they were lost in their own thoughts. Vince felt an overwhelming love. Whatever happened, he needed Audrey in his life. Driven by needs hitherto unacknowledged, he exulted in the conviction that this lovely woman actually seemed willing to spend her life with him.

They carried gear from the car to a patch of shade near the pool. While Audrey unpacked the picnic, Vince spread out groundsheets and tinkered with a portable radio he'd found. Rejecting stations that offered eastern variations on western music, he found one that played jazz, set the radio on the groundsheet and looked up. His mouth went dry.

Audrey's jgs were heaped on the end of the groundsheet as she wriggled out of a piece of non-regulation pink lace. 'Quick swim before lunch,' she announced airily and in time to the music, bopped self-consciously towards the water. At the edge of the pool she turned, with a wicked grin. 'Come on! Be in the water in one minute – or I'll come back to splash you! And,' she added provocatively, 'you won't get lunch – or other goodies!'

Transfixed by her beauty and the perfect ambience of this place she had brought him to, he suddenly felt uncomfortably confined. Tearing off his clothes, he ran after her.

They embraced and wrestled, laughed and ducked each other in the chilly water. Gasping for breath, she took him in her hand. 'Oh, you poor thing, you're frozen stiff! Let's go and put you somewhere warm.'

They ran laughing to the groundsheets. Efforts to dry each other were abandoned in favour of eager loving until, sated at last, they drifted into a contented sleep. Vince woke as Eartha Kitt purred 'C'est Si Bon' in his ear. He listened drowsily. It seemed too perfect; he felt like an intruder in someone's dream of paradise. Audrey slept with her head resting on his chest. Tendrils of still-damp hair tickled his cheek deliciously while his left hand cupped one lovely breast. On her face a smile of sweet contentment revealed a dimple he had not noticed before. After a few moments her eyelids fluttered open.

'Oh yes,' she murmured drowsily. 'Eartha got that right. It is *so good*!' Abruptly she was on her knees, rubbing her body. 'Ouch, let's get dressed and have lunch. The midges have found me and we need to talk. Tomorrow I'll probably be away all day,' she paused before continuing sadly, 'and you'll go back to Taiping on Saturday.' She stepped into her panties.

Refusing Vince's offer to kiss away every itch of the insect bites, she whispered huskily, 'Keep that thought, sweetheart, it makes lovely shivers run down my spine. But we wouldn't get lunch or have time for talk. We have to sort out what we want to do.'

As they dressed, Vince could not resist peeking. She caught his gaze and smiled. 'Don't worry, darling, I'm being an exhibitionist – but I adore the way you look at me. It makes me feel all warm and loved. I'll always be happy as long as you look at me like that.'

Audrey had wheedled from the hospital cooks a selection of cold chicken, sandwiches and fruit. They ate with the healthy voracity of young animals and washed the food down with stubbies of Anchor beer that had cooled in the pool. Drowsy from food, beer and loving, Vince wanted only to doze in Audrey's arms, but acknowledging their need to talk, allowed her to drag him to his feet.

They marshalled their thoughts while they wandered around the clearing. Halfway around Audrey stopped and seized his hands. 'Do you think we really *can* stay together?' Her voice was anxious – almost fierce. 'I know I haven't been fair, keeping things from you that you have to know. I'm too much of a coward to look at your face while I tell you, but last night I wrote everything down and I'll leave it in my retreat for you to read tomorrow while I'm down in the valley.'

Vince's thoughts were confused. He pushed away the vague concerns in the back of his mind and squeezed her hands. 'Sweetheart, look...' he began, gently, 'we haven't known each other long, but I reckon we've got to know each other pretty well. You're the centre of my life now and nothing's going to make me risk losing you.' He affected a quizzical stare. 'I can, I hope, Madam, exclude any possibility that you aren't an escaped mass-murderer, an ex-Nazi concentration-camp guard, or... or a transvestite, back from Sweden after unusual surgery?' He shrugged. 'I guess it's too late to worry anyway. If so the surgery was a total success. Possible objection withdrawn.'

Despite herself Audrey giggled. 'I believe, sir, that you can verify that all my bits and pieces are original issue and haven't been interfered with... er,' she stumbled, her face crimson, 'I meant to say, modified in any way.'

They resumed their walk, holding hands and making plans. When Vince returned to Taiping on Saturday they would keep in touch by mail. As soon as possible they would synchronise leaves and meet in either KL or Singapore. If possible they would marry there and in the meantime each would covertly try to find out how to make the arrangements. Nervous and excited, they resolved to somehow turn their dreams into reality.

'I'd thought about re-enlisting,' he mused, 'but if you'll come to New Zealand I'll take my discharge next May. We'll probably all be back by the end of November and posted to Burnham Camp – near Christchurch, in the South Island.'

Audrey squeezed his hand excitedly. 'I'll resign at the end of my contract next July and fly out to New Zealand as soon as I can. If I take my discharge here the service might provide my airfare to New Zealand instead of to England. Darling, if not – you said you've never been there. Maybe you could join me there and meet...' Her shoulders slumped. 'We'll have to think about that; maybe it wouldn't work.'

Everything was disturbingly vague and speculative, but they were comforted by dreams that shaped a future they both wanted. Between them they created an exciting foundation of ideas on which they could build a life together. Caught up in the excitement of planning a future, Vince worried about economic reality. 'Look, sweetheart,' he mumbled. 'I – I haven't got much. All I own is a building site that's not worth a lot and a few hundred pounds.' He scuffed the ground moodily with his foot and brightened a little. 'I've still got my woodworking tools. I'm a trained carpenter and I should be able to get work. We won't starve, but to start with it won't be easy.'

Audrey was supremely confident. 'I've got enough saved for emergencies and between us we'll earn enough to have our own home within a few years. Then,' she said with a determined gleam in her eye, 'I'm going to retire and you'll keep me pregnant until we have at least two little duplicates.'

All too soon it was time to leave and with the treacherous slope to the road negotiated they contested for kisses. One would quote from Kipling's *Barrack-Room Ballads*; the other tried to name the poem. When Audrey parked outside her hideout, the score was even. Desperately, Vince scoured his mind for a chance to win a final point. 'I know...

'I left my cap in a public-house, my boots in the public road,
'And Lord knows where, and I don't care, my belt and my tunic goed.'
'More,' Audrey demanded.

'Sorry, sweetheart, it's too late and I can't remember any more, but it's from "Cells".' As she stopped outside her flatette, Vince demanded his reward. He extracted it, but she complained.

'You cheated! You'll have to give that back.' He did so willingly until they were both laughing and breathless.

With the car unpacked and the gear carried inside, Audrey went to return Mr Wu's vehicle and give him his keys. From the doorway Vince watched her reverse down the narrow lane beside the shop. When he was back in hospital attire, Audrey returned – the keys still in her hand. 'He's not home. I'll give them to him later. Now, you get back to the hospital; I'll stay here and tidy up. If I can give Mr Wu his keys back and thank him, it'll save having to come back later. Now shut the door so I can kiss you goodnight.'

'I'll hate not seeing you tomorrow,' she whispered. 'Perhaps when I get back we could play cards? No… first I'll have to know how you feel after reading my letter.' Vince was dismayed as her eyes filled as her voice caught.

'Ah-h darling. I know that you don't want to have secrets. But it can't matter this much. Tear up the letter and we'll say that the world didn't start for either of us until last Sunday.'

She shook her head and sniffed. 'No, if only… no… you have to know… before things go any further. Just… when you read it, please try to understand. Now darling,' she sobbed, 'please go. I love you.' And he was pushed out the door.

Unwillingly, he allowed it to shut against him and decided to leave Audrey to sort things out. Troubled by her distress, he felt at a loss. I'll try to control my curiosity, he thought, and tear the bloody letter up in front of her unopened. Jeez, we had such a wonderful day; there can't be anything that'd make her this upset.

But his uneasiness persisted, and he was afraid that curiosity would drive him to find out what caused her so much pain.

Waiting for the dinner bell, he suffered a good-natured ribbing about his absences. Sister Sonya Bretucci had fobbed off enquiries by saying that Vince had to undergo some unspecified therapy. Jay-Jay enquired solicitously after Vince's health and suggested enviously that he too would benefit from similar treatment.

When Bryson came in to chat with Angelo, he examined Vince critically.

'You're looking great, sport. Are you getting special care denied us poor squaddies?' Vince was looking out into the fading daylight and was surprised to see Audrey hurrying down the street. Ah, he thought – she must be going to return the car keys.

His eye caught movement in the shadows behind her. A bulky figure in a dressing gown that flapped around its knees followed her with a peculiar lurching gait. Danty?

'Jesus Christ! Danty's going after Audrey! Cover me, eh?' Heart thumping, Vince pounded from the ward, down the stairs. Further down the road a figure skirted furtively around the light of a streetlamp. He ran towards it. Minutes later he paused, panting, at the corner of Audrey's street. Somewhere a door slammed. Oblivious to passers by, he rushed to her doorway. A sound – short and piercing – alarmed him further. A choked-off scream? He ran to her door.

Confused – unsure what to expect – he shouldered his way into the shadow-filled room. A figure sprawled unmoving across the settee: Audrey? Another crouched by the portal. It rose and lunged. Dressing gown billowing and teeth bared in a grimace of fear and fury, Danty was upon him! In the dim light from the street his face appeared contorted like that of a fiend – a gargoyle, a demonic fugitive from a psychopathic nightmare.

Half-remembered instructions from youthful judo exponents in Taiping sprang into Vince's mind. Automatically, he stepped to one side, throwing his right leg across Danty's path while his left hand seized a flailing left wrist. His own right hand gripped Danty's left sleeve. Time ceased. Danty, off-balance, squealing like a pig anticipating the knife, found himself driven headfirst and with unforgiving deliberation into the doorjamb.

The impetus of their combined weight deflected Danty, flinging him headlong into the street. Vince rushed after him, but Mr Wu, observing the disturbance, was there first. He brandished a meat-cleaver that threatened further and terminal danger to Danty's health. Vince felt a primitive need to kill Danty, but more urgently he must care for Audrey.

'No!' he yelled. Danty did not matter, but he did not want Mr Wu arrested for his slaughter.

More figures appeared: Bryson, Angelo, and others from the ward. 'Jay-Jay's ringing the cops,' Bryson puffed. 'Is Sister okay?'

'Unconscious,' Vince grunted. 'Make sure the screws bring a doctor.' He gestured as Bryson cursed and launched a kick at the figure on the pavement, – 'No unexplainable injuries, eh?' – and hurried back to Audrey.

He flicked on the light. She remained in the same position. With fingers fumbling anxiously, he felt for her carotid artery. Although she seemed lifeless, a steady pulse beat under his fingertips. He inhaled a great breath and bent to kiss her right cheek. She lay awkwardly, one leg over the arm of the settee. He moved her to the recovery position, re-arranged her skirt and choked with rage at the sight of a livid bruise on her left cheek.

Fighting anger and tears, he let himself crouch for a moment with his head on her shoulder, praying that nothing was seriously wrong. Anxious for the doctor to arrive, he stood and saw a pale blue envelope propped on the bookcase. Knowing what it must be, he crossed to pick it up. It was addressed to him and, unwilling for anyone else to see it, he slipped it into his dressing gown pocket.

He turned back to Audrey. The kris he had admired two days earlier lay on the floor by the settee. Vince bent to pick it up, but stopped. Hello, what's that? he asked himself. On the blade was a dark smear that could be blood. He looked around. Beside the glassed portal other dark drops stood out against the beige floor; others led towards the door.

Bloody good! Good on you, love – you fought the bastard off! He sagged, knelt beside her once more, cursing his urge to weep. There he remained until a uniformed captain with RAMC insignia strode through the open door. Behind him two redcaps stared silently from the doorway.

The captain nodded brusquely. 'Dr Baxter.' He looked around. 'You must be Corporal Tanner: recovery position, good, hmmm. Did you move her head? How's her pulse? Steady? Good.' As he spoke he took a stethoscope from his bag, asked the two military policemen to wait outside and proceeded to perform a careful examination.

Vince replied to the staccato questions as best he could. When he admitted moving her, his voice faltered. Frightened that he may have inadvertently aggravated a spinal injury, he began to shake.

The doctor sensed Vince's distress and turned from examining Audrey's eyes. 'Don't worry, young feller, you've done well,' he grunted, with a wave of a small flashlight. 'Seems to be no damage to the vertebrae. Now, I would like you to sit here and hold her head for me.'

Clearly Audrey did not need her head held. She was unlikely to make any independent movements in the immediate future. Doctor Baxter, though, was an innately kind man and understood that Vince needed to feel involved. He turned back, frowned and shook his head. 'There's no sign of concussion, but I can't rule it out. She's had a severe blow to the left cheek but, other than the resulting haematoma, there's no indication of bleeding.'

Quickly Vince told him of the bloodied kris and the trail of blood drops. Dr Baxter looked at them, shook his head and murmured, 'Good girl, put up a fight didn't you?' Then he turned to Vince. 'I don't think it's her blood, but let's check again anyway.' Together and working with great care, they moved the limp body sufficiently to confirm that the blood was not Audrey's.

Thoughtfully, the doctor put his equipment away in its case, straightened and turned to Vince. 'Look, Corporal, I'm going to arrange for Audrey to be admitted as a patient. I do not believe that this condition is life-threatening, but I must conduct a more extensive examination. I fear that if I am correct, it may be some time before a clear prognosis can be available.' He gnawed his bottom lip for a moment. 'The provosts will want a statement from you, and that may take some time.' He paused. 'I'd be very grateful if you would come and see me as soon as you are free. Er, did you find a letter from Audrey?'

Vince nodded, surprised, and the doctor, looking relieved, asked carefully, 'May I ask that you wait until you see me this evening before you read it? Audrey is a long-standing patient of mine and told me that she intended to write that letter. I have some understanding of its contents and it may be helpful if I am there when you open it. Now, my office is on the ground floor of the hospital. Go in the main entrance, turn left, and mine's the first door on the left. Don't worry if it's late, I shall wait. If the front door is locked, ask for directions, upstairs. All right?

'Now please look after Audrey until I get back.' He picked up his case, nodded, went out the door and returned with a pair of stretcher bearers. Close behind was a provost lieutenant with the two redcap corporals Vince had seen earlier. Vince watched numbly as Audrey was moved onto the stretcher and carried to a waiting ambulance. The redcaps busied themselves taking blood samples from the floor, bagged and tagged the kris and took photographs of the room.

The lieutenant, after a few words with his men, strutted over to stand in front of Vince. 'Stand at attention, Corporal!' As he drew himself upright, Vince unconsciously rolled his eyes. Christ, that's all I need now – an arsehole like this. The lieutenant reddened. His voice rose an octave. 'Corporal,' he squealed, 'did you roll your eyes when I spoke?'

'Yes, sir, medical condition, certain noises affect me that way. If you object, perhaps it won't happen if you stand back a little – sir.' He rolled his eyes again and the lieutenant took an involuntary step backwards. He trembled with fury as his voice rose to a still higher note. 'Are you trying to be impertinent, Corporal?'

'No, sir, certainly not, sir, absolutely no effort needed at all, sir.' The lieutenant turned to his men and shrilled. 'You men are witness to this!' They controlled heaving shoulders to chorus, 'Sorry, sir, witnesses to what?' Both gazed innocently around the room. One, screened from the lieutenant's gaze, rolled his eyes and gave Vince a weary wink.

The lieutenant spoke through his teeth, controlling himself with an obvious effort to hiss, 'I require a statement from you regarding the night's events – including your relationship with Lieutenant Mathews.' Vince became seriously irritated. He wanted to walk away, but suspected that they would arrest him and glared into the lieutenant's eyes.

'Yes, *sir*. Unless Lieutenant Mathews or myself are to be charged with an offence, I shall confine my statement to the attack upon her. As you may know, the lieutenant was the subject of a brutal assault and it was I who apprehended her attacker.' He continued over the lieutenant's sounds of outrage. 'If you want to charge me, I believe Captain Baxter will be present at my interrogation and of course I would need notes for my defending officer at any subsequent court-martial proceedings. In the meantime, I would be grateful if you would take my statement now… sir. I have an appointment to see the captain.' He rolled his eyes again. 'Besides, I can feel another attack coming on… sir.'

Muttering imprecations and threats, the puce-faced officer stalked out, leaving his corporals to take the statement: an unadorned account of the evening's events. Vince carefully evaded any inferences that he and Audrey had shared a personal relationship. His questioners were reasonably polite and sympathetic despite their prurient curiosity remaining unsatisfied. They advised him to remain available to sign the statement and allowed him to leave.

He crossed the road to thank Mr Wu for his support and to tell him what had happened, but the shop was in darkness. Feeling sick, and worried about Audrey's situation, he realised that the queasiness in his gut was due to hunger as well as the aftermath of an adrenaline rush. Night had fallen like a gallows trapdoor and the streets were in darkness.

Not just dark and dimly lit, the streets were almost deserted as he trudged unhappily towards the hospital. Other pedestrians were of no more substance than passing wraiths as he worried about Audrey's welfare, the plans they had made, the letter that still rested in his pocket and the forthcoming meeting with Dr Baxter.

The hospital entrance was unlocked and the foyer still illuminated. His stomach grumbled noisily. A glance at his watch indicated that it was almost 1925 hours. There was no difficulty in locating a room with a nameplate that read: Capt. G. Baxter. Diffidently, in the silence of the corridor, he knocked and a low, growly voice bade him enter.

Dr Baxter stepped from behind the desk where he had been working, turned on the main light and shook Vince's hand firmly. 'I'm pleased you came, I hope the provosts were not too objectionable. They can display a talent for confusing military regulations with their personal views of morality. Please have a seat.' He indicated two easy chairs half-facing each other, with a small table in between. Vince thanked him and sat.

The doctor proceeded without preamble. 'I know you're worried about Audrey; I last saw her about thirty minutes ago and I'm afraid she remains in a deep coma. We've confirmed this with a test that involves examining the patient's response to ice water being dripped into the ears. A contradictory and encouraging sign is that her breathing remains, as we observed before, steady and regular.'

'But, sir, she's going to be all right, isn't she?'

'The prognosis...? Well... I have a high level of confidence that she will eventually make a full recovery. I base this on my knowledge that she is a young woman of great character and indomitable will. I also understand that you and she have plans for the future: plans that are supremely important to her. Audrey is presently unaware of her surroundings, which is to say unconscious, but I believe that her subconscious is fighting to return to normality and the glimpse you have given her of a possible future.' He paused awkwardly. 'Sorry, I didn't mean to imply that you have any special responsibilities – just that I believe that she has the necessary strength and will to recover.

'Now, as a doctor I am concerned about your blood sugar levels and I am also going to give you something that should not be taken on an empty stomach.' He moved over to a cupboard and returned with a plate of sandwiches that he placed in front of Vince. 'From the hospital kitchen,' he said, and added slyly, 'They're not bad; I believe you had some earlier today. Sorry, that was thoughtless of me.' He gestured towards another door. 'There's a toilet and washbasin in there if needed.' Thankfully, Vince excused himself and went into the lavatory.

When he returned, the doctor, who was again seated at his desk, looked up and nodded, smiled and returned to his papers. Back in his seat, Vince found himself to be hungrier than he had thought and ate the sandwiches as he covertly examined Dr Baxter.

Slightly taller than Vince, he was slim, in his mid fifties and thickening around the middle. Thick brown hair receding slightly from his temples was sprinkled with white. A determined chin, full lips, enquiring brown eyes and a slightly oversized nose completed a pleasantly benign and friendly face. He exuded a sense of caring tolerance. Overall, he looked like the favourite uncle that all children would like to have.

Examination and sandwiches both completed, Vince stared at the crumpled blue envelope. He admired the neat script in which it was addressed, turned it over slowly to examine the excellence of its design. The flap once dampened with Audrey's saliva he pressed against his face, and he tried to stem the tears he found he could not control.

chapter five

When he regained his self control, he found a letter opener on the table beside the empty plate. Despite his feelings he smiled; the doctor was a thoughtful man. Reluctantly, he took up the opener and slit the envelope. With the pages spread, the script seemed distorted, like the world viewed through wet glass. As his vision cleared he began to read:

Dear Vince,

I know it is fruitless to wish, but I do truly wish it were not necessary to write this letter. Since last Sunday when you and I saw each other for the first time, my life and hopes for the future, perhaps yours also, have undergone a complete change. Now I have the self-imposed but difficult task of trying to convince you that I am worthy of your lifetime commitment.

Well, I guess I had better start taking the 'monsters out of the cupboard' and let you see them. As you know I was not as open with you as I asked you to be with me when I insisted on mutual revelations. This time I shall try hard to be completely honest. Here goes:

Soon after my posting to Cyprus in 1956, I met a young lieutenant in a cavalry regiment. His name was Derek Cunningham. He seemed very much the dashing young cavalry officer and I believed that we were both very much in love. Foolishly, I thought that he really wanted to marry me; we became engaged and lovers. It was only much later that I learned that while professing his love for me, he was also flying a pair of my knickers from the antenna of his scout car as a trophy of his conquest.

Vince already disliked Lieutenant Cunningham; now he was nauseated. He looked up; Dr Baxter stood over him, with a sympathetic smile on his face and a tumbler of amber fluid in his hand. 'I think you should drink this. It's a single malt, but I took the liberty of adding some water. You may need fortification. I certainly would. Umm… you may not know this, but for some time I have been Audrey's therapist, I admire her greatly and believe her to be the most courageous person I have ever met.' Vince took a gulp of the aromatic liquid and gasped, but relished the strength it gave him to return to the letter.

One night we had arranged to meet at a taverna where we'd met several times before. When I arrived, two young troopers, wearing 'Cavalry' insignia, got out of a waiting car. They said that Lieutenant Cunningham had sent them to pick me up and take me to meet him elsewhere.

Stupid and unsuspecting, if rather indignant, I went with them. When I realised that we were leaving the city I protested. One climbed into the back with me and forcibly restrained me from screaming, or jumping out the door.

They took me to an isolated area in the countryside outside Nicosia. Without a word, other than to curse me, they dragged me from the car, beat and kicked me, tore my clothes off and took turns to rape me. Throughout all this I was helpless and too terrified to resist. Finally they threw me down on the roadside like a heap of garbage and left me there.

A family of Greek peasants, heading for town in an old truck, found me still lying there next morning. Despite the anti-British feelings of the time they took pity on me. The women covered me with some of their own clothes and they took me to a Greek hospital in Nicosia.

Although barely conscious and scarcely able to speak because of the damage to my jaw, I was apparently able to convince a Greek doctor to contact the BMH. They strapped my ribs and an ambulance took me there. I was found to have two cracked ribs, a cracked cheekbone, multiple bruises, abrasions and internal injuries.

Two days later I was declared fit enough to be interviewed by the police,

*both military and civilian. During this nightmare of humiliation and pain
I tried to contact Derek. I believed that he must be worried about me and
I so much needed his support.*

*He had left the island the day after I was abducted and brutalised. He
must have known that he could not be meeting me that evening. Curiously
enough, some time later, someone 'thought I should know' that she had
heard him describing me in the mess as 'damaged goods', the very evening
I was raped.*

Vince's eyes became too blurred to read. As he felt tissues pressed into one
hand and the now empty glass removed from the other, he realised he was
sobbing.

'I believe you need a top-up,' Dr Baxter rasped gently. When the replenished glass was returned, Vince took it gratefully. He had never before tasted
single malt whisky, but enjoyed the smoky, peat flavour and most of all the
anaesthetic effect he needed to counter Audrey's calm report of a horrific
experience.

*I was told I attempted to slice my right carotid artery with some scissors.
Perhaps I didn't try hard enough. Any competent nurse should be able to locate
the carotid without difficulty. I went into a deep coma for almost a year.*

*My first memory, after Cyprus, is of the hospital in England, to which I
had been evacuated. When I was finally discharged I had a long period of
recuperative leave, which I tried to spend with my family. They attempted to
be supportive but were unable to cope with what had happened to me. I finally
left and stayed in a boarding house.*

*During my period of unconsciousness, the two men who had violated me
were caught and brought to trial. Fortunately my evidence was not necessary
to obtain a conviction. They had stupidly kept items of my underwear and
some articles from my purse as 'souvenirs'. Their defence claimed consent, but
when my medical record and sworn statement from Nicosia were read out, any
possible defence collapsed. The publicity upset my family. Although they wanted
to help me they didn't know how.*

*After considerable psychiatric evaluation and a medical board, I was offered
early retirement or another posting. I chose Malaya and here I am!*

*Whew! That was not easy. But there's worse to come. Please take a deep
breath, my darling, and try to forgive me.*

Since I have been here I have become a promiscuous seducer of young patients.

It sickens me now to realise what I became but it is something you must learn from me before someone else tells you.

Dr Baxter, a Senior MO here, is also a trained and experienced psychiatrist. He sees me every week for therapy. He has told me that my despicable behaviour fits a well-documented range of pathological behaviours exhibited by people who have been severely brutalised.

Oh, my darling! What have I done to us! You must understand why I could not say all this to your face and read the disgust in your eyes. I would never speak to you about the men; it was my fault, not theirs. At least I was sane enough to choose decent men. Please believe that at no time did I see in them anything like I found in you.

Perhaps, if you can overcome your revulsion for me, we could see Dr Baxter together on Thursday or Friday. There is something else for me to ask forgiveness for. I have already told the doctor about our relationship and he wants to meet you.

He says that during this last week I have made enormous advances in perception of my place in the world. Much more, he said, than in the previous two years.

He also said that he has never seen me so happy and that I am behaving exactly as a young woman in love should. The best sign, he says, is that I want to share my life and have children, with you. He even described you as the best possible therapy and claimed that you should be available on prescription for distressed young women. That idea I vetoed immediately!

Goodnight, my darling, I look forward with both fear and joy to seeing you on Thursday night.

All my love,

Audrey

Emotionally drained and half-drunk, Vince stared uncomprehendingly at the damp blue papers on his lap. How could anyone deliberately inflict such vicious brutality upon another living being? His shocked mind lurched in confusion. Dreadful things occur in warfare and other acts of mass stupidity. But this was different. What species of creature could deliberately physically and mentally violate a trusting young woman? Oh sweet Christ – some bastards, somewhere in the world, are doing this all the bloody time!

He looked up at Dr Baxter's polite cough. 'It's not easy to have a loved one suffer the evil of others.' He continued in the same, mild tone, 'I wonder if you would allow me, as Audrey's therapist, to read her letter? It may contain something that would help me to help her. Yes, while we are at it, may I also regard you as my patient?' He smiled. 'No formalities, you only have to say "yes" and it's done. All it means is that you will be protected by patient confidentiality and I cannot be obliged to disclose what you tell me.'

Vince nodded. 'Yes, gladly.' He tidied the pages as best he could and handed them across.

As he read, the doctor frowned sadly, shook his head and then with a look of revulsion, 'It's sad to know that so many of one's own gender fail to meet the most basic requirements of being human.' He shook his head again. 'The brutes who violated Audrey were cowardly failures in every way. She was and always will be their superior in every possible sense.' He grimaced. 'Lieutenant Cunningham may even be a personification of true evil. I think all three are psychopaths and should be deleted from the gene pool.'

He looked closely at Vince. 'How are you feeling?' When Vince hesitated, he added, 'Remember, you are my patient now. You can say anything you like; it won't be repeated.' Expectantly, he leaned forward in his chair.

Vince rubbed his face. 'I...I...don't know. I know that it must be true. I just can't believe it. What those bastards did to her... poor, lovely Audrey.' He jumped to his feet to pace around the room. 'That prick she was engaged to needs killing: I'd tear his guts out! He said he loved her; betrayed her and threw her to those other filthy bastards!'

Tears streamed down his face and he began to sob. The psychiatrist watched in silence. 'I can't believe it,' Vince repeated, dully. 'I can't bear the thought of Audrey, my Audrey, willingly making love to – fucking – all those other guys. Oh Christ! She must have taken them to where she took me and done with me what she'd already done with them. I'm just another bit of meat in a passing parade. How could she really think of me – separately – differently from all those others?'

He slumped back into the chair, head bowed, and stared brokenly at the floor.

The doctor rose to refill his glass. 'This had better be the last. A hangover won't help in the morning. Don't worry; Audrey saw you *quite* differently. You were her "white knight", come to deliver her from a life of torment. And still are – if you want to be.'

Vince sagged miserably into his chair. 'Okay, I'm being stupid and irrational, but... but, all right, she – she had sex with others. I have too, without any commitment. Why should it matter to me this much?' He gulped his scotch and wanted desperately to die without needing to solve the dilemma.

He groaned and put down his glass. 'What the hell've I been on about?' he thought aloud. 'When she comes out of her coma, she'll still be the same lovely person I wanted to marry this morning – and still do. What she did before – of her own free will – doesn't matter a damn, although it makes me sick. But by Christ I want to kill the rotten bastards who used her like a lump of meat. How can we share the planet with such scum?'

Shoulders bent, he mumbled, 'Sorry about the tantrum, shock and jealousy, eh? I don't reckon I've any right to criticise her. She put herself through a lot to make sure I knew the truth about what happened to her before – and… and before we met.'

Dr Baxter looked thoughtful. 'I don't believe you need to berate yourself, but there are several things you should know. She told me she was taking you to the waterfall today because she thought it a wonderful place. She had only been there with other nurses and wanted it to be a very special day. She told me that she was going to leave this letter for you to read while she was up in the valley.' He looked at the floor and grunted. 'I'm sure you had a wonderful day.'

He looked up with a grimace. 'Sorry, sometimes the relationship between therapist and patient becomes more complex than either realises. Anyway, I'm pleased that you let me read that letter. What she said is true. I'm certain that her promiscuity was a direct result of the degradations heaped upon her. Such behaviour is frequently reported in psychiatric papers. Unconsciously, victims try to take responsibility for their own suffering. In Audrey's case there was probably an element of "revenge" against men in general. Once her lovers left the hospital, she refused further contact and destroyed their letters unopened.

'Brutalised people commonly have a diminished perception of self-worth. As though they are saying, "See how terrible I am. This must be why I was treated so badly." They'll grasp at anything, even create evidence of personal faults to explain the cruelty of their persecutors.'

He thought for a minute. 'Two things occur to me. One is the improvement of her self-image since you two… well, became close.' He smiled thinly. 'The other is her desire to "marry and have children with you" somewhere far away from her unhappiness. These factors may prove catalytic in returning her to consciousness.'

Half-drunk and emotionally overloaded, Vince had difficulty in understanding all that was said. He puzzled briefly over the remark concerning patient-therapist relationships. Some things needed more thought. The psychiatrist's next words, however, caught his attention immediately.

'Tomorrow morning, if you wish, I shall take you to see Audrey. I hope that this coma will pass relatively quickly. She now has a reason and desire to return to a world that has much more to offer her than it did at the time of her previous coma. With your help we will hopefully hasten that return.'

'Is there something I can do? When I see Audrey – I'd feel a lot better if I could do something – anything – to help.'

Dr Baxter smiled. 'Good. I have an old tape recorder. If you make a recording that we could play to her each day.' He nodded, 'personal chat… well, rather than intimate, if you know what I mean. All sorts of people are likely to hear it, I am afraid. I have an idea that hearing might be the only sense still available to patients in deep coma. Your voice, talking over any plans you have made together, may well hasten the recovery process.'

Discussing plans for the next day, Dr Baxter took Vince back to his ward. As they climbed the stairs, he commented that he might have to put up with remarks about the scent of whisky that wafted around them. 'I always claim,' he said, 'that single malt is the best opiate for distress to the emotions. Not all my colleagues agree with me, of course. Perhaps it explains why I may be the oldest captain in the British Army.'

In the morning Vince had to put up with sympathetic but inquisitive remarks from other patients. By inference it was clear that his relationship with Audrey was no secret. Typically, Angelo, Jay-Jay or others came up, patted his shoulder and muttered words of encouragement together with condemnations of Danty, whose fate was summed up with a contemptuous 'good riddance'.

Bryson stated darkly and with unusual restraint, 'You did a good job on Danty, sport. Pity it wasn't more permanent. We're all upset about the sister, but. She's a great little sheila.' He lowered his voice confidentially. 'I heard she put up a fight and got him with a Malay dagger, bloody good eh? She's got real guts; she's gonna pull through okay.'

Vince bit his lip. 'I wish I'd remembered what Danty said the other night. I just never thought even that bastard would stoop so low as to try to rape her.' Bryson clapped his shoulder, shook his head sadly and left.

Nurses, too, whispered reassurances, insisting that Audrey would soon recover. He was grateful that nobody even hinted at her past dalliances. He knew they could not have been completely secret. Only the dark-haired Sonya referred directly to their few days together. She smiled and whispered, 'When Audrey's better, Angelo and I would love to be at the wedding…?'

Well, Vince thought ironically, but not uncomfortably, I guess my mind was made up for me anyway.

The same two redcaps arrived after ward rounds, armed with typed copies of his statement, which he signed after making a few minor corrections. When they departed, Dr Baxter arrived and took Vince to a two-bedded room in another part of the hospital. He found himself shaking. Chronologically speaking, it was a short time since he had last seen Audrey, but so filled with emotion that ages could have passed.

Audrey lay propped up on pillows. A tube protruded from her nose and she looked so small and vulnerable that he gulped and his eyes stung. Despite her pallor, she could almost have been in a normal sleep. Her hair was tied back and she lacked even the nominal makeup she normally wore.

On an impulse he stepped forward, knelt and reached under the sheet for her hand. It lay inert between his, but for a moment he imagined pressure in return. A nurse he did not know moved to intervene, but Dr Baxter waved her back, tapped Vince on the shoulder, gestured to a chair and whispered, 'We'll be back in fifteen minutes.'

Grateful for the privacy, Vince kissed Audrey's soft, warm cheek and whispered their shared dreams: of love, marriage and happy, laughing children. Avoiding the naso-gastric tube, he kissed lips that tasted of moisturising cream. There was of course no response and as the doctor returned, he shrugged mentally. No-one ever said I was a handsome prince.

Vince blushed as the analyst winked and said, with a mischievous smile, 'Never mind, it was worth a try. You *do* have to be psychic to be a psychiatrist, you know. Come on, let's go and make a recording.' He took Vince's arm and led him to a small room that contained a chair and a desk that held an old reel-to-reel tape recorder.

All morning Vince worked on a tape to be played to Audrey after he left. The therapist demonstrated the operation of the recorder, made a few suggestions and departed leaving Vince to decide on the tape's contents. During lunch break, he retrieved his copy of *Barrack-Room Ballads* from his gear for use during the afternoon session.

By afternoon's end and after many erasures and alterations, he had a completed tape that he was reasonably happy with. Avoiding anything intimate, he talked of their plans for a life together and talks they had shared. Carefully editing it all, he used any key words he could think of that might elicit a response. He invoked names: Dr Baxter, Mr Wu, Sonya, Bryson, Angelo and even Ishmael. Memories of their magical day at the waterfall he guarded jealously.

He discussed life in New Zealand: the building and furnishing of a house, interior decorating. What colours would she like? Children's rooms, what pattern of wallpaper? How to furnish them? Interspersed with it all, he read favourite poems from Kipling, always trying to speak as though he was enjoying a private conversation. He risked no reference to her past. When the psychiatrist stopped by to check on progress, they agreed that he would refer to Audrey's letter only in saying that nothing could affect their future together.

Exhausted by late afternoon, he left the tape for further editing the next day. Until dinner he held Audrey's unresponsive hand, whispered apparently unheard endearments into her ear and talked of their magical hours together.

The next morning, Friday, Vince first spent thirty minutes with Audrey before joining Dr Baxter for further editing. Although amateurish, it flowed smoothly enough to provide reassurance therapy. Vince's monologue and poetry readings, together with contributions from the doctor, provided a tape that would run for just over an hour. When duplicated, it would be played to Audrey through earphones, at least once daily for a month. At that time the medical staff would review its further use.

While the duplicate was rewinding, the doctor was called to the telephone. He returned looking disturbed and silently busied himself with the tapes. When they were in their boxes and the machine ready to be moved he turned to Vince. 'Listen, I probably shouldn't tell you this, so please keep it confidential. That call was from a colleague. He was called to the secure infirmary where Danty was held. He just pronounced him dead.'

'How did he die?' Vince blurted the question, recalling his savage delight as the doorframe had impacted with Danty's skull.

'Unfortunately, that's not clear.' The doctor shook his head. 'In the circumstances, I think our only misgiving should be that in the absence of an obvious cause of death, a postmortem will be required.' He gave Vince a sidelong glance. 'You should realise there is a chance an autopsy might reveal that death was due to subdural haematoma – bleeding into the brain cavity.'

He gazed pensively at a spool. 'I don't think we need worry unduly. The autopsy might reveal some hitherto unsuspected natural cause of death. Even if there is evidence of a brain haemorrhage, the coroner will surely find that it was sustained during the commission of a crime and there the matter should end.'

He brightened visibly and patted Vince on the shoulder. 'He may even believe, as do I, that you deserve a medal for your defence of Audrey. Anyway, on the bright side, there will be no court martial for Danty. That would have carried the risk of Audrey's unhappy past and your relationship becoming public.'

Vince shook his head despondently. 'No, Audrey fought him off. I only helped him on his way, but I'll never regret what happened to him.'

'Hmmm,' replied the Doctor dryly. 'I hope you never feel obliged to say that in court.'

After lunch, Dr Baxter had the tape recorder set up in Audrey's room, and demonstrated how it would be used in the forthcoming weeks. Vince was increasingly appreciative that the doctor was making a great effort to support him and make him part of the general effort to effect Audrey's recovery.

He tried to allay Vince's concerns: he showed him the oxygen bottles kept in readiness, in case of any disruption to her breathing; explained the routine of hourly checks of respiration and heart function. The regular movement of Audrey's limp body from side to side to prevent blood clots and bedsores was described. Even the use of the urinary catheter and care for all bodily functions were carefully explained beyond limits that he found comfortable.

Impressed as he was by the care provided and the acceptance of himself as a protagonist in therapy, he felt frightened and alone. In less than a week, too much had changed. He had lost control over his own future and acquired responsibility for someone who was helpless and suddenly immensely important to him, of whom he really knew very little.

Trouble might arise over Danty's death, but he felt no remorse – only a bitter enmity towards him and the brutes that had harmed Audrey in Cyprus. Had she not defended herself so bravely she might have suffered similar abuse from Danty.

After dinner he spent another hour with Audrey, worried about how hard it was to retain positive feelings for the unresponsive figure on the hospital bed. His breath caught in his chest each time he saw her. He loved her and would do anything he could to protect her, but they shared too little common history and memories for sessions such as this to continue. Miserably, he accepted that it was as well that he must leave tomorrow.

Dr Baxter's arrival made Vince feel better. Over the last couple of days they had established an odd rapport. He thought that the doctor also loved Audrey in some way. Not really jealous, he was appreciative of the extra dedication to her welfare.

With a bob and a smile, the doctor checked Audrey's pulse and respiration, glanced at her chart with a satisfied nod and made a note. Then he turned back to Vince, taking in his dejected look and the slump of his shoulders. 'Come on,' he said. 'Audrey's as fine as she can be – you can do nothing more today. I prescribe a dose of my favoured opiate. If you don't mind me saying so,' he added quietly, 'you look as though it might do you some good.'

With a forced smile, Vince acknowledged the invitation, stood and replaced Audrey's hand on the bed. Resisting a desperate impulse to throw himself on the bed and cuddle her, he kissed her lightly, whispered in her ear and followed the doctor from the room, feeling as useful as a spare tyre in a canoe.

In Dr Baxter's office, Vince sat where he had that terrible evening only two days before. The analyst busied himself pouring drinks, remarking, 'While it may be a sin to put water into single malt, it does make the flavour go further.' He handed Vince a glass with little room to add water from a glass beaker. Vince topped it up, without spilling more water on his dressing gown than went into his glass. As no whisky was lost it seemed like a reasonable outcome.

He sipped his drink and half listened to the doctor propound the virtues of various malts. As he prattled, Vince began to relax. The doctor commented, 'You're going back to your unit tomorrow.' He took a thoughtful sip and leaned forward. 'I want to reassure you on three counts. Audrey will have the best possible care. If there is any change in her status I'll let you know through your Orderly Room: five platoon, Bravo Company. Correct?'

'Yes, sir,' Vince replied, in a subdued voice.

'Good, next point,' he handed Vince a folded square of paste-board. 'That contains my name and position, how to contact me, and a statement that I am your psychiatrist as well as your medical doctor. It asks that I be contacted in any matter concerning your physical or mental health. Keep it with your ID card. It may prove useful. Get in touch if there is anything I can help with. I don't expect anything to go wrong, but you are recovering from a serious illness and have been under considerable strain.

'Third and most important, as you will agree: without scientific evidence, I have every confidence that Audrey will recover and when she does it will be largely because of you.' He held up his hand. 'It's a gut feeling, based on intuition and experience, but I believe I am right.' He nodded. 'Keep this thought with you. You are not leaving her in the lurch, dreams of a possible future with you are what will bring her through.

'Oh,' he smiled, 'one other thing. When we are alone, please call me George. I feel as though I should be wearing mutton-chop whiskers and a top hat when people I like call me "sir" all the time.'

'Thank you, sir – George.' Vince replied with sudden awkwardness, and rushed on. 'I can't tell you how grateful I am for what you have done – for us – both Audrey and me. I feel bad about leaving, but you've made me feel better about that too, and I've not much choice.' He stared at the floor to try to stop his voice from breaking. 'Without you, sir… George, I don't know how I could have got through the last couple of days.' They shook hands warmly and agreed to meet in Audrey's room after breakfast the next day.

Packed and ready to go the next morning, Vince held Audrey's hand, whispered in her ear and struggled to keep his worries from showing on his face.

Dr Baxter breezed in, lab-coat flapping and excessively cheerful. 'Excellent news! Danty's post-mortem examination was performed yesterday evening. The pathologist, who knew of my interest, rang just now.' He beamed happily. 'Natural causes: undiagnosed aortic stenosis – a blockage in the outflow tract of the left ventricle. He probably had rheumatic fever as a child.' He smiled at Vince's baffled look. 'Never mind, it's natural causes and an inquest is unlikely.'

He turned to the bed and began his usual examination, with a cheerful, 'Well, Sleeping Beauty, why don't you open those lovely eyes and give your young man a wonderful going-away present?' He paused, then continued in his kind, rough whisper. 'Not ready yet, eh? Never mind, I'm sure he'll wait, just don't keep him waiting for too long.'

He watched for some flicker of response, and then turned, disappointed, to Vince. 'Your transport will be leaving soon, son – say your goodbyes. I'll be back in ten minutes.' He swung on his heel and left the room.

When he returned Vince had scarcely moved. Unable to trust himself to speak, he blinked away tears, shook the doctor's hand stiffly and walked like an automaton from the room.

Numbly, he collected his gear from the ward. Men milled around, gathering bags and saying goodbyes. Nothing was real. As though caught up in a bad film, he tried to choke out words of farewell for the few he thought of as friends. Several nurses assured him quietly that Audrey's care would be a priority and Sonya kissed his cheek.

Bryson pushed through the crowd, booming, 'What's this, sport? You trying to steal *all* the sheilas?' Then, without compunction, he gave Vince a vigorous hug. 'Don't you worry, sport. She'll be all right, she'll be better in no time. Take care, eh?' And he too disappeared into the throng. Vince shook hands with Jay-Jay, and Angelo who, to Vince's dismay, not only hugged him but also kissed him on both cheeks.

Eventually they were on the bus and bumping down the hair-raising road towards Tapah and Taiping. Vince found a seat near the back where he was least likely to be disturbed and feigned sleep. Overwhelmed by feelings of helpless ineptitude, he craved solitude.

In one short week, he had won the loveliest woman he had ever met. Unable to protect her, he had lost her and she lay beyond his reach, like the living dead. Willingly, if perhaps foolishly, he felt responsible for her. Somehow he must find the means and a strength he was not sure he possessed to honour a commitment he wanted to last forever.

Chilled at his own inadequacy in the face of seemingly insurmountable mountains of responsibility, Vince fell into a troubled stupor, surrounded by ghosts of recent experiences. They flashed through his mind, the good, wonderful and terrible, like beams of energy that seared his mind with their passage.

The stirrings of desire when he saw Audrey for the first time; their long talks; the jokes and loving. That glorious final day at the waterfall and the enormity of its ending; his distress, compassion, bewilderment and rage when he read her brave letter. He relived the confrontations with Danty and his aching hatred for the vile and malevolent brutes responsible for it all.

In a deeper sleep, he dreamed of a simpler life. Beside a smoking fire, a flame-lit figure spoke soothingly of the elementary nature of man.

The bus jolted to a halt outside the hospital and Vince, startled awake, felt easier in his mind than he had since that ill-fated Thursday evening. The relief was temporary. By military standards it did not take long for the formalities of discharge from hospital to be completed. Soon, along with other post-convalescents, he was packed into a Land Rover with a Kiwi stencilled on the side and returning to the regiment a mile or so down the road.

chapter six

Although it was late afternoon, Vince needed to report to the Company Orderly Room. Because Tom Andrews had warned him in hospital that he might be grabbed for extra duties, he did so reluctantly. He was required however, to be recorded on company strength and also needed to collect the keys to his footlocker.

'Ah, Corporal Tanner,' the CSM smiled ominously. 'Welcome back to the real world. I hope you're fully recovered, because we've lots for you to do.' He gestured at the movements board on the wall. 'Four and five platoons are both in the bush so, apart from you, we have only six platoon to draw on for NCOs and one of theirs, Corporal Atkins, is on a course.'

Unhappily, Vince decided to bring up the matter of pay. When made Lance Corporal, over a year before, he had demurred at accepting acting unpaid rank. Over his protests, the CSM had ordered him to wear the chevron on his sleeve, with assurances that he would receive extra pay backdated to that time 'when the papers came through'.

The increase, little as it was, would be useful and a principle was at stake. Now he put his case to the CSM. It was he who had directed him to wear the stripe in the first place. The warrant officer appeared uncomfortable. 'Yes Tanner, all right, it's high time that you were paid for it. Something's gone wrong; you're due for a second stripe about now. I'll take it up with Major Bennett when he returns from leave and ask him to speak to you.'

Disgruntled, Vince decided not to hold his breath. The CSM then went on. 'The company is to provide light security for an Officers of the Brigade function. It will be held in marquees erected on the playing fields and will last for three days from Monday. There will be three two-man pickets deployed to patrol under your supervision, between 0900 and 1700 each day.'

Vince sighed. This was what Tom had warned him about. 'What men will I have, sir?'

'They'll be garnered from the odds and sods, the sick, lame and lazy who, like you Corporal, are not in the bush with their platoons. Report to Lieutenant Tracey at 0800 outside the marquee on Monday. He'll tell you what's required. Then return here. Your guard detail will be paraded outside Company HQ at 0830, to be deployed by 0855.'

Feeling highly pissed off, Vince trudged to barracks – bashas, as they were called. Each rifle company occupied five, eighteen-bed dormitories laid out in a U pattern with concrete paths and a strip of grass between. The buildings had thatched walls and roofs over a timber frame. Double doors at each end provided access and unglazed windows with shutters, together with ceiling fans, provided ventilation.

At the open end of the U stood a tea wallas' hut. Usually Pakistani, they were purveyors of tea, toasted sannies, soft drinks, cigarettes, and other sundries a squaddie might want and have the money to buy. They also organised the cleaners and the dhobi wallas for the laundry. For these services, each soldier contributed a few cents each day.

The basha was deserted. Only two bed-spaces near the far end held items of clothing or personal possessions. The others had folded mattresses with mosquito nets drawn back over them. Vince noted with pleasure that the roof and wall thatch had been replaced. During his last month here, the mosquito nets had saved slumbering squaddies from being smothered in gecko shit. The thatch was so infested with little lizards that sky was visible through the roof and everything below had become layered with the digested remains of their diet.

Alerted by lengthening shadows, Vince glanced at his watch, swore and grabbed eating utensils. As he neared the mess hall he heard mugs and eating irons being drummed on the wooden tables as unhappy voices chanted contempt for the food. Bloody hell, another food protest! Although the New Zealand ration scale was higher than the British, meals were poorly cooked.

Eating field rations or in a Brit camp meant two ringits a day extra in the pay book. Kiwi cooks were so poorly trained that the food was often scarcely edible. Some squaddies preferred to scrounge ration packs and prepare illicit meals behind their bashas.

An orderly officer and his sergeant, each wearing a scarlet sash to indicate his temporary position, arrived ahead of Vince. Over the head-throbbing racket, a grossly overweight sergeant-cook was looking self-righteous and displeased as he complained over the uproar.

Ignoring indignant protests from would-be diners, the officer climbed onto a long mess-table. He took a deep breath and bellowed. 'SILENCE! WHO CALLED THE COOK A CUNT?'

A few seconds of profound quiet was followed by a roar that rattled the roof thatch, almost lifting it from the rafters: 'WHO CALLED THAT CUNT A COOK?'

Red-faced and irate, the officer departed, followed by the sergeant fighting to hide a grin. Tension broken, the mess hall soon emptied to leave Vince and a few other dedicated diners. He foraged amongst the serving trays for scraps to stay his hunger, washed his mug and cutlery and returned to the basha. As he walked through the gathering darkness, he thought nostalgically of all the good hospital food he had eaten during the last four weeks and of the extra fifty-six Malay ringits that increased his pay account.

He woke to the screams of monkeys in the forest on the other side of the sports fields and training grounds. Sleep had been disturbed by the return of his two companions after the NAAFI closed, then by recurring dreams expressive of the turmoil in his mind. Men, grunting and cursing as they brutalised a lone woman in darkened countryside. Her whimpers of pain and fear, her unheeded pleas, left him powerless to help as he lay sweating, sick, and shamed, his heart pounding with impotent fury.

When sleep returned, his dreams were better. He was in a longhouse beside a smouldering fire, the scent of half-cured tobacco in his nostrils. Opposite was the halak. Fire-lit eyes stared into his as he whispered instructions on how to recruit a gunig and bring it under control. Oddly, the halak's lips seemed not to move. Later, he would wonder if this was when he'd first thought of the jungle as a refuge: a haven of escape from an intolerable world.

He had no duties other than to make sure that fresh uniforms were ready for the next three days. After breakfast he sorted his gear, sat on his bed and wrote, as warmly and as cheerfully as his mood would allow, a letter to Audrey via Dr Baxter. He posted it, then wandered listlessly around the camp, ate lunch without enthusiasm and lay down for a nap.

As he dozed he was alerted by the sound of his own name. Voices drifted from an open shutter in the six-platoon basha across the way. Straining his ears, he heard, '…dinkum, saw him in the mess hall, haven't seen him around for a bit. Nah, he was cas-evacced during five platoon's last op. Been in hospital ever since. Hey, did you hear about the strife in the Highlands? Yeah, some trouble over a sheila. They reckon some Brit who was mixed up in it died later on.'

Another voice: 'Yeah? He never seemed a bad sort of joker for a lance-jack. He got me out of the shit a while back, eh. That time I came back to camp pissed, the screws threw me in the lock-up. I kicked the door open but, and ran for it. Tanner was Orderly Joe. He saw me take off and found me under me bed. Pissed silly, eh? Anyway he made me get into bed and marked me present at lights out and they never knew I was the guy they was after.' He paused ruminatively. 'The only guy on a charge that night was that silly bugger Tamati, and he asked for it. He came in pissed later on – and then abused the shit out of Tanner!'

Vince grinned. Hapi *had* been pissed out of his mind and the RPs hadn't the wit to identify him before trying to lock him up. As a B Company colleague he helped when he could. He was not happy, though, that events in the highlands were camp gossip.

Three days of guard duty passed with little to alleviate the tedium. The CSM seemed happy enough and rewarded Vince by indicating his name on the Orderly NCO roster for the forthcoming week. Vince groaned and again mentioned his currently unpaid NCO status. The CSM replied impatiently. 'It will be dealt with. Go away and enjoy your four free days.'

The next nights he spent in the NAAFI drinking cheap schooners of draught Tiger beer that left a sour taste in his mouth and smoking too many issue cigarettes. He did not feel sociable, but sat with groups of drinkers in order not to be conspicuous. Feeling himself an object of rumour and speculation, he did not want to answer questions. Sudden silences and odd changes in conversation when he appeared made him start to feel paranoid.

On Friday evening he went with others to the Paris Bar for a drinking excursion outside the camp. They were back in camp in time for curfew at 2359 but, too restless to sleep, Vince found the usual gap in the fence and returned to town. Despite the time in hospital he felt surprisingly fit. He jogged towards the town, hugging the side of the road bordering the rubber plantations. Whenever headlights appeared he disappeared into the monsoon drain, fearful that they might belong to an MP Land Rover. He sought a bar that ignored the curfew and remained open as long as there were drinkers with the cash. Past the prison, he peered down poorly-lit streets in search of his destination. He had been there only once before, but finally found the road and the dingy entranceway.

A middle-aged Chinese man answered his banging on the heavy teak door and with a show of reluctance led him down a gloomy corridor to a smoky room at the back. There were none of the usual bargirls, only the barman who had let him in and seven drinkers.

The room reeked of tobacco smoke, alcohol, sweat and testosterone. The air ached with tension. Vince bought an Anchor beer and as his eyes adjusted to the light, he recognised some guys at a table on his right, near the bar. They were all Maori and he knew a few of them slightly; one waved in casual recognition, which he returned. On the other side of the room a lone figure leaned against the bar. Instead of the white shirt and dark trousers of required recreational dress, he stood out in sweat-stained jungle greens and worn jungle boots.

Vince recognised him as the pommy sergeant of the tracking platoon, a good-looking man a few years his senior. Standing at the bar, he had a beer in his hand and a belligerent look on his face. Vince guessed that there had been some dissension between him and the Maori.

Soothed by the beer he had consumed earlier and sweating healthily after his run, he felt more relaxed than he had since the awful aftermath of Danty's attack upon Audrey. She was never really absent from his mind, but for once her problems were not in the forefront of his thoughts.

He tried to engage the tracker sergeant in conversation, but after being told to piss off, turned his attention to the Kiwis near the other end of the bar. They at least were affable and waved him to a seat, but it soon became apparent that they were being polite and his presence intruded upon their conversation.

The man next to him turned, nodded towards the sergeant and said quietly, 'Friendly bugger eh? When we got here, about an hour ago, he wanted Chan the barman to kick us out.' He winked. 'Sweet chance eh, man?' He stuck out his hand. 'I'm Hiwi. I reckon you're from B Company.' He thought for a moment. 'Mmm... Tanner, eh?'

'Yeah, Vince, eh.' He shook hands around the table with Martin, Peka, Bert, Hone, Tama, and of course Hiwi. He tried to remember names, but knew that by morning he would be lucky to recall half of them.

Hiwi beamed. 'I knew your name had something to do with leather, eh.' Satisfied that they had fulfilled any obligations of hospitality, they returned to their conversation.

It revolved around the desire of iwi to regain control of tribal lands seized by the Crown after the New Zealand Wars of the last century. Hiwi leaned towards Vince with a grin to show that he meant no offence. 'We're plotting,' he whispered, 'to get back the land you Pakeha buggers pinched off us, eh.'

Vince finished his beer and returned the empty bottle to the bar. Before he left he wanted to thank the group for their friendliness and ordered seven more beers. As an afterthought he ordered another for the sergeant, who still stood at the bar, muttering darkly to himself and glaring malevolently at the shelves of bottles.

To murmured thanks he distributed six bottles around the table and returned to the bar for the others. With a bottle in each hand he stepped towards the Sergeant to place the bottle on the bar beside him. 'Here, mate, have a beer with us.'

His words were scarcely spoken when, eyes burning redly, the sergeant turned. 'Don't yer come near me wiv a fuckin' bottle in yer hand, yer cunt!' he screamed, snatching the full bottle and slamming it across Vince's head.

In stunned amazement, Vince stumbled against the bar and fell, half-conscious, to the floor. The sergeant stood over him and kicked viciously at his head. Desperately, Vince grabbed at the flailing feet, grateful that they wore rubber-soled jungle boots rather than heavy leather ones. A kick smashed into the side of his head that had already encountered the bottle and he lost all interest in footwear. The night became a nightmare: he felt himself dragged, pulled, carried and jolted about in a kaleidoscope of happenings entirely beyond his influence.

Vince woke feeling like one great bruise. A hangover of near-terminal proportions seemed to be complicated by the aftermath of an aeroplane crash. Experimentally, he opened his eyes, and quickly closed them again. There was too much light in the world. There was also a vaguely familiar figure sitting on the next bed and gazing idly out the open window.

Vince racked his scrambled brains to match the figure to a memory. Wearing day uniform, bare torso, uniform kepi, shorts and socks rolled down over the tops of leather boots, strong Maori features, muscular, olive-skinned. Last night, perhaps? Sitting at a table talking? He thought of pictures he had seen of Hone Heke, the famous warrior chief of the Ngapuhi. That was who it was – Hone, one of the guys who had shared their table with him last night.

Cautiously, one after the other, Vince opened his eyes. Hone examined him with interest and shook his head. 'How ya feelin', mate? Better than you look I hope, eh?'

'Not great,' Vince croaked, 'you were in the bar last night – Hone? Did you bring me back?'

Hone nodded. 'Yeah, me mates and me brought you back in the cab with us.' He chuckled. 'I tell you what: you wasn't helping much. You wanted to go back and kill the pom that hit you with a bottle. Not a great idea. We'd already pulled him off before he kicked ya head in. He got knocked around enough then anyway. Serves the mad bastard right.'

Vince grimaced. 'Thanks for bringing me back – Christ, I must have been a mess.'

'I reckon you still are, mate. D'you still want to punch me head in? Last night ya said ya was goin' to. I said I'd come back and give ya a chance today. What d'you reckon?'

Vince spoke through a sickly grin. 'I wouldn't have said that if I hadn't been out of my skull in the first place. Sorry mate, right now I'm in no condition to even think about it. Bloody hell! I can hardly move. Thanks again for bringing me back. Sorry I was such a pain in the arse.'

With a groan he struggled up, swung his feet to the floor and shook hands with Hone, who nodded. 'Don't forget, mate, I came back like I said to give you a chance to thump me out. It's good ya decided against it. No hard feelings eh? See ya.' He stood and walked out the door.

Vince still wore clothes from the previous night. The shirt was a write-off. The trousers looked as though the drycleaner might be able to save them. It was too late for breakfast but he stripped, wrapped himself in a towel and with his toilet bag limped to the ablutions. After a shave, shower and two mugs of water, he thought he might live. At midday he crawled into buff order and went to the mess. Two cups of tea and an egg sandwich cajoled from a cook's assistant helped him to feel better despite a sore jaw and a massive bruise on the side of his head. All relics of the sergeant's footwork. On the serving-tables were boxes of paludrine tablets. Standing Orders had changed, making it an offence to take less than two of the malarial suppressives each day. Without thought, he slipped a couple of bottles into his pocket, together with some plastic sachets of salt.

Almost unconsciously, he began to acquire a supply of easily carried items essential for an extended stay in the jungle. Following a mental checklist, he collected salt (vital in a hot climate), water-purifying tablets, and hexamine fuel tablets for a camp cooker. Fishing lines and hooks, too, and matches; as many packets of vitamin enriched rice from the ration packs as he could carry; dehydrated mushrooms, tea, sugar, instant soup powder and dried onion.

Time passed. So did his week as Orderly Joe, with nothing worse than near-lethal boredom. He had a friendly letter from Dr Baxter, cautiously optimistic but disclosing no real changes in Audrey's condition, and wrote one in return. He also wrote to his father and sister but made no mention of Audrey or the troubles in his life. By the end of the week most of his injuries had disappeared. He no longer limped; the soreness in his neck had gone. Only the bruise on the side of his head remained. Once Vince saw the tracker sergeant on the path leading to the encampment he shared with Iban trackers, dog handlers and their dogs. He was pleased to see he still limped. He had not got off scot-free at the hands of Hone and his friends.

He entertained a brief fantasy of ambushing the sergeant along the track with a baseball bat. At first his movements did not seem regular enough. Then it seemed hardly worth the trouble.

On Monday Vince reported to the jungle firing range on the fringe of the jungle on the other side of the sports grounds. He was required to refresh his immediate action skills, as the rest of the platoon had done while he was in hospital. The range covered perhaps five acres of jungle with concealed targets scattered around its trails. Some were stationary cutouts of human figures peering through the foliage. Others popped up abruptly at the release of a spring, glided past on invisible wires, or swooped from overhead branches when a cord was pulled.

At the end of the day he was told to return next day to assist with range control. This kept him occupied and was enormously preferable to orderly duty. Off duty he became increasingly introspective, brooding guiltily about being unable to help Audrey, even worrying that he was not worried enough. He tried to read, but haunted by idyllic memories of that last day with Audrey by the waterfall, could not concentrate. Emptily, he yearned for her laughter, longing to share her confidences, their lovemaking, her loveliness.

Too often he woke from nightmares of Audrey as, violated by grunting brutes, she wept and screamed while he could make no move to help her. Sometimes he stood, a mere shadow in her living room, as she gave herself to faceless men. He lay sleepless, miserable, wondering if they shared enough history to endure together. And if he had sufficient strength of character to wait for her return to consciousness, to help her recover from the horrors of her past.

Each week Vince exchanged letters with Dr Baxter. He liked the doctor, but sometimes his letters seemed little more than an umbilical cord that joined him to a helpless woman in a distant hospital bed. Memories of her haunted, tormented and confused him. Could he cling to her essence, the quality that had shone from a stranger in a white uniform, and invaded his heart – a stranger for whom he now felt real love and a lasting responsibility?

chapter seven

Five platoon returned. The basha filled with uproar, odours of sweat, machine oil and soiled gear. The thatch thrummed to laughter and ribaldry as they sorted equipment, returned ammunition to the armoury, cleaned and returned weapons to the arms-cote and generally disrupted the peace. Everyone was friendly enough; some, like Barry, were clearly delighted to see him. Yet he felt isolated. Time and events since he had last seen them had made them almost strangers.

An outburst of coarse laughter was centred on Short Storey. The platoon had flown out of Fort Chabai. A shack attached to the outer wall of the fort housed an attractive young Senoi woman whose presence provided food for prurient speculation. On the last night, when they were camped nearby, Short had boasted of an assignation with the lady who had become known, after a currently popular song, as Dark Moon.

To avoid being shot on his return, Short had ostentatiously arranged signals with a sentry before disappearing into the night. Next morning he looked smug and satisfied, until they all filed past Dark Moon's quarters en route to the airstrip. All heads turned for a glimpse of Short's putative paramour. A slim figure in a blue sarong was draping laundry over the fence to dry. At the sound of the passing patrol she turned, straightened, and a ripple of laughter ran along the file. Instead of Dark Moon's pretty face, lustrous hair and lissome body, this was a much older woman. She was bony, with sparse curly hair, a heavily lined face and flaccid breasts that hung over her sarong like leather socks. As they called, 'Good morning, Mrs Short' and other pleasantries, she waved and grinned, to show teeth like a broken picket fence.

Vince couldn't suppress a smile. Poor Short; he couldn't help inviting derision by his boasting and odd ways. When the platoon stopped to camp, it was a popular pastime to watch him set up his hammock and rain shelter. An unfortunate soldier in a preceding battalion had been dragged screaming from his hammock in the dead of night by a hungry tiger. Short had developed a pathological dread of encountering the same fate. Hoping to be overlooked by any passing tiger in need of a tasty supper, he hung his hammock as far as possible above the ground. The process became a continual source of enter-tainment and evoked much unwanted advice. Short maintained all the good humour he could muster, but the hassling was beginning to test his temper.

'Shut up, you bastards! Like I told yous before, I was jokin'. I just spent a couple of hours playin' cards at the fort.'

But the comments had persisted: 'What deodorant do yer use, Short? I wish I could find a sheila like that.'

'Hey, Short, find out if she's got a sister.'

'Nah, find out if she's got a granddaughter!'

'Hey, Short', called another voice, 'did she make a run for it when she saw your spare leg?' This had provoked another burst of hilarity.

After mess-call Vince joined Barry and Bobby Kendrick for beers. The NAAFI was noisy, smoky and reverberated with the celebrations of platoons back from ops as they drank copiously and recounted stories of doubtful veracity. A group formed around the piano and the room shook to lewd refrains: 'Round and round went the great big wheel, in and out...'

Barry found a quieter table being vacated in a far corner, but some self-styled hard men from the MG Platoon pushed aggressively past and sat down with belligerent glares. 'Shag off,' one advised unpleasantly. 'This is our table!'

Bobby paced his beer on the table, leaned over and spoke with exaggerated clarity. 'No-it-is-not! Piss off and take your drinks with you before you wear them!' Taking note of Bobby's size, his confidence and the way he moved they picked up their glasses and slunk away.

'Good on yer mate,' Barry and Vince grinned in unison. Barry told Bobby the latest episode in the Short Storey saga and they chortled into their beers.

Bobby turned to Vince. 'How about you, mate? Are you okay?' He hesitated.

'A guy in my platoon was in hospital while you were. He reckons you've been in some sort of strife, something – something about one of the nurses.' He looked awkward. 'He reckoned there were rumours about you having trouble with a pom that died later on.'

Vince stared at the table. He was still too upset and confused to want to talk about Audrey, but he needed to unburden himself to sympathetic ears. He looked up. Barry was round-eyed with curiosity, and they both waited expectantly. 'Well... okay. Taihoa while I get some more beers.'

He carried the glasses to the bar and struggled back through the melee with three schooners of beer. Barry and Bobbie waited, tense with expectation. An open can of cigarettes and a box of matches in front of his seat indicated that he would not be permitted further procrastination. Wordlessly, he placed a glass in front of each of them, raised his own glass and took a ruminative sip.

Barry broke the expectant silence first. 'Well...? What, er, what's all this Cameron Highlands stuff about, eh?'

Bobby had watched Vince shrewdly and sounded disgusted. 'The bastard's trying to wind us up, Barry. Come on, Vince, spit it out.'

He told them the bare bones of his week in the Highlands. Even without details about Audrey, it seemed a full week.

He spoke of how they had walked and talked together and of their growing affection. They were more interested in Danty, their squabble, and his subsequent attack upon Audrey, resultant injuries and eventual death. During a brief, hushed pause Bobby went for more drinks, with the exhortation, 'Wait till I get back.'

With fresh drinks they wanted to know more. Vince felt obliged to embellish a little and they growled approval: 'Good on yer, mate', 'Served the bastard right!'

When he told of how Audrey had defended herself with the kris, they were gruffly admiring. 'What a sheila eh?' 'Yeah' – a little wistfully – 'she must be quite a woman. You're a lucky bugger, mate.'

When he told them of Audrey's present condition – her helplessness, her vulnerability, the tubes and catheters, the coma that could drag on for years or forever – Vince's voice trembled. He glanced up, at their silence, and saw that their eyes were not completely dry either. Awkwardly, they leaned across the table to pat his shoulder. Barry stood to hug him and at the next table a group who thought this hilarious muttered 'poofs', but Bobby's silent glare made them recall urgent business elsewhere.

They agreed that a week at the battalion beach camp would be preferable to barracks and cheaper than post-operational leave in either Penang or Ipoh. It was also tacitly understood that this would avoid the temptation and expense of seeking transient comfort in the arms of whores. Erected by the engineer platoon, the beach camp was an overdue attempt to provide a leave environment sans prostitutes and public drunkenness. A basic affair, with thatch shelters where men hung their own hammocks, it had an open-air mess under a canvas roof and a general-purpose thatched communal area with simple tables and chairs. Several miles of rutted boggy track from the road were enough to discourage most ladies-for-hire or lust-driven squaddies.

Meals were barbecue style and relatives of the char wallas dispensed their usual fare – plus cold canned beer at NAAFI prices. The sea was warm and the coarse golden sand welcoming. Thick jungle extended to the beach and in the evenings troops of monkeys would drop from the branches to play on the shore. Bravely they scampered on the sand, until fear of the great open watery space sent them scrambling back to the security of the foliage.

One evening Vince took his beer can for a moonlit walk along the empty beach. After a few minutes he realised that the char walla's little black mongrel was tagging along. At the water's edge, the mutt stopped from time to time to dig furiously in pursuit of crabs. When it tired, with only its rear protruding from an exceptionally deep hole, Vince knelt, setting his beer can aside to help. When it was rested, the little beast tapped his shoulder with a paw to signal its readiness to take over again. So pleased were they with this shared labour that they continued it to the end of the beach where Vince lit a cigarette and stared at the lines of white foam, hissing as they raced up onto the sand.

A sickening maelstrom of images whirled through his mind, transforming the beach from a place of beauty to a world of torment. Audrey in a silk blouse with sunlight gleaming in her hair; naked and lovely; smiling, amidst clouds of butterflies; unconscious, a plastic tube protruding from her nose, a thread of saliva gleaming on her chin. A halak with glowing eyes, whose voice inside his head was dictating his dreams. The snarl of a tiger. Brutish men abusing a woman beside a dark road. Danty's grimace of fury turning to pain, and an unknown young officer's contemptuous smirk as he destroyed the life of the woman he had sworn to love.

As the havoc in his mind was becoming intolerable, despite the tropical warmth a small form nestled into his side. Absentmindedly he stroked the soft fur around the dog's neck, found comfort from its closeness and wondered if its small soothing noises were sounds of canine compassion.

* * *

A carefully maintained beer intake kept troublesome thoughts and dreams subdued until they returned to Taiping to find that Bravo Company was to provide a quarter-guard for Minden Barracks in Penang. Feelings were mixed. On the one hand, guard duty was irksome and boring. On the other, when they weren't on duty, the fleshpots of Penang would be at their doorstep. Vince despised guard duty, but when he saw his name amongst the others on the B Coy notice board he knew there was no appeal and he hurried to prepare his gear.

The guard detail of twenty-eight men included the two sergeants Rarangi – brothers – and sergeants of four and six platoons, with Tom Andrews as guard commander. They were on Penang Island and at the barracks in time for lunch the next day and soon assigned to their duties.

Since the winding down of the Emergency and the subsequent reduction in British personnel, the barracks complex had become mainly officer and married accommodation. There was little foot traffic and only non-Europeans were required to produce identity cards at the gate. Although full security regulations had not been formally rescinded, orders were to stop and check only suspicious vehicles. If any failed to stop when signalled, the guard was to use the direct phone in the sentry box to contact the guard commander.

At 2100 Vince and Mac Burrows were posted to an hour of boredom, taking turns in the sentry box while the other stood at the gate. Traffic was intermittent until Mac halted a car being driven so erratically that it almost tipped him into the monsoon drain. It was full of British service wives on a girls' night out. Filled with gin and ribaldry, they were quick to indicate their readiness to indulge in any mischief available. They would not leave until Mac, amidst a barrage of drunken giggles, succumbed to demand and checked the ID of the blonde driver who had parked it deep in her cleavage. Even then they would not leave until Vince assured them that they could find at the guardhouse a sergeant with the libido of a rabbit and the stamina of a bull.

Fascinated, they watched the taillights of the car weave their erratic way up the slope to the guardhouse and stop. Five minutes later the phone whirred angrily. 'If you bastards pull a stunt like that again,' said the sergeant unpleasantly, 'I'll have your guts for garters.' His voice softened slightly. 'Still, I might forgive you. The blonde with the tits reckons she's nervous while her husband's away. She wants me to check tomorrow night and make sure she's okay. It's our duty to make sure the ladies rest well at night.'

Mac and Vince decided to go into town during the afternoon. They rested during the morning, but Vince's sleep was still disturbed by phantoms of memory. In case they were back late, they left their uniforms prepared for the next morning. At 1500 hours, amidst good-humoured abuse from the guards, they hailed a trishaw at the gate. It had the advantage of economy as well as being a good way to see the sights. They would check out some tourist attractions later, but for now they directed the driver to take them to a bar.

* * *

Vince's head rested on something hard. Voices spoke quietly nearby. From a jukebox, a feminine Chinese voice lisped the final lines of 'Makeway', a popular song: 'East is east and west is west, the twain must ever part, flower of Malaya, you have my heart.'

Opening his eyes, he raised his head and looked cautiously around. This was the bar he and Mac had visited earlier. Memory gradually returned. They'd been drinking with some Australians who had decided to visit the Britannia Club in Georgetown. Mac had accompanied the Australians, while Vince had planned to return to barracks for an early night. But as with their earlier plans, good intentions had gone awry as he had a couple more drinks and brooded over Audrey's plight and their future.

Two girls, who looked Thai, had asked if they could sit at his table. Their names were Suzie and Nancy and they chatted casually for a while. When he bought another drink he offered them drinks also. They both asked for Coca-Cola and thanked him nicely when the drinks arrived. Vince had studied them across the table. Both were less than five feet tall with straight black hair. Nancy's, thick and coarse, was quite short, with a fringe that fell almost to her eyebrows. Suzie's was long, shiny and gathered at the nape of her neck to hang down her back. Nancy's face was round and moon shaped. Although attractive, she was plumper than most Thai women. Suzie, on the other hand was petit, with a narrow face and a slim, graceful figure. She was almost beautiful, with the natural grace and understated good looks of many Asian women. Her English was also clearer than her friend's.

Both girls wore the neatly brocaded sam fu – the ubiquitous pyjama-suit of tunic and trousers. Probably factory workers, he'd thought, out to supplement lousy wages with a little casual prostitution. His guess seemed correct when they asked with grave politeness, 'You like please stay long our house tonight?

Not far, ten-fifteen dollar all night – you say okay?'

He had smiled. 'Thanks, but I have to get back to barracks.' He tapped his glass. 'Too tired and too much rum, but I enjoyed talking to you.' A little later they thanked him again for their drinks and left. Too drunk to think rationally, he'd ordered another rum. That was all he remembered until he woke with his head beside a half empty glass of rum and coke.

He stared blearily at his watch. Jeez, 2100. I've slept for an hour! No wonder my neck's stiff. He closed his eyes again to subdue the throbbing in his temples, rotated his shoulder and kneaded his neck with his right hand. Unexpectedly, another hand touched his, rubbing at the knots in his shoulder muscles. He froze, but relaxed when he recognised Suzie's voice.

She scolded gently. 'You much silly boy. Go home sleep, not on table. Now poor back all sore. Sit still. I fix.' And fix she did. It was astonishing how soon her soothing fingers massaged the kinks from his muscles. He was left without room to manoeuvre when Suzie, helped by Nancy, who had also appeared, took control and helped him to his feet. 'No dollar,' Suzie assured him sternly. 'Too silly boy, drink too much. We take care you, then you go back to army.' She looked around suspiciously. 'First look in pockets. See no bad mans take things while you sleep.'

Embarrassed protests were ignored as they took an arm each and helped him to the street. He tried to signal a taxi, but both women shook their heads. 'No, no, not far. Walk together okay. No need taxi.' With movement and fresh air Vince's head began to clear and he convinced his escorts to walk arm-in-arm with him rather than as if they were in charge of an invalid.

It was pleasant to stroll publicly with two attractive young women and ignore the knowing glances of passers by. As the girls had promised, their destination was only a short distance away in an area of rickety looking buildings and small stalls selling Chinese noodles, chicken curry, nasi goreng and sizzling satay grilled on bamboo skewers.

Suddenly ravenous, he persuaded them to join him for a meal. They found a tiny table by the kerbside, lit by a paraffin lamp. His companions refused meat and chose noodle soup and rice gruel, but Vince had skewers of satay with peanut sauce and nasi goreng. He ordered a bottle of beer, but the disapproval was so intense that he joined the girls in cups of green tea instead.

After the meal they moved on to a large single-storey building only a few minutes away. Sparse light from street lamps showed it to resemble a disused warehouse with only a pair of locked double sliding doors at the front. Nancy produced a key and the smiling young women urged Vince into a corridor almost as dark as the street. A cream-coloured wall stretched in both directions, punctuated only by plain wooden doors. Some, partly open, allowed light to escape into a corridor dimly illuminated by one bare bulb.

Vince was steered to the left where the faint light showed a turn in the corridor. Sobered by the short walk and food, he wondered why his companions were so solicitous for his welfare. This did not seem to be a brothel. There were no semi-clad tarts, or provocative suggestions. Rather, the building had the air of a hostel that provided cheap, clean and secure accommodation. Nor could he believe that his charming escorts intended him harm.

Suzie opened the second door from the corner and led him inside. She clicked a switch and Vince looked around curiously. It was small, barely large enough to hold a three-quarter-size double bed in the corner beside the door, a small closet, a chest of drawers, an unreliable-looking chair and still leave a little floor space. In the far left corner another door evidently led into the room on the corner of the corridor.

The girls indicated that he should sit on the bed. He did so and was astonished when Nancy knelt to remove his shoes and socks while Suzie undid his shirt buttons. When he demurred, they made little soothing noises and continued as though undressing a child. Suzie admired a milky greenstone hei tiki that Vince habitually wore on a cord around his neck. 'Like jade,' she remarked approvingly, as she slipped it over his head. 'Ver' nice.'

'Yeah, a sort of jade, it's New Zealand greenstone,' he murmured, as relaxed as if he was enjoying an erotic dream.

When his underwear was removed and his responsiveness to their ministrations was revealed, the bed-maids exchanged glances and small sounds of approval. Suzie indicated that he should lie face down, and she massaged his back while Nancy folded his clothes and draped them over the chair. He was startled when Suzie slipped off her shoes and trousers, climbed onto the bed and inched her way along his spine, manipulating his vertebrae with her toes. Her feather-light form was no burden and apprehension gave way to bliss as he surrendered to the treatment.

With a remark that he did not catch, Suzie stepped from the bed and slipped back into her trousers. Pleased, puzzled and also a little disappointed, he saw that Nancy had stripped to lie down beside him. It had seemed likely that one would be his bedmate, and he had hoped for Suzie. Nevertheless, Nancy naked was more desirable than he had thought at first. Her breasts were firm and she had the robust sensuality of a healthy and vigorous young woman.

As Suzie slipped through the door into the adjoining room, Nancy slid beside Vince, looked into his face for a long moment and smiled. 'Don' worry, we be ver' good, nice. You like.'

She drew Vince's head to her breasts and gently urged his body over until he lay happily between her thighs. 'Yes,' he responded. 'I like!'

He dozed, wondering about the noises from the next room, a fairly continuous click-clack, like the sound of hard objects against a similar surface, punctuated by exclamations of annoyance, pleasure and sometimes laughter. He had first noticed them as Suzie stepped out the door, but Nancy had diverted them from his mind. Still none the wiser, he fell asleep.

An unknown time later a sound disturbed him. He strained his ears. The noises from the next room continued; he could hear faint sounds of traffic from the street. That was all. The space beside him was empty. 'Probably gone next door too,' he thought. He listened carefully: what was that? There it was again, a whisper of cloth.

There was a movement in the darkness, 'What... Suzie?' Softly, a slim smooth body pressed against him. Yes, it's her perfume, Vince thought. Whether soap or scent, it augmented her sweet femininity and stirred his senses dramatically. Wordlessly, she moved over him, lips caressed his neck and chest as an exploratory hand slid down his stomach until its objective rose to meet it.

He quickly reached up for her breasts. Small and firm, his fingers told him, as nipples pressed like pebbles into the palms of his hands. She rocked forward; sharp teeth nibbled at his neck. With a long gasp, she reared back as he threw his own head back and groaned. When he was almost asleep he felt her sliding from the bed, and he whispered, 'Suzie, could you make sure I wake up? I have to be in barracks before six o'clock.'

There was a whisper in reply, but he was asleep before he heard it.

Worn out by dream-disturbed nights, excessive drinking and recent exertions, Vince slept deeply. Occasionally he woke to the clicking and laughter, his curiosity piqued by why these delightful girls had been so kind to him. Hoarse, cackling laughter woke him again. The noises next door continued; this was much closer. A hand groped him intimately and his eyes jerked open. The light was on and beside the bed crouched a frail, ancient wisp of a woman with sparse grey hair hanging over an old kimono. Bony thumb and fingers gripped Vince's flaccid manhood and dreadful laughter tumbled from her toothless gums. With a horrified groan, he jerked away, pulled the sheet over his head and fell back into sleep.

When next his eyes opened, a faint morning light filtered through a skylight he had not noticed before. Nancy was asleep beside him and Suzie's voice was in his ear. 'Veence, Veence,' she whispered anxiously. 'Is time for army. Is five o'clo'.'

Befuddled by sleep, he wondered why he was in a bed surrounded by young women. Then gathering his wits, he climbed from the bed, being careful not to wake Nancy, whispered his thanks and fumbled for his clothes. They were on the chair where Nancy had left them, still neatly folded with his watch, wallet and pendant, his dog tags and small change. Under the chair were his shoes, side by side, with socks tucked tidily inside them.

Quickly, if clumsily in the near darkness, he pulled on the clothes. He was aware of Suzie's eyes but the poor visibility and the frolics of last night made false modesty ludicrous. Within minutes he was dressed. Suzie took him by the arm to lead him into the corridor and around the corner.

She indicated the door to an ablution room that he dimly recalled visiting the night before. It was spotlessly clean. A raised dais, in one corner, held an eastern toilet with raised footrests. In another corner was a tall cistern with a curved front from which hung a dipper, presumably intended for flushing the toilet and as an alternative to a shower. He urinated hastily, used the ladle to flush, splashed water on his face and joined the Suzie in the corridor.

He still could not fathom why the girls had been so kind to him. They had given him shelter, offered their bed and bodies in open generosity and massaged the aches from his muscles. Now Suzie seemed to have stayed awake to make sure he did not over-sleep. He felt flattered, his male ego pampered.

Although at first they had offered to take him home in exchange for payment, they had later made it clear that they wanted nothing from him. Rather, they seemed genuinely concerned for his welfare. In his wallet were two twenty-ringit – Malay dollar – notes, but he did not want them to believe that he thought of them as prostitutes. It was a dilemma. Particularly so, because those two notes were his last until his still-distant payday.

Nevertheless, as Suzie unlocked the door he slipped a twenty from his wallet. She opened the door to indicate the route by which they had got here. 'By bar we meet, plenty taxi. Go quick now, much late.' She pulled his head down to kiss him sweetly on the cheek.

She went to close the door, but he took the pendant she had admired the night before, slipped it over her head and returned her kiss. From his pocket he took a cigarette lighter, with a music box mechanism in its base, which played a Strauss waltz and slipped the watch from his wrist. He pressed them awkwardly, into her hand together with the twenty-ringit note. 'Suzie, thanks for being so kind to me, and please say goodbye and thanks to Nancy. Here are gifts for you both. You're lovely people – bye.' He turned and hurried away.

After a few steps, he heard a small cry and she ran up behind him, a tiny figure in a pink kimono and bare feet. 'Veence', she said, gasping, 'you ver' nice man. Presents ver' nice, from frien'. Not money. Last night we all frien', nice.' A little sadly, she added, 'We take money, then las' night we prossie. Now go quick.' She pushed the bank note firmly into his shirt pocket, turned and ran back to the open door.

He found an empty taxi near the bar where Suzie had suggested. It was a short ride back to the barracks and if the clock on the dashboard was correct, it was 0532 hours when he thrust a five-ringit note he had found in his fob-pocket at the driver. The guard sergeant stood by the guardhouse. 'Bloody hell, Tanner,' he swore disgustedly as Vince staggered past. 'Get yer arse into gear man, yer on parade in fifteen minutes.'

A quick cold shower, the only temperature available, followed a record-breaking shave. He was grateful that his gear was ready to climb into. He lined up outside with the other three guards, only seconds before 0550. Lieutenant Andrews inspected each man carefully. When he reached Vince he regarded without favour the pale face and pouched, bloodshot eyes. When his eyes fell to Vince's neck, he took a step backwards. 'Jesus, Tanner! What the hell's *happened* to you? You look as though you've been garrotted! Are you fit to go on duty?'

Miserably wishing he had the courage to say the reverse, Vince replied, as smartly as he could 'Yessir.' It was a croak, but Tom Andrews appeared not to notice.

'Holy Christ,' he muttered in awe, 'those are hickeys and those are tooth marks. My God. There's at least two different sets of tooth marks. What sort of women *do* you associate with?'

Embarrassed, Vince ignored the suppressed amusement on either side. He had been vaguely aware of marks on his neck as he shaved, but had no time to think about, let alone examine, them. 'Very good and close friends, sir.' he replied, a little primly. He recalled Nancy nibbling fervently at his neck and sometime later Suzie had behaved similarly.

The lieutenant shook his head. '*Very* close, evidently. God, I shudder to think what the rest of you must be like.' He turned, stalked off a few paces and prepared to accept the salute.

Vince ignored ribald comments from the rest of the guard, told Mac that he would explain later, crashed on a bunk and fell into an exhausted sleep. Sergeant Rarangi, as a wise and compassionate commander, altered the roster to place Vince on the third shift so that he might be fit to go on duty. He slept for over two hours.

The sergeant had also decreed it ridiculous to march a single man to and from the gate. So at 0855 Vince found himself marching as smartly as his body would permit down the slope to the sentry box. That ninety-minute duty passed with the speed of cold treacle spreading across a flat surface. When he was relieved at last, he marched back up the slope on unwilling rubber legs.

Mac burned with curiosity to find out what had happened, but he fobbed him off with a squalid tale of an encounter with an unusually exuberant whore with the propensities of an oriental Dracula. Disappointed, Mac went to play cards and left Vince to get whatever sleep he could. His next duty proved more fraught. Thirty minutes into his shift, as he paced outside the sentry box, a piece of paper blew against his leg. As he stooped to look at it, a Land Rover with kangaroo insignia swung in the gate. He took no notice until it halted a few yards past him.

'Corporal,' screamed a frenzied voice. 'Here, *at the double!*'

Vince strode over and executed a belated salute. 'Sorry, sir. I didn't see you in the vehicle.'

The captain spluttered with anger. 'You failed to salute an officer,' he fumed. 'You were reading on duty. You're a disgrace to your uniform!'

Vince tried to explain, but the captain erupted from the Land Rover and marched on the offending piece of paper. As he turned away, his driver spoke from the corner of his mouth. 'For Christ's sake, mate, don't get him all upset! That's Black Jack MacRoberts. He's as mad as a meat-cleaver and we've got to live with him.'

Captain MacRoberts returned, dramatically flourishing evidence of the crime. 'A comic,' he cried in triumph. 'You were reading a comic on sentry duty!' Again, Vince tried to explain the circumstances, but the seemingly deranged captain refused to listen. 'I'll have your stripe for this,' he hissed maliciously as he climbed back in the vehicle. 'Failure to salute an officer. Reading comics on duty!'

Suddenly, Vince had had enough. 'I am still waiting for the salute I *did* give you to be returned – sir,' he replied quietly. 'As for the stripe, you're welcome to it and I know where you could best wear it.' He gave the smartest salute available, turned and marched away. As the vehicle moved off he heard a cry of outrage from the officer and what may have been a snort of muffled laughter from his driver.

Vince waited by the sentry box until the telephone whirred angrily. Sergeant Rarangi burned his ears with the required dressing-down, and then heaved a great sigh. 'All right, Tanner, tell me what actually happened.' Vince explained in detail. The sergeant questioned him closely and again sighed mightily. 'You're a silly bugger, Tanner and Captain MacRoberts is as mad as a rabid dingo. Here's what's happening. To keep the mad bastard quiet you're on duty for an extra hour. Stop every vehicle that comes in the gate and check every identity card. We'll enforce every regulation in the book. Oh, Tanner…'

'Yes, Sergeant?'

'FOR CHRIST'S SAKE DON'T MAKE ANY MORE TROUBLE FOR ME!'

By late afternoon Vince was sick of the line-up of cars, the hostile and indignant officers, wives and dependents. Accustomed to driving through the gates unchallenged, they rebelled against displaying ID cards. Those unable to produce them were especially indignant at being required to stop at the guardhouse and prove their identity.

Throughout the shift Vince's sense of fragility increased while he struggled to remain stoic in the face of anger and abuse. Mac relieved him, fully aware of the unrest and with gleeful reports of Sergeant Rarangi greeting complaints from pompous officers or shrill wives with a wave towards standing orders posted on the guardhouse wall.

'Bloody hell, mate,' he whispered, turning to stop a racy sports car, 'if this is what happens after one night shagging your brains out, warn me when you get seven days' leave eh?'

That night Vince fell asleep with unsurprising swiftness, but not before reviewing the previous night's events. As remote as dreams now, only his scars, exhaustion and various other discomforts attested to their reality. He recalled Suzie's fragrance, her teeth on his neck and a flash of intuition revealed the source of the noises from the next room. He sat upright. Bloody hell! the realisation struck him full force – I was entertainment for the dummies during a bloody mah-jong tournament! That racket was their tiles being slapped down!

* * *

The nightmares remained, exacerbated now by guilt at his libidinous behaviour. On Thursday, a free day, he declined suggestions that he join a crowd to visit a brothel cum bathhouse near Telok Bahang. He wanted a market where he could buy a cheap watch to replace the one he had given Suzie. A bus into Georgetown would stop outside the gates at 1000 hrs. He wanted a day to himself, but when Buddy Tamati asked to come along, he agreed.

Buddy was a hard man to dislike. Of Tainui from the Waikato, he was of middle height with tight, curly black hair. His skin was a smooth dusky brown over clear facial features and he had a fine physique. He seldom drank to excess or raised his voice except in laughter, and his good-humoured common sense had earned him widespread respect.

Vince had resolved to reduce his drinking and pull together the unravelling strands of his life. Since the attack on Audrey, alcohol had helped him to avoid the spectres of her past, the reality of her condition and his own frailty. Danty had re-created for her the mental agony of the earlier assault and betrayal. His problems, compared with hers, were nothing. But he could not control his dreams.

They left the bus at Lebuh Carnavon when Buddy spied a market area that seemed promising. It was not very extensive but they wandered around to check prices and then took a trishaw to another a few blocks away. Here the prices seemed more competitive and after a look around the stalls, they began to haggle for what they wanted.

To Vince, bargaining only complicated shopping, but he had soon found that there were two options. You haggle, buy what you want at an acceptable price and get treated with respect – or pay the asking price, at least twice the real value, and be treated with derision. After a considerable drama, he paid ten Malay ringits for a watch he liked. The vendor swore he was being driven into bankruptcy and his children would starve. When the deal was completed, he brightened at once and presented Vince with a musical cigarette lighter. It was similar to the one he had given away with his old watch and on an impulse, he bought three more for a final price of one ringit each.

His new watch looked quite elegant. It had a nice leather strap, bore a well-known brand name, but was of doubtful authenticity. If genuine, it would be worth ten times what he had paid. Buddy too had completed negotiations for assorted gifts to send to his people in Ngaruawahia. Lured by the delicious aroma, they bought sticks of satay with peanut sauce, served on newspaper, and entertained other patrons by sitting by the vendor's stall, eating the satay directly from the bamboo skewers and washing the meal down with bottles of Anchor beer. Vince enjoyed Buddy's company. They got along well without intruding on each other's privacy.

Until a final guard duty on Friday night, Vince avoided booze. He spent his spare time gazing at a novel or browsing through Kipling's verse. Too often he stared into space and thought of how that last day with Audrey had begun as the best of his life and ended as the worst.

One day, while he was immersed in Kipling, Vince became dimly aware that someone was speaking. He looked up. Buddy stood at the foot of his bed, shuffling uneasily.

'Sorry mate, I didn't mean to bug you, but are you okay?' Vince nodded yes. The normally calm-faced Buddy looked embarrassed. 'Look,' he began, 'I…ah…well…' The words would not come.

Vince patted the bed beside him. 'Sit down and spit it out, Buddy. What's the problem?'

Buddy sat. His normally tan face reddened with mortification. 'Look – uh – maybe I should just piss off. It's none of my business – I don't want you thinking I'm being a stupid Maori – but a lot of us believe in things Pakeha call superstition.' His ears glowed as his discomposure increased. 'You know makutu?'

Vince nodded cautiously. 'Isn't that black magic?'

Buddy shook his head. 'Not black, just magic – stuff we don't understand, like religion.' Vince confined himself to a puzzled look as Buddy examined the toes of his boots and looked as though he wished he were somewhere else. Then he raised his eyes and spoke slowly. 'Okay, you'll think I'm crazy, but my granny told me to give you a message, eh.'

Seeing Vince's puzzled expression, Buddy grimaced wryly. 'Okay, you don't know my tupuna Hine. I'll have to lead up to things a bit. She raised me in Ngaruawahia and she was the only parent I knew. Since I was a potiki – a baby – she was always telling me stories of our people. About tupuna of long ago, like Maui, who fished the North Island of Aotearoa from the sea. He's the fella who tried to kill Hine Nui Te Po, the goddess of death. He tried it eh, so that nobody would have to die any more, but the piwakawaka, the little fantail, eh, it laughed just as Maui crept into her body and he was nearly crushed to death when she woke up.'

Buddy held up a hand when Vince moved restlessly. 'Taihoa e hoa, I'm getting to it. The old lady, she told great stories,' he said wistfully, 'and most of them she really believed, eh. She said she spoke with dead people. I think she really did.' He shuddered and his voice dropped. Involuntarily, Vince shivered also. 'She reckoned that Hine Nui Te Po came to her at night and whispered secrets that she should know without having to wait to die. That way she could tell other people things they needed to know before *they* died.'

He looked thoughtful. 'Last night my tupuna came to me in a dream. She said I should tell the Pakeha I was worried about…' he was looking defensive now '…Well, I've heard talk about trouble you've been in and you've been looking crook and pretty upset. S'pose I wondered if you needed help and she picked up on it. Anyway she says to tell you three things.'

Touched by Buddy's evident discomposure and concern, Vince remained puzzled. 'Did you tell your grandma about me in a letter?'

Buddy shook his head sadly. 'Nah, she died, must be two years ago, eh? That's why I joined up. She always reckoned I needed something like the army to knock me into shape. Anyway I better tell you before I forget and the old lady gets mad at me. She say you're okay, not a bad man, just a man and your woman's hurt bad, but not too bad. She say too, that in the bush you'll find the wairua, the spirit, of your woman and get it back to her.'

He shuddered again and looked at Vince reproachfully. 'Hey boy,' he shook his head reprovingly, 'this is pretty heavy stuff, eh?' Vince sat rigid, trying to make sense of the message, and Buddy nodded. 'Oh yeah, another thing.' He looked puzzled. 'I think she said, "Tell him to listen for the voice of the tiger".' Buddy shrugged. 'Well that's it, mate. If she asks, I can say I gave you her message.' He looked askance at Vince and gave his head another shake. 'I tell you what, mate, if any of this makes sense to you, I'm glad I'm not living inside *your* head.'

With a nod, he walked away. Vince felt bewildered. He had never had a message from a dead person before. It was unsettling.

Is Buddy making all this up? he asked himself. Nah, why would he bother? He wouldn't anyway, Vince thought. But it was strange; some bits seemed to make a crazy kind of sense. A chill touched his soul. Something beyond his knowledge or control seemed to be nudging him in a direction that he might possibly have considered, but without really meaning to follow it. What was it Buddy had said? Hurt maybe, but not too bad – that could mean Audrey. Okay, he thought, somebody could have pieced that together from hearing about what happened in the Highlands. But who in hell could know that I dream about tigers?

He shivered.

chapter eight

Ten days after returning to Taiping, five platoon was on patrol in the highland forests between Perak and Kelantan. Single-engine Pioneer aircraft of the embryonic Royal Malayan Air Force, little planes capable of landing and taking off on the short jungle airstrips with three or four passengers and their gear, ferried them into Fort Chabai.

Deployment took three days. High country, wreathed in low cloud, made flying hazardous. Fortunately the pilots were skilled and Vince was happily unaware of any untoward crashes. At dawn each morning they assembled at Sungei Siput airfield to wait for the cloud to dissipate. On the third day, bored with waiting in the heat of the open aerodrome, Mac, Barry and Vince hitched a ride in a plane headed back to Butterworth for lunch. The ex-Luftwaffe pilot had them admitted to the mess for a meal of beer and sandwiches and on the return trip to Sungei Siput he received a radio message. A colleague had found a clear passage into Chabai. They would follow him while it was still open.

They wound through the narrow valleys, trying not to flinch when the wingtips seemed about to touch giant trees looming from the steep hillsides. Trying for an aerial glimpse of Chabai, Barry exclaimed sharply and Vince turned to stare into the eye of an elephant wrenching unconcernedly at a tree-branch mere yards from a wingtip. Minutes later they climbed stiffly from the plane with the sight of the great beast, seemingly close enough to touch the wing with its trunk, still engraved on their minds.

Joe Savage, corporal of two section, Short, Buddy and Jimmy Te Pania met them. They had disembarked from a plane that had landed minutes before and taken off again. They, unlike Mac, Barry and Vince, who had only rifles and ammunition pouches, had crammed into the little plane with full gear. Short complained of being stuck in the middle, with packs piled over him. Joe shook his head sympathetically. 'Poor Short, if only we'd known you was there. We thought it was just an ugly lump in the upholstery that we piled our gear on — and we was right,' he declared with a whoop of laughter.

'Bugger you, Joe,' Short grumbled bitterly. 'You had your rifle in me ear from the moment we took off and Jimmy farted whenever we hit an air pocket. I hoped you'd pull the bloody trigger!'

As they gathered their gear, a Malay police captain emerged to meet them. He had heard by radio that the clouds had closed in again and there would be no further flights until tomorrow; an empty hut and spare hammocks were available for them. They declined further hospitality, preferring to prepare their own meals from ration packs and balance their supplies when the other packs arrived. No sooner had they reached their billet, than a drumming on the roof-thatch announced the afternoon deluge.

The basha had a rustic table, plank seats and enough posts with steel hooks to support ten hammocks. The communal toilet seemed less secure — a small jetty projecting over a stream flowing through the compound. At the end were a rail to perch on and a post to hang on to. The ablutions and water point, strategically situated upstream, were equally luxurious.

They settled in to prepare a meal before dark. After the garrison's call to stand-to, Mac, Jimmy, Joe and Barry began a game of five hundred. Vince and Buddy sat in their hammocks to read, taking advantage of the electric light before the fort's generator turned off for the night. Short rummaged in his pack and came up with a pack of playing cards. From over his own cards Mac nodded amiably. 'G'night, Short, see you in the morning.'

'What are you talking about, you silly bastard?' Short demanded, tapping his cards impatiently.

'Oh.' Mac smiled kindly. 'I thought you was off to shack up with Dark Moon's granny again.'

His face dark with resentment, Short stamped off to take advantage of any policemen sufficiently misguided to play poker with him.

Vince woke to the sounds of night. Water dripped from saturated eaves, geckoes rustled in the thatch. Muted sounds denoted a change of sentries and the background chatter of the swollen stream. He thought of Audrey: another letter had arrived from Dr Baxter. It was couched in the same optimistic tones but there was no change in her condition. He had written again to her, reiterating his love and reminding her of their plans. Afterwards he had stared at his words and felt a hypocrite. Then he'd thought, No. Damn it! Maybe I did get pissed and screw my brains out, but I've said nothing I don't mean with all my heart. At last he had taken up the pen and added that he would be on ops and would be out of contact for some time.

As he waited for sleep, he recalled the strange message from Buddy's tupuna. It made no more sense than it had before. He tucked it away for future thought and reviewed his interview with the Major Bennett.

On the Monday after returning from Penang, the CSM had called Vince into the Orderly Room. 'Corporal Tanner – you wanted to see the major – you've an appointment at 1100 hours tomorrow. Be here ten minutes before.' He glanced at the programme board. 'Five platoon will be revising ambush drills; speak to Sergeant Jones and allow yourself time to get back. Oh, jungle dress will be okay, but be tidy!'

News spreads. After lunch Tom Andrews stopped him for a word. Vince had spoken to him twice already about his acting unpaid status. The lieutenant had reported back, 'Something's gone wrong with the paper trail. You should've had your second stripe by now and I've recommended that promotion be immediate.' That had been months ago.

This time, after the mandatory exchange of salutes, he had spoken quietly. 'Look, Vince, when you see the major tomorrow, watch your tongue. You didn't help yourself with that balls-up in Penang, but you should have a second stripe by the end of the month. I don't want to lose you as an NCO and I expect to see you go home with sergeant's stripes.'

Vince had gazed over the playing fields towards the jungle-shrouded hills. 'Will I get backpay, sir?'

The lieutenant looked embarrassed and shook his head. 'I doubt it,' he said unhappily. 'But even if you lose your temporary third stripe you'll still be a lot better off when you get home.'

Vince had shaken his head in frustration. 'Sorry, sir,' he said stubbornly, 'it's a matter of principle. If promises aren't kept there's no trust. I'd rather take my discharge.' They had parted uncomfortably, which made Vince unhappy. Tom was a good officer who tried to avoid pulling rank.

Precisely at 1100 hours the next day Vince had marched into the major's office. Rubber soles squeaking on the varnished floor, he stepped to the desk where the major sat, halted, left turned, saluted and waited.

'Stand easy, Tanner, sit down.' The major sounded weary. He was not having a good day. 'Now if you wanted to see me about your second stripe, you can put it up as soon as the colonel signs the order. Anything else?'

'Yes, sir, when I was ordered to put up the stripe as an acting lance-corporal I was told that I'd be paid back to that date when it was confirmed. It's been more than a year, sir.'

The major went red in the face. 'You're pushing your luck, Tanner. This is the army, we don't do back pay. You're lucky Lieutenant Andrews spoke strongly on your behalf, or there'd be no thought of a second stripe.'

He flicked the papers on his desk. 'I've checked your record. Hospitalised: head injury while on leave, again with malaria; hospitalised again – this time scrub typhus. We don't get much use out of you when you're in hospital all the time. There's also too much correspondence concerning you,' he scowled and picked up some papers from the desktop. 'A complaint from a provost officer in the highlands: insubordination. Another one: this time an Australian captain in Penang – insolence – dereliction of duty. Mr Andrews assures me, however, that the captain is an excitable sort of fellow. Yet another, this one a medical officer, also in the Highlands; he at least seems to think highly of you. Claims you defended one of his officers and behaved most commendably.' He snorted. 'Thinks you should get a medal.' He snorted again. 'That letter is the only reason I let Lieutenant Andrews convince me about the second stripe. There's no question of back pay! If there's nothing further, you can go.'

Inwardly seething, Vince came to attention. 'Yes, sir, there is something. I request permission to remove my stripe and revert to private.'

The major jumped to his feet, livid with fury. 'My God, Tanner,' he exclaimed, his voice rising, 'you've got a confounded cheek! Request granted. Now get out of here!'

Stiffly, Vince saluted and marched out. He was not surprised to find the CSM on the veranda outside surveying the B Company notice board. From his own experiences he knew how thin the walls were.

The warrant officer shook his head sadly. 'You're a silly bugger, Lance-Corporal Tanner, you've tossed away a good future in the army by being too bloody stubborn. Okay,' he added quietly. 'I thought I could get you back pay – I was wrong. But if you take the corporal's stripe now, I think we can square it with the major and you could still make sergeant in a year's time.'

He gave Vince a quizzical stare.

After a moment's hesitation, Vince replied. 'Thanks, sir, but no thanks. I've changed my mind about re-enlisting.'

The CSM shrugged his shoulders. 'Well, it's up to you. Just don't forget, you will have the duties and responsibilities of an NCO until you get orders to the contrary – until then you will wear your stripe.'

'Thank you, sir,' Vince answered with weary irony and walked away to prepare for lunch.

* * *

'Holy Christ, what's going on!' Mac's yell startled them from sleep into wide-eyed terror. An unintelligible loud chanting from the blackness sent them fumbling for weapons, tripping over each other in the confusion of darkness.

'Settle down, you silly bastards.' Joe sounded smug and comfortable in his hammock. 'It's only the Imam calling his flock to morning prayers.' In ignominious silence they crawled back into their own hammocks, carefully ignoring Joe's dry chuckles. Over the forested ridges, the sun broke through to a chorus of hoots from the tribes of gibbons living nearby and the cries of birds that rallied to attack the rich food resources of the forest canopy. By 0800 hours, breakfasted and ablutions performed, they had packed their gear when the police radio operator brought a message. Two planes were in the air with others of the platoon. The entire unit should be deployed by mid-morning.

By 1100 hours the platoon had assembled, crossed the stream and begun the trek up the valley to the ridges and to their designated patrol area in the northeast. Their objective was to search the high country between the Sungeis Puian and Yai, rivers that rose in the highlands to flow into the State of Kelantan, north and east of Perak.

The remnants of Chin Peng's rebel regiments had withdrawn to camps on the Thai side of the international boundary. The patrol's mission was to deny any rebel attempt to re-establish a toehold on Malay soil. They would follow the Puian as it descended into the valley of the Nenggiri River. This they would follow south, upstream to its confluence with the Yai and follow that back into the high country to finally cross again to Chabai. They carried eight days' rations and part way down the Puian valley would be re-supplied by Auster aircraft. Further supply drops would be received at the end of each operational sector.

Two days' march took them to a ladang where they kept their rendezvous with the Senoi guides who would carry their heavy equipment. The fifth night was a dry bivouac at the top of the dividing range. At an elevation of some six thousand feet the nights were chilly and they were grateful for their half-blankets, as with nowhere to hang their hammocks, they made themselves as comfortable as possible on the stony ground. The porters in their low lean-tos of attap leaves seemed the only ones able to sleep peacefully through the night.

Each day after setting up camp, Tom Andrews dispatched two patrols to check as large an area as possible before returning by stand-to. On the final day he pushed the platoon to reach the planned re-supply site early; in order to sweep a larger area in advance of the air-drop.

The chosen site was an old ladang where only scrub needed to be cut to make space for fluorescent recognition panels. No one wanted to find that they had inadvertently dropped supplies to a group of particularly cheeky terrorists. Nearby, an orange balloon, inflated from a canister of moistened chemicals, would be released on a tether, to guide the approaching aircraft to the drop site in the vastness of the jungle. The Auster would first fly over to check that the panels were laid in the stipulated pattern. On the second pass, a coloured Verey flare provided further identification.

It was nice to have fresh rations and an issue of rum, but the two days spent at the drop site became memorable for other reasons. When the evening situation report was transmitted, incoming signals in the routine orders included that: 'L/Cpl. Tanner promoted to Cpl.'

Tom Andrews smiled tiredly. 'Have strength, Vince, they sometimes get it right.'

Sure enough, the next evening's signal read: 'Cpl. Tanner reduced to Private at own request. Private Burrows promoted to temporary L/Cpl.'

Also, Vince's sausages, ready to fry for breakfast, were stolen by a felonious musang. Outraged when his breakfast disappeared from his mess-tin, he suspected someone of playing tricks. Then he saw it, more like a fox than a civet cat, its brushy tail held triumphantly in the air. Evidence of its guilt hung from its jaws as it vanished into the bushes.

Over mugs of issue rum, Mac and Vince joined in an amicable transfer of section responsibilities. Vince felt an inexplicable pang of regret, but was pleased at Mac's gratitude for the chance of promotion and his eagerness for advice. Tom Andrews moved him to two section, led by Joe Savage and currently under-strength. He explained that it was only fair to Mac. Vince agreed. He liked Joe and was happy to be in the same section as Barry. They were still friends and Barry often asked after Audrey, but Vince thought that even he had begun to eye him strangely. Everyone seemed to nowadays.

Alone on sentry duty, he brooded about Audrey and his constant nightmares. He seriously wondered if he were going mad. After waking his relief sentry, he lay tortured with uneasy dreams. Visions of Audrey, assailed by tormentors, or sweet and innocent in a white bathrobe. Halaks and tigers glowered from the haunted night through eyes that bored into his soul. He woke in darkness, wet-faced and miserable. Dear God, he thought, I'm losing my mind.

Their next camp placed them about half a day's march from the Nenggiri. The ridge had become precipitous and guided by the porters they followed an easier route down a spur to the south bank. In late afternoon they found a suitable campsite by a small spring that bubbled from the ground in a shallow gully.

The next day's order of march placed two section at the rear of the column. Vince was Tail End Charlie, the last man in the patrol. The river ran high and fast, a rushing, roaring torrent forbidding any attempt from the shallows. An uneven path that led along the bank sometimes required them to splash through shallows, or ford rivulets rushing into the river. At last they reached an area where the downgrade was less steep and the roar of the river decreased. The path was easier when it diverged from the river. The Nenggiri and a campsite seemed within striking distance. Tom Andrews ordered an increase in the pace of march so they could find the river and a suitable area to halt before dusk.

It was then a series of minor events took place that changed Vince's life. His right foot caught on a broken tree root, breaking a bootlace. His trouser legs, tucked into the tops of the high-topped canvas and rubber boots, were laced to the top and tied to make the junction of trouser and boot as leech-proof as possible. The lace had broken and it took minutes to shed the cumbersome pack and re-tie it.

As he hurried to catch up with the rest of the section, he came to where a rivulet had gouged out a section of bank. Large sloping boulders jutting from either side left a gap about three feet wide – an insecure bridge used by the rest of the platoon. Vince barely hesitated, gathered what momentum he could and hurled himself across the gap.

He made it, but with barely enough traction to avoid falling back into the gap. Sprawling, face down, rifle in his right hand, he scrabbled with his left, barely obtaining enough purchase to prevent the weight of the pack from dragging him into the stream. He scrambled to his feet, the nails on his left hand torn and broken, his heart pounding with exertion. He leaned against a tree to recover his breath.

Alarmed, he realised that he was alone. A newcomer to the section, his absence might not be noticed immediately. Breaking into a shambling trot, he rounded a bend in the trail to find a fork in the path. Looking for a sign to guide him, he tripped, staggered and tumbled headfirst into a tree-trunk. His head struck, and his pack crashed into the base of his skull.

When his eyelids opened, a large ant was balanced on its back legs, trying to climb into his right eye. Shutting his eyes and jerking away, he found himself pinned by the weight of his pack. As he rolled over to remove it, he knew that this was the moment for which he had subconsciously been waiting. Like a somnambulist he clambered to his feet, his hat sticky with blood from his scalp, and stumbled to the right-hand fork. Footmarks showed that this was the route the platoon had taken. He nodded, retrieved the pack and returned.

Some hundred yards along he stopped by what appeared to be a reasonably clear, unmarked, but possible access to the other track. He removed his hat, throwing it to fall on the opposite side and off the trail. Stepping carefully to avoid leaving signs, he moved towards the other pathway. Choosing a zigzag route, he glanced back to make sure he had left no visible tracks, veering towards where the tracks had diverged. It cost him time and distance, but he did not want to miss the other path if it swung away unexpectedly.

When he did find it, he worried: the light's going, he thought. I'll have to find somewhere to camp soon or sleep on the bloody ground. Hurrying, he heard sounds of rushing water. Aha, he reasoned, this trail must follow along the river.

The water sounds became stronger and through the foliage he could see an expanse of water that shone silver in the fading daylight. Again he left the track and checked his back-trail for signs of passage. The river was less than a hundred yards from the trail and considerably wider here. Also shallower, it was less turbulent than further up the valley. Large rounded boulders lay scattered across the river-bed and along the banks like marbles abandoned by giants grown weary of their game. Several formed a U shape, with one parallel side only yards from the water. Within them grew several trees; two were ten or eleven feet apart. Hurriedly in the uncertain light, he unrolled his waterproof cover and hammock. By the time he'd set them up, darkness was almost total and he needed the flashlight to prepare a meal.

Gingerly, wary of snakes and scorpions and with minimal use of his torch, he filled the water bag and boiled water for tea. Cold rations would do, but he needed the comfort of hot sweet tea. A yellow crescent hung above the treetops. Guided by its feeble light, he circled his camp to see if the glow from the little stove showed between the rocks. None. He blessed his good fortune in finding such a campsite before full darkness had descended.

After a meal of cold corned beef and biscuit he took his mug of tea and felt his way to sit, rifle across his knees, and gaze at the silvery reflections on the water. The stream whispered and chuckled its way across its stony bed and around the standing stones. Guiltily, he clasped the tea mug and wondered at the enormity of what he had done. He had gone wilfully missing: he was a deserter.

chapter nine

Wryly, Vince recalled a favourite saying of his mother's. 'Well,' she would say, 'you've made your bed – now you must lie in it.' Impatiently, he thrust his doubts and fears into the strongbox at the back of his mind, rinsed the mug and went to his hammock.

Sleep, lured by the river's soothing murmur, came quickly. Yet several times he woke, anxious in the darkness and listened to the noises of the river. No longer comforting, they were the sounds of intruders; armed and merciless, who waded mutely through tumbling shallows to bring him harm. Feeling foolish and frightened he reached under the hammock for the rifle propped against his pack, eased back the cocking lever and waited. Finally, he released the safety catch and slept, cradling the weapon comfortingly across his body.

In the morning he felt better rested than for some time. The moon, now behind the ranges they had traversed days before, cast a faint glow over the eastern forest, heralding the dawn. He lay in the comfort of his hammock, taking stock. The doubts and guilt of the previous night remained locked away. Sometime reality must be faced, but in the meantime he would not allow himself to be found.

On the edge of his consciousness Audrey remained a constant concern, but even she needed to be set aside for the moment, until… Vince paused, puzzled. Until what? What was the plan? He was disturbed – almost despairing. What had he meant to do?

Deliberately, he shrugged the mood away. I'll think later, he told himself. I need to eat and get out of here. I'll cross the river and follow it back upstream to where the other stream… Again he paused. He couldn't remember making plans, or any streams flowing in from the other bank. There's no way I could have, he reflected. He shook his head in self-derision, set his rifle to safety and climbed from the hammock. As he groped for his daytime clothes, the chill grey light of impending dawn began to separate the boulders around him.

He swallowed a breakfast of biscuits with the remainder of the corned beef and washed it down with water. He struck camp, leaving personal wastes and other refuse in a depression under a stone he rolled back into place. A quick check for any telltale signs and he waded the river before the day was fully born.

A stout sun-dried sapling on the riverbank caught his eye. About six feet long, it became an invaluable support against the tumultuous current that sometimes reached to his waist. On the other side he emerged dripping, to rest in the shelter of a boulder while water drained from his boots and trousers. When the warmth of sunlight on his shoulders told him it was time to leave, he moved into the shelter of the trees.

The stony surface retained no marks of his presence and the trail of moisture would soon evaporate. Avoiding visible traces of movement between river strand and jungle fringe, he followed a little-used path upstream. It felt bad to run from his comrades, who by now would be searching vigorously, but something drove him on.

Despite the compulsion not to leave a trail and the narrowness of the path, his progress was good. He avoided patches of soft ground where a footprint might show. When he squeezed between trees or bushes, he examined them to ensure that no scraped or broken greenery would betray his passing.

At midday Vince thought he must be somewhere opposite where they had descended to the riverbank the previous day. For over an hour he had climbed steadily. Now he was tired. He needed food and rest, but decided to cross the spur before stopping. An hour later he reached a tributary of the Puian where a bend in the rivulet let early afternoon sun penetrate the forest canopy, to sparkle the water and make pebbles in the streambed gleam.

He looked for signs of humanity, saw none and eased off his pack. As he filled a mess-tin to make tea, he admired a cloud of red, yellow and blue butterflies fluttering around a limpid pool. His stomach churned as a giant hand squeezed his heart. He gasped, trembled and eyes brimming, staggered, to sit head in hands on a nearby stone.

Jesus, what's wrong with me? He asked himself. Yes! Those butterflies: it's like that last day with Audrey!

Disturbed, shaken by the power of recollection, he gathered his wits and prepared a meal. Still dazed, he resolved to straighten out his memories of Audrey as soon as he could.

From the can he ate cold baked beans with the spoon he carried tucked in the top of a jungle-boot, and chewed crackers with his hot sweet tea. His mind cleared of distracting memories and he dozed until the dappled sunshine was no longer warm on his skin. Reluctantly, he re-assembled his gear, hid the rubbish and other traces of his presence. Then – on a sudden impulse – he followed the stream upward towards the north.

It was two hours before he found somewhere to stop for the night. His path had again dropped from the spur to the stream. From here it traversed a gentle slope and fell in a series of rapids towards the now distant gorge. In an open area nearby was a rough stone fireplace beside a shelter of thatched nipa palm leaves. It seemed to have been unused for months, but was a reminder that others had thought this a desirable resting-place. Vince crossed the stream, balancing on convenient stones and fifty yards from the water found a suitable site screened by trees and a rocky outcrop.

He checked for dead limbs – a falling branch could wreck his waterproof cover – strung his hammock between two tall trees and stretched the green plastic above it. To discourage the multifarious insects, he cleared away the sparse greenery and leaves for several yards in every direction. Flat stones became a seat, a low table, and a rough shelf that kept his backpack off the ground. Forked sticks pressed into the ground held his rifle within reach.

Vince filled his waterbag and put water on the burner to boil. Some time he would run out of fuel tablets, but he might as well use them and save a few for crises. Similarly with rations; heavier tins he would use first. Dried or small containers of highly flavoured foods he would keep until last.

While the water heated he made a circuit of the campsite. He inspected uneasily the outcrop of rocks screening it from the stream. I can't see any, he thought, but that's just the sort of place where vipers or scorpions might breed. A memory made him quail – don't king cobra live in places like that? They're not supposed to be dangerous if you don't disturb them. He edged away. They reckon the buggers grow up to fifteen feet long. Oh shit, what did that joker at the museum say? '…while the female incubates her young, the male patrols aggressively around the area of the nest.'

Vince eyed the rocks warily. When *do* the bloody things mate?

By the time a can of stew had heated in the water destined for his tea, the light had faded. He ate listening to the calls of forest creatures. Gradually, these gave way to wind sounds as leaves rustled and branches began to sway. The roar of an approaching squall sent him scurrying to get his gear under cover and off the ground, while heavy raindrops slapped the plastic like bullets and the wind ravaged the canopy.

Fat drops of water drummed on his shelter as Vince struggled into his spare jgs and changed the jungle-boots for night-time hockey boots. They were intended to supplant his daywear when the latter were washed or replaced in camp. By torchlight, he checked his body for leeches. In themselves they were no problem, but nobody enjoyed the attentions of the slimy creatures and he cursed that he had not been better prepared before darkness fell. Finding none he savoured the tea, salvaged before he fled the downpour, and considered how leeches terrified grown men. The brutes could worm their way through the eyelets of jungle-boots or the weave of socks or flannel shirts and find their way into the most intimate hollows and crevices of the human body. A slimy little hitchhiker might be sucking one's blood at any time; they secreted an anaesthetic that allowed them to gorge while their host remained unaware. Plucking one from the skin, and leaving its head behind could result in a nasty ulcer. Happily, insecticide, salt or the touch of a lighted cigarette made them fall harmlessly away.

De-leeching in infested territory required some mutual co-operation. 'Jesus, Harry! Will you get this thing off my balls? NOT WITH A CIGARETTE LIGHTER, YA MAD BUGGER!', 'Pass the salt someone – a little bastard's crawling up me arse!' Sometimes an ashen-faced squaddie would be seen, staring transfixed with horror at a leech's tail protruding from nature's noblest one-way passage.

Suddenly, Vince felt himself the focus of alien eyes.

It's just because I'm thinking about leeches, he told himself. Maybe some insect's eyeing me up for dinner? Holy hell, I hope it isn't a family of vipers – or cobras in the rock-pile deciding I'm a trespasser! Reluctantly, he surrendered to nervousness and flashed a light around the campsite: nothing. Hang on, he thought: something's there! Again he ran the beam over the rocks. Still nothing? Yes: something on that branch, gleaming in the torch-light.

He focused on the limb. A feline shape stretched along the branch, eyes burning coldly in the torchlight. No markings were visible, but at about five feet long it had to be a leopard. Its tail flicked as gleaming teeth showed in a snarl. Quickly he flicked the light off – then wished he could still see where it was. It was the first leopard he had seen, but popular belief held them to be shy animals that did not attack humans.

Well, this one's not so shy! Edgily, he recalled reading that in northern India more people were attacked by leopards than by tigers. Five minutes later, he could restrain himself no longer. He flashed his torch on again. The leopard had crept away. Maybe it doesn't like my smell?

The downpour, which had paused, recommenced with renewed vigour. He made sure that his rifle and other equipment remained dry and crawled into the hammock to listen to pelting raindrops and the steady grumble of thunder in the hills.

He missed the company of others, the security of knowing that some poor squaddie guarded him while he slept. He missed the comradeship and the irreverent humour of his comrades. He even missed Short's ceaseless boasting and the ribald laughter as the others teased him. Most of all he bitterly missed Audrey, whom he had only known long enough for her to take his soul to somewhere he could not follow. With a wrench, he forced these thoughts away and fell into troubled sleep.

Terrified, he jerked awake: a leopard was at his throat! Instead, he found himself struggling with the square of camouflage netting he wore in lieu of a hat. The rain had lost its ferocity but remained steady and hard. Several times he woke again, alarmed, and reached for the rifle convinced that something, its sound concealed by the roar of the swollen stream, stalked him in the darkness. Instead of the commonplace noises of human society, he was habituating to the sounds of the jungle that replaced them.

Morning revealed a dismal world of mud and dripping trees. Snug in bed he reviewed his situation. If search parties thought he had headed back up the Puian – and he could think of no reason they would – the storm should have eliminated any sign. On the other hand, the path would be soft now and he would be unable to avoid leaving an obvious trail.

Vince climbed from his hammock with a sigh. At least the heavy rain had grounded the mosquitoes. He had no fresh bites and the water bag was full with run-off from the shelter, thus saving sterilising tablets. He grimaced, drawing on socks still wet from yesterday, half laced his jungle-boots and stepped gingerly across the sodden earth to last night's fireplace. Rifle in hand, he took the mess-tins to the stream to wash them, while fat drops from the foliage dappled his dry clothes.

He had expected the stream to be flooded, but was surprised that it had spread almost to the heap of rocks and the stepping stones had been covered. What had been a gentle stream was a muddy, tempestuous torrent, roaring wildly as it tumbled stones and tree-trunks into the gorge. Vince scoured the tins with mud, rinsed them and eyed the flood with disquiet. He would have to wait for it to abate.

Thankful for rainwater instead of muddy floodwater, he breakfasted on crackers and jam, sacrificing a sachet of instant coffee to the demands of his taste buds. He ate, buckled on the web-belt and with machete, water bottle, ammunition pouches and rifle, reconnoitred for an alternative route across the flooded stream.

An hour later he returned. He had been unable to find another trail, but he did locate an area of bedrock half a mile upstream. Perhaps when the flow subsided, he could cross there without leaving tracks. He sat under the shelter to clean the rifle and sharpen his machete and clasp knife. Restless, he looked again at the creek but could see no change.

Over lunch he glanced at Kipling's verse, and then fell into a reverie on the hammock. In it, Audrey and he were reading, sharing their delight in the poetry and each other's company. He felt a strange peace; for the first time in weeks he could think of her without anguish.

Eyes closed, he dreamed of love, feeling that Audrey was somehow able to share his dreams. Refreshed and peculiarly content, he woke to a brighter world. Beams of sunlight penetrated the canopy to daub the forest floor with patches of light. Further inspection of the creek showed that the water was receding, leaving the tops of the stepping stones visible again.

While his evening meal heated, he ran a length of cord from the hammock to his latrine. This was a hole in the ground, on the side away from the pile of stones and covered by a large rock that could be rolled aside. Should he be taken short in the night, he had no desire to wander and upset any king cobras living in the outcrop.

After the rain, and with the onset of darkness, mosquitoes were out in force. Squadrons of bothersome creatures patrolled the area, ready to attack exposed skin. Their bites, not merely irritating, could leave an exposed head resembling a knobby pumpkin and ruin his sleep. Worse, alone in the bush he might not survive another attack of malaria.

Despite his afternoon rest, Vince slept extraordinarily well. Day had broken; a family of gibbons breakfasting in the tree tops disturbed the peace with their hooting. Scraps of half-remembered dreams danced tantalisingly through his mind. He struggled to remember them. Warm and loving? Yes, he and Audrey, their heads close together, sharing intimate thoughts. That was all, but for the time being enough. For now the ghosts were exorcised and he could believe that he had received a message of love.

Something evaded recollection. He looked around and glimpsed the limb where the leopard had lain. It aroused a memory. A tiger had spoken to him; given him instructions. He shook his head in amusement: what had it said?

'Go upstream, take the first branch northeast and follow the track up the spur and down to another stream. Continue until you reach three rivulets close together, and follow the third.'

He almost laughed, but paused uneasily. There was that other weird message, the one that Buddy reckoned he got from his tupuna. That was in a dream too. Something about finding Audrey's spirit in the bush? He shivered. There was something else he was not anxious to recall, so of course it came to him quickly: 'Listen to the voice of the tiger.'

Breakfasting, Vince determined to dismiss the dream from his mind. Try as he might to do so, it popped back with increased incongruity. Sickeningly, another thought occurred. The voice in *his* dream lacked Buddy's rounded Polynesian vowels. It was an older voice, more confident, accustomed to being obeyed and with an educated, slightly clipped English accent.

Bending to put tealeaves into the boiling water, his eye registered an anomaly. He stooped, brushed away a few loose leaves – and trembled. Pressed firmly into the soft rain-pocked earth was the enormous paw print of a cat. Shaken, he looked away and back again. It was still there. After that dream, it was too much to assimilate. He struggled to reassure himself: Aw, come on! It can't mean that there was really a tiger here last night, talking to me – can it?

Unsteadily, he stumbled to his bed and as it swung gently under him, began to relax. Rationality required an answer that didn't involve talking tigers. I know, he thought. There was a tiger here before I was, and I didn't see the print – or maybe I did register it subconsciously and that brought on the dream?

This line of defensive reasoning was encouraging. He stood, cast a furtive glance around and grabbed the rifle. Weapon in hand, he glared belligerently towards the trees before scrutinising the soft ground. He did not need to look far. Full sets of prints entered the area from the direction of the creek. Others indicated that the beast had later resumed its nocturnal ramblings from a point opposite. Worse still, it had evidently walked around the hammock.

Probably, Vince thought resentfully, having a good sniff while dictating my hiking itinerary.

Still worse, there was no doubt that the prints were fresh. Some overlaid marks from his jungle boots. When he realised that the beast had carefully avoided the cord leading to the latrine, another block of ice slithered down his vertebrae – it had taken care not to wake him!

With knees like jelly, he used the rifle to steady himself and lowered himself into his hammock to think. Light-headedly, he began to giggle. Imagine sleeping peacefully while a tiger paced around giving instructions. A few minutes later, he felt better and told himself, It's just a matter of getting things into perspective. Hell, in a short space of time I've been pretty crook, fallen in love with Audrey, lost her, been beaten up – and been screwed silly by a pair of Thai dolls. To wind it all up I've tossed in a military career, got a weird message from a dead woman I've never met through her grandson and rounded everything off by deserting.

A tiger in the camp providing travel advice in a BBC accent? What could be more ordinary? Vince dragged himself to his feet to prepare breakfast. As he quieted his stomach, he decided to follow the route prescribed in his dream. The directions must be nonsense of course, but his curiosity would be placated. Otherwise he would always have an itch in the back of his mind that he could not scratch.

Encouraged that overnight the stream had become negotiable, he had the camp dismantled and the site returned to its original condition in less than an hour. Before walking off into the trees, he turned for a last look and was satisfied that no casual passer-by would know that it had recently been occupied.

The crossing point provided a good footing that retained no visible tracks. When he found the trail again, it was stony and firmer than he had dared hope. Before midday he reached a branch stream flowing from the northeast. He diverted from the path to investigate it, followed a little-used track to the top of the spur and stopped for a meal. If the voice in his mind had been correct – he didn't know whether to think of it as a tiger, or just as a voice – there should be another path that would lead to another stream.

It's a test, he decided. If there's a path leading into the next valley I'll follow it. If not, I'll head west and try to reach Chabai. I'll tell them that I woke up with a cut on my head and hadn't a clue what had happened. Anyway, I have to find out how Audrey is.

The climb was more arduous than expected. As it became steeper the track zigzagged, but remained a long and taxing climb. When by mid-afternoon he reached the top of the spur, Vince was exhausted and the pack on his back was a hated encumbrance. Wearily, he moved aside from the trail and found a place to rest and eat.

When he felt rested, he looked for a way down the other slope – and found it with conflicting emotions. On the one hand he was pleased that the exhausting climb, together with the entire unplanned diversion to the northeast, was not a total waste of time. On the other, he was alarmed. Something – something spooky and beyond his control – was urging him towards a destination that he was not convinced he wanted to reach.

It was the time when a downpour could be expected. Although he was on the eastern slope of the ranges, supposedly sheltered from the prevailing monsoon winds, a goodly share of their recent moisture seemed to have fallen on him. Vince shrugged; he might as well camp where he was. There were trees to support his shelter and hammock. The water bottle contained enough water if used economically and he might be able to catch some rainwater should a deluge occur.

It came with a roar, heralded by a rainsquall. Suddenly, swollen raindrops pounded the leafy canopy. The first plump drop struck him only paces from his shelter. When he reached it he was saturated, but positioned the water bag which filled in minutes.

Soaked, he fumbled in the sudden gloom to prop his gear up away from any seepage while water heated for a meal. He had missed lunch and needed hot food and drink to counter the clammy chill of wet clothes. In the confined space he struggled to change and to dry his equipment without knocking over the burner.

By the time his meal was ready darkness was complete. By torchlight he fished in the pack for a precious candle, to eat and tidy up by. While he chewed, he thought about the oddly articulate and informative tiger. While searching for candles he had found some nylon fishing line bought, together with a considerable length of cord, in the Taiping market.

At once he conceived the idea of using a 36 grenade to construct a booby trap to defend the camp as he slept and warn him of intruders. He quickly abandoned the thought. The danger of setting it off by accident was too great – flying shrapnel would be a threat to him as well as the tiger if it returned. It could easily have killed and eaten him earlier and he hated the thought of any animal, maimed by a blast of jagged metal fragments, dragging its torn body away to die an agonising death. There was also another reservation: measures taken against the tiger would indicate acceptance of its existence.

Plagued by a full inventory of flying pests attracted to the candle, Vince spread his day clothes on his hammock strings to at least drain by morning, and snuffed out his light. In spite of his determination to sleep lightly in case the tiger returned, he slept soundly. No sooner was he marinated with insect repellent and relaxed, than the monkeys began their raucous morning serenade.

Dawn was still little more than a thought of the day to come, but birds aided and abetted the gibbons to make further sleep unlikely. He swung his hockey-booted feet to the ground; incredulous that he had slept through the night yet still felt unready to face the day. With gritted teeth, he changed into yesterday's damp and soiled clothing.

While making a thorough and suspicious survey of the site, Vince tried to recall his dreams, but had only a warm fuzzy sense of closeness to Audrey. He found not animal tracks, but a smallish snake coiled at the base of a tree. Dark coloured with yellow bands, it wriggled away with a bad-tempered hiss when disturbed. He was content to see it go. It looked like a venomous krait. Are the buggers solitary, or do they live in pairs? Until he left the site he took care to move noisily and to look where he put his hands – or his backside.

When sunlight was visible above the trees and the heat was already apparent, he was ready to leave. The track descended in a series of oblique angles that were much more benign than yesterday's ascent. Vince was relaxed enough to enjoy the awe-inspiring, pristine jungle. Great trees supported a leafy ceiling, admitting only a diffuse greenish light, so de-energised that it reached the jungle floor too idle to cast a shadow. He felt like the sole occupant of a vast and gloomy cathedral.

High in the foliage he heard but could not identify bird and monkey calls. Noisy hooting sounds probably came from siamang, black-furred gibbons that live out their entire lives high in the canopy. It was so idyllic that he stopped, slipped off his pack and gazed around him.

Giant lianas hung from the trees like massive and untidy ship's rigging. A coluga, the flying lemur, disturbed by the rowdy siamang, glided on the wing-like membranes between its limbs and body to a more peaceful location. Scattered, once-brilliant blossoms lay amongst fallen leaves, silent evidence of a different world that existed high in the treetops.

Although still uncomfortable to be obeying instructions from a phantom tiger, he followed the next stream. It contained a respectable volume of water and its banks showed that it had recently been swollen with floodwaters.

Upstream, where it widened, he found a shallow area and crossed to the other side.

Vince stopped for a meal behind some large rocks that screened him from the trail. As he ate he was startled to hear loud splashing and sucking sounds, like a giant cow pulling its hoof out of a bog. The source became clear when he peered over the stones. Forty yards upstream the river had widened. Integrated with silt washed from the hillsides, it formed a sloppy morass that had attracted elephants. Now they were wallowing in the dark mud. A cow and calf emerged from the forest to join in the frolics and the creation of farmyard noises. Soon a trumpeting from the gully announced that the master of the harem was arriving.

Watching the animals with moody interest, he was reminded of the last ambush in which he had been involved. One night, a herd had invaded the camp from which the ambush position was maintained. Only six months ago, he worried. The buggers only wrecked some rain covers and scared the shit out of us. He looked wearily around the surrounding jungle. The worst thing was those tracks we found after the ambush was terminated. Three men, probably the sods we were after. They're all supposed to be across the border now, but I'd better watch out. They probably have a few patrols out still and I'd be easy meat.

Before leaving shelter, Vince noisily tossed stones into the water to avoid appearing furtive and dangerous. The herd watched with interest but betrayed no overt concern other than moving to shield the youngster.

Less than an hour later he forded another stream, only half the volume of the one he'd followed. His gut tightened as he crossed it; if his dream was true he should soon reach three rivulets. As he climbed, the stream had reduced in size. It diminished still further when he crossed another rivulet and he became distinctly apprehensive. When he stepped across another he felt ill. At the third he trembled and sat down before his legs failed him.

He was frightened. More even than when he'd dreamed of a tiger and found its pugmarks embossed in the earth. This was evidence of another intelligence, strange, frightening and invading his mind!

Oh, settle down! he told himself – come on! Maybe it's coincidence, but I can't turn back. I've got to find out where this trickle leads to, and why my dreams are taking me there.

He chewed some biscuits and took a few sips of water. When he felt a little better he looked around. The main watercourse, like the one he was to follow, had become a mere trickle.

There was no evident track in the direction he intended to follow. Screened by shrubbery, he slipped out of the pack straps and knelt to examine the stream banks. On the left there may once have been a trail, now a narrow trace threaded its way between the trees and bushes beside the rivulet. The path was far from clear-cut; sometimes stones, perhaps pressed deliberately into the crumbling hillside, formed rough steps that were the only indication of its existence. A short climb took Vince to where the sky was visible and slanting rays of afternoon sunshine splashed the tree trunks with pale orange light.

A final struggle took him up a last rocky escarpment to a small flood plain. The forest gave way to large surfaces of rock and grass, where repetitive flooding had largely stripped away the soil. In the openness he felt exposed and, shaking with exhaustion, he moved to the shelter of nearby trees to recover. Before him was a plateau laced with streams that he realised must be the source of the last two rivulets he had crossed.

Beyond, stretching back into the dividing ranges, lay a considerable valley. Craggy heights grasped garlands of white cloud, escaping shred by shred to drift away with the seductive breezes. Puzzled, he looked around again. At some time in the remote past, a great geophysical event must have moved huge quantities of rock to raise the valley floor and block the entrance. Subsequent cycles of erosion and forest regrowth had conspired to conceal its existence. Something else nagged at his mind. These three little streams, he thought, aren't enough to drain a valley this size. Somewhere they must have diverged from something bigger.

Too tired to travel further, he camped under the trees and thought about food. It must be about six days since the last re-supply, I ate fresh rations for two days so there should be three day's rations left, he calculated. The thought provoked a tip-out of the pack. An assessment of its contents revealed more edibles than expected. His daily menu might become monotonous, but there was enough to keep him going for another seven days. Perhaps fourteen if he kept his meals to the minimum needed for survival and supplemented his larder somehow.

Before leaving Taiping, he had traded most of his canned meat rations for rice. Each sealed plastic packet contained a cup of vitamin-enhanced rice. He still had five of these, plus a similar number of dehydrated packet soups. He had four small cans of sardines and three of canned fruit, all bought at the tea walla's hut, four little packets of dried raisins, three cans of baked beans and some small bags of tea and sugar.

Also in the bottom of the pack, a plastic bag held handfuls of tea, sugar, salt and coffee sachets purloined from the mess hall. Underneath were two small packs of biscuits, two sad-looking lumps of 'plastic' cheese and three Mars Bars from the ration packs.

As he reorganised his load, his eyes settled on a small packet containing cigarette lighters, some small mirrors, fishhooks, nylon fishing lines and three cheap clasp knives. Driven by thoughts of food, Vince took a fishing line and used the machete to dig grubs from a rotten log. Soon he had five, white and fat, that he put in an empty plastic sugar bag. With only the rifle, a fishing-line and the bait, he checked the pools visible on the rocky flood plain for fish, but they were mere pans of sun-heated water left by the stream after the last rainfall.

Not far up the valley he found a large pond. Formerly hidden by a bar of heaped gravel and rock, it was from here that the three rivulets drained. The waters had cleared since the last flood and he was excited to see fish swimming languidly in its shadowy depths.

He glanced at the trees along the edge of the jungle. Feeling uncomfortably exposed away from shelter, he moved to the shadow of a large rock that stood half-embedded at the water's edge. Eagerly he worked a squirming grub onto the hook and watched the line sink to where the fish continued their restless patrol. They treated the bait with disdain. Without exception, they swam lazily past. For twenty fruitless minutes, he urged the infuriating creatures to join him for a meal, then gave up in disgust, rewound the line and returned to further diminish his provisions.

When night fell, the valley resounded to peal after violent peal of thunder. Flashes of lightning lit the hills, charging the atmosphere with their energy. It was too easy to imagine scenes of cataclysmic conflict as titans locked in battle behind the darkened peaks. In anticipation of a deluge, Vince fumbled in the darkness to get his gear under cover and position the waterbag to catch run-off, but no rain fell. No moonlight showed to help him. Nothing but lightning flashes relieved the totality of the night.

He woke to find trees on an easterly spur backlit by morning sun. Siamang hooted in the distance, joining the birds in their salute to the day. Much closer, a troop of macaques chattered and squeaked like a giggle of pre-teens at a slumber party.

When there was sufficient light Vince took his machete and dug more grubs from the log. Unwilling to face dressing in the stinking clothes he had worn for a week, he took them, the bar of laundry soap, the fishing line and bait, to the nearest of the shallow pools.

While the soaped clothes were soaking in the still tepid water, he returned to the pond to fish. The change in behaviour was incredible. No sooner did his hook hit the water than one of the brutes raced off with the bait, leaving only the hook behind. Gone was the torpor of yesterday; these piscatorial predators demanded their breakfast. Vince gritted his teeth and re-baited the hook. This time he craftily tied the grub on with a nylon thread from his hammock. It worked. Within minutes he gloated over two ugly monsters thrashing on the rocks by his feet. Each was about eighteen inches long, whiskered and plump. Probably some sort of catfish, he decided.

Although partly screened by the standing rock, he felt uneasy and exposed. Rapidly gutting the fish, he threw the innards into the water and looped his catch onto the nylon line for carrying.

Back in camp, he hung them on a branch, scrubbed and wrung the water from his washing and laid it to dry on stones, under the trees but exposed to the morning sun. He had heard helicopters and light aircraft pass overhead. No doubt at least some of them were searching for him. If he was sighted, he would have trouble explaining why he had not actively sought their attention. He was not sure himself.

Laundry completed, Vince turned to breakfast. He had decided to dry-grill the fish in an effort to preserve them, since he lacked sufficient salt to smoke them properly. It did not take long to gather sufficient dry driftwood for a good fire in a rough fireplace he made in a stony area under the trees. He split the fish and rubbed them with what salt he could spare. He threaded them onto shaved green rods between forked sticks, then grilled them over glowing coals. Salivating hungrily, he put water on to boil for tea while he turned the drying laundry and set about dismantling the camp. He enjoyed one fish and, while he breakfasted, the other dried over the fire's cooling ashes. With boiled rice it would be his dinner.

By mid-morning the clothes were dry and his packing completed. Leaving only dead embers as evidence of his stay, he followed the stream into the valley. Keeping as close as practicable to the forest fringe, after about a mile he entered another area of scattered rocks. Here the stream fell towards him in a series of cascades. Behind the sounds of the tumbling water was the authoritative roar of a far greater volume of water crashing onto rock.

He scrambled up the boulder-studded slope, looked over the crest and stopped dead. Before him a large stream divided into two. The larger branch rushed off to his right and accounted for the roaring sounds; the stream he had followed was a mere run-off.

The lone figure of a man drew his attention. He stood at the end of a rocky promontory that protruded from the far bank where it created a pool of calm water before the torrent poured around it and rushed down the slope. He was of the Orang Asli, the original people, the people of the jungle. Either Senoi or Temiar; Vince was unsure of the distinction other than that Senoi seemed to be from lower country where they had more exposure to the outside world.

The Temiar, on the other hand, were said to inhabit the high mist-shrouded valleys and to have little contact with outsiders. Generally taller and lighter skinned than their lowland brethren, their hair was frequently wavy with a coppery tinge. This young man was tall by Senoi standards and quite pale skinned, but a cloth wrapped around his head concealed his hair.

chapter ten

The youth was fishing. Above his head he twirled a finely woven net that he launched to spread flat on the water. Dragged down by weights around its edges, it sank quickly and it was soon apparent that he had netted a fish. Rigid with concentration, he manipulated a cord to manoeuvre the threshing net towards him.

A wave swept down towards him. Only about eighteen inches high, it still bore amongst other debris an uprooted tree trunk studded with stumps of roots and branches. It may have obstructed the stream for days until enough water pressure had accumulated to carry it along with the torrent. In the grip of the current it swung lazily towards where deeper water should drag it past the fisherman and to the rapids.

So engrossed was the young man with his fish that he was unaware of danger. The log seemed about to sweep harmlessly past when a rock caught a submerged branch. It swung from the water and lifted, seeming to reach for the unsuspecting man. Vince shouted again and again, but his voice went unheard in the roar of rushing water. Frantically, he threw off his pack and reached the next level in time to see the figure of the fisherman snatched and flung into the swirling water like a helpless doll.

Shaken by the impending disaster, charged with adrenalin and driven by an instinctive urge to help, he clambered across the uneven stones. As the full realisation of the youth's predicament dawned, he halted indecisively. The log had jammed between the rocky shore and a line of stones that partially blocked the stream. Like the fangs of a huge beast they protruded unevenly through the frothing water and held the log against the current. Caught in a forked branch where the stream narrowed above the rapids, the fisherman's head was partly submerged in bubbling water as he struggled to disentangle himself from the tree's murderous grip.

Hurriedly Vince assessed the situation. He hoped he was correct. Time would permit no second guesses, for the unfortunate youth might drown in minutes. The tree's roots seemed securely jammed against the far bank; the branches caught in the rocks were held there by the current's pressure. The young man's struggles were weakening. An underwater branch gripped his neck and his legs also seemed to be entangled.

Vince threw a nervous glance at the rushing water, lay down the rifle and slipped the pouches from his belt. Crouched, with only the scabbarded machete slung diagonally across his body, he knew that if he slipped he would be soaked and bruised, but the young man could be dead. He sprang to the first rock. His impetus carried him further; a skip; another jump and he steadied himself against rough stone. His feet had found an almost flat surface under an inch of water.

Hanging the machete from a handy limb he tore off his shirt, tied the sleeves together at the cuffs and lay across the rock. Under the water he fumbled the improvised sling beneath one slippery arm. Gripping it, he strained to lift the youth's gasping head from the water. Now closer to the rock the drowning man scrabbled with frantic fingers as Vince tried, with desperate machete strokes, to weaken the branch and wrench it aside.

At last the barely conscious form floated with the current. Vince staggered to retain his balance on the slippery rock and cursed as his machete disappeared into the greedy waters. Vital though it was, he could not spare it a glance as he struggled to grip his shirt and the body it supported. Almost despairing of getting ashore with his burden, he was resigned to them both following the machete, to take their chances amidst the rapids. Involuntarily, he almost did so but unexpected hands steadied him and his burden against the drag of water. A startled sidelong glance revealed a grizzled head and lined face inches from his own. They topped a sinewy body that pressed firmly against his side helping to hold him upright.

The head indicated two tribesmen struggling to hold another log at right angles to the current. He saw their intention. If they could keep it positioned across the stream without dislodging him or his companions, the current might hold it securely enough to help them struggle ashore.

Between them they half dragged, half carried the inert and barely living body of the young fisherman onto the rocks and rolled him unceremoniously onto his back. Vince struggled to recall demonstrations of resuscitation procedures. He grabbed an ammunition pouch, placed it under the youth's neck, turned his head and cleared his mouth with a finger. Without further thought, he pinched the unfortunate's nose, tilted his head back and inflated the lungs. Too late? No! A few unaided breaths rewarded his efforts – and he jerked back to avoid a jet of water erupting from the young man's stomach.

Emotionally drained and physically exhausted, Vince put the other pouch under his own head and sagged onto the unwelcoming stone. The few minutes since the log had swept the young fisherman from the promontory had stolen more vigour than a day on the toughest trail. He did not understand the words and ignored the chattering voices.

* * *

When Vince sat up he found the recovered youth crouching nearby, staring with curious intensity into his face. At Vince's glance he turned away embarrassed, before edging even closer. Still crouching, he held his hands together, touched to his forehead. It was a gesture similar to those Vince had seen used by Indian and Thai people in making respectful greetings.

The older man, who had helped them crouched also and made the same gesture. The youth pointed to himself: 'Andor.' He waited expectantly.

Vince pointed to his own chest, resisted an impulse to say 'me Tarzan' and gave his own name. Andor nodded happily and repeated: 'Ints.' Then he turned to the older man and pointed. 'Muda,' he said, then pointed at Vince again. 'Ints.'

Believing the introductions to be over, Vince smiled and nodded, but there was more.

Now Andor indicated Muda and said something Vince did not understand. At Vince's blank expression he tried again, speaking slowly: 'Bapa.' He indicated himself again. 'Ana laki laki.' The words were vaguely familiar and after a moment Vince understood. Muda and Andor were father and son. At once the family resemblance was clear; but Andor was still not finished. He leant forward, placed his hands on Vince's shoulders to press his nose into each side of Vince's and inhaled deeply. Vince tried to conceal his surprise at both the intimacy of the gesture and its resemblance to a Maori hongi.

Again Andor sat back on his heels and pointed at Vince. 'Ints tepeh,' he declared. Then he held his levelled hand high above the ground and indicated himself. 'Peh,' he said, this time holding his hand lower. Vince wondered if he looked as baffled as he felt. Patiently, the youth turned back to his father, indicating both Vince and himself. 'Bapa, Ints bapa, Andor bapa, Ints tepeh, Andor peh,' he said, again with his hand held high and then low.

At last Vince understood. He had been welcomed into the family as Andor's elder brother. Hoping they would understand his Malay, he thanked them, holding his own hands to his own forehead. 'Terima kaseh Muda, terima kaseh Andor.' They beamed happily and returned the gesture, repeating in unison, 'Terima kaseh Ints, terima kaseh.'

With the formalities apparently over, Vince began to feel less exhausted and remembered the loss of his machete. Concerned too for the rest of his gear, he clambered to his feet. He need not have worried. No sooner had he turned than one of the tribesmen was before him, the machete flat across his palms and the still wet scabbard dangling by its belt from his shoulder. His companion squatted behind him supporting Vince's pack.

They both grinned cheerfully when he thanked them and Andor introduced them as Batu and Angah. When, with more happy smiles, they chorused, 'Selamat siang,' Vince realised that despite their isolation, these people of the high valleys spoke quite a lot of Malay.

Anxious to be on his way, but unsure how to take his leave, Vince assembled the pouches, scabbard and water bottle on his belt. He retrieved and checked his rifle and moved to lift the pack onto a rock and slip his arms into the straps. To his surprise Batu would not release it. He grinned, said 'tidak, tidak' – no, no – and swung it with apparent ease onto his own scrawny shoulders. The others watched with benign amusement.

His eyes sparkling with humour, Muda squeezed Batu's skinny biceps, did the same to Vince and shook his head. 'Makan,' he said and shook his head again. 'Makan,' and nodded judiciously, joking that in order to carry his own pack, Vince would have to eat well and become as strong as Batu.

Gesturing for Vince to follow, Muda set off along the stream with Vince, Andor, Batu and Angah in file behind him. A ten-minute walk along a well-worn and unusually straight path through heavy jungle led them to a cleared area. Here, more light filtered through the trees and they stepped into bright sunlight. After the shade of the forest Vince squinted against the light and saw that all the land in a bend formed by the stream was cleared for gardens. This must be the same stream in which Andor almost drowned. It had swung to the east and now formed a curve of water that gleamed below them.

To their left was a fold in the ground, where sunlight struck flashes of light from a rivulet that raced to join the stream below. Straight lines of ridged roofs showed through distant shade trees betraying the positions of two longhouses built end to end, about twenty yards apart and some fifty yards from both streams. Indistinct figures moved between them in the shadows of the trees. Beyond, the stream disappeared into forest which, in one direction climbed to the rim of the valley and in the other stretched forever into a misty green haze and the distant South China Sea.

Muda paused for them to gather and they moved together down a slope strewn with sun-bleached tree trunks. Vince gazed curiously around. The cleared space covered about twenty or thirty acres. Some of the dead trees bore blackened scars from the fires that had burned away leaves and branches to enliven the soil with their ashes. He thought of a graveyard of great creatures, their bones expelled by inhospitable soil. Felled trees lay where they had toppled, making progress under the hot sun tediously difficult. To Vince's astonishment Batu, his wiry body bent under the weight of the pack, scrambled over the obstructions with ease.

Occasional trees were still standing like a silent memorial to their fellows and Vince was astounded at the devastation wrought by small springy-handled axes in determined hands. Over time a balance had been achieved between the forest and its human inhabitants. A cleared ladang was used for a few years then, when those it had nurtured moved on, regenerated as fresh forest. Hundreds of generations of humanity had left little impression on their forest home.

On the hillside was tapioca, grown in profusion for its starchy roots, hill rice, corn, sweet potato, and tobacco. On the flatter land closer to the water were pumpkin, cucumber, peppers, green onions, bananas, paw-paw and flax. As their party drew closer to the settlement they heard the clucking of hens and the crow of a chronologically confused rooster. High-pitched children's voices piped from behind the buildings, where they played on the banks of the stream or splashed in the water. Then Vince heard the deeper inquiring tones of adults, to which Muda replied. Soon children were watching with shy curiosity from the bushes as they passed, then trooped behind them toward the longhouses.

It was a relief to step under a large shade tree between the buildings. Muda waved Vince to one of the logs placed there as seating and he slumped happily as his eyes adjusted to the shadow. Batu put his pack beside him and was thanked with a nod and a touch on the arm.

He leaned his rifle against the pack and looked around. It was a communal space, but the packed earth under the tree was free of debris and all but a few leaves. Some dozens of people gathered around, while more peered from the buildings, their eyes fastened on Vince. He shrugged; although this attention was understandable, it seemed more than simple curiousity. He felt a sense of expectation, as though something as yet undisclosed might be required of him.

There was something else also. Their looks suggested gratitude and, he thought, maybe they're pleased because I helped Andor. Trouble is, they seem to expect me to do something else interesting. Jeez, is this how wandering performers feel when they get to some remote village and the yokels all stand around waiting for them to do headstands?

Gathered in orderly piles were stacks of jungle produce, flax, leaves and flowers; all seemed to be in the process of being turned into head bands and other decorations. He wondered what was to be celebrated. Maybe this was the night of the new moon, when they danced away the demons and saved it to make another cycle?

Breakfast was a distant memory and Vince became conscious of his rumbling stomach. Even the thought of the fish remnants now fermenting in his pack stimulated his appetite. A girl, perhaps twelve years of age and almost adult, emerged from a longhouse. She carried a tray of woven rattan covered with banana leaves; on it was a melon sliced into succulent pink segments. At a nod from Muda, she offered it first to Vince and then to the rest of the returning party. It was not filling, but very thirst-quenching, with an unusual salty cucumber flavour and an aftertaste of watermelon.

After days of isolation it was good to have company, but the closeness of so many excited voices began to make him uncomfortable. If the activity were for a celebration that night, would he be invited to attend and be expected to stay in the longhouse? The thought bothered him. After a week alone he was unsure how he would cope with being cooped up with so many strangers amidst the noise and crowding of communal living.

Alone, amongst a group of people who chatted words he could not understand, he drowsed. In his thoughts he was by Audrey's hospital bed, holding an unresponsive hand and gazing at her face with frightened, despairing love. In this reverie, a finger twitched between his, long eyelashes fluttered opened, closed and opened again. His heart rattled against his ribs. He was so lost in dreams that the feel of hands on his shoulders nearly convulsed him with shock. With an almost physical jerk, he dragged himself back from his fantasy of realised hopes to the reality of a tiny community in a remote jungle valley.

On either side of him stood Muda and Andor, whose touch had startled him. Before him a small and aged man regarded him curiously. Dressed in a loincloth, a rolled sarong over one shoulder and a leather pouch hanging from a cord about his waist, the old man appeared to be ready for travel.

Vince overcame an eager desire to return to his reverie and was about to stand up, but hands on his shoulders deterred him. He settled back to see what would happen and to examine the gnome-like yet striking figure in front of him.

He saw a deeply lined face below a thick pelt of short grizzled hair, a small nose and ears and wide mouth. The face was dominated by eyes like obsidian marbles dark enough to make the pupils seem invisible, yet flickering with orange lights. The darkly shining eyes and the erect youthfulness of the small body made Vince revise his first impression. In spite of the lined face this was not an old man: he was ageless and largely untouched by the vicissitudes of long years.

Muda spoke. Amongst other words he did not understand Vince heard his own name. He heard 'Abu' and took it to be the name of this sprightly little man who bent forward to touch foreheads with him. As the little man did so, he murmured 'Ints' in a quiet, clear voice and smiled to display healthy-looking, but uneven teeth stained with the juice of the betel nut.

Struggling to reply, Vince quailed at a kaleidoscope of images that flashed through his mind as their foreheads touched. Himself dragging a limp, unconscious Andor from the water; a confrontation between a tiger and a cobra; Audrey, thin and lying still in a hospital bed; Audrey again, sitting, smiling; and then, amazingly, himself and Audrey walking arm-in-arm along a city street.

Shaken and bewildered, Vince felt no doubt that Abu had in some inexplicable manner communicated with him. A message, odd but welcome, that seemed to say 'thanks for saving Andor; your woman will recover'. Ponder as he might though, Vince found no meaning to match the image of the tiger and snake.

What was it; another sign of madness? This old guy's pretty impressive, Vince acknowledged, but how could he know anything about Audrey? And how the hell could he put picture messages in my head anyway?

Suddenly he needed to be alone, to get his head straight, rid himself of a claustrophobic feeling of being hemmed in – and to eat! The melon, which had only teased his appetite, was all he had eaten since breakfast.

With a sinking feeling he realised there was more to come. Muda and Andor remained beside him. Abu moved away, but others began to approach. Aw bloody hell, he thought, don't tell me the whole damned mob want to give me the once-over.

In the background, Abu wore a small sly smile. My God, I think the old bugger really is reading my mind. The solemn wink he received stirred the short hairs on his neck.

Each villager approached with a token gift. A palm-leaf headband, a feather, a flower, butterfly wings, fruit. Batu re-appeared, to stack it all dutifully beside Vince's pack, while the donors smiled and touched Vince on a hand or arm. One little boy presented a well-used wicker ball, then reached up curiously to touch the whiskers on Vince's cheek. The boy jerked away, startled by the bristles, and this evoked a ripple of kindly laughter.

He could not tell if he was being thanked, welcomed into the saka, or greeted as an honoured guest, but was touched by their spontaneous warmth. A parade of naked breasts passing only inches from his nose became uncomfortably diverting. He smiled and tried to ignore them while murmuring meaningless thanks, but feared that his increasingly uncontrollable and lascivious interest might betray itself.

A pair of particularly enticing brown nipples jiggled before him. When he looked guiltily away, Abu smiled with open amusement. Vince felt his cheeks and neck glow. From around him came a murmur of concern and the young woman responsible bent to see what was wrong. One nipple brushed his cheek and he could not suppress a groan, which provoked concern and solicitous murmurs from people who did not understand the source of his discomfort.

Vince smiled at his audience and jumped energetically to his feet, rubbing his right leg as if to dispel a sudden cramp. Neither Muda nor Andor seemed convinced by this. A few words created a flurry of activity; Batu took the pack, others gathered up the gifts. Andor closed his eyes, placed his hands beside his head and mimed sleep, indicating Batu's retreating back.

Fearful that those around him were intending to carry him, Vince grabbed the rifle and hurried after Batu. When they stepped across the rivulet he had noticed earlier, it was barely a trickle and he wondered if it had been diverted for irrigation purposes. They traversed an area where bananas and melons grew and Vince wrinkled his nose. The space outside the longhouses had smelled of smoke and damp bamboo; here the air reeked of fish scraps dug into the soil as fertiliser. They ascended a slight slope and behind a small copse was a hut.

Unlike the longhouses it stood barely a foot above the ground and was only about ten feet square. Framed with rough poles, it had a palm thatch roof and walls of flattened and coarsely woven bamboo. Vince recognised it as a pano hut, a death house, built whenever somebody in the community might be dying. If they expired in the longhouse it would be destroyed for fear that their spirit – their semangat – might linger there instead of progressing to the afterworld. Easily built, these death houses could be burned without substantial loss. The custom isolated the sick in a place where they could be cared for, and limited the spread of infectious diseases.

By the time Vince, Muda, Andor and the assorted retinue of well-wishers arrived at the hut, Batu had deposited the pack inside and was waiting in the doorway. At a few words from Muda, the others surrendered the items they carried to Batu, who put them inside the hut with the rest of Vince's gear and with smiles and waves, dispersed towards the longhouses.

Indicating that they would return later, Muda and Andor followed soon after. Alone at last, Vince inspected his lodgings. Although the house was windowless, a twelve-inch gap between wall and roof provided enough light for him to see a clean, springy bamboo floor, a sleeping platform, a table and a shelf along one wall. All were made from the same material as the floor. He had seen death houses before, but had not been inside one and wondered uneasily why it was so well appointed. Why shelves and a table? For a visitor? For me? He shivered and checked his gear. There were too many unresolved questions, including that of his own sanity.

Sturdy posts supporting the ridge pole enabled his hammock to be strung above the platform. Much of his gear he emptied onto the shelf. Then he propped the pack against the wall and took out the remnants of the fish. After a dubious sniff, he decided it seemed edible, and washed down with a few mouthfuls from the water bottle it was surprisingly good. A bamboo rectangle leaning against the wall fitted the doorway; he wedged it into place and slept.

From a tiny hole in the thatch, a slanting ray of late sunlight touched his cheek to wake him. He swung in the hammock and tried to analyse the many oddities that bothered him. Those tiger dreams. They started after that first visit to a longhouse. Yeah, and what about what Buddy said? Christ almighty! A dream message from a dead old lady I've never met. Now some old bugger's creeping around to draw pictures in my mind. That bloody tiger too. It talks to me in my dreams and gives me instructions in a bloody Oxford accent! It was all so frightening and ludicrous that he didn't know whether to laugh or cry.

chapter eleven

A short distance away Abu engaged in his own soliloquy. He had been eager to meet Vince, to inspect his mind directly, but now he was disturbed. There seemed little doubt that the stranger possessed the latent ability to be a halak, but he seemed both curiously naive and unaware of his potential abilities.

Almost two cycles of the lunar orb had passed since Abu had become aware of an unusual spirit that roamed restlessly in the forest. On impulse, he had entered into a trance state so his own spirit could follow it and he had been astonished. It was a semangat, not of the Temiar, but of the strange pale people who lived in distant places outside the jungle.

Its bodily home lay neither alive nor dead, but in a state to which it could neither fully return, nor leave without help. As he puzzled over her condition he became aware of the man he now knew as Ints. An accidental communion, while his brain was affected by illness, had allowed him to absorb knowledge from a powerful halak on the other side of the mountains. *That* halak's gunig was a tiger spirit. Abu's own gunig dwelt in the body of a cobra.

He thought about this for a while, but remained uneasy. Many times had the moon been reborn since his sister, his teneh, had borne a son – Muda, Andor's father.

In Temiar society, close blood-ties became blurred and his relationship with Andor was that of a grandfather.

They had been close from the first and as the child developed Abu watched closely for signs that, as had many of his bloodline over the millennia, the boy might have the potential to be a halak. Such signs became evident during the boy's adolescence and Abu recalled the pride he had felt as he gave earnest thanks to the forest spirits who had sent him a successor.

He became the boy's mentor and had led him to an understanding of animist theology far beyond that of other children. He taught Andor to respect the spirits that might reside in anything within the forest world, and how to avoid the blandishments of malignant spirits seeking to steal his soul – to face them and drive them away. He learned the use of pharmaceuticals derived from the roots of some plants, the bark, or leaves of others, and which of them could be used for healing – or killing – and which assisted entry into a state of trance. He learned how to solicit advice from helpful spirits, and how to evoke the power of dreams.

Having guided Andor along the path of the halak, even helping him to recruit a gunig – one that had taught him a song and a dance of power – the irony was that Abu had created for himself a rival. Tonight the people, the sakai, would dance to save the moon and for the first time in living memory two shamans would compete for the loyalty of the dancers. Andor had the spirit guide he needed; it was a tiger, and it had taught Andor a strange and powerful dance.

That Ints's mind had unknowingly become imbued with a fragment of a tiger shaman's power was of grave concern. Even in his meditative state, Abu sighed with frustration. During a long-ago trance he had experienced a dream in which a vision of great evil was revealed to him. He had seen a future where strange men desecrated the great forest with weird and terrible metal monsters. A time when the world of his people would be raped and pillaged and left a wasteland.

When that time came he hoped he too would have been taken by Sankal and would in his turn have descended the dark tunnel to the underworld. Yet he wanted to ensure that another strong halak would be here to help his people mourn their loss. The sakai must be protected, not only from the destroyers, but from also the fury of jungle spirits dispossessed by the invaders.

Andor was the only halak competent to lead the ruwai and comfort the sakai in the last days. The thought was sad, but there was pride and affection also. There was not and could never be, any envy or malice between us, but

I am not yet ready, Abu thought with pride, to surrender the power and responsibility of being shaman. Another thought struck him: perhaps we can serve the saka as halaks together? Such a thing is not unknown.

Did I make an error in leading Ints here? Another sigh. No, I had no choice. When the ular sedok told of the water-spirit's intention to drown Andor, the serpent also revealed that Ints could save him and my decision has been proved correct. He brooded over the scheming he had shared with the tiger halak from the distant saka – he who had somehow left his thumbprint on Ints's mind.

That halak also had an interest in leading Ints here – to save his daughter, Amang. Was it the work of the spirits or just blind chance that led Andor to her and caused him to bring her here as his woman? *His* gunig had said that Amang was in danger from a more tangible enemy: the despised Chow-Chow. Those pests had infested the ulu for a long time. They ordered the people around and stole their food. Sometimes, when they protested, the Chow-Chow even killed them. Worst of all, thought Abu morosely, they have even stolen the semengat of some of the people and made them as themselves, to be their slaves.

He muttered crossly. How was Ints supposed to save Amang, and from what? Why would the Chow-Chow want to harm Amang anyhow? As he asked himself that question he had a sick feeling that he knew the answer. Rape was a disease that had never infected Temiar society. Like most other violent crime, it affected the jungle only from the outside.

Squatters settled on the jungle's edge and entered the forests in search of wild rubber trees to tap for latex, or of any other valuable jungle produce. At times lone Temiar women had been violated by such riff-raff. These were among the few instances when the indigenes had used their blowpipes with lethal intent to exact revenge from violators, but using violence always took a great toll of the well-being of their ruwai, their group spirit.

* * *

Vince derived no more satisfaction from his thoughts than did Abu. The ray of sunlight disappeared, as the shadows grew deeper. Soon the area would be lost in the shadow of the central ranges and he should prepare food before it became dark.

Carrying the rifle and waterbag, he pulled the door aside and stepped outside, intending to fetch water from the stream. To avoid the contaminated water downstream he would have to go to the other side of the village, so he turned towards the rivulet, however, laid out on banana leaves by the wall of the hut were a gourd of clean water, a bunch of small, ripe bananas and a charred length of bamboo the size of a rolled up newspaper. The bamboo held cooked tapioca and there were even green onions provided to give it flavour.

Vince carried the food into the hut and shaking his head uneasily, set about heating water. They really are looking after me, he thought. I guess it's because I was there to help Andor. Father and son both seem to be held in some sort of easy-going esteem.

A phrase popped into his mind – first among equals, yeah, that's what their status is. And Abu, he's pretty important too. Vince shivered. There's nothing threatening about him, he seems good humoured enough. Yet it's scary how he seems to know what I'm thinking and puts messages inside my head.

He finished his meal, tidied away and listened to drumming sounds from the longhouses. He felt uncomfortable. What should I do? he wondered – go over to the longhouses, or stay here and try to sleep? A chanting began; male then female voices rose and sank to the demanding rhythm of a remorseless bamboo beat. He stood undecided in the doorway of the hut and longed for the comfort of a cigarette, anything to allay the sense of loneliness and keep him company in the increasing blackness of the night.

Through the trees a flickering light appeared and he watched with interest. Yeah, he realised, it's coming this way, what's going on? Yeah, they're heading here all right… three people with flaming torches. Bloody hell – they've crossed the rivulet and they're definitely heading here.

He nervously picked up the rifle and slunk into the deeper shadows behind the hut. The figures drew closer. In the uncertain light from the sparking brands, were four distinct figures. Three had torches, while one carried a dark bundle. They halted by the doorway.

'Ints, Ints.' Vince recognised the voice and feeling foolish, stepped into the torchlight. It was Andor. He, Angah and Batu all carried torches. The fourth person it took Vince longer to identify as the young woman who had distracted him earlier. All were adorned in party finery – headdresses of leafy crowns or bands of dried grasses. The men wore loose kilts of dried palm leaves over their loincloths and Andor had a necklet of plaited grass.

They propped their torches against stones. Andor handed the bundle he carried to Batu, took the girl by the arm and brought her forward. They made an attractive couple. She was tiny, her head barely reached to Andor's shoulder, but she was nicely proportioned. As far as Vince could see by the torchlight, her face was very attractive with full lips and eyes that sparkled in the torchlight. Over her hair she wore a wreath of green leaves and a similar kilt over her sarong. Between those troublesome breasts hung a posy of orange-coloured blossoms.

For an awkward moment Vince was afraid that Andor was offering the woman to him, but realised that on the contrary he was being introduced to Andor's wife.

'Amang,' Andor said. He began to say something else, stopped and shrugged his shoulders. 'Ints,' he said, speaking now to Amang, and adding, 'Andor tepeh.' He spoke a few more words and Amang stepped forward, looking demurely at the ground. Then she stood on tiptoe, rested her hands on his shoulders and greeted him as Muda and Andor had that afternoon.

Vince stooped to accept the greeting and enjoyed the experience more than seemed strictly proper. She smelled of citrus, ginger and fresh leaves, and he groaned inwardly. For God's sake, you fool, he told himself, this girl's your sister-in-law. He attempted to ignore the brief pneumatic pressure of bare and softly pointed breasts against his chest.

After a second, Amang stepped back.

With a shaky grin, Vince spoke to them both. 'Amang, Ints neh,' he said, meaning Amang was his young sister.

He was shocked at Andor's vehemence. 'Tidak! Tidak, Ints, tidak Amang tepeh. Ints Andor tepeh!' Puzzled and a little put out by Andor's passion, Vince took him to mean that he, Vince, was Andor's elder brother, but certainly not Amang's. Mildly irritated, he gave a mental shrug. All right, little brother – sister-in-bloody-law then.

Smiling once more, Andor turned towards Batu and spoke a few words; Angah picked up one of the still burning torches and they both entered the hut to retrieve the bundle they had brought. Angah replaced the torch on the ground and Vince watched uneasily as he selected something from the pile. This, when Angah held it up, he saw was a headdress of dried grass stalks that stuck up in the air like a wavy crown. With a smile Angah settled it on Vince's head and nodded, pleased with both fit and effect.

Andor indicated for Vince to remove his shirt and draped a sash of loosely plaited fibres across his shoulders; next Andor motioned for him to remove his trousers. This he did unwillingly, unsure how to refuse and grateful that he was not wearing the high jungle boots. To have to stand on one leg to unlace them would have been a further affront to his dignity.

He stood in the flickering light of the torches miserably conscious of skinny white legs protruding from baggy green underpants. A memory of childhood imposed itself upon the bizarreness of the situation and almost made him break into hysterical giggles. He heard his mother's voice: 'If you don't wear clean underwear, you'll wind up in hospital one day and everyone will know.'

Hah, he thought, Mum, I'll bet even you never thought your wayward son would end up half-naked in a jungle clearing with a small crowd eyeing his grubby underpants.

The three viewed him, rather too critically Vince thought, before finding a kilt of palm leaves to cover his underpants. At last everyone except Vince seemed satisfied with his appearance. After relighting a torch that had gone out, they turned back towards the main buildings. Vince took his rifle, but worried about the other gear, grenades and ammunition left in the unsecured hut. He was also all too conscious of the ludicrous figure he must appear in Temiar garb, with orange hockey boots on his feet. That his erstwhile comrades were not present to pass vulgar comments on his appearance was a limited consolation.

The celebration was in the area between the two longhouses. The logs, where they had sat earlier, had been moved aside to seat spectators and large bamboo mats formed a dancing surface. Clear of trees and buildings, leaping flames illuminated an impressive sight. Women and girls dropped bamboo sections endways onto hardwood logs to produce a strange cadence. Rather than a steady beat, the tempo rose and fell to promote a writhing motion and the odd rhythm was reflected in the movements of the dancers. Fifteen male figures dressed in a similar way to Batu, Angah and Vince himself, writhed and swayed to the beat.

Alone on the other side of the dancing area, Abu moved with a sinuous twist that was hypnotically repetitive, and belied his apparent age. As he tirelessly gyrated and swayed to the music, several young men contributed the throbbing wail of nose flutes.

Vince watched, fascinated, as Abu maintained his rhythm yet moved more and more like a marionette. His tiny frame mimicked that of a cobra swaying to a snake charmer's flute.

'Sssssst!' His back arched, his head darted forward and his spittle struck the end of a longhouse with a force audible in the sudden silence. Seemingly unaware that the music had ceased, the dancers continued their movements, but Abu crumpled to the mat to writhe and hiss through foam-speckled lips.

Soon he rose, glided to his feet and sidled through the crowd. Undulating, Abu hissed at some, whispered words to others. He passed near Vince and swayed towards him. Vince's hair bristled as he heard inside his head the words: 'Intsss, the tiger may triumph but the cobra will endure. We three need each another, be well, we will all care for your woman.'

With another twist of his body, Abu slipped into the crowd only to reappear amongst the dancers. One by one, they responded to his whispers as he moved amongst them. Some collapsed to the mat themselves and thrashed jerkily, before climbing back to their feet and rejoining the melee of leaping shadows.

Vince stared into the crowd, his eyes unfocused and the scene a blur. That Abu — now he's *talking* in my head as well as drawing pictures — but what does he mean?

People changed position, dancers joining the spectators, while others replaced them on the matting. Freshly costumed figures came from the shadows and gathered on the mats. The bamboo orchestra began their glockenspiel-like music in a rhythm that seemed hauntingly familiar: Da-da-da-da–dadida–da-di-dadadadada–da-da-da-da-dadidadidadi–dadi–da-dadada…

Blindly, Vince groped for support and, unmindful of the roughness against the back of his thighs, dropped heavily onto a log. What *is* it about that beat that's so bloody familiar?

Andor moved onto the mat and, as Vince watched with the bothersome music prancing through his mind, crossed the dancing area in a series of steps that struck another chord of memory. Four steps, pause, three short quick steps, pause, seven steps, pause, four steps, three more quick ones, reverse… the dance continued. Vince became lost in the shifting cadence of movement and the beat of bamboo. Andor's eyes were almost closed. The flautists stepped forward to contribute their wails and the lone dancer turned, almost in waltz step, before stepping back in the original direction.

Other dancers formed pairs, holding each other's hands, left in left, right in right, paced to the music, turned and retreated. Flutes wailed and Vince gaped. The couples faced each other like ballroom dancers. My God! he nearly shouted, as his mind reeled back in time. Khyber Pass Road: St Sepulchre's Saturday Night Dance. The band, what was it? Eppy Shalfoon's 'Melody Boys'? They were playing… what…? Holy Christ! These mad buggers are all dancing the Maxina!

Gradually the numbers strutting across the mats increased until the dance area expanded to accommodate Andor's new adherents. More converts joined the acolytes, drawn by this novel dance. Slowly Andor succumbed to trance, but his movements differed from Abu's. Rather than emulating the sinuous writhing of a serpent, his steps were like the measured pacing of a tiger.

He maintained the cadence of the dance while giving occasional loud interrogative coughs as, like a great cat deciding which prey to pursue, his gaze swivelled across the crowd. Abruptly he stopped and the musicians fell silent. He raised his head and from his throat erupted a roar that seemed too great to have come from such a small, though muscular, frame. With a feline slouch he turned and stalked through the crowd, his head turning from side to side and harsh rumbles sounding from deep within his chest.

People stumbled from his path, yet here and there he would halt, fix someone with a stare, utter guttural sounds and move on. With nervous admiration, Vince watched his approach. Andor's appearance had not definably altered, yet advancing towards him was not the cheerful, pleasant youth he had rescued. Nearing him was the spiritual personification of a great predatory, carnivorous animal – and he trembled.

When Andor reached him Vince was mesmerised by the transformation in his 'young brother'. He forgot the beliefs of his upbringing. Andor had exceeded his humanity to become a spiritual force expressed through millennia of belief in the elemental power of forest spirits. Here was a human, apparently no more than a personable young man, who displayed the power and natural authority of a jungle predator.

Andor embraced Vince fiercely; his grip was surprisingly comforting and Vince returned it with equal, but nervous fervour. He felt a strange surge of brotherly pride. It was as though this unusual creature was a true brother. One with whom he shared a history of sibling affection tempered now with awe. It's almost, he thought bewildered, as though my kid brother turned out to be a bishop, a rabbi, or the grand-bloody-Mufti of Jerusalem.

As he had with Abu, he experienced an eerie feeling, and without hearing them, he felt Andor's words spoken within his mind. 'Ints, you will dream what you must know; we are linked together to help each other. Semangat of tiger and serpent will guide us.'

When Andor moved away, Vince thought again of being marooned in someone else's dream. He sat exhausted and stared blankly at the knuckles of his right hand, blanched white by their grip on the rifle. There he remained until Batu and Angah reappeared and indicated with smiles that they would take him to his hut. With a nod and smile of relief he accepted. Armed with smoking brands from a fire, they lit him to his resting place.

He removed the greenery. It irritated his forehead and made the skin around his middle itchy. By candlelight he rubbed ointment on the itches, applied insect repellent to his face and hands and put on his semi-clean nightwear. For both solace and thirst, he made a hot drink and, to discourage insects, threw his leafy finery outside before snuffing the candle.

On his hammock, he set the torch handy and sipped his drink. A recurring theme bothered him: am I going crazy? I don't feel mad, he thought sickly, but how would I tell? He clasped the still warm mug and stared at the top of the walls where feeble starlight tempered the blackness of the night. Only an occasional human sound disturbed the stillness. People were close by, but he felt more alone than ever. With a sigh, he rose, threw the lees from his mug out the doorway and fumbled the door into place. He tried to compose himself for sleep, but instead stared into the darkness and wondered at the qualities of madness.

He found some comfort in attributing the voices inside his head to individuals. Okay, he decided, the messages come from either Abu or Andor. How do they do it? God knows, but does it matter? If either of *them* got a radio message, they wouldn't understand how it happened either, but that wouldn't make them crazy. Not knowing wouldn't alter the message's meaning, even if they couldn't believe it. *No*, I don't *want* to think about how I can understand thoughts in a language I've never learned.

He recalled Bible stories from his childhood: heavenly voices – like Saul taken to task by God on the Damascus road. Yeah, that was a bit different though, because others heard it too; but how about when Herod has Peter tossed into prison and an angel tells him to be quiet and walks him out past the guards? That Old Testament – it's full of inner voices.

And what about that old Abraham? *His* voice told him he would be the Father of Nations, – so the old goat puts his wife's Egyptian au pair in the family way and when a voice tells him to sacrifice the kid – Isaac – on a hilltop, the crazy old bugger's ready to do it! Holy Christ, I hope I'm never *that* mad! Moses too, he was a real beaut. Spoke to disembodied voices all over the place. Yeah, that chat with a burning bush must have been a beauty!

Vince smiled in the darkness. Right, take these tablets until you feel better!

Thought transference from a tiger? Okay – not easy to explain, but hey, is it worse than taking instructions from a fire? Hang on, what about that little dog at the beach camp? He and I understood each other about digging for crabs. Couldn't *that* be some sort of thought transference?

At last he gained comfort from his thoughts, slept and dreamt of childhood.

In the morning he felt in a positive mood. Any dreams were indistinct memories without negative overtones. Again he found fresh water, bananas and a small round melon, similar in flavour but sweeter than the slice he had tasted the day before, placed outside the door.

He breakfasted gratefully, his mind running back over last night's thoughts. His head shook at the complexities of religion. For these guys, he thought, their beliefs seem to work better for them than those of other religions. They're nice people, and they don't seem to do anyone any harm. I've never heard of anyone else with a religion so tolerant of other people doing their own thing.

With the remains of his meal tidied away, Vince wandered down to wash at the stream. He wore only his underpants, towel and hockey-boots and carried the rifle and toilet bag. For several days he had conserved razor blades and he wanted to scrape away the accumulated growth of whiskers. As he considered how to locate the water point, washing and latrine areas, he sensed movement from behind nearby bushes. He was being observed.

Sure enough, there's a bunch of kids keeping an eye on me, he thought. Little buggers, I should have expected it. He smiled to himself, then flushed. Oh hell! The little bastards must have been watching me all the time. That rustling in the bushes while I took a crap wasn't just some meandering musang! Mortified, he wondered how to even the score. There had been no malicious intent, but he still felt foolish and embarrassed.

He reached into the toilet bag. Sure enough, there was one of those lighters from the Penang market. He palmed it, withdrew his hand casually and pressed the switch in the base. Even over the gurgling of the nearby stream, the clear, tinny notes of 'Greensleeves', sounded unnaturally loud. Vince looked amazed. He halted, peered about and switching the trick music box to his left hand, jumped in the air to grab at imaginary flying insects.

His attempt to match his movements to the cadence of the music was like some ungainly dance as, with a final great jump, he pretended to grab something from the air and dash it to the ground. A sidelong glance revealed three naked urchins who watched with wide-eyed concern as he stamped viciously on the empty ground.

A few steps later he looked back. The children crouched, open-mouthed and puzzled, to examine the ground where he had staged his pantomime. Gotcha! He grinned, switched on the re-wound trinket and swayed off down the path in time to the music. The children remained to watch and ponder.

There was no problem finding the bathing area. Another group of children played there in the shallows or jumped from the bank. Further downstream women rinsed sarongs and slapped them clean on smooth boulders. Self-consciously, Vince sought an isolated spot to perform his ablutions. He could have saved himself the trouble. Soon he was the focus of bright eyes studying his every move. Their fascination reached new heights when he began to shave. When he'd finished, his cheeks red from the scraping in cold water, a youngster reached up like the child had the day before and exclaimed at the new smoothness of his face.

* * *

Seemingly welcome to remain indefinitely with these hospitable people, Vince adjusted to Temiar life and pondered his options for the future. Unless he could find a way to return to the regiment, he would never know if Audrey had recovered. If he did return he might be locked away for desertion.

One day he went with Batu, Angah and another young man to check pig-traps. Set along game trails, these lethal devices consisted of a powerful bow mounted horizontally on a rigid framework. When a pig trod on sticks laid artfully over the trigger, a sharpened arrow was propelled with great force about fifteen inches from the ground. Vince knew that several soldiers had received serious leg injuries after triggering pig traps. Fortunately, the missiles were never poisoned and when traps were set, crossed sticks were stuck across the path as a warning to be wary. Now that, he thought, is something we should have learned during jungle training!

No traps had been sprung, but the day was saved when Angah halted suddenly, held up his hand and stepped to the middle of the trail. With practised ease, he slid the eight-foot blowpipe from his shoulder to his mouth and pointed it into the branches at a target Vince could not see. A deep breath, an explosion of air that seemed to come from both lungs and stomach, and a poison-tipped dart flew into the leafy shadows. Next minute, grinning modestly, Angah picked up the corpse of a male monkey that had fallen with a thud at their feet. It was a long-tailed macaque with soft fawn-coloured fur, its eyes glazing quickly in death. They offered a prayer for its semangat, and Angah slung it over his shoulder to carry back as a contribution towards the evening meal.

Another day they went fishing. Shortly after sunrise the four of them climbed the path up through the ladang that they had descended the first afternoon. Andor led the group, a blowpipe slung over one shoulder. Vince followed with Angah and Batu, each of whom carried a fishing net. Their intention had been to cast them in the place where Andor had almost drowned, but when they reached the pool no fish could be found. Vince had fastened hooks to several lengths of nylon and tied them to finger-sized pieces of wood, and now with gestures persuaded them to follow him to where he had fished previously.

He set his rifle aside and, as they watched in bewilderment, attacked the same rotten log and gathered a handful of fat white grubs. He wrapped them in a large leaf and led the others, still mystified, to the pool where he had caught fish before. They exchanged looks.

Bloody hell, they think I'll do something silly – like feeding the bloody things!

Where the shadow of the rock broke the reflections on the surface, Vince peered anxiously into the pool. Ah, a movement, a flash of silver as a fish turned, then another – good! At least they're still in there. From a pouch he took the prepared lines and beckoned the others. When a grub was threaded on a hook they began to grin. Now they understood, and they watched excitedly as the first baited hook dropped below the surface.

With excruciating slowness it sank into the murky depths. They leant forward to watch its descent and stared expectantly at the spot where it had disappeared. Suddenly, the line jerked taut and Vince, off balance, almost went into the pool. He fought to control the threshing, struggling creature on the line. He blessed the thought that had made him tie toggles on the lines, but he wished he had left more length so the fish could run with the line and tire itself out.

Eventually he dragged ashore a fishy giant, nearly three feet long, which he guessed to weigh about fifteen pounds. Vince killed it by pressing the point of his machete into the base of its skull as the others held it still and they stared at it in awe while Vince mumbled a self-conscious prayer of thanks to its semangat.

Now they were all wild to fish. Vince tried to make them all aware of the needle-like barbs on the hooks, but soon had to remove one from Batu's thumb – he had been too eager to get his line into the water. The concept of the fishing hook was well known to them, but they had no experience of hooks as efficient as these.

By midday they had caught all the fish they could carry. Any survivors exercised a belated caution and refused the bait. Jubilant at their morning's success, they were even more so when, after rolling up the lines as Vince showed them, and politely returning them, he gave them back for future expeditions. Vince had tried some of the monkey that Angah had killed the day before, but had difficulty in swallowing it. It was not so much the gamey flavour as the fact that, skewered and grilled over the cooking fire, the carcass distressingly resembled that of a skinned and cooked infant. That evening, they dined on delicious, freshly grilled fish.

On his fourth day at the ladang, Vince sat outside his hut with pieces of bamboo, making whistles for the children. When their initial shyness had been overcome, the three who had spied on him became frequent visitors and now watched him closely as he worked. Already he had collected the materials he needed. Now Vince cut pieces of bamboo to length, made notches in them and filled the ends with wooden plugs. These were shaved to leave a shallow slot to blow through and then fixed with tree resin. When the resin hardened, he shaped mouthpieces and had a whistle for each of the children and a couple of spares.

As Vince finished the whistles, more visitors arrived: Andor, accompanied by Amang and his regular companions, Angah and Batu. The three men wore loincloths with machetes in the waistbands. Andor and Angah both carried blowpipes and at their waists wore bamboo cylinders containing darts tipped with ipoh poison. Batu carried a long spear. Each wore a rolled sarong across his body in the manner of men about to set out on a journey.

Amang was dressed like most of the women, with a simple cotton sarong tucked in at her waist and a string of red seeds around her neck. Her hair looked as though it had been recently dressed with oil and it fell to below her shoulders in shining waves. Above her left ear was a scarlet blossom from one of the flowering vines growing on the jungle fringe. On each wrist she wore several silver bands. As they came nearer, Vince tried to ignore the charming manner in which her breasts bobbed as she walked and the way the sunlight created coppery ripples in her dark hair. He groaned in silent discomfort. Oh, Holy Christ, don't start reading my mind now!

They all looked quite serious Vince thought, but greeted him and the children affectionately and squatted to watch as he completed the whistles, demonstrated them and gave one to each child. Off the youngsters scampered towards the stream, each trying to outdo the others in a range of birdlike sounds.

Andor seemed amused, so Vince gave him one also and, as only one remained, gave it to Amang. She, to Vince's surprise, glowed with pleasure. Soon, she and Andor laughed like children as they tried to outdo each other in producing new sounds. Angah and Batu watched tolerantly, if impatiently. They seemed anxious to get going.

At last the novelty of their game waned. Andor took Amang by the hand and turned seriously to Vince. 'Ints, tepeh,' he struggled to find words to convey his meaning and reverted to mime. With a swing of his arm, to indicate the high misty ranges to the north and west, he raised the blowpipe, stretched his arms to their fullest extent, held up three fingers, then shrugged and held up a fourth.

Vince gathered that the three friends intended going into the hills to search for the special bamboo from which longer and more prestigious blowpipes could be crafted. They apparently expected to be away for three or four days and he wondered if he was expected to remain at the settlement until they returned.

He was becoming anxious to return to the regiment. Perhaps Audrey was recovering and he should try to allay any problems arising from his separation from the platoon. He wondered why Andor hadn't spoken directly into his mind as he had done before? A glance at Amang made him pleased that he had not. Having a wife who looked this sexy and seductive wouldn't make mind reading a very comfortable ability.

With an impulsive movement, Andor led Amang forward. 'Ints, Amang saya punya – perempuan, malam empat – Amang kama punya perempuan jaga,' he said haltingly. Vince listened with limited understanding, but an unsettled feeling. It sounded like... He ran over the Malay words in his head: saya punya... my... kama punya... your... malam empat...four nights... perempuan... woman...jaga...guard.

'Hey Andor, wait!' But he was too late. Andor had turned, waved and disappeared with his companions into the trees. Vince was left to mull over what seemed to have been said. Vince, Amang (is) my woman. (For) four nights, Amang (is) your woman (to) protect.

chapter twelve

When he looked at Amang, Vince's stomach fluttered nervously. She wore a small smile and was peeping from under her eyelashes. He stared helplessly as the aureoles encircling the tips of her breasts swelled, the nipples growing like small creatures with independent lives.

Afraid of doing something he should not, dry-throated, he tore his eyes away and turned to stumble into the dark interior of the hut for his water bottle. He took a quick swallow and remembering his manners offered it to Amang, who had followed him inside. She examined it, sipped and returned it with a grimace at the metallic taste.

Indoors, her proximity became even more disturbing; his heart pounded and he wanted to hold her for support. Then he had a brain wave. I'll wash my clothes and soak myself in cold running water. That'll give me a reason to get away from her for a while and sort out how to cope while Andor's away.

Hastily, he scooped up the laundry soap with his soiled clothing and tied them into a bundle. Unable to change his clothes, he was glad he still wore the towel over his underpants. He grabbed the rifle. Amang looked puzzled and indicating that he intended to wash his clothes, he waved her towards the longhouses and turned to the doorway. Before he could reach it, an inexplicably irate Amang snatched the bundle from his hands and stormed from the hut.

He hurried to follow her but, worried about the children, paused to push the door into place. Oh Lord, now what? he asked himself. I've offended her, I should have thought. I guess she thinks she has a duty to do the same chores for me now that she does for Andor. Oh bloody hell!

He hastened after her.

Amang had disappeared. Confused, Vince looked around and glimpsed her trudging up the slope. Despite the bundle on her head she moved rapidly and he hurried to overtake her. Her mouth was set in a tight line and she was clearly still upset. Mystified as to where she was taking his soiled clothing, he tagged contritely behind.

She followed a barely discernible path up the slope and through the trees. Another hut came into sight on the far side of a small clearing covered with uneven, knee-high grass. He thought this was their destination until he saw the figure squatting on a platform in front of the building.

It was Abu. Apparently unaware of their presence, he oscillated from side to side, his hands clasped above his head. Amang's arm became a barrier, holding Vince back. They stood, scarcely breathing, as Abu swayed to his feet with a fluidity that reminded Vince of a snake charmer moving in unison with his pet serpent.

His eyes were drawn to a movement on the periphery of his vision. A lithe form, some fourteen feet long and as thick in the middle as a man's thigh, slid like thick rippling fluid from the branches of a tree. Sunlight glistened on its scaly hide as it slithered to the ground. His own antipathy toward snakes drove Vince to shout a warning, but Amang's hand upon his arm forestalled him.

'Tidak Ints,' she hissed. 'Ular sedak – gunig!' The cobra was Abu's gunig – his spirit guide. Lips clenched, Vince stared with horrified fascination. The king cobra rose on its tail and moved with alarming speed towards the platform, where Abu continued to sway and writhe, a good part of its body visible above the scrubby grasses.

It was a disquieting sight. Moving to music they alone could hear, man and serpent engaged in a weird choreography. Vince was both charmed and repelled by the eerie scene. Totally absorbed, he unknowingly clung for human contact to Amang, whose head had tucked comfortably under his chin, the bundle of laundry at her feet. Somehow his hands came to rest on her hips. The closeness of their bodies more enjoyable than he cared to admit, he moved slowly away to pick up the rifle that leaned against a tree.

Amang heaved a great sigh, gathered up the laundry, muttered something inaudible and continued up the trail. Vince followed, his mind filled with the image of man and reptile bobbing and swaying in silent communion. He shivered and hurried after the very human young body that swayed gracefully ahead of him.

Only five minutes' climb from the encounter with Abu and the king cobra, they reached a clearing where a rivulet had formed a pond the size of a room. Amang untied the bundle of clothes, soaked them in the pond and soaped them. Vince was ignored and, rather put out, looked around him. This must be the trickle that runs past my hut, he decided; so I was right – somewhere they must divert some for irrigation.

Amang, with a stern look, indicated that she wanted the towel from around his waist. With scarcely a thought he handed it over. Then, feeling suddenly exposed, he sat down in the pond. She pursed her lips and pointed imperiously at his baggy green underpants. She wanted those also.

Pursing his own mouth, he wriggled out of the underpants, embarrassed and wretchedly uncomfortable as his buttocks encountered the rocks and gravelly bottom of the pool. She accepted the soggy garment gravely, soaked and scrubbed it, then returned to stare openly through the lucid water. Shamefaced, Vince followed her gaze and struggled to prevent his erection from breaking the surface. Tossing her head, she waded back to spread the washing over fallen branches to dry.

The wet sarong clung to her body so alluringly that Vince felt at once avid and self-righteously elated at having resisted temptation.

What's she doing now?

She had crouched on the coarse sand at the edge of the pool with her back towards him. With a swift movement she undid the sarong and knelt upon it. With buttocks elevated, she turned her head to send him a bold and challenging smile.

Totally rigid on the bed of the pool, he stared back unbelievingly. So blatant was the gesture, yet so open and innocent, that he scarcely knew what to do except stare at the neatly rounded orbs of her bottom until she turned her head again with an impatient pout. That and the view of her smooth thighs was enough. Good resolutions forgotten, he scrambled to his feet and waded like an automaton through the shallow water, his member guiding him like a compass needle. Wet and trembling, he folded over her in an embrace that reached fulfilment all too soon.

Drained of energy, he sagged against her back, eyes closed and her alluring breasts in his palms. Although she breathed a sigh of apparent satisfaction, Vince knew that her pleasure had not been complete. Gently he turned her towards him. At first resisting, she realised his intention and relented. Reunited, he could see her face. Kissing was new to her, but she came quickly to enjoy it and her satisfaction became so plain that Vince feared that Abu might arrive with attendant serpents to discover the source of the commotion.

Wonderfully relaxed by their encounter, they eventually disentangled to huddle companionably together. Too soon the persistence of a swarm of tiny sweat-bees forced them to move. Vince, trying to suppress guilt at having made love to his 'brother's' wife, thought uneasily, When he's away its okay by their rules. It's just the way I was brought up that… Yeah, it was wonderful, but Audrey… Oh hell!

Returning to the hut was very different from leaving it. Mutual attraction, reinforced by successful lovemaking, rendered frequent physical contact vital. Wet clothing dried on their bodies as they walked and Amang again bore the bundle of laundry upon her head. They saw no sign of Abu or his gunig. When they halted for a rest, Amang swung her bundle to the ground; kissing was a novelty that required practice and she was again aroused, but showed no resentment when, to his chagrin, Vince was unable to match her ardour.

By the time they reached the shack it was mid-afternoon and Vince was ravenous. While Amang draped the wet laundry over a cord strung between two trees, he made tea and prepared lunch. She sipped a little sweet, sugary tea and nibbled a biscuit, but rejected baked beans with a moue of distaste.

After a short speech, of which Vince understood not a word, she went off to the longhouses. Feeling confused, he sat outside the doorway to complete his meal and ponder. His increasingly complicated relationships with Andor and Amang had spiralled out of control. The person with first claim upon his thoughts should be Audrey. Pangs of guilt aside, he felt physically content and relaxed, for Amang had proved an eager, generous lover. He was flattered that she had initiated the proceedings, but admitted to not being an unwilling participant.

Despite the inherent impossibilities, Vince allowed himself to daydream. To settle in the jungle, among people for whom he felt a great liking and respect, seemed ideal. To do so with a lovely and unspoilt girl like Amang would be almost idyllic. With Audrey it might be possible, he thought wistfully, if we could do without all the stuff we've learned to need. The Temiar are okay – they evolved into a forest world and didn't need any industrial revolution; they've got too much bloody sense. Metals and medicines would help them, but the forest has everything they really need.

In late afternoon Amang returned. There was no fanfare of trumpets or any attempt to conceal their new relationship. She arrived with two other young women, carrying some possessions, together with provisions for an evening meal. Between them the women gathered palm leaves that they spread over the sleeping platform to form a springy mattress. Amang was moving in.

Vince raised his eyebrows. Back home, adultery was usually pretty sneaky and dishonest. They mightn't encourage it here, but it seemed to be accepted as a fact of life. Hell, at home everyone knows it goes on, he thought, but they pretend it only happens to other people. The rules here allow everyone to be human. Yeah, they reject real evil, but accept that people, who are imperfect, aren't necessarily bad.

Amang and her friends had brought a short length of bamboo containing a glowing coal. They formed a stone fireplace, gathered firewood and placed the coal on a bed of dried palm fibre. A few puffs and they had a flame that became a cooking fire.

With shy smiles and downcast eyes, the young women departed, leaving Amang to prepare a meal: python steak grilled over coals with tapioca cooked in bamboo sections amongst the same coals. Snake flesh tasted rather like oddly textured fish and was greatly improved with salt from his pack.

When they had eaten, the light had disappeared from the sky. They threw their meal scraps into the fire, sat close together in the cool evening air and stared at the dying embers in companionable silence. Amang had drawn up her sarong and Vince's sleeved arm was around her bare shoulders. Her head rested under his chin and her hair, smelling pleasantly of wood-smoke, felt smooth against his throat. Adjusting her position, she mischievously began to practise her kissing on his neck. Eyes closed, he enjoyed the sensation, surrendering his thoughts to the pleasure of the moment.

She twisted away, fumbled in the shadows by the fire and rose with a resinous torch aflame in her hand. Bewildered, he thought, I guess she's decided to go back to her own bed. Just as well – maybe I'm enjoying being with her too much.

But she turned towards him, transformed in the wavering torchlight from a young woman of the jungle into a Lilith, an Eve, the epitome of man's atavistic and erotic dreams. The torch held carefully to one side, she took Vince's arm and urged him into the dark interior of the hut.

With brisk, confident movements she propped the flaming brand upright among a few stones and closed the doorway. Turning without affectation towards him, she undid the knot that held the sarong above her breasts and let it drop to the floor. Vince sat on the sleeping platform and watched entranced.

Dancing shadows enhanced her mysteries and he felt like a worshipper at the shrine of a pagan goddess.

Lovemaking was sweet and satisfying and they slept, limbs entwined on the spread-out hammock, covered lightly by Amang's sarong. When he woke during the night her head rested on his chest and he recognised the fragrance of ginger and lemon. *That's funny, I haven't noticed that scent since this morning. I guess it's her own natural body smell when she makes love. The first time I noticed it… An irrational pang of jealousy stabbed his belly. Yeah, right, that would be when she came with Andor and the others to get me dressed up for the dance contest.*

Careful not to awaken her, he turned away and tried to repel unwanted thoughts.

Amang was out of bed before it was fully daylight and gesturing towards the doorway. It took Vince minutes to shake the cobwebs from his brain and understand that she mimed the experience of a dream. He had heard of Temiar dream conferences, where adults and children reported their dream experiences and halaks interpreted their meanings and significance for both the dreamer and the ruwai.

He took a few swallows from his water bottle, but Amang demurred. By way of breakfast they ate some small bananas as they walked towards the longhouses where everyone had gathered between the buildings. Groups assembled around cooking fires, welcoming their warmth against the coolness of the morning. Smoke drifted around them and collected in the foliage. People wandered, singly or in small groups with sarongs held over their shoulders, talking and waiting for the sun to appear above the trees. Sleepy-eyed children played desultorily with a wicker ball. They all waited and Vince thought of roll calls and awaiting the command: 'Get on – parade!'

He and Amang were greeted with casual smiles and morning salutes. Vince felt relief. Nobody seemed concerned that they had spent the night together. Nor were there sniggers, or disapproving looks. Struth! He looked at everyone attending to his or her own business and shook his head. *Imagine this happening at home! Your brother's away, and in the morning you come out of the bedroom with his wife and everybody smiles, good morning, did you have a nice night?* He had to cover his mouth and cough to conceal the bout of hilarity that the thought evoked.

Amang moved away to speak to another young woman. Muda and Abu emerged from a longhouse and sat together under the tree. Each caught Vince's eye, raised a hand in greeting and nodded pleasantly. He returned their salutes and joined others who began to gather around them. Curious, he waited to see what would happen.

Quietly, Abu spoke a name. A woman replied with a few sentences, hesitated and then continued. When this happened several times, Vince guessed they were dreamers reporting follow-up from past sessions. After each report Abu looked thoughtful and spoke a few words. Then individuals, probably those with lucid dreams to recount, spoke. The first, a young boy, spoke and received as much attention as had the adults. Abu replied kindly, perhaps providing advice or explaining the dream.

Understanding little, Vince had difficulty in remaining focused. His mind drifting aimlessly, he recalled his dream of a talking tiger and the pug-marks left in the ground as proof of its presence. I wonder what Abu would make of that dream, he thought. Then two almost simultaneous occurrences destroyed his peace of mind.

Abu darted him a look as though he had said something odd, and he realised that Amang was speaking. As heads turned towards him, he became hot with embarrassment. Bloody hell, what's she saying? Okay, maybe she's just telling about a dream that's got nothing to do with me. Yeah? Then why's everyone looking at me like that?

He again sensed Abu's voice. 'Be easy Ints, we do not mock you. Amang shares a dream that you saved her – as you saved Andor. She feels grateful to you as we…'

The message tailed away as Abu spoke gently to Amang, as if quietening her fears.

When the dream session ended, Amang had disappeared and Vince decided to escape to his hut. Although no one seemed in the least bothered by their liaison, he still struggled with a feeling that he had breached a personal code of honour. Also, although the words appearing in his mind had been benign, they were intrusive and he still worried that some form of mental illness drove him to imagine them.

So confused was he that he decided to put a notion to the test. He would try to instigate telepathic contact with either Abu or Andor. Suddenly he longed for the empathy he had shared with Audrey, and that set him wondering further. With the abilities that Abu and Andor seem to have, couldn't they break the barrier between her mind and body and bring her back to life? Immersed in his thoughts, Vince responded automatically to friendly greetings until he felt a touch on his shoulder and heard a deep voice in his ear. 'Ints, saya ana laki laki, selamat pagi – Ints my son, good morning.'

He turned at Muda's voice and fumbled a dutiful reply. 'Selamat pagi, bapaku – good morning my father.'

Muda looked pleased and smiled, 'Datang saya, makan Ints,' he said and gestured towards the nearest longhouse.

Vince was invited to breakfast. His heart sank; he wanted to be alone to think, but lacking linguistic skills to produce a credible excuse, smiled hypocritically. 'Terima kaseh Bapu.'

Muda, with a flourish worthy of a maitre d', ushered him up wobbly steps and into the gloomy interior of a longhouse.

When Vince's eyes adjusted to the shadows, he peered around. Beams of light slanted through hazy smoke from a glowing fire, but failed to penetrate into the corners. It seemed similar to the one he had visited before. God, was that only… what… three months ago? It seems like a lifetime, he thought. This is a bit different, but not much.

Muda touched his arm and indicated for him to sit on a log by the fire. When they had entered he had heard low voices, but he and Muda had seemed to be alone in the large room. Now he saw with surprise that the deep shadow across from him was in fact a small man: Abu. He squatted unmoving. Vince sat awkwardly and waited for him to speak, irritated that he felt at a disadvantage and determined not to be first to break the silence. With a low murmur Muda passed him a piece of banana leaf, on which were bananas and a still warm bamboo cylinder of cooked cassava.

Vince accepted the food, muttered his thanks and began to eat. On the other side of the fire Muda ate also. Abu remained silent and immobile. Squatting like a bloody garden gnome, Vince thought grumpily. Hungry as he was, the bland, unsalted tapioca needed water to wash it down. He enjoyed the bananas but they could not quench his thirst. Bugger it, I've left my bloody ammo pouches, as well as the water bottle and machete in the hut. Christ, if Amang starts poking around… He glared at Abu, who still squatted, unmoving, eyes shut, beside the fireplace. Come on you silly old bugger, I'll have to go before Amang…

Abu's obsidian eyes flicked open and a monkey smile spread across wrinkled cheeks. 'Thank you, Ints.' Vince could hear Abu's words clearly inside his own head. 'I am old but not a bugger, whatever that is. Be peaceful, Amang will not do what you are afraid of and be hurt. That is not her fate. I did not mean to worry you, but wondered if you could speak to me as I speak to you now.'

The voice in Vince's brain was wistful. 'I could wish that you could stay with us. It would be a great thing to have two grandchildren as halaks who would lead our saka into the great change. You are of us and here your semangat should rest. We will be sad to see you go, but once more our moon will shine upon us together.'

He stood and stretched. More words appeared casually in Vince's mind. 'Andor will return in two days.' And, gently, 'Amang is his woman, she is yours only to protect for a short time. Your fate is to leave here soon and again earn our gratitude. Our ruwai will never forget what you have done and what you are yet to do.'

Vince found himself outside again, feeling dazed and unable to find explanations for anything that had happened to him. He stared at the rifle in his hand and thought of the grenades waiting for curious fingers to find and create disaster. Filled with thoughts of self-doubt and inadequacy, he hurried back to the hut.

Everything was in order and Amang had not returned. He had not really expected disasters, but still a thread of relief ran through his gut and he sat down for a while to allow accumulated tensions to drain away. The sky was opaque with cloud but the sun had enough strength to imbue the area with a golden-green glow. He gazed towards the heights and thought about the morning.

The general unconcern about his relationship with Amang was a relief, but deep down he had a 'guilty little boy' feeling that he had managed to get away with something that he would eventually have to answer for. The thought provoked another guilt attack. Bloody hell, I should be doing something to help Audrey instead of enjoying myself here in the bush.

That thought took him by surprise. Yeah, I am enjoying myself. Except for those days with Audrey, I've been happier this last week than I can remember.

A feeling of sadness made him gulp. Not since childhood, had he felt such a sense of something precious and irreplaceable being taken and placed beyond his reach. Trying to throw off this depression, Vince paced about the hut and thought to make some tea.

Grubbing amongst his supplies, he realised how depleted they were and resolved to cut back to one tea or coffee a day. There were plenty of sterilising tablets and paludrine; he had scarcely touched his food supply since arriving here, but few fuel tablets remained. When it was impossible to make a fire he would need them too – the last box of matches was less than full. From the glowing coals in the fireplace, he coaxed a flame and thought of the little cigarette lighters. They were only novelties, their fuel containers were ludicrously small, but even without fuel they could produce a spark. He had one in his toilet bag and two more were in the pack pockets. There should be another somewhere, but where? He shrugged, squatted beside the fireplace, he scraped fine shavings of dry bamboo for tinder and experimented. After a few abortive clicks a spark caught, enabling him to blow life into the smouldering fibres.

Cheered by the small triumph, he sipped tea and reviewed the morning. Those last two messages from Abu seemed less troublesome now. Perhaps the last was a subvocal exchange of thoughts? He considered his relationship with Andor's wife.

Bloody hell! I don't want him picking up my thoughts about his wife!

The apparently supernatural way in which Abu knew about Audrey and her situation frightened him. That's not all! He shuddered. They all seem to have expected me to be here when Andor might have drowned. Yeah, now Abu's hinting that I'm supposed to do something for Amang, too – God knows what! Bloody hell, maybe we're all nuts.

Amang returned to find him shaking his head abstractedly. Sensing his mood, she seemed troubled. Lacking verbal communication and not wanting her upset, he activated the tiny music box in his pocket. 'The Ding-Dong Song' sounded and Vince sang along. 'Each time you say, love me, then I know its time for ding-dong to chime – ding-dong ding-dong…' rolling his eyes, he seemed to search for the source of the music.

Her initial astonishment dissolved into giggles that had charming side effects. To distract himself from these seismic quiverings, he capered about as though in pursuit of a fairy butterfly. When he stopped for breath, she suppressed her smiles with a stern look, shook her finger in an admonitory way and held out an upturned palm.

Her message was clear; she knew of the act Vince had put on for the urchins. He grinned and handed her the lighter, but she could not make it work. For a moment he let her fumble, then gently took it from her to demonstrate how to rewind it. Then he placed it back in her hand and guided her finger to press the button in the base.

The effect was immediate. Amang held the trinket as far from her body as she could and gasped at the music. Rapt with the sounds seeming to emerge from her clenched fist, she trembled while her face lit with fear and delight. The gaze she fixed on Vince was so filled with awe that he felt a complete fraud.

Bloody hell, she thinks I'm some sort of halak. Scruffy little Taiwanese factories stamp these damn things out in millions, but how many industrialised people can do what real halaks can? It saddened him that a race having evolved an almost utopian society steeped in practical spiritualism, might yet be driven to extinction by those obsessed with producing things like this.

Looking away from her trembling torso, he took the lighter from her hand. With a flick he created a spark and demonstrated how to light the tinder. Amang's eyes lit up at technology she was able to relate to, but minutes later the music was re-wound and playing: '…love me ding-dong…' Amang prepared a lunch that looked like grilled rat, but tasted better. He ate, wishing that Amang would throw that bloody contraption away.

Then Amang broke into excited if incomprehensible chatter and ran off to show the new wonder to her friends. Restlessly, Vince decided to explore the path that ran past the pool where they had become lovers. Someone seemed to have mentioned a cave in a rocky outcrop further up the hill. Baffled as to how he could have heard of it, he wanted to see if it actually existed.

He passed Abu's 'spirit hut' with an apprehensive eye out for cobras, but was pleased not to encounter either him or his gunig. At the pool he paused for a nostalgic sigh. His thoughts dwelled on the complexity of life for youth in societies that expect them to practise sexual abstinence when their bodies are programmed to demand the reverse. My God, he thought, no wonder we're half crazy compared with the Temiar… The thought was never completed. He rounded a bend, saw a rocky outcrop, the dark mouth of a cave visible at its base and in the middle of the trail, completely relaxed but enormously threatening – an immense tiger.

Vince halted. His heart tried to climb from his throat and run screaming down the trail. His scalp prickled, his hair felt as though it stuck out in fibrous spikes like a sucked mango seed and he feared his bladder would fail him. For moments, neither moved. It was like a tableau depicting a jungle hunting scene where it is not clear who is hunting whom. Vince trembled. Can I get a shot off to frighten it – it's only a few yards away; could I kill it with one shot? Oh Christ! Is my safety catch on?

He almost collapsed when the tiger seemed to speak to him in smooth British tones that were strangely familiar. 'Please don't try, dear boy,' it said mildly. 'I would be on you before you could raise your rifle and I might not be able to disarm you without serious harm.' As an afterthought it added, 'Your safety catch, by the way, is definitely in the "on" position.' A sidelong glance proved the tiger correct, and Vince thought wildly, Surely there can't be two English-speaking tigers in the jungle – and it didn't harm me last time.

'L-Look,' he said. 'I'm a bit shaky.' He nodded towards a rock near the cave entrance. 'I'm going to go over there and sit down – okay?'

The tiger gazed back at him expressionlessly. 'My dear chap, of course, I am sorry, I'm afraid I must have given you quite a start. Please relax. I'm sure we shall get along famously.'

Vince could imagine the hearty smile that should accompany such a voice, even an unspoken one. Suddenly the absurdity of the situation induced in him a fit of giggles that only increased as he tried to stifle them.

'For heavens sake man,' the voice inside Vince's head was stern. 'Do try to control yourself. You sound like a schoolgirl at a class picnic. We have much to discuss, which is why I, er, arranged that we meet here.'

'S-S-S-Sorry.' Vince wiped his eyes on his shirt sleeve. 'It-It-It's j-just s-so...' He took a deep breath. 'Sorry, but this is just so bloody ridiculous!' Unexpectedly he slumped, almost toppling from the stone. 'Why,' he whispered plaintively, 'am I sitting in the middle of the Malayan jungle talking to a tiger?'

'Yes, all a bit irregular I know. I should have introduced myself. Colonel Charles Cuthbert. Late of the 17th Punjabi Rifles. Sorry I can't shake hands, old boy.'

Vince stared with open scepticism, fighting an urge to seek further refuge in hysteria. 'Look mate, you don't look like a colonel to me, even if you throw your weight around like one. To me you just look like a bloody tiger.'

The voice seemed tired. 'Please let's not bicker. I'm sorry we got off on the wrong foot. I have some explaining to do and there is limited time. All right?'

Shamefaced when confronted with reason, Vince too apologised and the tiger continued.

'I was here in Malaya with my regiment, as a company commander, at the time of the Jap invasion. With other Indian, British and Australian units we were deployed in Kedah to resist the enemy advance from Thailand. Somewhere north of Sungei Patani we engaged them on our front, but were outflanked by a larger force with tanks and heavier artillery. We were being cut to ribbons and our CO ordered surrender.

'Those of us still alive surrendered our arms... Before the Japanese began to slaughter prisoners, a few of the chaps dragged me into a paddy field close by, and we escaped into the jungle.' The voice paused. 'Only two of us survived, a Sikh corporal and I. We joined survivors from other units and made it to the coast, where we pinched a motorised fishing boat. Much later, a few of us made it to Australia.'

He sounded drained. 'It's a time best forgotten. Those of us who survived the journey spent a long time recuperating. A year later I was recruited into Force 136 and after training, landed from a Dutch submarine south of Port Weld. I was to deliver a pile of arms and equipment to the Chinese communist guerrillas, who met me at a pre-arranged rendezvous. Malayan People's Anti-Japanese Army – MPAJA – which is what they called themselves. Terrible the addiction the blighters have for long titles.

'My further instructions were to train the guerrillas in military tactics and the use of the weapons. Eventually I was to act as liaison between them and the Allies when we invaded the Peninsula, while they harried the Japs from the rear.'

The narrative intrigued Vince, but it did nothing to explain why he was sitting on a stone and listening to the reminiscences of a tiger. It did remind him, though, of the stories that he, Bryson and others had been told at the Planters' and Miners' Club outside Ipoh.

The beast lay across the trail like some domestic cat afflicted with gigantism. It gazed pensively towards the entrance to the cave, licked its paw and, after a long pause, continued its unspoken narrative. 'Hiroshima and Nagasaki made invasion plans irrelevant. After the surrender, there was rounding up of Japanese forces, war-crimes trials and repatriation. By the time it was all over I'd had enough. After the massive losses we had suffered at Patani and India's impending independence, the regiment was disbanded. I took my discharge with the rank of lieutenant colonel, returned to Malaya and purchased a run-down rubber estate in northern Perak.

'I'd been able to locate some men from the regiment who had survived both the massacre at Sungei Patani and the prison camps. Some dozen of them agreed to come and form the nucleus of the work force for my new venture. With us was the bride I brought back from Australia. Willie and I met while we were both convalescing in Brisbane. She had escaped from Batavia as the Japs were about to invade. Her father, a Dutch administrator in Sumatra, sent his wife and daughter to Java to escape the inevitable Japanese attack. Thank Christ they made it onto an old freighter that limped into port at Brisbane weeks later.'

With an impatient movement, the tiger rose to its feet, stretched and began to pace up and down as it continued its tale. 'When the Emergency began, we fully expected to be targeted by a band of CTs that Special Branch warned us operated in our area. The fact that we weren't was probably due to their being led by a chap called Ah Fut. That was also the name of the leader of a group that I dealt with in Force 136. A jolly decent chap, unlike some scoundrels I encountered. Anyway, in the final months of the war I had been instrumental in saving him from an ambush set by the Japanese Kempetai. They were rather like the Nazi Gestapo, y'know.

'What they would have done to him had they captured him doesn't bear thinking about and he was extremely grateful. I suspect that he saw me when we moved into the plantation and restrained his men. God alone knows how, but our establishment never became an operational target. We lived charmed lives while the same CTs harried the other Europeans in the area. I certainly got some funny looks at the Planters' Club.

'Look, I'm sorry to go on, old chap, but I'm almost done. I thought you deserved some background on what's been going on. I'm sure you've been puzzled.' It halted for a moment to rub its haunch against a handy tree then continued its pacing. 'In 1958 one of Ah Fut's band was identified and captured while covertly visiting his family in Grik. As was common, he promptly sold out his comrades for the reward money.

'Before he could find out that his henchman had been taken, Special Branch directed a platoon of the Gurkha Regiment to a village where the guerillas would be soliciting money and supplies. In the subsequent ambush Ah Fut, with two of his men, was killed; another two were wounded and taken prisoner. Two or three escaped, but the band was effectively eliminated as a menace in the area – or almost so.

'Oddly enough, these events were my own undoing. Two days after the ambush the others were still celebrating. I couldn't. Ah Fut was a terrorist, but he had also been an honourable man. It was then that I was ambushed on the plantation and killed.'

Clearly disturbed by the memory, the great cat shook its head in sudden violent jerks, then flopped down onto its belly in front of Vince. 'I assume that the surviving CTs thought that I was connected to the ambush. Their camp was later located in the jungle only a mile or two from our plantation. I obviously have no direct knowledge of what occurred next, but have put some of the pieces together.

'All I knew was that my conscious mind was suddenly in another body.' The great form gave a massive shudder that flowed from head to tail in a tsunami of fur. 'I was terrified. I had no idea what had happened. The whole world looked, smelled and sounded totally different. I thought I had become insane. Perhaps I had.'

The huge face shook sadly. 'The situation couldn't have been much better for my hostess either.' The great head hung unhappily. 'Yes,' the voice seemed bitter, 'as you may have noticed, she's a female. I imagine that I'm the only trans-species transvestite in creation.' The voice paused once more, then added fiercely. 'Don't even consider asking what happens when she's in heat. It's bad enough to try and deal with hormone surges at other times and, in the absence of a Y chromosome, to think clearly at all.'

Vince assured the tiger that he wouldn't dream of being so offensive as to ask such personal questions.

The tiger, mollified, continued its story. 'In any event, we seem to have worked out a reasonable compromise. She does the hunting and,' the voice contained a fastidious tremor, 'all the nutritional side of things. At such times I retire and sleep, as I do during…' here there was an even more distinct tone of distaste, 'more intimate occasions, which fortunately are few and far between. God!' he groaned, 'whatever will I do if she becomes pregnant?'

'Anyway, it's a strange way to exist, but immensely preferable to the logical alternative.' The tiger tensed and stood suddenly. 'Must go, old boy, she's waking up; the old belly's a bit empty and she might think you're breakfast. Much more to tell you – I'll be in touch.' It trotted rapidly down the path and disappeared around the bend. Vince remained sitting on the stone until he realised how excruciatingly uncomfortable he was and stood to ease the numbed muscles of his buttocks.

Not only was his bottom numb; his brain was unable to cope with what he seemed to have learned. Am I daydreaming? he asked himself. Could it be that those stories from the Planters' and Miners' Club, and dreaming about tigers, have really got to me?

He stretched to flex his back and leg muscles and examined the area where the tiger had paced and lain down. The hard dusty soil revealed nothing. Was that good, or bad?

Vince shrugged. Something that showed a tiger had actually been there might indicate that he was sane. However, if what seemed to have happened actually had, insanity might be preferable. Had he been drugged? How to compare this view of reality with one that was chemically inspired? To be on the safe side, he resolved to be alert for any sign that a tiger had recently been nearby and to watch what he ate.

His heart heavy, he trudged back down the trail, examining the ground and wishing that the beast had gone in another direction. I don't want to be around if she wakes up hungry, he thought. Maybe, being crazy enough to attend a meeting with a phantom tiger is better than being a meal for a real one. Bloody hell, I'm getting really confu…

Abruptly, he knelt to investigate a sign of recent movement. Near the bend where the cat had disappeared there was a sharp indentation where something had been dislodged. A movement in the undergrowth startled him and he swung around nervously before searching for whatever had left the hole. A few feet away he found it: whatever had dislodged it was going in the same direction as the tiger – and himself. He picked it up and it fitted the depression exactly, but it was not a stone.

Interested, he inspected it more closely. It was a well-smoothed piece of bone or pig's tusk almost three inches long. Hello! He took a swig from his bottle, spat some water onto whatever it was and rubbed it on his trousers. Yes! It was some sort of artefact. It even had a hole to hang it by. I wonder how long it's been lying there? Diverted by his find, he headed homewards. The problem of the tiger, if not forgotten, was at least set aside.

Amang was not at the hut. He felt a sharp pang at how much he had come to rely on her company – and at the prospect of facing Andor when he returned. He sighed and walked through the bushes to the rivulet to find some fine gritty mud and energetically used it to polish his discovery.

Further upstream was a natural pool in which he washed it. The pool had been enlarged by the construction of a stone dam and some large bamboos, notched to clear the obstruction at their joints, had become water pipes. Supported on rough tripods, they bore the water some fifty yards across the slope. Its very crudeness increased its efficiency as water constantly splashed and dribbled out along its entire length to provide even irrigation.

Washed and dried, the object was transformed and its original high lustre largely restored. An unknown artist had wrought a figure that, whatever way it was turned, suggested the shape of a voluptuous woman. This sophisticated artistic concept formed a sensuously charming pendant that would be his farewell gift to Amang.

Back at the hut, the sun formed long shadows across the valley while cloud clung to the loftier peaks. Amang had lit the fire and the air was fragrant with the scent of grilling meat. Vince did not care what it was; he was hungry and it smelled delicious.

The meat tasted like venison and, sprinkled with salt, was as tasty as its fragrance suggested. With the ubiquitous tapioca and bananas, it became a banquet beside the dying coals of the fire. When insects drove them inside they lay together without need of words. They made gentle love in the darkness, and did not wake again until dawn.

In the morning when they had eaten, Amang made a long speech and skipped off to the strains of the 'Ding-Dong Song'. Vince occupied himself with minor chores and dozed until lunchtime. He ate and strolled along the riverbank, to discover a trail that led up a side stream towards the head of the valley. When he returned, Amang welcomed him with a big smile and chattered excitedly. She kept on for a full two minutes, but the only word he could understand she repeated three times: Andor. He stemmed a sullen stir of jealousy. Oh sure, he's your man and you'll be pleased to have him back, just don't rub my nose in your pleasure.

Vince swallowed his chagrin, realising that Amang owed him nothing. He was in debt to her, and to Andor and their society, for the hospitality, friendship and loving he had enjoyed. Amang stood in front of him, so close that he could feel the pressure of her nipples through his shirt. When she looked up into his face, her eyes were damp with tears and his heart thumped with the realisation that she too might regret their parting.

She reached up, linked her hands behind his head and drew down his head to show her mastery of the art of kissing. Vince thought, this shouldn't be happening – not now. Oh god, yes it should! Maybe it'll never happen again, but I can't reject such a lovely gift. With a groan, in which lust and tenderness shared equal places, he cradled her tiny form in his arms and carried her into the hut.

Dinner became overcooked, but neither cared. They huddled together in the evening cool and gazed at a band of moon riding above the ridge. Their time together was ending, but each was happy with the moments they still shared. When Vince slipped the pendant over her head, strung on a piece of nylon, she displayed all the delight of a western lover presented with a diamond necklace. It looked perfect lying between her breasts and he admired it anew. Tenderly he drew the piece of blanket across her shoulders and marvelled at how loving sex could replace language as a means of communication. They slept locked together, knowing that when they awoke a significant phase in their lives would have ended.

That afternoon they were both pleased to see Andor, with Batu and Angah, when they appeared from the forest. The men were tired but cheerful. Each carried, lashed together over one shoulder, lengths of boluh sumbitan, the special bamboo from which were crafted the finest blowpipes. The minute they arrived, Amang ran to Andor and embraced him. Troubled, Vince watched her kiss Andor and speak excitedly before turning to Vince.

From between her breasts she lifted the pendant for her husband to admire and he shot Vince a look of startled appreciation. For two long breaths the adoptive brothers faced each other in silence. At last Andor stepped forward, smiled and they exchanged brotherly hugs.

'Terima kaseh Ints, terima kaseh,' he said, turned and without a backward glance went off to the longhouses with Amang and his friends.

Vince ate alone, staring moodily into the fire's embers. He slept fitfully, missing the small form that was not there to press against him and fought a foolish and unjustified jealousy that gnawed at his mind. Soon after daylight, he was dressed, eating breakfast, sorting his gear and making plans to return to Chabai and the regiment. He put one of the grenades and a full magazine into the pack to reduce the weight of his belt pouches that had chafed his hips.

Knives, the remaining lighters, the mirrors and all but one fishing line he left out, together with some of the ringit notes that he folded and slipped into his shirt pocket.

chapter thirteen

When by mid-morning he was ready to leave, a group arrived from the village to wish him a good journey – selamat jalan. There was Muda, Abu, Andor, Angah, Batu, Amang and her friends with other well-wishers.

Vince's heart sank. There were not enough gifts for this multitude. He gave knives to Andor and Muda. To Abu he gave one of the lighters and to Amang and her friends little mirrors; for Angah and Batu there were two ringits apiece and he handed out fishing lines and ringit notes until none were left. Everyone seemed happy with their gifts; even those who received nothing but a smile appeared satisfied.

The farewell committee had not come empty-handed. They brought more provisions than he could carry and while they examined and compared their gifts, he stuffed his pack. He selected sticks of cooked tapioca or rice, a hand of bananas and a small melon. That was all he had space for and those things would improve his diet for days.

He looked up. People were still occupied with their gifts. Abu, his wrinkled monkey face alight with glee, listened to the strains of 'Lily Marlene' that seemed to float from his hand. Beside him, Amang stared fixedly at Vince. When he caught her eye she looked down, lifted her pendant, fondled it lovingly and glanced away again.

Oh bloody hell, he groaned, I've got to get out of here before Andor reads my mind. Forestalling Batu, who had moved towards the pack, he sat on a log, slipped his arms through its straps and heaved himself to his feet. Aware that a hush had fallen, he realised that Muda, Abu and Angah had all gathered nearby. Amang moved to one side, looking mildly upset and gripping the horn amulet. The remainder of the throng stood back a little, but there was no sign of Andor.

One by one they approached to embrace Vince, with smiles and soft words of which he understood few. Unable to see Amang – and with Andor also missing – he was about to turn away disappointed when Andor appeared from behind the hut. With Amang behind him, he strode forward as the crowd moved to let him through. In his hands lay the slim shining tube of a blowpipe.

Vince flinched. Bugger! He's read my mind all right and wants to blowpipe me! But Andor halted in front of him and bent forward with curious formality. With the long tube laid across his palms, he proffered it to Vince, who accepted it hesitantly.

Andor reached behind him to take a bamboo container from Amang. 'Ipoh.' He showed Vince the tarry brown substance on the tip of the needle-pointed darts inside, showed by word and mime that Ipoh poison was lethal, and handed that to him also.

Knowing the importance and status associated with a Temiar tribesman's blowpipe, Vince felt a fresh surge of affection for this strange, weirdly powerful brother he had acquired and, according to his own value system, betrayed. He had put his rifle aside to accept the gift, which he now passed to Angah while he stepped forward to hug Andor in thanks and farewell. Andor returned the embrace, stepped aside and pressed Amang forward to say her own goodbyes. She stood on tiptoes with her hands resting on his shoulders as she had before and brushed his lips with a kiss that spoke only of friendship and affection. They both knew that their goodbyes were already complete.

Trudging up the path he had followed twice before, Vince felt mildly surprised that no one had offered to guide him on his way. He suspected that his friends believed that something was pre-ordained to happen and would not risk interfering with fate. The thought irritated him, but also made him uneasy. Around Abu's 'pano hut' he was watching out for cobras when his mind received two messages in quick succession. He halted in his tracks as both Abu and Andor etched similar admonitions, expressed slightly differently, into his mind: 'Heed the voice of the tiger.'

It became more than he could cope with. Sick and frightened, he stumbled to a tree and rested against it. He no longer cared whether or not the voices in his head, or the disturbing interview with a tiger, were hallucinations. If he had not yet slipped into a world of madness, the haunted dreams, the voices, the talking tiger, Audrey, Andor, Amang, his feelings of guilt, inadequacy and loss – all conspired to send him there.

When his eyes reopened, he was curled at the foot of the tree. Rifle, pack and blowpipe lay scattered around him. So shaken was he by the realisation that he had so abandoned himself to hysteria as to lie uncaring and vulnerable on a jungle trail, that it cleared his mind like an icy shower.

Sick and shamed, he gathered his gear and his wits sufficiently to continue along the track. Pull yourself together, you silly bugger, he ordered himself, or you'll die here – probably nastily. You'll be no help to Audrey, and if she ever recovers she'll think you betrayed her just as surely as that other rotten bastard did. The last thought, the idea that he might plumb the same moral depths as Lieutenant Cunningham, completed his rehabilitation. Mad or sane, he thought, I'm going to see Audrey again!

Without a glance he passed the pool where Amang had done his washing. By the cave where he had met the tiger he brewed tea from frugally recycled tealeaves. Clear-headed now and filled with a new sense of resolve, he wanted to understand what was happening to him. He broke open a tube of tapioca and tried to recall Buddy's dream – Yeah, it was about his Grandma, right, and she had some weird message for me that's niggling at my mind. That was about a tiger too, but what was it?

He sat upright, spilling the rest of his tea. Holy bloody hell, it was almost the same as the two this morning. Listen to the voice of the tiger.

All afternoon he climbed. He became tired and short-tempered. The blowpipe's length made it an encumbrance and to cap it all his boots began to fall apart. He halted to examine them. Time had become largely meaning-less, but he estimated that they had lasted for almost three weeks. His old pair had been dried and kept in the pack and he wondered how much use remained in them.

With a sigh, he took the tape used for repairing the plastic canopy and effected stopgap repairs that he hoped would extend the use of the boots for a few more days. He also made a cord sling for the blowpipe and hung it diagonally across the pack, making it easier to carry, but more difficult to get on to his back. As he struggled with the pack, a disturbance in the vegetation alarmed him. He looked around wildly, swung up the rifle and pushed the safety catch forward. Leaves moved above his head and he gasped with shock as a tiger's head beamed down upon him.

'You bloody idiot!' he screamed, in a release of pent-up terror. 'You scared the shit out of me and bloody nearly got yourself shot!' Startled at the sound of his own voice he tensed again and lifted the rifle, his hands trembling. What if it was a different tiger?

Relief mixed with anger as that now familiar voice etched words directly onto his brain. 'Sorry old boy, didn't mean to alarm you, silly really – should have thought, but I enjoyed so much talking to you yesterday. These local chaps are very nice but they lack an appreciation of British cultural traditions. Literary allusions are of course quite out...' The words faltered and stopped.

So contrite was he that Vince took pity: 'Lewis Carroll, I presume, or may I call you Cheshire?' Although the words were good-humoured, his tone was tart. Shaking twigs and leaves from its coat, the tiger emerged self-satisfied, to casually block the path and quite unselfconsciously proceeded to preen itself.

'You've absolutely no idea what a pleasure it is to converse in English with someone who has at least read a few books.'

Vince eyed him narrowly and grunted; he did not care to be condescended to by a phantom wrapped in a tigerskin rug.

Unperturbed, the tiger continued. 'Chaps like Andor and Abu are jolly intelligent and they do have amazing abilities.' The voice paused thoughtfully. 'Y'know, perhaps the lack of stimulating reading releases parts of the mind to develop differently. Anyway we'd better find you somewhere to camp.' The tiger rose complacently and ambled down the track.

Together they found a suitable site. The tiger watched with interest, but did not interfere. Vince ignored the beast and went through the familiar routines of setting up camp. As dusk began to thicken, the tiger rose to stretch. 'I'd better get along now, before she wakes up. I'll be back before dawn and I'd be grateful if you would refrain from shooting me. I think by then I'll have some information you'll want.' When Vince looked around again it had disappeared soundlessly into the shadows.

These subvocal conversations with the tiger had become strangely normal. Vince too, appreciated contact with a creature that spoke the same language and thought in a similar way. However, he was not pleased that it might return in the night. That would make it difficult to remain alert, for if he was disturbed he would not know if it were by the return of the tiger or some new threat. Its final enigmatic remark he ignored.

In fact, Vince fell asleep very quickly and was startled from a harrowing dream, when the tiger nudged the hammock with its head. 'Bad news I'm afraid. A group of bandits arrived at the ladang at nightfall and they seemed to know that you had been staying there. They have questioned the people and made threats.' He paused and Vince could hear the rasp of his breath, in the darkness. 'You did realise that the CTs collect food from the ladang occasionally in return for having helped with the original clearing? They've actually done some cultivating too and erected a bamboo aqueduct. Muda and his people don't like it but there's little they could do.'

Things suddenly came together in Vince's mind. An awful dream flooded back into his mind. The image was confused, but he knew now what it had meant. 'Oh Christ!' The recollected image sickened him. 'Look, the bastards have taken Amang to punish the whole sakai, I've just seen them in a dream.' He thought of what had happened to Audrey and shuddered with disgust. His gut twisted and he groaned. 'Her hands were tied behind her; they were prodding her along the trail and laughing. Oh God... I – I think they're going to rape and kill her.'

He tumbled from the hammock and scrambled around in a frenzied search for his clothes and equipment. As he struggled into his shirt, he hissed. 'Quickly, where're the bastards camped? I have to get there before it's too late.'

The reply in Vince's mind was firm and clear. 'They wouldn't move before daybreak, so your dream must be a warning of what is to happen. They're camped about three hours' march up the valley from the ladang, where the ridge we're on intersects with another that forms a buttress for the main range. Where they meet, there's a watercourse that eventually drains into the river below the ladang. Up past the first set of rapids, the camp is on a sort of headland. All you'll see from the stream is a rocky cliff about twenty feet high. From the path, on the southwestern bank, the entrance is obscured and almost invisible.' Thoughtfully, the tiger paused, then added helpfully. 'They'll most likely have sentries posted along that path – on each side of their camp. Any questions?'

'Yeah: can you guide me there?'

'Sorry, old boy, I can only lead you as far as the entrance to the gully where the stream leads to their camp.' He seemed uncomfortable. 'Because Andor is the halak and I the gunig, I must contact him first. My God, what a conflict: but I shall try to get back to you the minute he is alerted... perhaps you didn't know... he, Angah and Batu are hunting up in the eastern heights and aren't expected back until this evening. Perhaps Abu had an inkling of what was coming and sent them away.'

Vince fumbled agitatedly with his flashlight, trying to get dressed while sorting out the gear he needed. The torch batteries were failing and he had difficulty finding things. He rejected the idea of striking camp and taking everything with him. There was not enough time, it was too dark and he could travel faster without the pack.

Amidst the chaos of his thoughts, Vince tried to assemble items from a mental checklist and place them on the hammock where they could easily be located. First, he told himself, everything I carry on my belt. His fingers found each item in place and told him that the water bottle was almost full. Spare magazines and grenades? He fumbled the other spare magazine from the pack, but decided to carry only one grenade. Paludrine, sterilising tablets, the camouflage netting hat, first-aid kit – oh, Christ yes, fresh boots!

It took ten minutes of blind scrambling before his nervous fingers had finally laced the boots onto his feet. He groaned anew – food. He scratched around to locate the remaining bamboo tubes and took one. With the belt finally around his waist and everything stowed as well as possible he thrust the remaining bananas inside his shirt.

The tiger moved towards the track, eager to be away, but Vince paused for a deep breath to quiet the turmoil of fear and anxiety that surged within him. The sky showed no indication of sunrise, but a pre-dawn chill suggested that the first flush of light must be near. As he turned to follow the tiger, something made him turn back and grope around for the blowpipe and quiver of darts.

For an hour he stumbled and tripped along the darkened trail. Obliged to feel with his feet to stay on the path, he walked into the beast when it stopped. The growth on either side was almost visible as he heard in his head, 'Here we need to leave the path and move down the spur to the stream where the bandits are camped.' The tiger seemed doubtful. 'Can you see well enough to follow? It's only a game-trail so you'll have to watch out for your head as well as your feet.'

Almost too tense to reply, Vince said, 'Keep moving, I'll feel my way,' and silently cursed the blowpipe that continually caught on unseen obstructions.

When they reached the extreme upper reaches of the valley, daylight was nearly full. A boisterous stream tumbled from a gully that ran down from the main range.

'That's it,' the tiger told him tersely. 'Remember, at the first rapids look for a headland in the bend of the stream. That's where their camp is. There's probably a sentry on the left bank near the path and not too far upstream.' It paused thoughtfully. 'He wouldn't be there all night, so he could be taking up his position now. We'll be back as soon as we can. Good luck!' And the large beast padded into the shadows.

Heart thudding with anxiety, Vince moved into the gully and crouched beside a bush, ears straining for dissonant sounds and eyes alert for movement. Slowly he moved up the slope to his right, hoping to find a line of advance that would provide a view of the opposite bank. Where the gully narrowed below him was the white of cascading water, and he cursed that he could see little else. Working his way along an increasingly precipitous route, he observed, through the tree branches, several well-concealed bamboo and thatch buildings. He held his breath. Could this do for an ambush? No. His heart sank. Not enough visibility and they'd have too much cover. Even if I could get clear shots at the sods, Amang wouldn't be safe.

He retraced his steps to move upstream from further down the slope, hoping to find a way to bypass the camp and approach it from the other side. What he found was a cataract that poured over a seven-foot drop. Large stones and debris from the hillside had created a natural dam between the headland and the nearly vertical opposite bank.

A vagrant morning breeze carried the rank, unmistakable odour of hill tobacco, the only variety normally available to the insurgents. As he tried to detect its source, he noticed an oddity. Hanging from a dark hole near the top of the cliff, below where he had seen the buildings, was a thick, dark thread. Vince paused to absorb its meaning. Must be an escape route, he thought; they told us that all camps have them. Okay, there has to be a tunnel leading to it, or maybe a bunker under one of the buildings.

While he considered the escape route, he lost the scent of tobacco smoke and crouched to scan the opposite bank, hoping to pick it up again. With the breeze's gentle breath in his face, he continued to examine the bank as he moved back downstream. A ray of sunlight caught a pocket of grey mist and he strained to peer beyond it. There! A movement from left to right. Twenty seconds later, a similar movement in the opposite direction. Vince counted to twenty. There, the bugger's back again, pacing up and down while he has his smoke.

Slowly and warily, he moved back to the gully entrance. A faint trail seemed to lead towards where he had glimpsed the sentry. Cautiously, he crossed the current and moved up the bank to a position near where he had last seen the guard.

Silently he removed his equipment, placed it beside a large tree and laid the blowpipe beside it. Holding only his rifle, he squirmed slowly up the slope until he sensed movement ahead and to his right. Pulse throbbing with apprehension, he peered through the foliage.

About to sit on a fallen tree trunk was a bored-looking Chinese perhaps forty years of age. In khaki uniform – worn and frayed, but neat and tidy compared with Vince's – he looked like a museum piece from the early days of the Emergency. Beside him on the log lay a sweat-stained khaki kepi and on its front was a red star. Beside the cap a short-barrelled Lee Enfield jungle carbine rested against the log. On his feet were a rather incongruous pair of black sneakers, patchily waterproofed with raw latex.

Vince lay in the detritus of the jungle floor. Afraid to move in case Amang and her captors arrived, he hoped not to be disturbed. Particularly not by centipedes, scorpions, snakes or the huge bull-ants that could tear out lumps of skin and flesh. While scrambling after the tiger, he had forced down a few bananas. Now with the sun rising in the sky, his stomach growled alarmingly and he needed water.

Impatiently inert, he tried to make a plan. When the CTs arrive, they're bound to speak to the guard. Maybe they'll relax and with a clear field of fire and surprise, I might get two or three with five shots. That should give Amang a chance to make a run for it. Oh shit – if there are four of them and I only nail two – one will return fire while the other outflanks me. Maybe, he thought nervously, I'd better see when they get here. It might work if Amang's out of the field of fire.

Anxious and thirsty, he wondered if he should slip back for the spare magazine and water bottle. The decision was taken from him when he heard voices and sounds of movement. When they became visible, Vince saw the same dreadful scene that had disturbed his dreams.

There were four bandits; all were dressed like the sentry except for the leader; a small man, wiry and dapper, who swaggered along ahead wearing a uniform that looked newer and of better cut. Apart from him, they all carried Lee-Enfield rifles. He had an old Sten gun on a sling over his shoulder. Behind him walked Amang, hands bound behind her and obviously terrified. Bravely, she tried to keep her head high in the face of her tormentors, two of whom flanked her and amused themselves by continually jostling her. The last of the four slouched along in the rear.

The guard, in an apparent attempt to appear alert, picked up his rifle as his fellow miscreants approached. Now he sauntered forward, spoke, leaned towards Amang and with a leer pinched her right breast. She flinched away with a cry as Vince raised his rifle. Had she not been within his field of fire, the man would have died instantly.

The moment passed and with an exchange of words with the sentry, the four moved on with their captive. Shocked, trembling with rage and tension, Vince knew he must move fast if Amang were to be spared worse treatment. As the sentry watched the departing figures enviously, Vince crept back to his gear, reclaimed the blowpipe and darts and took a long swallow of water. Impatient but wary, he moved to be as close to the log as possible without becoming visible from the clearing.

Vince judged that when the sentry returned to sit, the distance would still be too great for him to have much chance of hitting him with a dart. He lay down again and sliding rifle and blowpipe before him, wriggled inch by cautious inch, until he was only five yards from the log. With infinite care his frightened fingers selected a dart from the quiver and slid the pipe between the leaves and twigs that screened him. Partly supported by the foliage, he directed it at a spot three feet above the log and waited. The sentry continued to stroll unsuspectingly around the open area with the carbine in his hand and seemed bored and restless. He moved towards the end of the clearing nearest the camp, to toy absently with a vine hanging loosely from a tree. Idly, he swung it backwards and forwards, appearing to mutter to himself.

Vince watched tensely. For God's sake you lout, come and sit down on the log. He stiffened. Holy Christ, I forgot – they'll have an alarm system and I bet that's it. A jerk on the vine will warn the camp! Come away you sod. Please come and sit on the nice log.

As though responding to a polite request, the man turned, ambled over and placing himself on the log took out his tobacco and stuffed his pipe.

Stealthily Vince aimed for the top of his head, hoping the trajectory would place his dart in the exposed neck. A deep breath, a hard *puff*! Vince watched, horrified. Lazily, the dart left the mouth of the blowpipe, wavered in flight and hit the ground a yard from the log. Disturbed, probably by the sound of expelled air, the CT glanced around incuriously, then returned his attention to his pipe.

Slowly Vince exhaled; took several deep breaths to allow his trembling to diminish and repeated the procedure. This time he emulated how Angah had seemed to expel air from both his lungs and stomach, and this dart flew true.

In slow motion it arched through the still morning air and as the guard turned towards the sound, embedded itself below his left ear. As though chasing away an insect he waved his hand. Puzzled, he brought it back to pull the dart from his skin. For a long, uncomprehending moment he stared at the ipoh-poisoned missile. With a grimace of horror, he jumped to his feet and ran towards the hanging vine. Vince grabbed his rifle and scrambled to his knees, determined to kill the man before he could reach it, but after a dozen paces he had slowed, stumbled and dropped to the ground, twitched, then lay still.

Stumbling himself on legs numb with cramp, Vince reached the body, slipped the magazine and bolt, from the rifle and threw them into the bushes. Was the guard dead, or…? With repugnance, he slashed the carotid arteries and, sickened, thrust the corpse down the slope, assembled his equipment and hurried towards the camp.

* * *

Along the outer edges of the headland, a hedge of thick bushes protected the site from casual observation. Now it screened Vince as he crept towards the buildings. He did not expect land mines, but trip wires, with alarms or booby traps, were likely. Every movement was carefully planned. When he heard voices, he worked forward on his stomach to peer into the camp.

He saw four identical bamboo and thatch buildings; each was rectangular and about fifteen feet square. They were in line, with the last hut on his right further separated to leave space for a small parade ground. A slim straight sapling buried upright in the soil served as a flagpole from which hung a red flag, listless in the morning heat. At its base slumped a small limp figure, wrists and ankles trussed to the post behind her in the most humiliating and uncomfortable position imaginable.

Amang was clearly distressed. She was struggling against gravity and mortal fear to remain on her feet and to hold her head erect. Vince remained still. His first imperative must be to deal with the four men he believed to be in the camp. Although distracted by Amang's predicament, he heard faint sounds of movement and voices coming from the last hut.

The huts were built on posts two feet above the ground. Side panels at the bottom of the nearest wall of the end hut had been removed to disclose an excavation that formed a sort of cellar underneath. Vince eased the 36 grenade from his pouch, checked that the pin had not stuck and blessed himself for wiping it with oil. As he again nervously checked his safety catch, a head appeared, closely followed by shoulders and forearms. The officer was ascending a ladder and about to emerge.

Vince shook. Suddenly he did not know what to do. But as the man reached the top of the ladder he saw a pale carved pendant hanging over his shirt: the one Vince had given Amang. He was outraged, and the man immediately decided his own fate. He turned and made a laughing remark, followed with a lasciviously obscene gesture towards the front of the building and his trussed and helpless captive.

Vince became icy calm. When the man turned to crawl into the open, Vince's shot took him full in the face. As the body tumbled backwards Vince grabbed the grenade. Despite the oil, the pin stuck. He heard shouts and as it finally came free, looked up in panic to see a startled face peering from behind a rifle.

Instinctively, as though throwing a stone, Vince hurled the grenade. The sergeant instructor at the grenade range at the Waiouru camp would have been outraged, but it did the trick. Struck between the eyes, the man was already dead when he and the grenade fell together into the trench. Two pounds of steel and explosives had dropped him as though he were a pole-axed steer. Vince lay on the ground, hands over his ears, as the explosion shook the flimsy building apart. Much fell into the pit, while the air filled with shrapnel and debris flew from the hole to scatter around him.

Shaken, but curiously remote from the destruction, he remained prostrate. The lightly framed building crackled, creaked and sagged deeper into the hole. Smoke and dust formed a cloud above. Feeling strangely detached, like a spectator at a second-rate movie, sceptical of what he saw, he at last rolled over and pushed himself upright.

From somewhere came a long sobbing groan. Using the rifle as a prop to help him to his feet, he gasped. Where'd that come from? Oh God – Amang! At the base of the flagpole lay a small crumpled heap. Anxiety clawed at his bowels as he stumbled towards it. Her breath was even; he found no sign of injury and sagged with relief.

Tenderly, he cut her bindings to draw her into a sitting position against his chest and held the water bottle to her lips until she swallowed. While he sponged her face with the dampened hem of her sarong her eyes opened widely. She tensed and stared, her mouth opening to scream and then her tiny body relaxed.

'Ints,' she choked, 'oh Ints,' and buried her face in his chest, clinging to him fiercely as her store of fear and anguish drained away in great wracking sobs.

Vince tried to think. Where's the other sentry? He'll have heard the gunshots and explosion. Will he think that security forces had attacked the camp and try to escape? Or will he be curious enough to creep back to see what's going on? He pondered. Two things were sure, there was at least one of the buggers still alive in the wreckage and he couldn't sit around in the open like this in case another one turned up.

He climbed to his feet and looked around with a wary, uncomfortable sense of being watched. Amang needed help to stand and clung to him fearfully as he guided her to shelter behind surrounding bushes. Struggling to support her, he scrutinised the trees, rifle ready, fearful of ambush. A part of his mind worried that she walked with difficulty. Is it cramp from being trussed up, or was she hurt after all?

He found a space enclosed by glossy-leafed bushes, where she should be safe until Andor and his friends arrived with the tiger. Crouched beside her, he watched through the leaves for signs of movement. It was difficult to concentrate and his vision was blurred. His head hurt and when he put his hand to his right temple, it came away sticky with blood. Where he had touched burned like fire and a crust of gore extended to his chin. Bloody hell, he thought, I must have hit my head – too bloody scared to notice. Anyway, a scab's forming okay; I'll check it later.

Amang had turned on her side, her eyes were closed, tears ran across her face and she was shaking. What's that on her sarong? Blood? And on her feet, god it's been running down the inside of her legs. Oh those filthy, stinking bastards! I was too bloody late after all! Suddenly it was part of an all too familiar nightmare. Vince shuddered, shook his head, sickened, and trying desperately to think.

When Amang's comfortable, he told himself, I'll check out the sentry deal and kill any bastards still alive.

In one of the huts he found a few blankets that were not too smelly. He tucked these under and around Amang to keep her warm while her abused mind and body emerged from shock.

As he passed the wrecked bunker, he saw a bloodied figure crawling from under the splintered bamboo floor clutching a rifle. Shakily, but without remorse or hesitation, Vince put a round through the man's head and another through his chest, mumbling crazily, 'Take that, Lieutenant-bloody-Cunningham, you rotten depraved bastard!'

Threshing sounds from the bushes sent him diving for cover. Urgently, he swung the rifle, searching for their source. A familiar voice called hoarsely,

'Ints, Ints.' A dazed figure tumbled from the foliage. It was in khaki, struggling to reach a dropped rifle. Vince's first shot took the man in the chest and the next tore away half of his head.

Breathing heavily, Andor emerged from the shrubbery clutching a tree limb like a club. They embraced quickly, 'Amang?' Andor's voice was hoarse with worry. Gravely Vince nodded, 'bagus.' He hoped he was not lying – but if not 'good', she was at least alive. From his waistband Andor took the whistle Vince had made. Two short blasts brought Batu and Angah from different directions. They stared at the corpse, grim-faced and frightened. Batu went to Vince and with little clucking sounds of concern, examined the wound on his temple. With a little smile he clapped him on the shoulder as if to say, 'You'll live.'

Andor fidgeted nervously. Vince gazed dazedly around, nodded and led them to Amang. He was cheered that she was sitting up and sipping water from the bottle he had left beside her. Woken by the shots, he thought dully. Her face lit at the sight of Andor, who dropped the club to fall to his knees and hold her close. Vince watched silently, confused and dizzy.

Unwilling to intrude and unable to keep still, he beckoned for the others to act as lookouts. He must be sure that there were no further threats. Cautiously he approached the bunker and paused to listen. Are those sounds of movement, he wondered, or just the noises of the building as it settles? He could hear nothing further; only the stream below the bluff and other noises of nature. Just the continual creaking, unnaturally loud in the sunlit silence, as the flimsy hut sagged into the hole below.

The corpse lay where it had crawled from the building, its legs still partly obscured by the wreckage. Vince averted his eyes from iridescent blue flies already forming a gorging mass over the grisly mess that had been a head. Hesitantly, he approached the shattered building and peered underneath. All he could see were dark shadows amidst still swirling eddies of dust pierced by narrow shafts of sunlight. Curious, with an urgent need to find and destroy any survivors, he slashed their bindings to pull away the remaining flimsy wall panels.

Satisfied with his labour he crouched to look again. More light reached into the hole, but he could make out little detail. The dust and abattoir stench of shredded flesh and body wastes were still too much to face at close quarters. As he clambered to his feet, dizziness reminded him that he needed food. The sun was high overhead and he had burned energy and adrenaline for the longest eight hours of his life.

The others were where he had left them. Batu and Angah had retrieved their hunting gear and grilled something over a fire. In spite of his hunger, the scent of meat made Vince's stomach heave. Andor crouched protectively beside Amang, who was asleep on the blanket. Gently he released her hand and rose to his feet to give Vince a powerful hug. 'Terima kaseh Ints, terima kaseh,' he repeated joyfully.

Vince was taken aback that Andor could be so cheerful. He nodded at the sleeping girl. 'Amang?' he inquired with an interrogative lift of his eyebrows and more sharply than he had intended.

'Bagus,' Andor replied and squatted beside her again. Even as he touched the hardening blood drops that had seeped through the cloth of her sarong, his smile did not fade. Vince shook his head, noticing that the bloodstains had been washed from her feet – and gaped. Andor was swinging his arm in an arc from east to west. Vince stared dumbly as he repeated the movement several more times. At last Andor brushed a space clear of leaves, took a stick and drew a series of symbols. A circle, then an ovoid, a crescent, another crescent and finally another full circle. Vince stared until he finally got it.

Andor was showing him the phases of the moon. He too grinned; next to finding Amang alive, it was the best news he had received all day. He had after all got there in time to prevent her from further abuse. Andor was telling him that the blood was from her period.

He forced himself to eat a tube of rice and a fruit that Batu gave him. It tasted like mango, sweet and juicy, but Batu insisted that he first cut out the seed and throw it away. When he had eaten he lay down, rested until mid-afternoon, and then went back to the bunker. With Angah and Batu to help, they soon cleared away the bamboo and thatch to admit sufficient daylight to make exploration feasible.

The stench had not improved, but Vince decided to descend the surprisingly intact ladder before it worsened. Neither of his helpers would dare the spirits of the dead, so he clutched the rifle, held his breath and went down alone. Flies, disturbed from their feasting, rose to meet him. He gagged as they circled and swarmed around his face

Stepping fastidiously over the corpse of the officer, partly covered by the man hit by the grenade, he soon confirmed that all were dead. Much of the officer's face was missing and Vince had no intention of examining exit wounds. The body lying across him was the least marked of all. Only a fist-sized depression in the middle of his forehead testified to how he had died. The third, having received most of the grenade's blast, was scarcely recognisable as human. The sight of his eviscerated torso and shredded face filled Vince with a horror that he knew immediately he would never entirely banish from his mind.

While he had been resting, it had occurred to Vince that this might be a circumstance that could ease him back into the good graces of the regiment. But I'll need proof to back up my story, he thought. Some papers maybe? I can't carry all the weapons, but the breech mechanisms shouldn't be too heavy; I'll gather them up.

He avoided lifting the officer's shattered head by cutting the sling to remove the Sten gun that still hung around his neck. The CT struck by the grenade still clutched his rifle and, even in the heat, the rigor of death made him unwilling to release it. When Vince worked the bolt a spent cartridge leapt from the breech and over the reek of death he smelt recently exploded cordite. Falteringly, he put a hand to the hardened blood on his temple. The bugger got one off! Jeez, he said to himself in wonder – I'm bloody lucky!

He tossed the cocking mechanisms and magazines out of the bunker. He would collect them later. The ammunition he did not want detonating as the bodies cremated, for another thought had occurred to him: this camp's big enough to house a full platoon. If more are around, I don't want to be here when they get back. And if they do come back, I don't want them to figure out too quickly what's been going on.

Driven to haste, he took a notebook from the officer's shirt pocket and cut the cord holding Amang's pendant. On a rough table at the back of the dugout were a few maps. Those on top were stained with substances he chose not to contemplate. Those underneath were less damaged. He added them to his collection. An object protruding from a gap in the floor above proved invaluable. It was a canvas backpack containing a treasure-trove of papers – the commander's document cache.

Okay, that's enough, he thought as he glanced around. Hello! What's this?

To the left of the ladder, a patch of darkness seemed deeper than the shadows around it. Closer inspection revealed a screen of split bamboo over a hole in the wall. It was neither very high nor wide and Vince felt disinclined to investigate it much further.

He remembered the rope hanging from the bluff.

It's pretty narrow, he thought, just high enough for a crouching man to scuttle through in hurry, so okay – just a bolthole. But what the hell's that?

Squinting into the deeper gloom of the tunnel he made out a line of objects hanging from spikes driven into the wall. Fearful of snakes and scorpions, he reached with a tentative hand. Fabric – clothes? Carefully he lifted one from its peg. Heavy – very heavy. Now even more curious, he dragged it out for a better look.

Some sort of jacket, like a canvas waistcoat with two pockets on each side. He couldn't see enough to identify it properly, so out it went with the other stuff. He threw it, the pack of papers, into which he had also put the notebook, together with the weapon parts, into the daylight. Carefully avoiding the bodies, he clambered up the ladder, grateful to escape the reek of carnage and the increasing swarms of loathsome, buzzing flies.

Like a child with buried treasure, yet puzzled by his own excitement, he squatted to open the pockets. He was disappointed. What? Bits of brass? He felt the weight. Suddenly, he was eying the yellow glow of the bars with awe. 'Bloody hell! They've got to be gold bars!' Startled looks from Batu and Angah, who had withdrawn to the shade, told him he had shouted aloud.

Within minutes, twelve vests lay empty on the dusty ground. Forty-eight gold bars: each one maybe half a pound. Jesus Christ, he calculated that must make about twenty-four pounds of gold! Vince looked at the pile of waistcoats and thought of all the live bodies that could be accommodated in the camp. Time to get out of here.

He threw the waistcoats into the bunker, packed eight of the bars together with the weapon parts and papers into the pack, and set it aside. The magazines and loose rounds of ammunition were thrown into the surrounding bushes. With eight of the bars in his arms, he stumbled awkwardly to the end of the promontory, found a suitable place and tossed them into the pool below the cataract.

Back at the bunker, he enlisted the willing help of his watchers who were happy to assist if they could do so without offending the semangat of the dead. He loaded them with ingots, showed them where to throw them and left them to dispose of the remaining bars. Vince returned to the corpse of the CT clubbed by Andor and dragged it without ceremony to the bunker to topple in with the others.

In the clearing, he dropped the pack, gathered the blowpipe and quiver and as Andor helped Amang to her feet, indicated that it was time to go. Someone had collected useful items from the camp: a few blankets, cooking pots and blankets and it gave him an idea. I'll check their food supply; they might have some rice. He wrinkled his nose, thinking, Hell, if it's in with those bodies, I'd rather go hungry!

Amongst the coals of the fire a two-foot length of wood still blazed at one end. With a gesture to his helpers, Vince took it to the pit, ignited and threw in armfuls of dry thatch and followed them with the still burning branch. He watched with satisfaction as the flames took hold. Quickly, Angah and Batu understood. They slashed more vine bindings and threw more fuel into the growing inferno.

While the fire blazed, Vince did a quick recce of the contents of the other buildings. Two were dormitories, where he had found the blankets; the third had been used as a kitchen and mess hall. There were two bags of rice. One was already open and infested with weevils, but the contents of the other looked edible. He poured out the surplus and tied the bag to be carried as a gunnysack. Swirling smoke stung his eyes as he paused by the pole where Amang's bonds still lay. A machete stroke severed the cord that held the red banner and it joined the rice inside the sack.

There was one more task to perform. With the bag slung wearily over his shoulder, he checked on where the gold was dumped. Fancying he saw a yellow gleam through the disturbed water, he added more rocks. Finally satisfied, he took a piece of palm frond and walked backwards towards the flaming buildings, using it as a brush to eradicate any marks leading to the dumped gold.

They headed down the valley towards the ladang, very conscious of the conflagration behind them. There was little smoke, but a rattle of reports from burning sections of bamboo sounded like rifle fire. Not wanting to leave tracks leading to the ladang, Batu took them on a little-used track that swung up the side of the valley and here Vince turned to see if the fire was still visible. There was a flash and an explosion. Clouds of smoke and dust rolled above the treetops while a gust of hot wind swept over them, scattering leaves and bending the tree branches.

For a full minute they stared in astonishment. Oh Lord, Vince thought sickly, I should have checked what was stored in the bunker. I could have killed us all by being too bloody squeamish to search the place properly before setting it alight.

It was almost fully dark when they reached the ladang, where knots of people gathered anxiously by torchlight. Like waiting for visitors at a railway station, Vince thought. I guess we're expected. Worried voices reached them as they neared and two figures stepped forward. As Muda spoke authoritatively, the others fell silent. The smaller shape was Abu and Vince felt again that strangely familiar sensation as words were imprinted upon his brain.

'Terima kaseh, Ints, terima kaseh. You have done much for our ruwai.

Andor and Amang will produce another halak to help us through the hard years ahead.' When Vince went to speak aloud, Abu held up a hand and continued. 'Your woman's soul is saved from Sankal and restored to her. Soon you too will have children to raise. They too will be of our ruwai. Your soul lives always amongst us and our saka is yours.'

Vince was thrilled by the implication that Audrey had stirred from her coma. Despite what his rational mind told him, Abu's words had an authentic ring. There were, however, other thoughts he must convey. 'If the bandits return, they might blame the sakai for the destruction of their camp, the killing of their people and the removal of the gold. The yellow metal hidden in the stream is highly valued and they would kill you all to get it back. Batu and Angah know where it is concealed and you must leave it there until it can be hidden elsewhere. Andor must ask his gunig how best to use it, for gold has the power to save the sakai when bad times come.'

Staggering with exhaustion Vince mumbled his goodnights and stumbled to the hut he had occupied before. Mercifully it was as he had left it. The pack, rifle and other gear he dropped onto the table and himself on the sleeping platform. He needed to think, but fell asleep wondering what had happened to the tiger.

When he awoke, still fully clothed, Vince wandered to the river to wash and was besieged by small children who ran about blowing whistles with a fervour that hurt his head. They watched solemnly as he knelt to wash away the blood that still encrusted his face, and then ran off in response to some other interest. The wound was painful, but shallow. Ouch! It doesn't seem infected, he decided; I'll put on some antiseptic when it dries.

Ravenous, he was delighted to find food and water laid out beside the hut again and ate hungrily. Replete, he took his limited first-aid kit and gingerly smeared antibiotic ointment onto the wound, also swallowing a couple of aspirin to stifle the throbbing headache that had blurred his vision since he woke.

As he readied himself to leave, a small party approached from the longhouses. Vince recognised Muda, Abu, and Andor, together with Angah and Batu. He felt a pang at Amang's absence, but understood. Whatever an inscrutable fate had intended for them, the episode was over. Before the solemn-faced party was close enough for speech, Abu's voice scratched words upon his brain.

'Ints, we wish you selamat jalan. Today we leave our ladang for another part of the ulu, until the Chow-Chow have gone forever. You must reclaim your woman.' They stood silently around him while the voice inside his head persisted. 'She will need your help to recover. Any who escape the grasp of Sankal need time to get better, but her strength will return.' Abu stepped back and one by one the others came forward to embrace him and to wish him a safe journey. 'Selamat jalan, Ints, selamat jalan.'

chapter fourteen

Vince set a steady pace and by mid-afternoon reached the campsite he had abandoned in darkness. Everything was how it had been except for a tube of tapioca, dropped in the darkness and completely emptied by ants.

He felt driven by an urgent need: to cross the divide, make his amends with the regiment and discover if Abu was correct in implying that Audrey was really recovering. As if he had woken from a deep sleep and was anxious to catch a train for a journey, long planned and too long delayed, he set about re-packing.

From the pack taken from the terrorist camp, he removed the papers he had shoved indiscriminately inside, rolled them carefully and replaced them. With breech mechanisms and flag, they became a lumpy weight in the bottom of his main pack. Is that enough to get them to overlook me going missing for a few weeks, he wondered: who knows? Maybe a bit of CT gold would help?

The gold distracted him. He could not recall handling the metal in any quantity greater than a nine-carat ring before. It glowed in the last scattered rays of sunlight and felt oddly buttery to the touch. Their weight and feel were mesmerising and he thought of all he had heard about the lure of gold.

Each of the eight ingots was about two inches long, an inch and a half wide and perhaps a quarter of an inch thick. He hefted one in his hand. Hey, I reckon that's heavier than I thought. Could be more than ten ounces there! He stared at the bars hanging heavily in the middle of his hammock. Has to be around five pounds of gold there! Maybe I should have kept more.

His fingers found marks stamped into one surface. Unclear in the fading daylight, they seemed to be in Chinese characters. He wrapped them in his spare clothes and wondered uneasily to what lengths the previous owners would go to regain them.

After a meal, another application of antibiotic and more aspirin, he cleaned his rifle and slept. Sleep came easily, but not before he revisited the tension-filled hours of the previous day. God, I've never killed anyone before, he reflected, but it didn't upset me – well not too much. If it wasn't for how they treated Amang it might have been different. Anyway, I'm bloody glad I killed the bastards. Christ knows what would have happened to her if the tiger hadn't... Hey! What happened to it, anyway? – it was going to come back.

He thrust away his disgust at the carnage he had wrought. That little prick – the officer – he asked for it. Bloody hell, they all had. They were like that arsehole Cunningham and his mates – worth nothing more than a quick death and a future as fertiliser.

Drowsily, he wondered about the blowpipe. Was it just a thoughtful gift? Or did Andor have some sort of premonition that I'd need it to save Amang? He shrugged. Something I'll never know. That morning he had cleaned the blood from Amang's pendant, replaced the cord and left it with the blowpipe on the sleeping platform. At first light he woke, eager to be on his way, but still wondering. What did happen to the tiger?

The trail was ill-defined, but not too difficult to follow. After two days of hard slog he could look down on the valleys and midday on the third found him on a well-used trail among the high peaks. Such tracks had served the jungle people for millennia. Lacking a map, Vince tried to visualise his position from memory. It was hopeless and he decided to continue south until he could work out where he was.

The likelihood of running into CTs was remote, but he travelled warily. Contact with security forces would not suit his strategy for returning to military life. If they were trigger-happy it could also prove fatal. Although alert, he travelled faster than normal. The well-worn pathways running from Thailand, as far south as Negri Sembilan, were easy to follow. Parts were worn into high, wind-swept ridges. Others clung to steep hillsides or wound their way through ancient, lichen-clad forests.

They were part of a labyrinth well known to the Orang Asli and developed through the consensus of a hundred generations of travellers. On this basis Vince assumed it to be the best route available. Perhaps it was, but he sometimes wondered, when he found himself scrambling up rock faces, or teetering across a log-spanned chasm.

On the high divide, the vegetation was different: the canopy was lower. Trees sometimes gathered tendrils of cloud, like cobwebs in a neglected house. Where sunlight penetrated the foliage, orchids glowed like jewels in the forks of trees or amongst the damp humus of the forest floor. Monkeys, probably gibbons, heralded the sunrise with their cries and when they became too confident – or irritated at intrusion into their territory – threw sticks, or worse, at him. He was watchful for beruang, the Malayan sun bear. Growing to five feet tall and fuelled by aggression, they were best avoided. There were sometimes signs of wild pigs or deer. Once he glimpsed a tiny mouse deer. It paused to stare, and then with a flicker of movement disappeared into the shadows.

Early on the second morning, he caught the scent of woodsmoke and approached the next bend cautiously. Pulses hammering, he prepared to step into the shadows at any hint of danger. A peep around the corner revealed a simple domestic scene where a pair of nomads had set up house beside a pool. Their shelter was no more than four feet high, a simple frame of saplings lashed together with lianas. A roughly thatched roof sheltered a bamboo floor, only inches from the ground.

A young woman, a girl really – she looked no more than thirteen years old – sat, legs crossed, inside the open front. She was pale-skinned with shiny black hair tied neatly at the nape of her neck. There were silver bangles on her wrists, but her only clothing was a checked sarong tucked into a cord around her waist. An infant nursed at her breast and her eyes were half closed, a soft dreamy smile on her lips. But something about the child seemed wrong.

A man stepped from the bushes to drop dead branches beside the fire. Scarcely older than the young mother, he was much darker skinned, no more than four and a half feet tall, with a slim muscular body and a thick cap of tight black curls. Wearing only a loincloth, with the naked blade of a parang through the waistband, he was clearly of the itinerant Negrito people who travel in small groups and seldom settle.

Vince hesitated. There was no way to avoid them without creating alarm or suspicion. He gave a loud cough and called calmly, 'Selemat pagi, selemat pagi,' stepped around the corner and halted. For a few seconds the couple remained very still and examined him. Then they both smiled and the young man spread his arms in a gesture of welcome. Vince stepped forward and stared. Goddammit! That's a bloody hairy baby – it's covered with soft pale fur. Hell's teeth, it's a baby monkey!

Amidst much miming and mutual incomprehension, Vince learned that the couple had stopped here while the girl delivered a stillborn baby. Sadly, the father had dug a hole, laid the mite in it and covered it over. The girl had wept, and her breasts had been swollen with milk. They had been hurting, so her man had taken the blowpipe, now tucked under the roof of the hut, and in the forest had killed a mother monkey with a tiny baby on her back.

Vince looked at the anonymous object sizzling over the glowing coals of the fire with dawning horror. He had eaten little but brown rice for several days and been very aware of a succulent aroma. When he was hospitably offered a nicely cooked haunch he shut his mind to its origin, accepted it with a smile and devoured it greedily. Well, there's a sort of symmetry to it, he decided – the mother monkey's still feeding her child…

In the afternoon of the next day, a tall cloud-hung gunong loomed through a break in the canopy ahead. To avoid it he decided to go no further south, but to follow a rivulet that should lead west and eventually reach the Sungei Perak, the premier river of the state.

Navigation was pure guesswork. This central range ran from north to south. A descent to the west should eventually bring him to the main valley of Perak where tributaries raised in the high country drain into Chendoroh Lake to feed the Perak River. Another range of hills ran along the other side of the lake and near their southern end lay Taiping.

Vince tried vainly to peer through the trees and think. I must have already passed where we crossed the divide, he calculated, looking for the Puian. I hope I haven't gone too far and missed the lake, but I'd hit the Sungei Perak – or Temor – anyway. Somewhere down there, around Gunong Besar, there should be more high country.

He tried to picture a map, but remembered only fragments. Okay, Besar should be to the northwest. I wish I could see into the valley and think more clearly. He kneaded his head through the sweaty netting. Mustn't panic; follow the lie of the land and hope for the best. Navigating between points in the jungle would be impossible without a reliable compass and a map. He was trying to find his way by blind guesswork and instinct, but he had a large target.

An hour of stumbling down steep streambeds drove him up a spur to search for a path. When he found one, he followed it until it was time to camp. Since leaving the ladang, Vince had walked like a robot each day and fallen exhausted into his hammock at night. He was sick of coarse brown rice, having cooked the unappetising stuff each evening, with mess-tins as a boiler and sardines for flavour, and his stomach rebelled. The only break in the monotony had been his encounter with the Negritos. He had scarcely thought of anything except how to get back to Audrey as quickly as possible. He was worn out, needed rest and craved food that would please his taste buds as well as fill his belly.

Sorting through his remaining rations, Vince's hands strayed to the biscuit-like ingots. Like a lover, he stripped away the rags of clothing and stroked the soft slippery metal that was revealed. A sudden mad desire urged him to rush back to recover the hoard from the pool. The impulse passed quickly, but left him shaken. He packed the bars away quickly. God! This bloody stuff really can drive you crazy, eh?

In a fit of unbridled consumption he opened a can of baked beans and followed it with a hoarded can of fruit, washed down by hot, sweet tea. Unusually replete, he sat back in his hammock, filled with a dreamy euphoria, to contemplate as the shadows thickened.

Tomorrow? Tomorrow I'll follow my nose and the lie of the land. The gold? Maybe it'll pay for a wedding? Oh God, what if Audrey isn't any better and I'm going to face a court martial for mislaying the platoon? How can I look after Audrey if she doesn't recover – or if I'm locked up in Kinrara? The latter was a hell-hole, a so-called 'corrective establishment', run for the brigade by the Australian Military Police. Vince knew guys who had served twenty-one-day sentences there for pretty minor offences. When they returned to the company they had been different: broken men.

That night he slept poorly, troubled again by frightening yet indistinct dreams. In them he was haunted by sobbing, tormented women; he himself was helpless, a lost and frightened little boy. It was a relief to be woken by the cries of gibbons and early morning bird calls before falling back into blessedly dreamless oblivion.

Hours later, he woke feeling better and gazed up critically at the waterproof cover. Black insulation-taped patches marked repairs to tears from falling branches and he worried that another hit would destroy the shelter. While he was fretting over its condition, he heard a faint, repetitive, rasping noise. Curious, he raised his head and started to swing his legs over the side of the hammock head to locate the source of the irritating sound.

Its origin became frighteningly obvious. Breath caught in his chest and his heart hesitated, then hammered his ribs at twice its normal rate. Close enough for him to smell a feral reek of carrion on its steady, noisy breath, eyes focused implacably upon his face, was a fully-grown tiger.

Thoughts scattered like spilt coins. Is it the Colonel, so far from where where I last saw him? Dunno, keep still, think; rifle safety catch? On! He suppressed a groan and visualised the rifle where it lay between two forked sticks. Waiting to be grabbed – on the other side of the bloody hammock!

The huge cat leaned back on its haunches. Christ, its going to pounce! He swung around, grabbed desperately for the rifle and – fumbling the safety to off – tumbled out the other side of the hammock. Winded, one foot caught in the hammock, expecting powerful jaws upon his throat, he struggled to bring the rifle to bear. Instead a familiar voice spoke inside his head.

'Awfully sorry, old man. Should have spoken earlier – thought you'd recognise me.'

Vince was furious. He had been terrified; had almost killed either himself or the tiger and felt thoroughly humiliated. Methodically, he set the SLR back to the safety position, untangled his foot from the hammock and climbed seething to his feet. 'You stupid bastard! I bloody near died of fright and you're damn lucky I didn't shoot you!'

Lowering its head, the tiger looked subdued. 'I really am sorry, I was so pleased to find you, but didn't want to wake you. I just didn't think that when you did wake up... well, I'm afraid that I forgot that you wouldn't see me as a human. You see, I've just been to see my wife. I go and watch her from the bushes every now and again like some grubby little voyeur and it always leaves me rather distraught.'

Well, what could he say? The huge feline gazed levelly at him, seemingly as imperturbable as ever. Yet in his mind he heard a mature man in the grip of a strong emotion and fighting to hold back tears. He wanted to offer sympathy and thought to embrace the great beast as he might a grieving friend. The voice became gentle. 'Thanks, dear boy but best not, I'm never sure what might rouse her and I should hate to be unable to stop her from eating you – anyway, I'm not at all sure how you'd taste.'

For a few minutes the cat groomed itself quietly. Recovered from his outburst, Vince made coffee and felt ashamed. Finally the tiger raised its great head: it looked lordly, but the words were tentative and uncertain. 'If you really are willing to humour an old man, I'd be hugely pleased if you'd listen to me for a while. I so much enjoyed talking to you before... You're the only person I've socialised with for more than two years.'

'Sorry mate, maybe I'm losing my sense of humour. Sure, I'm happy to have a yarn.' Vince sat on the hammock to listen as he ate.

'Willie and I were always very close,' the Colonel began. 'We married soon after we met but had only six months together before I returned to Malaya. I actually pined for her, y'know, until the end of the war when I saw her again.' He paused, as though thinking. 'We were never separated again – ever – until... until I was killed – if that's what happened to me. We wanted children, but couldn't, you see, so we became even more dependent on each other.'

'The... er, physical side of marriage was important to us both, it was just part of us. It doesn't bother me now, no testosterone you see, but I can't help worrying about Willie poor girl. I keep on going back and hoping she's found someone else, but there's no sign of it. Dammit! There were plenty of randy buggers at the Club wanting to make off with her while I was still around. Good-looking woman, and faithful too. Bet she's frozen them all off out of some misguided sense of duty. I might be envious, but I can scarcely be jealous. I'm a bloody ghost for Christ's sake!' The voice became despairing. 'It's just something else to drive me crazy. I want so much for her to be happy and I can tell that she isn't. If only I could make contact with her... but I can't, it might drive her insane too.'

Vince was greatly touched by the devotion shown by... by Charles – yes that's better than thinking of him as 'the tiger'– for the wife for whom his love had transcended even the grave. 'I wish I could help, Charles... do you mind me calling you Charles? Have you thought of contacting your wife through her dreams, like you did with me?'

Charles paused. 'Well yes, I thought about it, d'you think it would be all right? Wouldn't upset her, d'you think?'

After a long thoughtful silence, he began again. 'I wonder if... that is... would you consider... No, sorry, old man, not the sort of thing one can ask a chap. No – make me feel like a bloody pimp!' And he once more lapsed into silence.

Vince wondered if he should feel shocked. He suspected that he knew what had been on Charles's mind.

The two sat in companionable silence, each unwilling to renew the conversation. Finally, Charles's voice pressed gently into Vince's mind once more. 'I'm sure, dear boy, that you must be eager to see your lady again. She's such an indomitable spirit.' He said it again, pleased with his choice of words.

'Yes, an indomitable spirit is exactly what she was when I was so briefly in contact with her.'

Vince was startled. Charles continued, 'Yes, these Orang Asli chaps are quite remarkable. All this stuff about spirits and such. Well I for one think that sort of thing should remain between the pages of the Old Testament. Yet these chaps live out their beliefs every day of their lives.' Vince sensed what could have been a hollow laugh. 'Why, they even believe tigers have spirits with which they may exchange thoughts! Do you know if it weren't for Willie – and having to live in the body of a female cat with disgusting habits – I could enjoy learning from these people. Their spirit world is so real to them – no one's got around to telling them that it doesn't exist.'

The big animal stood, stretched and paced around the camp sniffing at whatever caught her fancy, before returning to its original position and assumed a sphinx-like pose. 'Do you know that old blighter Abu recruited me to become Andor's gunig? I don't know how they do it, but they both have abilities that would be totally beyond any boffins at the smart universities. He's set his heart on the lad becoming a great halak who'll save his people from some doom to come.'

Vince watched mutely as the beast attended to a particularly irritating itch on its right flank before continuing. 'D'you know Kaa – Abu's gunig? Damned great cobra! Ugh. Clever? Oh yes, but it has a mind like chilled slime. Anyway, he told Abu that water spirits – malicious devils by all accounts – intended to drown Andor. Well Abu went off to his pano hut and into a two-day trance while his semangat searched the spirit world looking for help. This is where you came in, for he found not only Sankal, the old giantess who guards the entrance to the underworld, but also a strange spirit like none he had seen before. Sankal's attendants were trying to lure it to the pit, but it wouldn't go.'

The tiger gave Vince a meaningful look. He was incredulous. 'Come on! You're not trying to tell me it was Audrey's spirit? In the middle of the jungle – the underworld?'

'Afraid so, old boy – seems she couldn't get back to her own body but was determined to wait – until – well, who knows?' The tiger gave Vince another interrogative stare. 'It seems to me dear boy, that she had an understanding with you that she was determined to honour. Anyway, old Abu followed her around and somehow, I don't know how, found out through Amang's father that you were susceptible to entering a trance state.'

Vince felt dazed. That he could be sitting in the middle of a tropical jungle listening – albeit inside his head – to a tiger holding forth on metaphysics numbed his brain. *Am I drunk, or dreaming? For God's sake pull yourself together; you've got to get back to Audrey.*

His voice was shaky and desperate. 'Charles, why do you talk as though you know Audrey – and how can you imply that she's better? I'm sure that she's an indomitable spirit, as you say. Her psychiatrist said the same thing, but how could you know that? It's simply unbelievable!'

Charles continued, quietly and unhappily. 'Nothing has been either simple or believable to me for years. Yet I have to accept that these things must be so, if only in the particular dream in which I exist. I was there with Abu, though not in the flesh of course, when he snatched your lady from Sankal's right armpit. Kaa and I distracted the attendant spirits, but it was Abu who did the dangerous stuff. God! Imagine tickling that gruesome hag.'

Vince was becoming more confused and agitated by the minute. 'But – but – where is Audrey – her spirit – now?'

'I'm sorry dear boy, I do wish I could say for sure, but I have little doubt she is recovering from what – some sort of coma? Abu saw her back to – I think – that Military Hospital in the Cameron Highlands. He watched her spirit re-enter her body and I've no doubt whatsoever that she will enjoy a full recovery.'

They fell into another companionable if troubled silence, each immersed in his own thoughts and worries, about what had been and what might yet occur. After a time, the great creature heaved itself onto all four paws and stretched like a domestic cat on a hearth-mat. Its tone was regretful. 'Well, old man, the belly feels a little empty, and the concierge will soon be awake and looking for dinner. Oh, do you know where you are now?' It was a rhetorical question, for he barely paused. 'The trickle you're following runs into the Sungei Temor, but this track will soon cross to the other bank and diverge to cross the foothills south of Gunong Besar. Eventually, it reaches Lake Chenderoh about fifty miles east of where we are now. From there you could raft or get a boat to Kuala Kangsar, only about twenty-five miles from Taiping.'

Vince's heart sagged. He had hoped he was closer to the lake. Still, on a track like this, he might cover ten map miles a day. In harsh, hostile terrain a patrol might be lucky to travel a mile or even less between camps, but most of this travel would be downhill. Now the situation seemed to require some formality: 'Goodbye, Charles, and thanks for helping Audrey and me. I wish there were some way to keep in touch and share the rest of the story.'

The tiger gave a single nod and vanished into the trees, leaving only its thoughts behind. 'Thank you, dear boy, thank you. We'll always be in touch, because we'll have much in common.' An enigmatic farewell and one that Vince felt instinctively would echo in his mind for years. As he puzzled over Charles's meaning, Vince realised he had forgotten the gold and that Andor, Abu or Muda, needed advice for its future use. He tried to project his thoughts after the now vanished tiger, but received no sign that his message was received. Nothing remained of his presence but the words fixed in Vince's mind: 'I have little doubt she is recovering…'

* * *

Days later Vince camped in hilly country near a pool that looked suitable for fishing. He caught three fish, all over a foot long, grilled one for dinner and dry-smoked the others for the next day. Extra protein was welcome and so was a change of diet, but more salt would have helped. He thought he was a little south of Gunong Ulu Sah, the highest point in the area. When crossing its foothills earlier, he had not seen Gunong Besar either, but felt sure that it had been no more than ten miles north of the track he followed.

The following morning he sniffed a mouth-watering citric scent on the air and followed it to where a sturdy lemon tree stood, the earth under it strewn with fruit as big as grapefruit. Presumably a passing bird had once dropped a lemon pip and, where a forest giant had fallen and the sun could at last reach, it had taken root in the damp humus. Dizzied by their aroma, Vince scooped one up only to find that it was largely pith, its juicy centre no larger than a golf ball. He bit into it, but the sour astringent flavour puckered his mouth. With enough cored to fill his mess tins, he squeezed a couple into his water bottle. Two squeezed over his dried fish lunch improved the meal, while the citric tang refreshed the chemically treated water.

* * *

As Vince went through the long-practised chores of establishing camp on the western slopes of the hills, he felt increasingly ill. Had there been something wrong with the fish – or the lemons? He had been faithful in sterilising drinking water and in taking two malaria suppressives each night. The semi-healed wound on the side of his head remained uninfected and past experience kept him diligent in protecting himself against scrub typhus.

It had been an hour earlier that he had first begun to feel unwell. Nausea and an intermittent unsteadiness progressed, by the time he had strung up the hammock, to almost total incapacity. He was feverish and a throbbing headache added to his misery. Gulping down three aspirins, he propped the rifle up beside him, placed the water bottle within reach and collapsed into the hammock. As the throbbing subsided, he fell into a haunted, fitful sleep. Trees and stones harboured malevolent spirits, all conspiring to thwart his desperate struggle to drag an unconscious Audrey from the grip of a hideous female ogre.

During the night he woke hanging from the hammock, drenched with sweat and desperately thirsty. Aware enough to swallow anti-malaria pills and more aspirin, he fumbled for the piece of blanket. Even in the lowland heat, he shook with cold. Night passed, and demon-haunted sleep alternated with periods of wakefulness. He was either sweating heavily, or chilled to the core. Daylight brought little relief. He struggled from the hammock, staggered to the rivulet to fill the waterbag, added purifying tablets and used the latrine, pleased that the nausea had passed without evidence of food poisoning.

He managed perfunctory ablutions and tried to eat. With little to choose from, all he could face was the last can of fruit. The label had long since gone, but he was happy that it contained pears. Their syrupy sweetness soothed his throat as he sat, hunched on his pack with the blanket clutched around him, and savoured each juicy mouthful. Exhausted by the effort of eating, he fell back into the hammock with both water bag and drinking mug nearby. The day passed much as the previous night had.

Nothing had changed when night fell again. Vince was still sleeping fitfully and waking frequently. Once when he woke in the night and looked around him, he was suddenly very frightened: where was he? Why was he here? And when memory returned, terror remained. He had awoken from a grisly dream in which strangers had stumbled upon the campsite: a stained and rotted hammock that held only bones inside the mouldering remnants of a uniform. They took the gold bars and left everything else. He shuddered. Even if, through the number on his rifle, the remains were eventually identified, no one would think to inform Audrey. For the rest of her life she would believe that he had walked away and deserted her.

He struggled from the hammock and to the stream. Without falling, he managed to splash water on his face. With mechanical movements, he heated water for tea, opened and ate what he could from a tin of beans and struck camp. Somehow, some time later, he was again on his way, stumbling along a trail towards an unknown destination.

chapter fifteen

Framed between open French doors, she stared dully into the garden. I should speak to the syce, she told herself – the pool needs cleaning, the hibiscus hedges need trimming and the whole damn place looks squalid. Oh well, I don't suppose it's really his fault, I haven't bothered… hello, why are the Singhs here? Who on earth…?

The woman stepped out onto the terrace, immediately grateful for the shade of the tall trees around the bungalow. Although it was still morning, the sun would strike a fiery blow on skin meant for cooler climates.

Three tall, well-built men approached from the shadow of the trees. The leader appeared to be in his early fifties, perhaps ten years older than the other two. They carried staves as tall as themselves and wore loose cotton shirts and trousers. Each carried himself like a soldier. Sheathed parangs hung from their belts and above their heavily bearded faces they wore neatly tied khaki turbans. They were Sikhs.

From the shoulder of the older man hung a pair of stained and worn army packs mounted on an A-frame. In his right hand was a military assault rifle. His younger companions supported, almost carried, a young-looking, dirty and unshaven man. Clad in torn and stained jungle greens, he looked ill and was mumbling incoherently.

'Jai Ram, who is this and why have you and the Singh brothers brought him here?'

'He is a soldier, Mem, we think maybe lost from his patrol. Ranjet and Surrinder Singh are walking with me in the forest when we are meeting this person. At first we are thinking him a dacoit. Oh my, it was being very frightful, Mem! He was looking and spokeing very wild and when we thinking he would shoot us, I knock the rifle from his hands with my stick. We are bringing him to you because we think that is what our sahib would have wanted us to do. We think he is maybe very sick.'

'Yes,' she said, 'you are right – that is truly what my husband would have wanted. Please – bring him in; Amah and I will deal with him.' She turned and called, 'Falidah!' Seconds later a plump, middle-aged Malay housekeeper hurried into the room.

'Falidah, please turn down the covers in the guest-room, Jai Ram and the Singh brothers have a visitor for us. Surrinder, would you and Ranjet put him on the spare bed please? Falidah,' she called again, 'please first put a waterproof cover over the bed; this man must have a good sponging.' As the others followed her directions, the woman turned to the older man. 'Jai Ram, please put his equipment in the wash room cupboard. Oh, you'd better make sure his gun is unloaded.'

Jai Ram nodded. 'Acha, Mem,' he responded, and removed the magazine, cocked the rifle, expertly catching the cartridge as it flew from the breech. He carried the gear around the corner.

Having disposed of their burden on the bed, the Singh brothers followed Jai Ram, steepling their hands respectfully below their beards as they went out the door. The woman watched them walk towards their own quarters, and she smiled as they gesticulated and bobbed their heads as they talked.

How fortunate I am, she told herself, that dear Charles left such reliable men to support and guide me after he died. Even now they have brought me someone to look after, to take my mind from my loneliness. What a pleasure to have something to focus my attention upon!

Between them, she and Falidah stripped the inert body and administered a comprehensive and much needed bed-bath. They worked efficiently and without fuss; in quite separate circumstances each had nursed injured soldiers before. They applied antiseptic to scratches and abrasions, washed caked dried blood from his hair and decided that there was nothing further they could do. 'That wound on right head looks healed good without infection,' Falidah said, 'but hair might grown in, should have cut off, too late now.'

'Yes,' agreed the European woman, 'this one not taking proper care of himself.'

'We shave him?' Falidah asked hopefully. She was enjoying herself.

'Yes, why not? Let's see how he looks without whiskers. But you stop looking at his dingle like that. You can see he's not Muslim.'

It was said teasingly, and Falidah giggled appreciatively. 'Yes, very strange to me, on little boy yes, not on grown man. Anyway, long time now I not have young man naked on bed.'

Between them the two women shaved Vince and put him into clean pajamas and checked his pulse – a little slow, and his temperature was high, but not dangerously so. The fever was burning itself out. They laid him on his side, covered with a single sheet. The overhead fan was set to slow, a glass of water was left on the bedside table and the door ajar. While Falidah prepared lunch, they speculated on how their patient had come to be alone and ill in the jungle.

Later they propped Vince up on pillows and attempted to feed him broth. Not all went down his throat, but they did persuade him to swallow paludrine and aspirin. Oblivious to them peeping in from time to time to check on him, he slept all afternoon. He woke in darkness, lucid, but alarmed until he pieced together some at least of what had happened since his struggle to break camp. Slowly, from blurred memories, he reconstructed the events that had led him to this place.

Big men with beards had taken his rifle and pack. He thought they meant to rob and kill him, but they had helped him and brought him here. He recalled women's voices, the touch of soft hands and two faces looking down on him, one brown and dark-haired, the other pale with hair so blonde it was like cirrus cloud framing a face of pale beauty.

He found and drained the water glass, listened to the fan beating the humid air and the occasional cheep of the geckos hunting insects on the walls and ceiling. Then he fell into a deep, healing sleep and stirred not at all when a kimono-clad figure slipped into the room. She regarded him for a few minutes by torchlight, refilled the water glass and went away as silently as she arrived. She wondered about the mosquito net, but decided to leave it tied back; the fan seemed to keep the pests away.

* * *

Back in her own room, the room she had so long shared with her beloved

Charles, she hung up the kimono and lay down on top of the sheets. They had so much wanted to have children together, but had come to terms with the fact that it was not to happen. Their delight in each other was its own reward and they had shared an intensely erotic love without need of outside stimulus. Since he had died, so suddenly and tragically two years before, no thought of physical desire other than for him had troubled her mind.

She remembered with disdain the men who had lusted for her since she was little more than a child. Yet Charles was the only man for whom she had felt a reciprocal passion, and that had endured throughout their marriage. Her least endearing encounters had been with acquaintances: post-war expatriates at the club in Kuala Kangsar. Some had been overly persistent in their attempts to seduce her. Worst of all were those who, under the pretext of being kind to an unhappy widow, had continued persisting after his death. These men she actively despised, and the worst of them was a neighbour on the other side of the lake.

They had all been repulsed with scorn and sometimes force, but now, lying in the darkness, she tried to analyse her feelings when watching her sleeping guest.

Something's changed, she was thinking – how and what, I don't know. But I feel different.

She tossed uncomfortably. Is it, she went on to ask herself, something to do with the dreams I've been having these last few nights? They are so unsettling because I can't remember them properly. Charles' voice, but…?

She sighed. Never had she been a woman to whom celibacy could seem a natural state. Often in recent years she had felt a desperate need for the consolation of physical love and repressed it as yet another aspect of grief for the lover who had left her a widow. He had been the only man with whom she had found sexual joy, and the fire that he had lit in her body all those years ago he had tended assiduously until his untimely death.

She moved restlessly in the humid darkness and wondered how it would have been if they had been able to have children. They had both been eager for parenthood but, no matter how hard they tried, she never became pregnant. She smiled in the darkness. Oh yes, how hard we tried. She permitted her memory to dwell on the pleasure they had found in each other's bodies during their unending quest for parenthood. A wave of heat raced through her body: her groin and breasts ached with a sudden, frightening need.

She thought of falling asleep within strong protective arms, the scent of male skin in her nostrils. A sudden mad impulse brought her upright, and she began to tear off her nightdress. It caught on an overlooked hairpin and the moment of struggle brought her to her senses. Oh, you foolish woman, she berated herself with a nervous laugh, it is well that poor young man is sick, or he'd have a crazy old woman jumping on him!

Eventually she slept, and she dreamed of tender nights of carnal pleasure that left her pregnant and content. She woke rested, but sad that she wouldn't really have a baby. The euphoria evaporated with her dream; only an empty sense of disappointment remained.

When Falidah brought the morning coffee at seven, her employer and friend was at the window in her kimono and staring out at the slightly run-down garden. 'Thank you, Falidah, I'll have it after my shower. How's our guest this day?'

'Selemat pagi Puan, he is much better, but he is still weak – I think not long ill before our Sikh man find him. He being very lucky man. I show him bathroom for shower and give him some of Tuan's old clothes like you say. They too big but okay.'

The woman gazed after Falidah as she left the room. How fortunate I am, she reminded herself, to have such a staunch friend. They had been friendly since Falidah first came to work on the estate ten years before, but since Charles had been killed she had become truly indispensable. It was Falidah who had urged her to engage a manager but retain overall control for herself of the estate. Since that time she had become confidante and adviser as much as housekeeper and friend. Today she wore one of the colourful kabaya outfits that suited her so well. She was someone who was always neat, competent and composed, regardless of her activity.

* * *

In his room, Vince looked from the window. Behind a grove of paw paw trees, a body of water reflected morning sunlight. That must be Lake Chenderoh, he realised with a pang of anxiety – by water and road, he calculated, it can't be more than a day's journey to Taiping. The Malay lady who gave me breakfast said this is the Chenderoh Plantation and that some of their workers found me in the bush.

His memories were hazy, but becoming clearer. He assessed himself: I'm a bit shaky and weak, he thought, but no worse than I've felt after a dose of 'flu. I reckon I'm just about fit enough to travel and they must have some sort of transport that'll get me to Taiping.

A tap on the door startled him. Must be the Malay lady, he guessed – what's her name, Falidah? But in spite of her sam fu outfit of green and orange silk brocade, the woman who entered at his call was clearly European. Her hair was tied back in a cap of blonde radiance and her figure was not one with which a sam fu was usually required to cope.

My God, Vince breathed, she's gorgeous. She'd make Marilyn Monroe look like a pretty average sort of sheila. He realised that she must be about ten years older than he was.

'Good morning,' she said, 'welcome and thank you for visiting with us. I am most pleased that you are seeming much better.'

Vince's tongue stumbled, but he could not stop. 'You – you're one of the angels, you and the Malay lady. I'm sorry, I mean I had this dream and woke up – and you were saving me, uh, looking after me.' He stood unsteadily. 'I'm sorry, I really should thank you for taking me in and looking after me, I've been a mess. Look, I should introduce myself. My name's Vince Tanner and I'm a rifleman in the New Zealand Regiment. I got lost from my patrol and I've been wandering around – for about a month, I think.'

'Really – a month on your own? Oh, now it's my turn to be sorry.' She stepped forward and held out her hand. 'My name is Wilhelmina and this is my estate. Charles, my husband, left it to me when he passed away a couple of years ago.' As they shook hands Vince felt an odd tingle of surprise, as though he recognised her touch, and Wilhelmina's hand jerked as he held her grip a second longer than he intended

With her words, the light faded from her eyes and he had an odd feeling that he knew her, but had temporarily forgotten who she was. Her hand was soft, warm and dry. He released it reluctantly. 'I'm sorry – about your husband, I mean. I can see you still miss him.'

She turned towards the window and looked at the suddenly blurred view of trees and the lake beyond. After a minute, Wilhelmina turned back with a tremulous smile. 'Thank you… Falidah tells me that you've already eaten, but won't you join me for a second breakfast? Or just coffee, if you prefer?' Her smile brightened. 'I would like you to make me informed of how you could survive by yourself for all that time in the jungle.'

While he sipped coffee, Vince watched Wilhelmina eat mango slices with cereal; she drew from him more than he had intended to tell anyone except Audrey. She was a good listener and asked intelligent questions that elicited a more comprehensive account than he had intended to divulge of his movements since separating from the patrol.

She was particularly interested in the lifestyle of the Temiar; knew of their dream beliefs and the accomplishments of halaks and sought greater detail. Vince was reluctant to admit that he thought he had experienced extrasensory communication with Abu. With Andor and the tiger, too, he thought helplessly... well, some things she's just going to have to take on faith, and I'm buggered if I'll tell her about Amang.

He told her about Andor's dance and when he described the solemn performance of the Maxina outside the longhouses, she giggled. When he described how he and Amang had passed Abu's pano hut and seen the giant cobra, apparently dancing with Abu, she shuddered, then looked thoughtful.

'But where were you going?' The question was innocent enough, but her next question was more perceptive than he cared for. 'Amang – was she not your adoptive brother's wife? Hmmm, is it true that it is proper for a Temiar wife to sleep with her brother-in-law during her husband's absence? Then...'

To Vince's relief Falidah entered the room to announce that lunch would be ready in fifteen minutes. He wondered what had happened to the morning, and quickly suggested that he would like some fresh air. They walked around the compound, past a processing depot and to the edge of the plantation. Wilhelmina explained how the latex was collected every day by teams of rubber tappers who visited each tree. They gathered latex from the holding cup and cleared the sloping incisions in the trunks to allow the next day's supply of sap to trickle into the replaced cup. The collected latex was treated, pressed into perforated rectangles, smoked and shipped to Kuala Kangsar on the plantation's old diesel launch. Vince listened politely, although he already knew much of what he was being told.

The gloom under the rubber trees was not as pronounced as that of the deep jungle, but the orderly rows of evenly planted trees marched in each direction amidst perpetual dusk, in which tappers glided from tree to tree like dryads. As they turned back towards the bungalow, Vince said, 'Wilhelmina, you mentioned a boat; do you have a telephone? I should contact my regiment or I'll be in deep... er, I could be in trouble.'

'That I understand, Vince. To you I should have mentioned this earlier. We have only one line we unfortunately must share with the plantation across the lake. The wife I feel sorry for – she has become married to a disgusting man, and I am sure he listens in to our calls. Soon, I hope, we will have a line to ourselves.' Wilhelmina glared towards the lake with distaste. 'The trouble now is that our line is not operating, and the boat is in Kuala Kangsar for an overhaul of the motor.'

In response to his questioning look, she shook her head. 'Mohammed Das, the boatman, said it might take a week. He left on Friday so, I'm sorry, you must have a forced holiday with us for maybe four days.' She touched his arm and smiled. 'You are a very welcome guest. For me, I am very pleased. Now I shall hear all of your story.'

During their chat over lunch, Vince learned that there was a ladang an hour or two away from the plantation and some of the Senoi residents were employed on the estate. They had links with a Temiar saka in one of the high valleys, which was how Wilhelmina and her husband had become interested in their customs.

After lunch, Vince followed his hostess's instructions to rest and he slept for almost two hours. When he awoke he lay in bed for a while, thinking: God, fancy being this close and not even be able to ring Dr Baxter! I've got to find out if Audrey's really getting better, like both Abu and Charles reckoned. Charles… funny that Wilhelmina's dead husband would have the same name… Wilhelmina …that could be shortened to Willie, couldn't it? He sat up, lay down again, stood up and walked to the window. Sheets of rain had started to fall in thick droplets that obscured the view. But with that white skin and silvery-blonde hair, she must be Scandinavian – she speaks very good English, but – bloody hell – yes! She could be Dutch.

He picked up the rifle. Falidah had shown him where his gear had been put and arranged for his clothes to be laundered. Spreading the piece of blanket over the rattan table, he stripped, cleaned and reassembled the SLR, emptied, cleaned and replaced the magazines – and thought, Bloody Charles! Is he still jerking me around? He thought about their last conversation. The bugger! He actually steered me here. Even if I hadn't got sick and been carried to the house, I'd have wound up here anyway.

At a loose end, he wandered to the kitchen and chatted to Falidah while she prepared dinner. He liked this plump, bustling woman whose oval brown face could suddenly break into the most radiant smiles. 'Puan catch up with accounts,' he learned, 'because manager away on leave,' and that dinner would be at seven.

Thanking her, he decided to explore the lakeside he could see from his room. He followed a path that led him to a dock, where he presumed the launch must tie up when at the estate. He wandered along the shore, constructing scenarios of what he might face when he got back to the regiment: the first thing to do, he decided, is to ring Dr Baxter, and then I'll have to show somebody – Major Bennett, the Intelligence Officer…? – well, somebody, the papers, the breech mechanisms…

Suddenly, he knew that he wanted to keep the gold. If he and Audrey couldn't marry, maybe it would help with her care.

He began to feel gloomy again and thought about returning to the house. He had strayed about a hundred yards south of the main building and wondered which windows were his and Wilhelmina's bedrooms. What a lovely-looking woman – and really nice with it! Well-off widow, Vince thought, but she's treating me like an honoured guest, not just some baggy-arsed squaddie who's stumbled out of the jungle.

He watched the sun, a great golden disk appearing to swell and slide behind the hills on the other side of the lake. Reminded of the time, he hurried to shower before dinner.

Wilhelmina asked him to join her for a drink before dinner. While she sipped a gin and tonic, he enjoyed a Tiger beer. How ironic! he thought. She chatted about running the estate, problems that occurred when the manager was on leave and how efficient Mr Townsend was. Her lawyers, supported by Falidah, had encouraged her to hire an estate manager after Charles had been killed. Vince only half listened, wondering about the absent Mr Townsend. Wilhelmina obviously liked him, and there was no mention of a Mrs Townsend. She spoke of him with respect, but never referred to him by a first name. It seemed he was an occasional dinner guest, but apparently not a frequent companion. While she chatted, Vince wondered if Mr Townsend might be one of those unfortunates who are immune to feminine charms.

He gazed at her. She was utterly charming in an olive-green skirt with matching bolero over a satin blouse as white as the hair that hung to below her shoulders. Jeez, he said to himself, how could any man not go bonkers over a woman like this? Stuck out here, the only other European in the compound, the poor bugger must need ten cold swims every day. Unless… no…

'Vince', her voice cut into his thoughts, 'you were shaking your head.' She smiled. 'Was I saying something not correct?' His face glowed as he heard a voice that sounded like his own blurt, 'No, oh no, I – I was just thinking what a beautiful lady you are.'

She turned very pink. 'Why, thank you Vince, that is very sweet.' She stood and crooked her arm, 'would you take me into dinner?' She squeezed his arm. 'Young men should learn care with compliments – old widows, like old tigers, can become man-eaters.'

During dinner the conversation drifted from topic to topic. Wilhelmina chatted about the Temiar saka in the hills and how tribespeople sometimes approached the local Senoi to become their intermediaries in trade with the outside world. 'Sometimes we buy from them the wild rubber – jelutong – and process it with our own, to help their economy a little.'

Vince soon excused himself, borrowed a book from the shelves in the living room and went to bed. He read for a short time, but was soon drowsy. His dreams were benign and his morning memories were of figures dancing between two longhouses. Somewhat disconcertingly, Audrey and Wilhelmina were both amongst those twisting, fire-lit figures.

At breakfast he asked Wilhelmina about the men who had rescued him, so that he could locate and thank them. When he found them, they were warm and friendly. He liked them at once. Jai Ram he thought particularly impressive and walked with him around the estate as he checked the workers and made notes about ongoing maintenance.

The ex-warrant officer remained devoted to the memory of his late commander. 'Ah, the sahib was being a true gentlemans. Because of him not one single mans in our company would bow down to the Japan devils. When war is end he gives us chance of new life, blessed be his soul.' He shook his head sadly. 'When those miserable dacoits kill him, all Sikh mens and other mens from regiment most sad.'

They walked back towards the bungalow and Jai Ram took Vince by the arm. 'Do you know, sahib, the banner of the Punjabi Rifles has on it a tiger? No? But then you must be coming to look.' He took Vince on a circuitous route around the house and close to where he had been standing the day before.

Jai Ram squatted under some trees and swept aside the leaves. There in the soft soil, sheltered from the rain, were the clear paw prints of a tiger. 'We are thinking,' Jai Ram whispered as Vince assessed the angle to the building, 'that the sahib now has the body of a tiger and returns to watch over us and the memsahib.'

After lunch Vince rested in his room. He dozed for an hour, and then took out his cleaning gear and with an old toothbrush set about cleaning the accumulated grime from the crevices in his rifle. He had been conscious of low voices from the living room and assumed that his hostess had a visitor. Unwilling to intrude, he paid the voices no further attention. Suddenly, a female voice was raised in anger. A sharp cry followed an angry male voice and what sounded like a sharp slap. He was already moving through the door when he heard Wilhelmina's voice raised in fury.

He peered around the living room door. A man he did not know stood in the middle of the room with reddening parallel scratches on his left cheek. His even white teeth were bared in a nasty smile. Facing him, her back to Vince, Wilhelmina sprawled across the rattan settee, one hand to her cheek, the tunic of her sam fu torn open. Her voice crackled with rage. 'Get out of my home, you scum. If you put a foot on my land again I'll ki…'

Vince was seen the second he pushed the door open, but the rifle at his side was concealed. Startled, the stranger quickly recovered. 'Hello – what's this, the resident gigolo? I suppose he's the reason my charms are so resistible.'

Angered, Vince stepped forward, rammed the rifle muzzle into the man's midriff and, as he bent forward, took a backward step and swung the barrel across the sneering face.

Hoarse with anger, he levered a round into the firing chamber. 'You heard the lady. She wants you out of here. But first you'll apologise to her. Now!'

'Apologise?' The stranger raised an eyebrow and sneered. A hand went to his bruised cheek. 'You impertinent colonial yob – I've a mind to…' Another smack over the ear with the rifle barrel silenced him.

Shaking with rage and nervousness, Vince slipped the safety catch forward. 'Last chance.'

The interloper, his arrogance overshadowed by shock, looked towards Wilhelmina. 'I-I'm sorry I hit you.' Mumbled through clenched teeth and clearly not heartfelt, the apology was accepted with a nod. Vince prodded the man into a shambling run, out the door across the lawn and to the dock, where an open speedboat bobbed at its moorings.

He stood back, rifle across his chest and watched the man fumble with the ignition. Blood dripped from his chin; his mouth moved without audible sound. When the motor fired, he turned and screamed something, incomprehensible over the roar of the engine. Suspecting that he was not being wished a long and prosperous life, Vince again flicked off the safety and fired a single warning shot as the boat departed. He hurried back to the house.

Wilhelmina was in the doorway, a hand to her bruised cheek and her eyes wet with tears. She had rearranged her clothing, the tunic now held precariously closed by its two remaining buttons. Though she tried hard to look composed, her voice trembled. 'I – I hear shot as boat going, is all right?'

When he stepped into the room, she threw her arms around him with a strangled sob. When her spasms of weeping ended and her breathing became normal, she stepped back and looked into his face. 'Thank you, Vince – for being here and for saving me from that pig. I thought I could handle him; I should have known better.'

Wordlessly, and as one would comfort a child, he wiped the tears from her cheeks with his thumb and kissed her forehead. He helped her to the settee, told her to try to relax and left the room.

When he returned he handed her a glass of water, sponged her face and held a kitchen towel folded over ice-cubes against her bruised cheek. She swallowed the water gratefully, put the glass down and turned to him with a fierce smile. Gripping his hands, she said. 'Thank you, too, for hitting him: that I would have liked to have done.' She added enviously, 'I scratched him, but you hurt him more.'

In another part of the house a door slammed and a moment later Falidah was in the doorway. 'I'm return Puan, what time…?' her voice trailed away as she took in the two of them sitting close together, Vince barefooted, Wilhelmina dishevelled, her face tear-stained and her top with barely enough buttons to restrain her breasts.

The swift flow of expressions over Falidah's face moved so swiftly from surprise, shock, and dismay to amused tolerance, that neither Vince nor Wilhelmina could restrain a splutter of awkward laughter. With averted eyes, Falidah turned to leave, but Wilhelmina halted her. 'Please wait, Falidah, I'm sorry, this is not how it looks.' She hesitated. 'Did I say that right?' She glanced at Vince. 'Our guest has been very good for me.'

As Falidah's eyebrows soared, Wilhelmina coloured. 'No – no, I must start again. This afternoon I was visited by the despicable Mr Cunningham. He said he wanted to talk about the telephone and I stupidly let him in. He said disgusting things, and then he attacked me. Vince came and drove him away. He is being my hero.'

She stood as Falidah, her face tight with concern, moved to embrace her. 'Oh, Puan, let's put some more ice on your poor face.' Vince watched as employer and employee reverted to being close friends. With grateful smiles in his direction, both women left the room.

He took the rifle to his room and moodily set about cleaning it once more. Several things troubled him. He had no regrets for the manner in which he had dealt with the handsome but obnoxious Mr Cunningham. He believed that had the situation been reversed he would be dead and probably Wilhelmina as well. No, it's not that, an inner voice insisted – I enjoyed holding Wilhelmina. No – it's that bloody Charles. He's still trying to use me… Well, all right, it was nice… her neck and hair… her perfume…

Out of the blue, it hit him. Cunningham: wasn't that the name of the bastard in Cyprus? The son-of-a-bitch who walked out on Audrey when she'd been brutalised, the rotten prick who might have actually set her up to be beaten and raped!

No, it couldn't be. How could he be here? But yes. It was possible. The strength went from his legs and he sat numbly on the edge of the bed. Oh Holy Christ! Have I really missed a chance to kill that bastard?

Falidah knocked on the closed door. 'Dinner in one hour. Puan say please to join her for stengahs in thirty minutes.'

'Falidah, can you give me a minute?' Without waiting for a reply, Vince drew her into the room. 'Who is this man Cunningham? How long has he been here? Do you know his first name?'

Her smooth brown face became perturbed. 'I'm sorry Tuan,' – an honorific not usually bestowed on an ordinary soldier, but Vince did not even notice – 'maybe two years. His name? I think maybe Drik? Maybe Derk? Maybe best ask Puan.' She hurried away to prepare the dinner.

Drik? Derk? – Derek – Derek Cunningham! Maybe it was the same evil bastard and he'd missed the chance to shoot the rotten shit. Sick with renewed anger, Vince put on the dressing gown provided, showered and changed into the fresh clothes laid out on the bed. Joining Wilhelmina in the living room, he felt better; at least he now knew where to find the odious Cunningham and could file his anger away for future use.

Stepping through the door, he found his hostess on the rattan settee. She sipped from a long glass and stared pensively through the French doors into the garden. When she stood to greet him with a radiant smile, he stared. Her mane of platinum hair had been drawn back and dressed into a tapered headpiece. Only the narrow straps supporting the black silk cocktail dress broke the clear paleness of her shoulders. Before narrowing to the waist, it struggled valiantly to contain her bosom before flowing over curvaceous hips to end just below her knees. Her simple necklace of black coral was not needed to draw his eyes back to the décolletage.

His own knees became liquid, his mouth opened without sound as he stared.

Wilhelmina was disturbed. 'Vince, what is it? Are you again not feeling good? What can I do?' He bit his tongue. 'Vince, please say something. Why are you…? Oh.' He watched in dazed fascination as a tide of pink coloured the skin from the roots of her hair to her neck.

'I'm sorry Wilhelmina, I'm truly sorry, I didn't mean to stare. I – well – I knew I was having dinner with a beautiful woman and I find myself in a room with her even lovelier young sister.' He could not stop. 'That dress is stunning. You'd add glamour to a royal wedding.' He found himself moving to where she stood, taking her hand and lifting it to his lips. Dear God, only foreign poofs do things like this, he thought distractedly.

Wilhelmina smiled uncertainly, 'Oh, Vince, are you sure you are all right? Those were lovely compliments and I am liking that you think my dress is nice. I was frighten that it was too daring for an old woman when I saw your look.'

He was incredulous. 'An old woman at nineteen? Just not possible!'

'Now stop being a silly boy and tell me what you would like to drink. Will you have a stengah, or something else?' Unwilling to confess that he was not sure what a stengah was, Vince opted for gin and tonic.

When they had recovered their equanimity, Wilhelmina sat back on the settee and Vince moved to sit across from her. 'No, no,' she said and patted the cushion beside her, 'Please sit here so that we can talk more comfortably.' He complied with mixed feelings. Some alchemy had transformed his hostess from a lovely and likeable older woman. She had become ageless: the beautiful and desirable goddess of an erotic cult. Pulse racing, he was afraid of again doing or saying something incredibly clumsy.

While they sipped their drinks, Wilhelmina eyed him worriedly. 'I hope that you are not unwell again. It must have been upsetting to be disturbed by that pig this afternoon – thank you for helping me.'

'No – no, I'm fine – just pleased I could help.' He cocked his head. 'I hope your cheek's better; most of the redness has gone anyway.' As she raised a hand to her cheek he rushed on. 'Who is this Cunningham character anyway? Has he been around here long?'

Wilhelmina wrinkled her nose as though at an unpleasant smell. 'The pig was coming here nearly three years ago.' She nodded. 'Yes, it was seven or eight months before poor Charles was killed. The plantation owner died when his car overturned a year before and Cunningham' – she spat the name – 'was hired by his widow as manager. By six months he was in the main house and master of the estate. The poor woman often wore bruises when she appeared in public afterwards, but now inside the house she stays.'

She shook her head. 'He is completely a swine. Once I heard him boast of how he treated the women – young girls even – on the estate. That same night – at the club it was – he told me he wanted me to… well, I slapped his face in front of everybody. He left before Charles returned or he would have been beaten.'

Their glasses were empty and as Wilhelmina replenished them, Vince asked casually, 'His name is Derek, isn't it?'

She looked surprised. 'Yes, it is. How did you know?'

'Well, it's a long story, but if I'd known who he was this afternoon, I'd have killed him.'

Her hand went to her mouth. 'Oh – he has hurt someone you love? Yes? Do you want to tell me about it?'

Surprised to find that he did, Vince told her of his romance with Audrey and their plans – destroyed by Danty's assault – and her subsequent coma. He omitted much from Audrey's letter, saying only that she had been brutally attacked years before and left by the roadside, and that he blamed Cunningham for betraying her – and possibly worse.

Wilhelmina pressed his hand and left for a minute. She returned to whisper that dinner was delayed – and Vince realised that he had been weeping. She soothed him, whispering words of comfort, and he knew a sense of peace he had not enjoyed since he was a little boy in his mother's arms.

When they had both recovered – for she had wept in sympathy for Audrey and the plight in which her coma had left them both – they rinsed their faces and Wilhelmina served dinner. She had sent Falidah home to her family. Although the food, which had been kept hot, was a little overcooked neither of them really cared.

She gave Vince a bottle of white wine to open for a course of fish in coconut sauce, later insisting that they must have claret with the beef. Unused to wine, Vince quickly felt unsteady. Noticing for the first time a wall-hanging that depicted the snarling head of a tiger over two crossed rifles, he nodded at it curiously. 'Is that the emblem of your husband's old regiment: 17th Punjabi Rifles?'

He realised his error when Wilhelmina stopped chewing and stared at him silently. After a few seconds, she resumed, swallowed and asked him directly: 'How did you know that Charles's regiment was the Punjabi Rifles? To you I said nothing of his military background. How could you have known that?'

To Vince's relief there was nothing accusatory in her tone; she simply wanted a solution to what seemed an impossibility. He thought to disclose what Jai Ram had told him, but recklessly decided to tell her of Charles' continued existence and the enduring nature of his love. How could he do this? He had to ask her to suspend her belief in the immutability of the world as it was thought to be. He took a swallow of wine, wiped his lips on the linen napkin and stared at his plate. When he looked up again she still stared, lips apart and trembling slightly as she waited for her answer.

'Well… it's a long and improbable story,' he began slowly, 'but it's only fair that you should hear it, even though it's pretty hard to believe. Maybe we should finish dinner first?'

She pushed her plate away and stood. 'No, no, I've eaten enough, I must hear now!' She paused, and her voice softened. 'But please, you must finish your meal.'

Vince shook his head, smiled and stood also. She picked up the wine bottle and her glass, to lead the way into the other room. He followed with his own glass, thinking, Oh hell – my big mouth – yeah, we might need the glasses. A few minutes ago we were both half-cut. Now we're as sober as a bench-full of judges.

This time she sat in the chair and waved him to the settee, replenished their glasses and sat back, silent and expectant.

chapter sixteen

Vince looked up from his wine glass and leaned forward. 'Did you like fairy tales when you were little?' Her eyes widened as she nodded, so he went on. 'Children love fairy stories because they're full of weird creatures and events that are thought to be impossible. They believe in them, because they haven't learned otherwise. Did you dream about beautiful princesses, dragons, witches and handsome princes?' Again she nodded with a small smile of memory.

'Then would you try to be that little girl again and attempt to believe that not everything can be explained by what we think of as common sense? I've had to do that, because otherwise I'd know I was crazy. Why not, anyway? People of many religions accept the incredible as everyday articles of faith.'

Wilhelmina studied Vince's face thoughtfully, then nodded twice.

He began his story. 'Once upon a time there lived beside a lake, on the edge of a great forest, a handsome Prince and his incredibly beautiful Princess. They both wanted very much to have a baby. A child to be their own little Prince or Princess, but try as they might to make one, it never happened. They told each other, "Never mind, we are together and very much in love" and they were still very happy.'

He glanced up; she was listening intently. A tear running down her cheek made him wince, but he continued. 'Sadly, a band of outlaws lived in the forest. They did many bad things, but perhaps the worst was when they stole the Prince from his adored Princess: they trapped him on a forest trail and killed him.

'But it so happened that a wise wizard was passing by. He wanted to save the soul of the Prince, but where could he put it?' Vince heard subdued sobbing, but ignored it; if he looked up he knew he might be unable to continue. 'Wizards have very large souls and he hadn't room for another. Then a tiger passed by. Tigers have pretty small souls, so there was plenty of room for the Prince's. Ink, pink as fast as a wink, the Wizard slipped the Prince's soul into the tiger and went on his way, content that he had done a good deed.

'But had he? The tiger was used to having total rule over her own body. Oh yes, it was a she tiger and not very happy about sharing her privacy with a trespasser. Our Prince could only have control when she was sleeping, or when he could persuade her to do what he wanted. He'd whisper that wild pig, the tiger's favourite prey, were plentiful in the jungle near the lake. In this way the Prince encouraged the tiger to travel back to his home by the lake on the edge of the forest, so that he would watch for his beloved.

'He could only watch her from afar. If he was too close, the tiger might waken and kill the Princess, so he could speak to her only in her dreams. Hopefully, he watched and waited, and hoped that his beloved would find another Prince and have the baby that they had sought together.

'He no longer felt the natural jealousy of a man; he was a man no longer. Now he was a human spirit in the body of a female tiger, who only wanted his beloved Princess be happy.' Vince stopped speaking and stared into his glass again for a minute.

'Of course, the story isn't over yet. The beautiful Princess has still to find another Prince and live happily ever after with him and their child.' He took another sip of wine and looked up. Wilhelmina's eyes were red and her cheeks were marked by tears drying in the draught from the overhead fan, but she was under control.

'Thank you for the fairy story; it is a nice story perhaps, but only a story. Why would I believe it?' She paused and her voice quavered as her bottom lip began to tremble again. 'Please make me believe it! I am needing something to believe in.'

He told her about his first dream of the tiger, how he had found the pug marks next morning. The way in which Abu and Andor had also spoken in his brain; the subsequent meetings with the tiger; Charles and what had been said between them.

Vince left the room and returned with a dampened towel and wiped away smudged lipstick and eye shadow that had mixed with her tears. She smiled. 'It is being my turn to thank you for being nice and for your stories, too. I think I am believing a little.' She shuddered slightly. 'It is not being easy, would you help me a little more?'

He nodded.

'Please try to tell me exactly what Charles said the last time you spoke to him.'

Vince thought. 'He said that you were married in Brisbane and that you only had six months together before he was sent back here to Malaya with Force 136 and that he pined for you until the end of the war.' He searched his memory and said gently, 'He told me that you both wanted children and that...' his voice faltered and he felt himself blushing.

She touched the back of his hand and whispered, 'Please go on.'

'Aw... he said that you were never separated again, that the... er, the physical side of marriage was important to you both and now that he can't be with you or feel jealousy he wants you to find someone else,' he finished in a rush.

Then he had a flash of memory, and affected Charles's voice: 'Bloody hell! There were enough randy buggers wanting to make off with her when I was still around. Good-looking woman and faithful too, bet that she's frozen them all off out of some misguided sense of duty.'

Wilhelmina laughed through her tears. 'Yes, yes, that's more like my Charles! Good-looking woman,' she mimicked, 'incredibly beautiful Princess! Sometimes, Mr Tanner, I am thinking you are being a big fibber – but also being very nice, and I think now I am really believing.'

Vince felt emotionally drained. He said on a sudden impulse, 'I've had too much wine and I need some fresh air to clear my head. Could I borrow a flashlight?'

After fetching a torch, Wilhelmina asked in a small voice, 'Can I be coming with you? I am needing fresh air also.' They passed through the French doors and strolled, arm in arm, towards the processing depot. Beneath the trees was the soft velvety blackness of night and the warm air was smooth on their skin. He had shone the torchlight on the path for fear of snakes, but outside the empty and unlit depot he flicked it off. They stood listening to the night sounds, watching fireflies cavort in the silent darkness.

She squeezed closer to him and he put his arm protectively around her shoulders. 'You know,' he said, 'I really like fireflies. We don't have them in New Zealand, so we weren't used to them when we arrived here. Our last exercise, during orientation training, was set up as a real jungle operation. I was a brand new NCO in charge of a section and not too confident. At stand-to, the men were positioned and I'd turned away from checking the bren-gun crew when I heard the snick-snack of the weapon being cocked.

'Alarmed, I turned back hissing, "Hold fire!" The gunner stuttered, "T...t...tiger." Then I saw it coming right for us. Two bright eyes shining through the darkening shadows. My hair stood on end and I cocked my own weapon. Then they turned and went – in different directions. Sometimes, I've been night sentry and seen a light, gliding along the path towards me like a lit cigarette – look – like that one th –'

A firm resonant voice came from the darkness. 'Goodnight Mem, goodnight Sahib, it is being a fine night for a stroll, isn't it?'

They grabbed each other in shock, but as they caught the scent of burning tobacco Wilhelmina recovered quickly. 'Goodnight Guptal Singh.' She did not move away. 'Our night watchman,' she whispered. 'He gave me a big fright. Please hold me a minute longer.' It was easy to comply. Enjoying the steady thump of her heart against his chest and her warm breath on his neck, he heard a throaty laugh. 'I think it's well I didn't do what was in my mind while you talked about fireflies.' Warm lips and a darting tongue touched his for a second, and she had slipped away into the warm darkness.

'Willie – Wilhelmina, wait,' he called after her. But she had disappeared into the night. Vince snapped the torch on, but caught only a glimpse of a figure between the pool and the house, moving towards the lakefront. When he caught up with her she stood by the pier gazing at the still, silvery surface of the water.

A sliver of moon provided faint radiance and Vince's breath caught at the thought that it must have been four weeks since he had arrived at Muda's ladang. He stood beside Wilhelmina and wondered what she was thinking. Why had she run away and left him.

A warm hand crept into his and she whispered. 'I am sorry I ran off just now. Very confused, I am – there's so much to be confused about.'

He could only agree.

The house was indistinct in the moonlight. 'Which is your room?' he whispered. She pointed to moonlight reflected on glass and he realised that it must be on the other side of the bathroom from his own.

'Why? ' Her tone was arch. 'Are you wanting to serenade me?'

Standing back, he spread his arms, put his head back and sang tunelessly, 'I am the Sheik of Arabee…'

A small hand clapped over his mouth and she whispered through her laughter, 'Oh you lovely fool, you mustn't wake everybody.'

'Okay,' he whispered back lightly, 'I'll finish it later, after you're in bed.'

'Shh – that should be all right – as long as nobody else hears you.'

They walked back to the house, once more arm-in-arm as he wondered, now what on Earth did that mean?

In the living room she rummaged in a dresser, emerging triumphantly with a bottle of cognac. 'This has been a much unusual day. We must be having a nightcap and go to bed soon.' Smiling, she handed Vince a generous measure. 'Outside, you called me Willie. No, no, it is nice, it was what Charles always called me and now you must.' She raised her glass. 'To the mysteries you have revealed to me and the others that we will open for each other.'

They took swallows of the delicious spirit and leaned against each other as it traced lines of fire down their throats. She took his hand, saying, 'bring your glass.' Still holding hers, she stared into his eyes and kissed him firmly on the lips. 'Please,' she whispered, 'please will you make for me a baby?'

As Vince choked, good brandy ran down his chin. His heart stumbled; he choked and swallowed. 'But – but, I can't,' he stuttered feebly. 'Audrey…'

'I am needing a baby now. Later you can make for Audrey a baby. Right now, Audrey isn't needing a baby.' She led him from the room, the brandy and his own throbbing pulses convincing him that she had constructed a very compelling argument.

It was almost daylight when Vince woke sprawled across the bed, his head nestling between Willie's breasts, one hand tucked behind her neck and the other on her hip. Filled with bliss and unwilling to open his eyes in case it was a dream, he felt wonderfully content; a little boy again, secure and loved.

Later, Willie was contrite as they talked. 'I should not have brought you to my bed, you are unhappy and feel unfaithful to Audrey. I don't think you are,' she touched him gently, 'from what you said, she wanted any understanding with her to be in abeyance until you had read her letter.'

'Ohhh, mmmm.'

'Oh, sorry darling, I forgot I was doing that.' She put her hands behind her head, causing him further palpitations. 'I know you love her and feel responsible for her, otherwise I wouldn't let you leave here.'

'Oh Willie! If I hadn't met Audrey and fallen for her, your staff would have to drive me away with cudgels to get rid of me.' His voice was muffled against her breastbone, but she heard and seemed content.

A tap sounded on the door.

'Oh God, Falidah!'

She bustled in with a merry, 'selemat pagi Puan, selemat pagi Tuan,' put coffee cups on bedside tables and drew the curtains. Sheepishly, Vince lifted his head in time to catch a roguish wink and a bland smile as she calmly inquired if they would like breakfast in bed.

When she had gone, Willie giggled. 'Heavens, darling, I think she is approving of what we do!'

Their strange affair continued in the pattern established on that night. Each evening they talked over drinks and dinner and went early to bed. Willie was a skilled and considerate lover. At first Vince had a sense of learning dancing from an accomplished artiste: one accustomed to performing with a single partner. Slowly he learned the moves and their rhythms merged as she taught him an entirely new choreography of lovemaking.

They did not speak of love or commitment, but shared a tacit understanding that the sole purpose of their union was to provide Willie with a child. Yet they addressed each other with endearments and slept locked in each other's arms. One thing did trouble Vince: he had discovered an unwillingness to surrender paternal rights to a child as yet unconceived.

A daily pattern developed. Falidah served them breakfast together, then Willie would work in the office attached to the processing factory. After lunch they would take a siesta and Vince would pursue his vastly enjoyable duties in search of procreation. Once, when they had just made love, Vince, who should have been relaxed and drowsy, felt unaccountably unhappy.

Discerning that something was wrong, Willie raised herself on one elbow and peered at him closely.

'What is it, dear lover, why are you being sad? Have I done something bad?'

He shook his head vehemently. 'No, Willie. No it's me. I'm all mixed up. These few days I've been happier than I can believe. It's a terrific compliment that you want to have a baby with me.' Vince struggled for words. 'It's just that I'm beginning to realise what a betrayal it'll be, to walk away from my own child.' His voice became bitter with self-condemnation. 'I love Audrey and have a responsibility for her – my choice. Yet, here I am in bed with you and dreading the thought of leaving you. I'm full of betrayals and terribly confused.'

'Oh, Vince,' Willie said, her voice low. 'You're not a person who'd mean to betray anyone – that's what matters. You're like Charles was. We're all human and we all can be tempted. Charles and I were always faithful because we didn't play with fate. We didn't give each other – or ourselves – a chance to be unfaithful.' She smiled gently. 'I know that you love Audrey – it's just that circumstances are, um, a little unusual.

'You are not betraying or deserting your child and I'll make sure that he, or she, never thinks that is so.' Willie sat fully upright. 'This is something I must be showing you.' She cupped her breasts and showed Vince slightly swollen and inflamed aureoles around each nipple. When he exclaimed with concern, she smiled. 'It is very good, darling – I think is meaning you have made for me a baby. Again you are being my hero.'

Thursday lunch was interrupted by a loud ringing: brrrr, brrrr, brr. They sat upright. Willie cried, 'Good heavens, darling, the phone – two longs, one short: it's us,' and she ran from the room. It was an old-fashioned telephone with a little handle on the side that one cranked to reach an operator. It hung on the wall just outside the kitchen, opposite the dining room, so Vince could hear Wilhelmina's voice quite clearly.

'Good, well done, Mohammed… Really! Well I'm pleased you got through in the end… Oh, finished. When? Friday? That's tomorrow… are you sure there's nothing further…?' She sounded resigned. 'All right, mid-morning then, and thank you again for going to the telephone company. One other thing, I might need you to return to KK as soon as the boat can be re-loaded. Goodbye, Mohammed.'

Willie returned with a face like an alabaster sculpture. She came to stand behind Vince's chair and rested her hands on his shoulders; her voice was troubled, but controlled. 'That was the boatman – Mohammed. When he knew that the launch would soon be ready, he tried to phone here but couldn't get through, so he went to the phone company.' Her voice rose. 'Our line was *accidentally* cut on the Cunningham property. I shall insist that they give us a completely separate line; this harassment cannot continue!'

Her fingers dug into his shoulders, 'Oh Vince, he will return tomorrow morning. You must go and I am not ready for that.' She bent to kiss his neck, spilling a veil of platinum hair over his face and enclosing him in a sweetly perfumed tent. He felt wetness on his neck and her voice became muffled, 'Please darling, please come and hold me.'

Their tender and protracted good-byes began. When Willie insisted on wine for a farewell dinner, they became maudlin. Vince wrote down his postal address in Auckland as well as his army one and Willie ensured that he had the number of her post office box in Kuala Kangsar. They were careful to avoid promises, other than to keep in touch. So much was beyond their control. Both felt terrible; neither was ready to be parted.

* * *

The launch that Mohammed berthed at the pier, promptly at ten the next morning, had the air of an elderly dowager. She bore her years with dignity, as though determined to set the world a good example. About thirty feet long, with a beam of twelve feet, she had a small forward deck aft of the helm – a roofed area with seats for half-a-dozen passengers and rolled tarpaulins to drop in bad weather. The rear deck was clear, intended for carrying cargo, and the stern bulwarks were removed to enable planks to be laid for loading and unloading. She was painted white with varnished teak rails and the name on the bow read: HRH *Wilhelmina*.

They had loaded the last of the latex sheets by 1300 hours and the *Wilhelmina* was ready to depart. The Singhs, together with Jai Ram, had shaken Vince's hand, Falidah had hugged him and he drew Willie towards the bow where they could speak privately. She handed him an envelope: 'This is for your CO. I thought that a letter from a Colonel's widow might do no harm. I was needing to explain how sick were you, and about telephone and boat so you couldn't return to your unit earlier. I've not mentioned more important things.'

Vince set his rifle aside to take her hands. 'I've left two gold bars under your pillow.'

Her eyes and mouth rounded as he squeezed her fingers. 'Okay, I know I forgot to mention that I had a run-in with some CTs; they had gold and I took some. Just don't tell anyone else. Anyway I've left a bar to be divided amongst the guys who found me in the bush and the other is a Christening present for our baby. Be discreet about cashing them, that's all.'

He started to turn away, and then turned back. 'Charles must have named the boat and he was right. You're a queen amongst women, and I'll never forget you.' With a quick squeeze, he kissed her cheek and stepped aboard. His eyes were too blurred to see where he was treading and he hoped he would not fall overboard.

chapter seventeen

Willie had introduced them with instructions to Mohammed to do as Vince asked. Vince now stowed his gear under the canopy and shouted. 'Okay, Skipper, cast off whenever you're ready.' They waved their farewells as the bow turned to the deeper water of the channel. It was a pleasant day. Light cloud broke the intensity of the sun and Vince idly watched a speedboat scrawl curves of white across the placid surface of the lake.

Except for Cunningham's, he had seen no leisure craft on the lake and as it circled nearer to the *Wilhelmina*, he became uneasy. Nervously, he checked that his rifle was cocked and a full magazine in place. When it drew closer Vince saw that it was red, and almost certainly Cunningham's. He hurried forward to alert Mohammed, who frowned and nodded at a shotgun on a rack beside the helm. As an afterthought Vince loosed the tarpaulins, leaving them to hang and conceal who was on board.

With a roar from its open throttle and a sheet of spray that temporarily blinded Mohammed, the powerboat shot across their bow. As it swung around the port side, Vince saw a man he did not recognise crouching in the stern. Vince assumed that Cunningham was at the wheel. As the craft crossed their stern the man stood up, clutching a Stirling SMC with its stock extended.

Raising it, he fired a burst at Vince, who automatically ducked, but the boat hit the *Wilhelmina's* wake and the whole 9mm salvo flew skyward.

Vince, who had pre-set his sights to three hundred yards, began firing two-round bursts: tap-tap, tap-tap. He aimed at head height where the man was standing so that as the boat drew away the trajectory would drop. He was rewarded when the man tumbled from sight. When the range became too great he hurried breathlessly to check on Mohammed, who was almost incandescent with fury. His pride and joy might be peppered with bullet holes. 'Crazy dacoits, they come back I fix good,' he yelled, waving his gun fiercely.

They did come back. Vince cursed as the apparently uninjured gunner loosed another burst as the red boat swung in a tight curve and sped away, leaving bullet-scarred woodwork. He checked his sights. A star in his pay-book declared him a marksman. So far he had fired eighteen shots, without evidence that he had hit anything except their boat. Also he was worried. They must have a plan that would make sense of their apparently pointless tactics.

He peered past Mohammed at the lake ahead. The channel seemed to swing in towards the bank on their port side, where a small promontory protruded into the lake. He hurried to indicate it to Mohammed. 'Might be man with a rifle,' he shouted over the sound of the engine, gesturing for their course to be altered away from the possible trap.

Mohammed shrugged. 'Sandbar – we stay in channel or go aground,' he yelled. 'Be like ducks on water – too late for outer channel.' Vince hurried to the stern and tried to drag out a stack of latex to shelter the helmsman. It was too cumbersome to move. Frustrated, he slashed the bindings with his machete and hauled several evil-smelling sheets forward to screen Mohammed from the shore.

Scrambling back to the stern he squeezed in between two of the stacks, rested the rifle on the top and watched the powerboat bearing down on them again.

He took it head on, leaving a pattern of holes in its Perspex windscreen. It lost power, skewed and wallowed in the water. Vince exulted. 'Got the bastard!' He turned to check the bank just in time. A series of reports, from a higher velocity weapon than the Stirling, made him cringe as rounds cracked overhead.

He held his fire, watching for a clue to the sniper's position, as they glided toward the point where he must be waiting. Patience was rewarded when a cautious head rose from behind a rock. Tap-tap, tap-tap; it disappeared in a cloud of rock fragments. A few more shots would get them out of sight behind the promontory. Then the newly-restored engine gave a series of bronchial coughs and stopped, leaving them to drift helplessly in the current. Vince grimly changed magazines.

While Mohammed struggled with the engine Vince watched in dismay as the motorboat again throbbed with power and headed for the shore. 'Bloody hell!' he shouted. 'I missed the bastard after all – only gave him a fright.' He watched helplessly, but his mind was working overtime: bloody Cunningham's realised the rifle would've been more use to him on the boat. He'll pick up his gunman, Vince thought, and what the hell can we do? With both weapons on their much faster boat, we're going to be in real strife. Even if Mohammed gets the motor working, they'll catch us on the river!

In a few seconds the point would hide them from view. Vince re-set his sights and aimed carefully. With the rifle, together with the SMC on the faster boat, we'll be dead. No chance the bastards would let us get to KK alive. He bit his lip. I'll aim for the motor, he thought. If it's out of action they can't chase us; if we can get to the police in KK, they can sort the bastards out.

Vince groaned. The range must be nearly a mile by now and a sick feeling in his gut said he hadn't a chance in hell. The target looked tiny and the current was still carrying them away. He reset the sights again, controlled his breathing and squeezed the trigger tenderly, his attention concentrated amidships: tap-tap, tap-tap. As the current carried them around the bend, a figure scrambled over the stern of the motorboat. Desperately, Vince squeezed off two final shots, tap-tap, cursed and prepared for the final onslaught.

Instead, the sky beyond the point lit with flame. A burst of energy echoed overhead as a pall of black smoke appeared above the headland. The sky filled with frightened birds and Mohammed peered from the engine hatch, his eyes round with awe. 'Sahib, did you do that?'

* * *

After a few more tries and much to Vince's relief, the engine turned over, coughed twice and settled to a steady thump. He knew nothing about diesel engines, but had been with patrols deployed by boats along the river and the prospect of trying to navigate the torrent while Mohammed worked on the engine terrified him.

Where the lake ended, the current became stronger as it swept them into the swirling waters and shoals of the Sungei Perak. Vince went forward to congratulate Mohammed on his mechanical skills and mentioned his earlier fears. Mohammed looked shocked, laughed and nudged Vince with his elbow.

'No Sahib, no! In river we tie up to bank for repairs. If Sahib steers, Mohammed jump overboard.' Manoeuvring the vessel through the current, alert for rocks and submerged logs, he became thoughtful. 'What we tell mata-mata? They be at wharf maybe.'

Bloody hell, he's right, Vince thought. The gunshots, the noise and smoke from the explosion must have been heard for miles. The main road, to Grik and Baling, ran along the other shore and somebody was bound to have called the cops. 'We'll just tell them the truth. Someone in a strange motor boat shot at us. Another madman fired at us from the shore and I shot back. When we were out of sight there was an explosion and we hurried to KK to tell the police.'

Mohammed was dubious. 'We never see boat before?' Vince carefully explained the distinction between that and not recognising it. He also pointed out the needlessness of mentioning that it probably belonged to a neighbour of Mrs Cuthbert. Mohammed shrugged. 'Okay, good not embarrass Memsahib; bad mans anyway,' he said and turned his attention to steering the vessel through the maze of rocks and shoals.

Thoughtfully, Vince returned to where he had left his gear. He emptied his pack and reached for the rag-wrapped ingots at the bottom. Unwilling to surrender them, he had planned to conceal them somewhere between Kuala Kangsar and Taiping. If the police were waiting at the wharf, he would not have that opportunity. He emptied the pouches on his belt, to divide the remaining bars between them. Grimacing at their weight, he made his way forward to the helm and stood beside Mohammed to watch the river ahead.

About a third of the distance between the outfall from the lake and KK, where the Sungei Temor entered from the east to pour its waters into the Perak, the river formed a dog leg. The Perak changed course, turning sharply northwest for a couple of miles before swinging back to the south. Where the Temor widened at its mouth, flood-borne debris formed a delta and created a lagoon beside the bank. The platoon had disembarked there on a previous operation and it was where Vince had decided to conceal the remaining gold.

The moment he spotted the bend, Vince gave a loud groan and clapped his hand to his belly. He snatched up a newspaper that was wedged under a seat and groaned again. Shifting from foot to foot, he tapped Mohammed on the arm and gestured urgently towards the bank.

Mohammed took in the look of anguish, the newspaper in Vince's hand, the need for haste written on his face and swung the launch towards the shore. The moment it touched, Vince was off the stern, up the bank and, trying not to show he carried extra weight, out of Mohammed's sight. Behind some low bushes he found a large rock that he rolled aside and, pleased to make full use of the situation, used the paper for its advertised purpose.

As an artistic touch for the edification of the curious, he rolled the stone back in place leaving a corner of paper protruding and descended to the river to wash his hands. Ensuring that he was practically invisible from the boat, he scraped a hole in the mud and gravel beside a big rock, pushed in the bars and covered them with gravel and stones. A few stones in the pouches to replace the gold, and he reclaimed the rifle and returned to the boat. He gave Mohammed a smile of happy relief and when they were under way again, dropped the stones quietly overboard and replaced the empty magazines.

An hour later, as they passed under the road and rail bridges above KK, Vince glimpsed the Sultan's palace perched high on the hill above the south bank. The marble palace with its towers and golden domes together with the larger glowing dome and elegant minarets of the nearby mosque were like fabulous buildings from the *Arabian Nights*.

When Mohammed swung the boat in towards a low dock close to the main wharf, a blue police Land Rover was parked by the end of the pier. As the boat neared, two uniformed figures emerged to watch their arrival. While Mohammed swung the launch around to reverse into a mooring recess in the dock, Vince saw that the reception committee consisted of a Malay inspector and a young Chinese constable, both smartly uniformed in crisp light-blue short-sleeved shirts, dark blue shorts, long socks and shiny black boots.

Quickly, Vince jumped onto the dock, helped to tie up and, rifle in hand, pack slung over one shoulder, hurried towards the approaching mata-mata. He addressed the officer: 'I'm really pleased to see you, sir; we thought we would have to find the police station. We've been attacked by madmen in a boat – and somebody shot at us from the shore too.'

The inspector spoke good English, but needed a few seconds to digest the words. 'Are you Private Tanner of the New Zealand Regiment?' he asked politely. When Vince had identified himself, the inspector went on. 'There is being a number of people anxious for you. We having a call from Mrs Cuthbert at Chenderoh Plantation. On estate hear big explosion after you leave and she worry for you and her boatman.

'Your regiment alerted us some weeks ago that you were missing. I have been on telephone with your colonel. Someone from regimental police is coming to pick you up. First you must be coming to the station. We will be having statements from you and boatman about happenings at Lake Chenderoh.'

None of this was as Vince had planned. Cunningham's homicidal idiocy had thrown everything out of kilter. 'Thank you, sir, I wonder if Mrs Cuthbert could be contacted and told that we are both safe?' He glanced back. The constable was speaking to Mohammed while some helpers unloaded the cargo and stowed it in a decrepit-looking shed. 'I would also be grateful, sir, if you would contact the regiment again and ask that an intelligence officer and my company or platoon commander could come down also. I have information of military significance and I will need their clearance before informing the police.'

The inspector's eyebrows almost disappeared under the visor of his cap. He was unaccustomed to people of little importance establishing conditions before providing information. Only innate good manners prevented him from saying so. He grunted. 'At station we see. First make statements about shooting and explosion.'

At that moment the constable approached with Mohammed Das in tow and reported, 'The launch is secured, sir; the coolies will complete unloading and lock the godown.' Then he excitedly whispered something to the officer. Inaudible to Vince, this made the inspector frown.

Aha, he thought, Mohammed's enlarged on what I said, and he's seen the bullet holes too.

'At the station,' the inspector repeated firmly. 'Bring Private Tanner's gear, Constable.' Vince did not want to be separated from the items from the CT camp. 'Thank you, sir, but I am responsible for my gear; I'll carry it myself – unless I'm under arrest.'

Taken by surprise, the inspector glared. 'All right, but you are being under police control; your weapon must be unloaded.' Silently Vince removed the magazine, double cocked, picked up the ejected round, pressed it into the magazine and put it in his pack. Although not looking altogether happy, the inspector nodded and they all climbed into the vehicle.

At the station, Vince and Mohammed were interviewed separately. As his statement was being typed, Vince wondered if Mohammed had mentioned the comfort stop at the mouth of the Temor. He had not mentioned it in his own statement, simply sticking to the bare bones of what had occurred on the lake.

He paced around the interview room. A silent Malay constable watched him impassively from the doorway, while also keeping one eye on Vince's gear, which was nearby. Vince was jittery. How's Audrey, he was thinking; what's going to happen when someone from the regiment gets here? Will I be blamed for the deaths of Cunningham and his goons? I don't care if I am responsible; I'll be mightily pissed off if any of those bastards survived!

How will I explain getting lost? The trick will be to say as little as possible and not get confused. He was still pacing when the inspector returned with a constable carrying a couple of chairs.

The officer held some sheets of paper and handed one to Vince. 'Please read and sign if it agree your statement.' Vince read it, signed and returned it. As if for the first time, the inspector compared it with the other sheet. He looked up casually. 'Mr Das's statement is little bit different. Why you not mention stop by Sungei Temor?'

Vince contrived an embarrassed grin. 'Well, yeah sorry, I was feeling crook, you know, all the excitement I guess,' he looked at the floor. 'It was pretty urgent.'

The inspector raised his eyebrows again. 'Crook, what means crook'?

Vince rubbed his stomach. 'Sorry, Kiwi slang, it means ill.'

The policeman shrugged his shoulders, but nodded sympathetically. 'It must be upsetting to know you just kill people.'

Vince managed a look of horror. 'Do you think I really killed those guys?' The policeman shrugged again and, seemingly satisfied with the reply, left the room, to return a moment later with two newcomers.

* * *

Vince had the presence of mind to jump to attention when Major Bennett was first into the room. Lieutenant Tom Andrews, who was close behind, seemed genuinely delighted to see Vince and shook hands with enthusiasm. 'Gosh, Vince, it's really great to see you. We were afraid you'd disappeared for good.' He turned to the major, 'Isn't that right, sir?'

The major shook hands with rather less enthusiasm. Vince sensed that had he not returned, the loss might have proved endurable. 'Pleased you made it back, Private Tanner,' he said with patent insincerity. 'Now you'd better tell us how you got lost in the first place and why it took so long to get back.' Tom Andrews looked startled and opened his mouth as though to speak, then shut it again.

'Oh, yes sir', said Vince, 'I have a letter from the widow of a Colonel Cuthbert. Her workers found me ill in the jungle. It's addressed to the CO, but can I give it to you?'

'Thank you, Tanner,' the major said with heavy irony, 'I am after all your CO. Now, do you think we could get on with this?'

'Yes sir, excuse me sir,' Vince turned to the inspector. 'Were you able to reach Mrs Cuthbert, sir?'

'Well yes, she was being very worried for you and for Mr Das. She was saying what a fine soldier you have being, struggling through the ulu all alone.' He gave the major a reproachful look. 'And how sick you have being when her men have founded you. She ask to wish you much good fortune.'

For the next hour Vince recounted a suitably edited account of his recent activities. When he had finished, the major looked distinctly unimpressed, but the inspector seemed at least entertained.

Tom Andrews looked thoughtful. 'Vince, this CT camp you mentioned. Can we go back to that for a minute. Would that have been about a fortnight after you got lost?'

'I think so, sir, but I was pretty confused. I'd hurt my head and lost track of the days.'

Tom turned urgently to the major. 'Sir, do you recall a report about three weeks ago? Somewhere between the Sungei Puian and Anak Reng – a Brit chopper pilot saw an explosion in the jungle?'

'Well… yes, I do of course, Mr Andrews, but you're not seriously suggesting that…' He looked at Vince in disbelief. 'No – dammit – we need a detailed map of the area.' He looked searchingly at Vince. 'As I recall, a squad of Gurkhas went in. They found a burnt-out CT camp and some bodies in a cellar of some sort. It was two days before they got there and by that time the corpses were all a bit nasty.'

'That's right, sir', Vince chipped in. 'Five bodies in the bunker and a sentry, on the edge of a clearing a couple of hundred yards downstream. All the weapons were there with their firing mechanisms removed.' He added helpfully, 'I didn't have time to do much with his rifle, the sentry's I mean. I just threw the bolt and magazine into the bushes with the rifle.'

They stared at him as though he might suddenly do something alarming. The major was first to break the silence. 'I suppose you removed all these weapon parts and hid them somewhere?' His tone was caustic, but his face was reddening.

'Oh no, sir. Excuse me,' Vince said as he rose and crossed to his pack. He suddenly felt in control. The others seemed to be holding their breath. They aren't sure whether I'm crazy or not, he thought. He resisted a mad impulse to take out the last grenade and juggle with it. Instead, he took out the weapon parts and documents he had brought from the bunker, walked back and clunked them onto the table along with the communist banner he had taken off the pole. 'I brought them with me. Sorry,' he lied, 'I should have shown you these earlier, I forgot. The papers were in the bunker.' My God, I'm babbling he thought, but he could not stop. 'I only took the ones that weren't covered with blood and guts,' he explained conversationally, 'before we set fire to everything.'

There was a long silence as they continued to stare at him.

The inspector spoke first. 'You are saying "we". Are you meaning there were other peoples helping you?' He hesitated and asked gently: 'Who are being these other peoples and from where did they come?'

Vince stared thoughtfully at the wall. 'Oh yes, there were others: there was Batu.' He held up four fingers, ticking them off one by one. 'Angah, Andor and Amang. Amang was there already. I'm not sure where the others came from – I didn't see them until after I'd been hit in the head again,' he added truthfully. 'But Andor and Amang were somewhere else when we did the burning.' He thought of the gold dumped in the pool and grinned vaguely. 'Batu and Angah were very helpful though.'

The others looked increasingly uncomfortable. They seemed to have arrived at an unspoken consensus: Vince had been through a great deal and should be 'looked after'. It was eventually agreed that the three New Zealanders would return to Taiping, while the papers would be left with the inspector to be evaluated by Special Branch. Subject to a medical clearance, Vince would be available for future questioning as required. They exchanged meaningful looks that were not lost on Vince, who fought to repress a smirk as he thought of mentioning his conversations with the tiger.

The Inspector expected a report some time the following day from a police party, dispatched to investigate the disturbances at the lake. He also told Vince that Mohammed would be released the following da on Mrs Cuthbert's surety and would return to the estate with the *Wilhelmina*. At the inspector's request the major agreed to the police temporarily retaining Vince's rifle for forensic testing. Vince thought that so far things had gone as well as could be expected. Quiet words were exchanged between the inspector and the major and Vince was taken to a side room. There a Malay constable inked his finger pads and, careful not to leave smudges, rolled them upon a prepared piece of cardboard. Vince returned wiping the ink from his fingers and was taken to the waiting Land Rover.

Tom Andrews drove back to Taiping; while he and the major talked quietly in the front seat, Vince sat in the back. Night had stolen away everything of visual interest and, unable to hear the conversation in front, he soon drifted into sleep. He did not wake until the vehicle stopped at the camp entrance.

Tom drove directly to Company HQ, where Vince's gear would be stored overnight. He inspected Vince appraisingly. 'You're in bloody good nick after all that time in the bush without re-supply. Who patched your jgs?' Vince explained about Falidah and Tom responded by peering ostentatiously at his throat. 'Hmmm, no visible scars anyway!'

Major Bennett, whose mood had mellowed during the drive back, studiously ignored this conversation. 'Tom,' he said, 'I think there's some mail here for Tanner. See if you can find it, would you?' To Vince he said, 'That doctor from the Cameron Highlands was trying to get hold of you – Captain Baxter, isn't it? He wants you to get in touch with him.' He shook his head in wonder. 'The Captain seemed quite perturbed to hear that you were missing. Oh, as were we all of course. Um… your next of kin haven't been told you were missing. We decided to wait until – well, until all possibilities had been explored, but Army HQ were going to send someone around next week if – well – just as well we held back, eh?' Sounding rather uneasy, he added, 'We'd better have the MO look at you tomorrow. Maybe he could have a word with Dr Baxter?'

As he spoke, cold reality clutched Vince's guts in icy fingers. Audrey, he was thinking: something's gone wrong. She's not better; Abu and Charles both lied to me.

Tom was standing in front of him with a handful of letters, staring. 'You've gone as white as a sheet. Are you okay?' He stepped to the water cooler and handed Vince a cup of water.

Vince's throat had suddenly gone dry; he gulped the water gratefully. 'I – I – is there a phone I could use… Please?' The two officers looked at one another perplexedly. 'Well,' said the major, 'if it's so urgent I suppose you could use the one on the desk here… or the one in my office… '

Tom Andrews looked suddenly understanding. 'Look, you'll be billeted in the officers' quarters until you've been fully debriefed. If you can wait until we're there you can talk privately before we get some dinner.'

On the short drive to the Junior Officers' Wing, Tom spoke over his shoulder. 'There's an empty room near mine that should be okay. I've got some spare gear that should fit near enough. What size shoes do you wear? Nines? No problem.'

On arrival, the major went to speak to the sergeant in charge of the quarters, leaving Tom to show Vince where he would sleep. It was tiny, with a narrow bed, bedside table, a wardrobe, a small desk and chair and one comfortable chair. On the table was a telephone towards which the lieutenant gestured. 'There you go. Dial nine for an outside line. There's a directory on the desk. I'll be back in ten minutes with some gear for you to try on and then we can get some dinner.'

Fingers trembling, Vince took the card that Dr Baxter had given him more than two months earlier from his shirt pocket, where he had kept it in the plastic envelope with his identity card. Although the night was moist and warm, his skin felt cold as he dialled nine, waited for a tone and dialled the number on the card. The phone rang, but nobody picked it up. After six rings there was a pause; he was about to hang up when it rang again. Nervously he tried to stop his feet from shuffling about on the linoleum floor.

There was a click. A crisp female voice spoke cheerfully. 'Nurse Thompson, Ward Four. Yes?' Vince was taken aback for a moment. 'Oh, I… I'm sorry, I was trying to contact Dr Baxter. I thought I was ringing his office.'

'I'm afraid he's not here. When he's away, his phone rings up here on the ward. Would you like to leave a message?' Vince's spirits sank even further.

'Thanks, would you tell him that Vince Tanner ra –'

'Vince! Of course I will. This is Denise – Denise Thompson. D'you remember me – we heard that you were missing. Are you all right?' Vince thumbed rapidly through his memory. 'Denise, small, curly fair hair?'

'Vividly,' he lied. 'Do you still have those lovely blonde curls?'

She laughed. 'Don't you flirt with me, you lecher, or I'll have Audrey scratching my eyes out… Wait, there's the doctor, I'll get him for you.'

Moments later the familiar voice was in his ear, filled with concern. 'Vince! Delighted you're back. Are you all right?'

'I'm fine, but Audrey – how's Audrey – is she all right?' Even to himself his voice sounded thin and edgy while his knees trembled with nervousness.

'All right? She's fantastic! She opened her eyes a fortnight ago, looked around and started mumbling. She kept on mumbling until Sonya – you'll remember Sister Bretucci? She realised that Audrey was trying to say "where's Vince?". She hasn't changed her tune since. That tape we'd been playing to her made her think you were here all the time. She understands that you couldn't stay, but she's really anxious to see you again.' Tom put his head around the door, raised his eyebrows at Vince's broad grin, dropped some clothes on the bed and withdrew. 'So she's completely better. Is she out of bed, when can I see her?'

The doctor gave a pleased laugh. 'Well, to answer in order. I believe so; yes, and as soon as you can get here. We were a little worried about some possible hallucinations, but I think they were just residue from dreams she'd had while in the coma.' He sighed. 'It was strange though. There were names – at least I think they were names – she would say in conjunction with yours. Let me see.' There was a short silence. 'Yes, I thought I'd written them down. Arboo, Andaw and Charles. She didn't seem to care much for something – or someone – called Arming. Hello, are you still there?'

Vince picked the phone up from the linoleum and grunted unintelligibly.

'Good. As for the other question: we've been exercising her manually and she was on a physiotherapy regime, being moved around in a wheel chair for a couple of hours each day and walking with assistance. Now she's walking on her own and taking solid food. How soon can you get here?'

Vince provided a rundown of the interest displayed by both police and military in his activities during recent weeks. He also hinted that he might be unable to leave Taiping and mentioned the major's remark about seeing the MO the following day.

'Look here,' said the doctor firmly. 'I'll get in touch and see if I can be in Taiping in time for your medical. The psychiatric as well as physical well-being of two of my patients have to be considered. I do understand the need for authorities to conduct their investigations, but I shall require a role in providing treatment as necessary.'

There was a long and awkward pause, while Vince assimilated what he had just heard. Did the doctor actually say that Audrey had memories that could only have come from spiritual encounters during her rescue from… what was it Charles said? From Sankal's left armpit – bloody hell, how'm I going to tell anybody that?

Doctor Baxter's voice intruded into his thoughts. 'Vince, are you still there? Good, there's something else I wanted to talk to you about, but I know Audrey wants to tell you herself. If I can arrange a telephone connection to her room, would you be able to speak to her tomorrow?'

Vince coughed and swallowed. Somehow he felt choked with emotion, elated, frightened and full of hope all at the same time. 'Yes, yes, thank you Doctor, I… I'm sorry, I think I'm feeling a bit odd. Yes, I do want to speak to Audrey and to see her as soon as I can. I'm fine, just a bit shaken up is all. I'd love to see you tomorrow, but I don't want to be a nuisan – All right, maybe tomorrow then.'

Tom Andrews reappeared as Vince was ringing off, bearing shoes and towels. 'C'mon, I'll show you the ablutions. When you've changed we'll get some dinner. I don't know about you, but I'm starving.'

Only a few officers were in the dining room – those who had been unable to dine at the regular time. Tom was as usual a pleasant and unpretentious companion, but Vince could not shake off the feeling that he himself should not be there. This was officer territory. He felt that the white-jacketed mess attendants who waited on them would agree.

The next day the MO, somewhat to Vince's surprise, came to his room after breakfast to examine him. He seemed mildly put out although not unduly concerned that Captain Baxter was including himself in Vince's care and would confer with him that afternoon. He asked questions, took notes and seemed particularly interested in the state of Vince's psyche. Preferring to deal with Dr Baxter, Vince, when asked if he was troubled by hallucinations, smiled blandly. 'Not really, sir, I quite enjoy them.' Captain Mulberry departed soon after.

He then underwent a two-hour debriefing by a pair of hard-nosed Special Branch sergeants. They were interested to know how he came to be in possession of the papers and weapon parts, but seemed unwilling to believe what they were told. They had seen the report from the Gurkha patrol that investigated the site and admitted it tallied with Vince's statement.

During a rest period after lunch there was a knock on the door and in response to Vince's call Dr Baxter entered. When they embraced, Vince was surprised at his depth of feeling for the gravelly-voiced devotee of single malt scotch who insisted on being called George.

George had hitched a ride on a Royal Navy chopper and needed to be back at the Taiping BMH by 1500 hours to catch a ride back to the Cameron Highlands. They had little more than an hour. Over Vince's objections, he was examined again, 'Just to confirm Captain Mulberry's findings. Other than the scar on your temple, there's no sign of any physical trauma that might account for the fever that laid you low. Anyway, it's gone now.

'You seem all clear, much as the Captain said and in pretty good shape considering your recent experiences. Now let's talk about these hallucinations. Dr Mulberry implied that you weren't very forthcoming on the subject.'

Vince looked at the door and chewed his lip. 'Yesterday, when I was interviewed at KK, there was a police stenographer present. I don't know how much he took down, but I've a feeling that before we have this talk, you might like to see the transcript.' He grinned, 'I wondered if I was hallucinating, but last night you gave me independent evidence that something else was happening, as I think you'll see.'

The doctor laughed. 'Stubborn young bugger, if I didn't need your help with a favourite patient, I'd recommend you for extra duties'. He glanced at his watch. 'I should have time to see if I can get a copy from the Colonel's office, I want to speak to him about taking over your treatment anyway – back in the Highlands.' He stood and shook hands in farewell. 'Any messages for Audrey?'

Vince turned pink and passed him an envelope. 'If you don't mind, sir… George.'

'Gladly lad, I'll try to get a phone set up for her tomorrow so you two can talk.'

Three further events occurred that afternoon. His barrack box, clothes and personal possessions were brought to his room; he received a message to report, dressed in Regimental Order, to the Colonel's Adjutant, at 1100 hours the next day and before dinner Tom Andrews dropped by to ask if he would like visitors.

'The whole Company wants to know what's going on. You were adrift for nearly six weeks and rumours are rife. One story reckons that you're being held in the cells for murder; in another it's mutiny.' Tom scratched his head. 'The best one is that you crossed the border and got into in a gun battle with the Thai police.'

'Did I rob any banks?' Vince asked wistfully. 'A little extra cash would be useful.'

Tom laughed. 'No, that's one they haven't thought of yet. What d'you want money for, anyway? You're in the army and you're not thinking of getting married or anything, are you?' Vince flushed, and Tom stared incredulously. 'My God, I believe you are. Is it this, what's-her-name, Fallydah, the bint that's been looking after you, eh?' He looked serious. 'Just don't rush into things, matey. Remember, you don't have to buy a brewery just because you like an occasional beer.

'Anyway,' Tom continued, 'some of your mates have been worrying about what's going on and they want to make sure you're not being stretched on a rack or worked over with hot irons. A few of them came to me to ask – I won't say demand – to see you. The major said it was okay and if you like I can bring them in after dinner.'

He hesitated, and then spoke carefully. 'I've told them and I've been instructed to tell you that the Official Secrets Act has been invoked. This means that you can't tell anyone about what happened after you got lost on patrol.' He shook his head irritably. 'You won't know about the flap going on in government and diplomatic circles. While we've been wasting our time swanning around in the boohai, some Federation ministers were organising secret talks with Chin Peng and his mates to try and negotiate a surrender of what's left of the insurgent forces across the border.'

He nodded at Vince. 'Seems they didn't expect some blood-crazed Kiwi squaddie to clean up a bunch of bandits still on Malayan territory. Now they're shit-scared that word'll reach the CT base in Thailand and their talks will be wrecked.' He spread his arms in frustration. 'That's the only reason you're holed up here instead of being in KL, having a bunch of gongs pinned on your shirt.'

He paced to the window and stared outside. 'You were in the KL parade to commemorate the end of the Emergency. Did you hear anything, in all those fancy speeches, about not shooting the sods if we came across them?' He did not wait for an answer. 'No, neither did I. Rules of engagement remain the same and they still issue us with things that go bang and kill people.' He turned and gave a sheepish grin. 'Sorry, I guess I'm pissed off because you're in my platoon and won't get the medal you deserve. Worse still – I won't get the promotion I deserve, because you're in my platoon!'

chapter eighteen

Tom left, saying he would stop by later and they would have dinner together. Vince sat in the easy chair and thought. He had been so concerned with the notion of using the encounter with the bandits to obscure the manner in which he had parted from the patrol that he had not thought the whole thing through. Bit bloody rude – last year they were hunting for guys to give gongs to. Now I've knocked off six of the bastards we're supposed to be after, he mused, and I can't tell a soul. Ah well, I met some interesting people and had the most exciting time of my life.

His mind returned to his bizarre experiences and his adopted family: Muda, Andor, and Amang. With a pang of guilt he remembered the strange sweetness of her scent in his nostrils. Of releasing her from the stake and the CT officer's obscene gesture before Vince shot him. He had a sudden thought: oh Christ, maybe I was too late; maybe she was raped and lied to Andor to make him feel better about leaving her alone. God! I could've made her pregnant too. I just can't believe how easily it happened with Willie.

That thought brought a memory of Wilhelmina lifting her breasts, delighted with her tender and swollen nipples, and provoked further redistribution of his blood supply. Oh my God, he thought uncomfortably. If I'm going to marry Audrey I must stop thinking about other women!

The phone rang. He hesitated and picked it up on the fourth ring. A voice whispered, 'How are you, my hero? I am wanting to know that you are safe and have spoken to your Colonel Rhumb. I have been telling him that you have done much fine things,' she giggled throatily, 'but not exactly all of the fine things.'

Then more seriously: 'I am really wanting to know that you are well and, ah – I'm wondering – Audrey, is she better?'

Vince passed on what he had heard from Dr Baxter. After a moment's silence, Willie murmured, 'I'm pleased for you both, please let me know if there is anything I can do.' Her voice lifted: 'I must tell you also that Charles or Charlene Tanner Cuthbert, will join me later in the year. I am very grateful my dear.' They bade each other affectionate good byes. Vince replaced the receiver and wondered if he were elated or upset by her news.

After dinner, Tom ushered in Barry Prendergast, Joe Savage and Mac Burrows. When the regulation hand shaking and shoulder slapping had been dispensed with, they stood about shuffling their feet for a few minutes. Like small boys visiting a sick friend, each managed to look simultaneously embarrassed, curious and concerned. Vince was pleased to see them, but knew that the world that they shared had changed forever, and he hoped that the same would not be true when he saw Audrey again.

Barry examined Vince's officer issue jgs critically. 'Jesus mate, you're all mockered up like a pox doctor's clerk. What've you been up to? And why are ya bunked up in officer's quarters?'

Desperate for a reply, Vince raised his eyebrows at Tom. 'Lake Chenderoh?'

Tom thought then nodded. 'Just remember, you guys – although this isn't covered by the secrecy order, it's still subject to a police investigation. Anything you hear from Vince and repeat outside this room could damage his chances if they decide to charge him. If you understand that, it's up to him.'

Impressed, they nodded their heads and Tom looked around. 'Okay, taihoa while I get some beers and another ashtray – won't be long.'

While he was gone Vince caught up on what had been happening during his own extended absence. Evil Eric Purcell had quit drinking and become a model soldier.

Joe shuddered. 'It's scary when they go like that. It might happen to any of us.' They all looked appalled. 'Major Heke's getting to be a nervous wreck, they reckon he's like a man waiting for a bomb to go off. And d'you know that Purcell hasn't been up on a charge since he got out of hospital?' As they discussed Short Storey's most recent peccadillo – a scheme for obtaining free samples from the ladies of the local horizontal dancing set – Tom returned with a tray of beer cans and ash trays.

Vince told them of the *Wilhelmina* being attacked by Cunningham and his cohorts. How they had tried to use the SMC and motorboat to drive them into an ambush close to the shore. Told of the repeated attacks, his friends were disgusted at Cunningham's incompetence.

'Silly pricks,' Mac grunted, 'they could've used their boat's superior speed and the rifle to drive you inshore and then shot the hell out of you at close range with the SMC.'

They all nodded, but Joe looked sceptical. 'Bloody hell, Vince, I thought you could shoot! How come you couldn't stop them with your SLR?' He frowned. 'They must have been within fifty yards at times and if you say your sights were set at three hundred, you must've at least been able to plug them by the time they passed that range.'

Stung, Vince defended his marksmanship. 'Aw, come on! It's not like on the firing range. Remember, both boats were moving and they're not stable shooting platforms anyway.'

Joe grinned and held up his hands in mock surrender as Barry broke in impatiently. 'Okay, you're caught in the inner channel. Even if you can keep the joker on the shore down until you get past, what's to stop them picking him up and having another go at you on the river with both weapons?'

'Yeah,' Vince nodded, 'I reckon that was their aim – and at that point the motor cut out and poor Mohammed's got his head in it and can't even use his shotgun. Anyway by the time we began to move around the bend, the range must have been about a mile. I knew I'd only have time for a few aimed shots and I felt pretty sick about our chances.'

He described those last desperate shots as the boat swung in the current, the subsequent flash and explosion. Joe broke the ensuing silence. 'Jeez, a mile eh? What a shot! Those silly pricks! It couldn't have just been petrol – the mad bastards must have had explosives and detonators on board.' He shook his head. 'Well, bugger me!'

The silence continued until Barry flapped his hand flirtatiously, 'That's very nice of you, Corporal, but I won't if you don't mind.' For a heartbeat, Joe stared at him incredulously, then grinned. 'Watch out, Private, I might have to make that an order,' and he threw Vince's pillow at Barry's head.

As the hilarity died away, Tom said, 'Okay, I bought the first round and Vince doesn't have any cash. Who's in the chair?'

With a lordly air, Barry dragged out some notes and handed them over. It was so unusual for him to have cash a week after payday that everyone stared. Barry looked smug: 'I played cards with Short and some of his mates in the four platoon basha last night. Silly bugger thinks he knows how to play poker, but he's always up and down like a whore's drawers telling everyone what to do.'

Joe grinned. 'Yeah, that's Short all right. The bugger's like a fart in a bottle.'

When Tom returned with the beers, Barry asked curiously, 'Who was this Cunningham joker, anyway? I can't make out why he'd want to get you. Who'd want to hijack a load of crude rubber? D'you reckon he was he after this Mohammed character?'

It was a question Vince did not want to answer, but he was surprised that nobody else had asked it. 'I think he was crazy. Mrs Cuthbert wouldn't have him on her property – I got the idea that he'd been making a nuisance of himself. Maybe the mad bastard thought I was cutting him out.' He laughed at the idea, and they laughed with him. Imagine a Colonel's wife taking a fancy to Vince? But Tom, instead of laughing, looked very thoughtful.

When they had gone, Vince opened the shutters wide to rid the room of cigarette smoke and beer fumes and stared into the night. I don't like to deceive friends, he said to himself, but what can you do? He prepared his regimental gear for his morning meeting with Colonel Rhumb and went to bed wondering when he could speak to Audrey.

At 1055 hours he presented himself to the colonel's adjutant at Battalion HQ. Captain Atlas, in defiance of his name, was a willowy, fair-haired young man who suffered from the unfortunate delusion that his character and physique were like those of a General Patton.

Received with a tirade of furious ranting, Vince maintained a morose silence. Making believe that he was in more congenial company, he repeated: 'Yes sir,' or 'No sir,' at appropriate intervals.

Then his attention was grabbed by a nasty smile and the words: '...fraudulently obtained leave and went off for a weekend with a nurse when you should have been training. Now you've gone skiving off in the jungle not to mention murderously assaulting civilians. What are you smirking at man, did I say something funny?'

'Certainly not, sir.' Vince replied, reminded of sweet, pleasantly plump and compliant Hine and two delightful nights away from Waiouru during winter exercises. How'd this twerp know about that anyway? 'Just recalling happy days training in Waiouru, sir.'

The intercom on the captain's deck gave a serendipitous buzz and emitted a tinny-sounding voice. The captain listened attentively. 'Yes, sir, certainly, sir, I'll bring him right in sir.' With a malicious smile, he looked up at Vince, whom he had kept standing at attention. 'The Colonel will see you now. Come with me.' He stood and turned towards a closed door. 'Walk this way,' he ordered over his shoulder. Vince felt himself to be subjected to unfair temptation. For one so slim, Atlas had an extremely ungainly walk.

Colonel Rhumb was behind his desk. Vince marched before him, halted, saluted smartly and stood to attention. The colonel stood and held out his hand for Vince to shake. 'Stand easy, Tanner, do please have a seat.' He turned to the adjutant, who gaped at the informality. 'Thank you, Captain, please don't let me keep you from your duties.' With a sigh, the outraged officer waddled from the room.

The colonel examined Vince silently for a long minute before he shook his head and spoke. 'You know, Tanner, running an infantry battalion is like running a fairly large business, the mission of which is homicide.'

Vince perked up; this sounded interesting.

The colonel continued. 'As in any large organisation, the executive officer gets to know some of his staff well and others less so. I've looked through your record recently – since you began attracting attention – and consulted some of my officers. You, at least, seem to have grasped what our corporate mission is about.'

He regarded his hands, which were clasped on the desk before him. 'Frankly, I'm puzzled. You have a good, but not outstanding, record. You chose to relinquish a lance-corporal's stripe and subsequent promotions.' He stared moodily out of the window. 'I've recently discovered that we may have handled that rather badly.' The colonel placed his hands flat on the desk and looked directly at Vince. 'Yet, to be honest, I also understand that you have got away with rather a lot since you enlisted. Yes?'

Vince hesitated, but the colonel waited for a reply. Vince sat forward with his hands on his knees. 'May I speak frankly, sir?' Taking a nod as assent, he drew a deep breath. 'After I joined up I learned that some officers in this battalion are rude, arrogant and incompetent idiots who should never have control over others. I'd be ashamed if I couldn't put something over such clowns.' He turned and looked pointedly at the adjoining door.

Colonel Rhumb sat upright while a red cloud of anger faded from his face. Relaxing after a moment, he exchanged it for a thin-lipped smile and tapped a folder in front of him. 'All right, point taken and although you've not been brought up on a charge since basic training, I'm beginning to understand why some people think you're a pain in the arse.'

He looked at his watch and Vince thought he was about to be dismissed. 'Now I want to hear everything that occurred from when you separated from your patrol, to when you reached KK.' He pressed a button. When the door opened to the obsequious Atlas, he said, 'Do you think you could organise coffee for Tanner and me, Captain? And some of those chocolate biscuits please.'

The captain threw a venomous glance at Vince and, with an air of injured subservience, withdrew. Vince was still arranging his thoughts when Atlas returned with a tray that he placed beside the Colonel, before leaving silently.

Colonel Rhumb poured coffee and gestured for Vince to help himself. 'Okay, fire away.'

For almost an hour Vince retold his story, pausing only to clarify details or answer questions. He edited much, but an increasing liking and respect for the CO made him avoid unnecessary lies.

When the intercom buzzed, the colonel leaned forward and growled: 'No interruptions, Atlas.' Moments later he buzzed Atlas back. 'Sorry, Captain, but please cancel anything you have down for me before 1300 hours and make it known that I'll be late for lunch.'

He walked over to the wall opposite the door and gazed at a large-scale map of the Malay Peninsula. 'Look. Come over here would you, Tanner?' He tapped the map with a well-manicured fingernail. 'Here, on the Puian, is where you were lost from your patrol. Then you popped up again here on Lake Chenderoh. You had no map or compass; you were by yourself and had only about seven days' rations. Yet you covered about a hundred and thirty miles. We know that in that sort of terrain we need to at least double the map distance, to allow for actual distances covered. Now what I need you to tell me is this...' He looked at the map again and shook his head. 'How the hell did you manage to average over four miles a day, feed yourself and still find time to clean up a CT platoon?'

Vince felt uncomfortable: 'I'm sorry, sir, I'm not sure what you are asking. Am I being accused of some sort of fraud? Ever since I got to Kuala Kangsar I've felt as though I've been under suspicion. Of what I don't know, because no one's told me...' Surprised by his own anger, he allowed his voice to taper away before he continued.

'No, it wasn't easy and most of the time I was scared out of my wits. I've never killed anyone before, but I did it as well as I could – the way I was trained to. I'd probably have detoured around the CT camp, but I was afraid that if I did, they'd pick up my trail and hunt me down. I'd most likely have died of fever in the jungle if Mrs Cuthbert's plantation workers hadn't found me.'

Ire thickened his voice, but he had to continue. 'Those mad bastards in the speedboat, who tried to kill Mohammed Das and me on the way to KK – people have implied it was my fault and that I might be charged with their deaths – if they're dead. I don't even know that. No one's bothered to tell me.'

When he had cooled down a little Vince was surprised to see Colonel Rhumb smiling – a little red-faced again, but smiling. 'Well,' he said, 'I'm beginning to understand Major Bennett's ambivalence concerning you – you don't accept perceived injustices lightly.'

As Vince was about to speak, the Colonel held up his hand. 'No, you've had your say and you're correct. We haven't kept you informed. I'll confess there was some doubt as to how you came to be missing. However, since your return all the evidence indicates that everything occurred exactly as you have described. We even had a second team go in by chopper. They located the other corpse – the sentry – exactly where you said. They also found his carbine, its bolt and the magazine, which had your fingerprints on it.

'There is no indication that you are in any way culpable for the deaths of your three assailants on the lake. Once again, your account of events and that of this Mohammed Das are substantiated by all the available evidence. As for your attackers…' He tapped one of the reports on the desk disdainfully.

'Sadly, one was a disgraced British ex-officer, who had been cashiered from a cavalry regiment. He was apparently born here, in Malacca, where his father was some sort of colonial official. The other two were troopers of the same regiment and had been imprisoned for a particularly brutal attack on a British nurse in Cyprus. The Malayan police are trying to find out how they were able to enter the Federation.'

Although his heart was filled with exultation, Vince felt the blood drain from his face.

Concerned, the Colonel crossed to the water cooler and returned with a waxed paper cup. 'Here, sorry – I didn't mean to bring it all up again.'

Vince nodded his thanks and lowered his face to conceal the delight in his eyes.

'The three bodies have been recovered, along with the wreckage of their boat. Forensic evidence shows that they actually carried plastic explosives and detonators together – a further indication that they were insane.' He nodded at Vince. 'We'll never know what set off the explosion but, if it was your bullet, you did the world a favour.'

He gave his watch another glance. 'This brings us to the crux of our problem. Under normal circumstances we would give you a medal for your actions in eliminating a CT camp and the regiment would bask in its share of the glory.

'The reality is, however, that although we know what happened, we have no witness who can make the necessary recommendation.' He drummed his fingers. 'I believe Mr Andrews has told you of the political difficulties that further complicate things?'

He smiled widely. 'A number of people, amongst them Lieutenant Andrews, Mrs Cuthbert and Captain Baxter, have hounded me to find some way of recognising your achievements. Um, I believe Captain Baxter has the solution. Mmm, if you were to be considering marriage – I only said, if – and the prospective bride were an officer – it would be extremely difficult unless you were one also…' He assumed an expression of concern. 'We don't mean to press you into marriage, but the Brigadier has seen my report and rang me this morning. He too thinks you should receive some recognition. If Tom Andrews' earlier recommendation had been accepted – and in retrospect it should have been – you would be attending an officer training course at Portsea by now. If we hadn't messed up your promotion to corporal you'd go home a temporary sergeant in a few months time, so there are some errors we can rectify.'

Feeling dazed, Vince stared at the colonel. He opened his mouth. 'But… sir.'

Again the Colonel held up his hand. 'I'm offering you a short-term commission as a first lieutenant. If you agree to sign on again, I'll want you to complete the course at Portsea and on completion keep the two pips, together with the accumulated seniority. We'd like to have you in our jungle-training wing.'

Vince replied quietly. 'Thank you, sir, but no thank you.' He turned and again looked at the adjoining door. 'If I can't require respect from officers like Captain Atlas, I would really rather remain a private.'

It was the colonel's turn to open and close his mouth in anger and astonishment. Then he placed his hands flat on the desk, put his head back and let out a loud bark of laughter.

The door opened and Captain Atlas poked a wary head into the room. 'What is it, sir?' He gave Vince an accusing glare. 'Is something wrong?'

'No, no', spluttered the CO, dabbing his eyes. 'G – glad you're here though.

Has a package arrived from the camp tailor? Good, that was quick work. Would you bring it in please?'

When the captain returned, the colonel looked solemn and waved him towards Vince. 'It's his.' Puzzled, the captain passed the large flat cardboard packet to the equally mystified Vince. 'Oh, Atlas,' said the Colonel, 'I'd like you to meet Captain Tanner. Captain Tanner is the most recent addition to our cadre of officers.'

As the mortified adjutant exited the office, Vince clutched the cardboard container on his lap, feeling equally upset. A familiar stirring in his gut told him that he had got himself into another uncomfortable situation. Colonel Rhumb walked around the desk with his hand outstretched and dazed, Vince rose to take it.

'Congratulations, Captain. Oh, the packet contains dress uniform and shirts. We had to guess at your sizes so they may need altering. Ah, yes – there are only two pips on the shoulders so the tailor will need to sew on another of those also.'

'But, sir,' Vince pleaded, 'I don't think I can do this. I've got no idea how to behave as an officer! I'll make a fool of myself.'

'For goodness sake, Tanner, you'll cope. Think of what you've dealt with in the last six weeks.' He lowered his voice confidentially. 'Anyway, considerations of ability don't inhibit some officers who, despite all evidence to the contrary, admit to no inadequacy. Why should they bother you?'

Again he glared at his watch. 'Now stop looking like a stunned mullet and pay attention; I must be out of here in twenty minutes.' He glanced at a check-list on the desktop.

'One: today is Sunday. Until Tuesday morning you remain Lieutenant Andrews' responsibility. He will give you a crash course in mess protocol and anything else he thinks you should know. The Quartermaster will issue your kit entitlement as a captain and Tom will arrange for the paymaster to have your pay and entitlements sorted out.

'Two: on Tuesday morning you will depart this camp and report to Dr Baxter at Cameron Highlands BMH for psychiatric evaluation. You will remain at his disposal for as long as he sees fit. You will travel in a Land Rover from the motor pool or, if one is heading that way, by chopper. Lieutenant Andrews will organise that for you also.

'Three: your substantive rank will be that of first lieutenant. You will hold the rank of captain in an acting capacity only. Hopefully your orders, travel vouchers, new ID card and commissioning papers will be available from

Battalion HQ before you depart.

'Four: Sorry, but I must go. Oh, one other thing – two rather,' he stood and reached for his red-trimmed cap. 'Please give my best wishes to Lieutenant Mathews. Yes, the other thing,' under his cap visor he raised an eyebrow in a quizzical look. 'What did you do that convinced Colonel Cuthbert's widow that you should be promoted to commissioned rank?' He studied the expression on Vince's face. 'Hmmm, sorry, rhetorical question. Don't answer.'

Vince straightened; they exchanged salutes and left the office together.

chapter nineteen

Like a giant dragonfly, the helicopter drifted to settle on the landing area behind the hospital. As it touched earth, Vince followed his bags out of the hatch, instinctively clutching his cap and ducking to avoid the thumping rotors. He peered, through tendrils of misty cloud not dispersed by the swirling blades, to establish direction. There were no other passengers. He had been picked up only a hundred yards from his recent quarters; the chopper had come in from the northeast, terminating a mission completely unknown to him. The loadmaster had waved him to a seat and they were aloft again within seconds.

As the land receded, they had swung over the area where a sapper sergeant had demonstrated the power of PE allied to instantaneous fuse and detonators. Behind was the jungle range, where targets unsettled the unwary by popping up unexpectedly. The craft gained altitude over the weaponry ranges where the platoon had sharpened its skills with assorted infantry hardware, and levelled over the Alpha and Bravo company lines.

With a course set for the south, they flew over jungle and Vince moved to dangle his feet into the void, enjoying the view and the buffeting of the slipstream. Rivers gleamed in the morning sunlight and limestone gunongs reared over forested valleys like wooded towers. Jungle, in multifarious shades of green, looked like tightly-packed heads of broccoli interspersed with the brighter green of cultivations. Beneath that canopy lay a separate world: one that he had come to love. He experienced a frisson of dismay. It was a world in danger of destruction by the terrible pressure of human avarice.

* * *

He waved to the crew, to whom he hadn't even spoken, picked up his bags and headed for the hospital buildings. He wore jgs with a peaked officer's cap; the loose sleeves on the epaulettes of his bush-shirt bore the still unaccustomed three pips of a captain. Though he tried to look relaxed, his feelings swung between euphoria and stark terror.

Since the interview with the Colonel on Sunday had ended so unexpectedly, his life had been turned about. That evening he had spoken to Audrey for the first time in nearly three months. He had expected Dr Baxter to call and connect him to an extension to speak to her. Instead, when the phone in his room rang, a feminine voice had whispered, 'Vince?' He had almost dropped the earpiece. His heart throbbed uncomfortably and his throat had gone dry. When he finally spoke, his words had tumbled out like peanuts from a split bag.

'Audrey? Audrey is that really you? I thought... Dr Baxter said... This is wonderful! I'll be seeing you in a few days. Unless – that is – unless you don't want to see me? It's been a long time...if you've changed your mind... Oh hell! I'd better let you speak for a minute.'

They talked for twenty minutes. Audrey was unequivocally positive that she wanted to see him. She had played the tape he had made – the one played to her while she was unconscious – until his words were no longer audible. 'But it doesn't matter – I still remember every word.' She sounded happy, but also as though she might be weeping, and he knew that he must sound the same.

Later, going over the conversation in his mind, Vince realised that the sound of her voice had carried him back to that other Sunday when he had first been drawn to her. Then he had been impressed by her poise and confidence. Now she sounded frightened and vulnerable. They had spoken with affection and reassuring words, but it had felt curiously formal as they both selfconsciously avoided the endearments they had previously shared. Nor had he discovered what it was that Dr Baxter had said she wanted to tell him.

* * *

He left his bags near the steps where he and Audrey had talked, and ran downstairs to Captain Baxter's office. Nobody there; nobody in the corridors. Men were playing on the badminton courts at the back, so the place was not entirely deserted. He approached a group of card players in the recreation area. They were so intent on their game that they did not see him until he spoke. 'I'm sorry to interrupt your game, but does anyone know where the staff have disappeared to?' They looked up and to his dismay started to scramble to their feet. He waved them back to their game but one remained at attention.

'Sorry, sir, didn't see you come in. I think there's a staff meeting, but there's one of the sisters through there,' he nodded towards a ward, 'what has stayed about to keep an eye on us. Shall I tell her you're here, sir?'

Vince shook his head, 'No thanks, Corporal. I'll have a look. You get on with your game.' He nodded and walked to the ward. Near the ablutions at the far end a nurse, clipboard in hand, checked the charts hanging at the end of each bed. As his eyes adjusted to the reduced light, he peered to see if he knew her. 'Excuse me, Sister, I wonder if…'

When she turned around he could not continue. It was Audrey. 'Good morning, sir, can I help you?'

He struggled to produce words but none would come, and he realised that with him silhouetted against the outside light, she was at a disadvantage. When he finally spoke his voice was thick. 'Yes, Sister, please come over here and give me a kiss.'

'Sir!' She drew herself up and glared at him. Then, doubtfully, 'Vince – Vince is that you?' She seemed to stumble and sat heavily on one of the beds. 'Vince, what are you doing in an officer's uniform?' To his consternation she began to sob.

He knelt beside her. 'Sweetheart, I'm sorry, I didn't mean to alarm you. It was such a shock to see you. I thought you'd still be in bed. I don't think you should be working.'

She laid a soft finger across his lips: 'I'm not alarmed, you great oaf. I'm overjoyed! I couldn't just sit around waiting for you to come; I've been as jumpy as a cat so I offered to stand in while Sonya attends a staff meeting.' She looked about distractedly. 'Let's get away from these beds before I give in to temptation and jump on you.'

She led him to the recreation room, where they sat at a table away from the card players, gazed at each other and talked. He explained his odd promotion, how he had been lost and sketched an outline of what else had occurred since he had last seen her.

Audrey told him how she woke up one day, thin, weak and unable to comprehend that she had been unconscious for more than two months. 'I couldn't believe that you weren't there. I'd been having a lot of weird dreams and in between them I'd hear your voice.' She gave a tremulous laugh. 'There was a funny little man who kept telling me to come back to you. I wanted to, but an awful, great big old woman, had me under her arm and...' She broke off at the sounds of voices, of movement and approaching footsteps.

The meeting had ended. Those staff members whom Vince knew were pleased to see him and agog at his altered rank. Captain Baxter shook his hand vigorously. 'I'm delighted they didn't make you a major – I'd have to salute you. Just don't you forget: I have seniority!'

Dr Baxter formally admitted him as a patient and then told him to go away. He turned to Audrey. 'You too, my dear. Mr Wu tells me he has kept your retreat as it was before you became ill, and he will have it aired out.' He grinned. 'Under the circumstances it won't bother anyone if you want to stay there together for a week or two. You'll have a great deal to talk about, and that's the therapy I recommend.' He looked at his feet. 'I'm sure you'll think of other therapeutic variations.'

When they were alone, Vince exulted. 'Great! I'll get my bags, what do you need? You can show me your favourite eating place and we'll spend the whole evening catching up with...' His voice trailed away at the expression on her face. Pale from her enforced seclusion, it had become ashen. 'What – what's the matter?'

Her face was composed but tears brimmed in her eyes as she stared miserably at the wall. 'I asked Dr Baxter and he said that you read my letter...the one I left for you... are you really sure you want to go there with me now... or – or – ever?'

A single tear overflowed and trickled down her cheek. 'Audrey – sweetheart – we've both done things we wish we hadn't. If excuses are needed I reckon yours are better than mine. Come on, let's get our things and get out of here.'

Her face glowed through her tears as she nodded wordlessly.

Much later, after a dinner at Audrey's favorite kebab eating-house, they sat close together on her settee. Vince broke a long silence. 'Okay – so when are we going to get married?'

Shaking, she turned and buried her face in his chest. 'Vince, there's no easy way to say this, but – but I have to – I can't put it off any longer – I'm pregnant!' Her voice was muffled and distorted. 'I – I can't even pretend that

I'm certain you're the father. I can only pray that you are. Oh my darling, how could I have been such a fool!'

It was a sickening jolt. After reading Audrey's poignantly distressing letter Vince had recognised that this was a possibility, but then in the wake of her continuing coma it had seemed an unlikely and irrelevant fear. Now – in a split second – he was faced with the need to view things from a different perspective. He thought of Willie, swallowed and lowered his eyes to hers. 'You'll be the mother – of course I'm the father.' He forced a smile. 'It's our child if you want it to be – and sweetheart, it's going to be a beauty.'

As they talked through the night, the extent of their shared occult experiences became more apparent. Audrey remembered dreams from her time of unconsciousness and Vince could sometimes match them with names, or places. Oddly she recalled Charles – helping to distract Sankal's attendant spirits – as a pleasant and courteous middle-aged Englishman. Vince thought this more incongruous than his own perception of Charles the tiger.

When they had finally talked themselves out over cups of tea, Audrey took a bundle of linen from a compartment under the seat of the settee and showed him how it converted into a double bed. All remaining awkwardness evaporated as the shared domestic chore became a solemn ceremony of commitment.

They were shy at first as they undressed, more so than when they had first made love. But when they held each other under the sheets, all reticence disappeared. At some time in the early morning he was wakened in inky blackness by burning kisses and a hot tongue that flickered and thrust between his lips.

Her passion startled and delighted him. When she slid down beside him, they clung together despite the heat and sweat of their exertions. Drowsily he turned his head to nuzzle her neck, whispering. 'Wow! I'll never ever let you out of my sight again!' She kissed his cheek and closed her eyes as he murmured. 'There's so much to tell you about the last couple of months and I haven't even mentioned the gold.'

As a forefinger of pale dawn slipped between the window drapes, he was lying there enjoying the way her breathing teased the short hairs about his neck. He thought she was asleep until he heard a dreamy whisper, 'Andor, Muda, Abu, Angah, Batu, but you haven't told me about Amang.' She sniffed. 'And I didn't catch the name of that Englishman's wife either. Sounded like a man's name anyway.' Vince was thankful for the dim light as his blood again redistributed itself, now to his face and neck. Bloody hell, Charles, he groaned inwardly, how can a tiger be such a damned blabbermouth?

* * *

Over the next few days Audrey and Vince spent many hours exploring and testing the rapport they had discovered months before. On their behalf, Dr Baxter made inquiries about obtaining permission to marry. He was suitably impressed by an assurance received from a staff officer at brigade HQ.

'The brigadier himself has ordered that any such application in those names should be granted immediately.'

Inevitably they discussed the weird spiritual world they had both encountered – Audrey in the frightening, occult world of spirits and demons; Vince, in more prosaic experiences of the flesh. Her memories were patchy, distorted and in the manner of dreams elusive, and to find that Vince hadwaking experiences to complement her memories of dreams was both fascinating and frightening.

When they had exhausted the recollections that they could share, Audrey tried to extend them. She would make seemingly offhand comments, or drop names dredged from her dreams: 'Amang' and 'Willie' cropped up regularly. 'It must have been lonely in the jungle. Even in the village you wouldn't be able to converse much,' she would observe casually. 'Surely there were comely Temiar maidens willing to teach you,' she teased. 'Didn't any appeal? I remember how you looked at that tribal girl when we first walked down the street together.' Each taunt carried an undertone of tension.

One evening Mr Wu invited them for dinner in his home at the rear of the shop. He had prepared a sumptuous Vietnamese meal enhanced with herbs and spices that Vince had not tasted before. As he sipped a deliciously piquant soup, he attempted discretely to pump Mr Wu for information concerning the covert gold market. Mr Wu remained unperturbed, but was clearly interested.

'Naturally, prices vary depending on what form the gold is in: flake, dust or bullion; its purity and of course, its provenance: where it came from.' He sat back, causing his rattan-dining chair to creak; his head was cocked to one side and he peered questioningly across the cluttered glass-topped table at Vince.

Unsure what to say, Vince turned toward Audrey, who looked perplexed. 'What's all this about gold?' She furrowed her brow. 'You said something about it the other night after...' she hesitated and went pink, 'well – when – sometime after you arrived.'

Vince hesitated. He glanced into their faces and nodded to himself. 'Sorry, love,' he said, turning to Audrey, 'I'd forgotten I hadn't explained this, but please keep it to yourselves.' They both nodded and he went on to tell them about the CT camp. Of their captive, the sentry he had killed, the others in the bunker, of finding the gold and what he had done with it. When he finished, he looked up to find them staring at him with expressions of mixed incredulity and horror. 'Sorry,' he muttered. 'I've said too much.'

'No...no,' Mr Wu replied. 'I now understand your interest in the price of gold and also your, er, new situation.' Delicately, he continued: 'Ah, I think perhaps I may be able to help if you wish to dispose of some.' They both looked at Audrey, who had continued to stare at the table, apparently still perturbed by the story. 'Please, let us sit more comfortably and then if you wish we shall discuss it further. Will you both take some green tea?' He ushered them into seats on more deeply upholstered rattan furniture and bustled from the room.

Mr Wu returned carrying a tray with teapot, translucent green porcelain cups without handles and a plate of rectangular shortbread biscuits. He fussed around for a few minutes pouring the tea and positioning cups and plate on a low table within reach. He left the room once more to return with a folder that he placed beside his cup.

They sipped in thoughtful silence while Vince cast worried glances at Audrey, who had not spoken since they left the table. He broke the silence abruptly. 'Most of the gold I had to leave behind, but I hid the six remaining small bars before getting to KK.' Looking up, he saw he had their attention once more. He spoke slowly, remembering. 'Each bar,' he demonstrated with his fingers, 'is about half an inch thick and two and a half inches by one and a half. I would guess they'd each weigh about, oh... maybe eight or ten ounces.' With an inquiring look at Mr Wu, he sat back and took another sip of tea.

Mr Wu was almost excited. 'Ah, I think I know what they must be!' He opened the folder. 'Because of their shape they are often called "biscuit bars" – they are similar in size to these shortbread biscuits.' He held a sheet from the folder to catch the light. 'Yes! Ten tael bars, measure sixty by thirty by twelve millimetres each – that's around the size you described, but these are a little heavier – nearly three hundred and seventy-five grams. Let me see,' he stared at the paper. 'Yes, one tael equals one point two ounces in weight – so ten taels are equal to twelve ounces.' He sat back and beamed.

Seeing the puzzled looks on their faces, he tapped the folder. 'One tael,' he spelled it out, 'which is an ancient Chinese measurement of weight, is equal to one point two ounces of very high quality gold. One such bar contains twelve ounces.'

Vince glanced again at Audrey, who had perked up a little, and turned back to Mr Wu. 'So what d'you reckon they'd be worth then?'

Mr Wu smiled. 'By a happy chance the seven main gold trading nations met recently in London and agreed to establish a Gold Pool, to maintain the price of gold at the pre-war level of thirty-five US dollars per ounce.' He stared at the piece of paper. 'That makes your six bars worth a total of about twenty-five hundred dollars US. Tell me, are the bars marked – stamped in any way?'

Vince thought. 'Yeah, there are some markings but I don't know what they are. The only time I really looked at them was by candlelight.' He turned to Audrey and grabbed her hand. 'Sometimes I felt like chucking them away, but I'm glad I didn't. They can pay for our wedding!' Seeming pleased, she squeezed his hand and kissed his cheek.

Mr Wu smiled benignly. 'If my guess is correct, they may be bars from the old Imperial Treasury in Shanghai. The Kuomintang Government had much of their gold reserve stored there, in the reconstructed National Central Mint. Remaining gold stocks vanished when the Communists took Shanghai in 1949. If they are old imperial bars, they should have a higher value and I may be able to return to you the official rate. If not, you might have to accept ten to fifteen per cent less.'

Vince smiled and shrugged his shoulders. 'Whatever you say. Of course we'll be grateful for whatever you can arrange, but first we'll have to figure out how to recover them from where they're hidden.'

Mr Wu spread his hands. 'I shall not need my car for the rest of the week. If you would like to use it, for whatever purpose... Well – I would be honoured if you would do so.'

Soon after, they thanked Mr Wu for the delicious meal and the offer of his car and left. When Vince took Audrey's arm to cross the road, he was disturbed to find her trembling. He shut the door behind them, but instead of turning on the light, she clung to him, her whole body heaving with the power of her sobs. Holding her close, her hot tears soaking his shirt, he searched his mind for whatever had upset her.

Tentatively, he edged her across the darkened room to the settee where he held her until her sobbing gradually gave way to sniffles. 'What is it sweetheart? Please tell me what's wrong.' Finally she drew away and a warm hand touched his face. His sigh of relief became a grunt, as a sharp smack stung his cheek.

He fell back in surprise as she wailed, 'You – you – b-b-bastard,' stumbled to the bathroom and slammed the door.

Alone in the darkness, Vince's mind seethed with conflicting emotions: sorrow, anger, pity and indignation. Confusion reigned. What have I done wrong? he asked himself. Is she having a breakdown after everything that's happened? Time passed; Audrey remained locked in the bathroom while his mood blackened with virtuous and unreasoned anger. What am I waiting for? She hit and swore at me, bloody hell! I think I'll just piss off out of here.

Just as he was thinking of leaving, the bathroom door opened and Audrey stood silhouetted in her white towelling robe. As his eyes narrowed against the glare, he saw that she had washed her face and tied back her hair. A pale and penitent figure, she looked like a little girl who knew she had been naughty and is afraid, but ready to accept her punishment. His heart melted and he rubbed his cheek. 'I knew you drove like an armoured corps veteran, but you didn't tell me that you'd majored in unarmed combat!'

Her eyes brimmed again and he jumped up to whisper. 'Please come and tell me what I've done to upset you.'

They sat silently on the settee until she said, in a small voice: 'I – I'm sorry I burst out like that and hit you. I know I'm not being fair, but I s'pose my hormones are all running around in circles while the little one in my tummy's screaming me, me, me!' He gave her a squeeze and she buried her face in his chest, muffling her voice. 'I – I really think I'm going mad with jealousy.'

She drew back and stared intently into his face. 'Oh... I don't really think I've any reason to be... It's what we were talking about before, my dreams – memories from when I was unconscious. When you talked about killing all those men – well, I knew that you had to, but then it came to me. You did it for Amang, didn't you?' He nodded silently. She looked down. 'Her name just sprang into my mind and I couldn't help thinking: why wasn't he there in Cyprus, to save me when I needed him?'

Vince sought for something to say, but before he was ready to speak, Audrey continued. 'You were right of course – I'm just jealous because you had an affair with her – didn't you?' He nodded mutely. They stayed silent until Audrey blurted: 'Do you love her?'

'No!' He pushed away thoughts of her doing similar things. He knew that was different and replied humbly. 'No, I liked her and yes, I lusted for her – somehow it seemed expected that we – and I was lonely and – and confused. I was filled with guilt, because of you and Andor too, but I think she – they – saved me from madness.'

He stopped and shook his head. 'It was all over between us when Andor got back. The next night I heard she'd been kidnapped and I… I just…' His voice belonged to someone else. 'Even if I hadn't known about what those animals did to you in Cyprus, I couldn't have walked away.' He wiped his eyes absently with the tissue she pushed into his hand. 'Yeah, I did think the same as you – I only hope I wasn't too late this time.' They sat not speaking for a little longer, then Audrey turned to him, stared into his face and kissed him firmly on the mouth. It was a kiss, not of passion, but of enduring love.

'No!' she said, 'you couldn't and I'm glad – I too pray you weren't too late… darling.'

She got up and he listened, mystified, while she moved things around in the kitchen until she returned to place on the coffee table an unopened bottle of black label whisky together with two glasses. After a moment's hesitation, she took a glass away and came back with it filled with milk and a jug of water. With a wry smile she nodded at the bottle: 'Bad for baby.' At Vince's inquiring look, she said gently, 'It was a Christmas present. Help yourself, you might need it.'

As he took an apprehensive sip, Audrey tilted her head to one side and spoke with a self-deprecatory smile that contained a hint of desperation. 'I'm sorry darling, I need to know about Willie – or would you rather write *me* a letter?'

They talked far into the night. He answered her questions without reserve and they both shared tears of sympathy. Audrey wept for the fate of Charles and Wilhelmina. To Vince's amazement and her own, she was pleased by Wilhelmina's pregnancy. 'She is a very lucky woman, it was very kind of you darling. I'm sure that Charles will be happy too.' She gave him a briefly hostile glare. 'I just want to be sure you didn't enjoy it too much!'

When he reached the point in the story where he and Mohammed Das reached Kuala Kangsar, she shook her head in bewilderment. 'I'm sorry darling, I don't understand why those men had been trying to kill you. What had you done to them?'

Vince shifted uneasily and refreshed his glass. 'I'm pretty sure that the leader was the guy who assaulted… er, Wilhelmina. I guess the others worked for him, or were friends.'

'Describe him for me again please.' Her voice was strained and Vince wished he had made his earlier description rather more vague. Her tone unchanged, she whispered. 'It was Derek Cunningham, wasn't it? I just know it was.' She spat the name. 'And – and those animals – the ones that…?'

Numbly, Vince nodded; he did not know what to say. 'I hope you don't mind,' did not seem to hit the right note.

Suddenly, the life seemed to drain from her. For a moment, she slumped like a lifeless doll. When colour returned to her cheeks, her eyes were radiant. 'I was afraid that I might want to grieve for him because I was once stupid enough to think I loved him.' She laughed with delight. 'I don't! I'm free, I'm free! Oh thank you, darling. For years I've been afraid – terrified that I'd see them in the street – in a bus, or on a train.' She gave a great shudder. 'Or worst of all, that I'd suddenly hear their awful braying laughter and feel those fingers gripping my arms. Thank you, my darling. You've given me a new life and now you've swept the world clean for me!'

The years to come might drift past like forest leaves in autumn winds, more rapidly as memories dimmed. That night, however, Vince knew would remain precious. A memory that they might never discuss, but one that Vince would keep available in his mind for happy contemplation.

Audrey made love to him with a single-minded intensity that blew the alcoholic vapours from his brain. The realisation that the spectres of her haunted past had been exorcised, and that he was forgiven his own transgressions, left him humbled and elated. It was an affirmation of love – and an assurance that he had at last done something worthwhile in this life.

 bibliography

Barber, N., *The War of the Running Dogs*, Arrow Books Ltd, London, 1971.

Holman, Dennis, *Noone of the Ulu*, William Heinemann Ltd, London, 1958.

Moore, W. and Cabbit, G., *This Is Malaysia*, New Holland Publishing, London, 1995.

Noone, R. and Holman, D., *Rape of the Dream People*, Hutchinson and Co. Ltd, London, 1972.

Rennie, F., *Regular Soldier*, Endeavour Press Ltd, Auckland, 1986.

Williams-Hunt D.D.R. (Major), *The Malayan Aborigine*, Kuala Lumpur Government Press, Kuala Lumpur, 1952.